FIRST *THE EXORCIST*
THEN *SYBIL*
NOW *THE OWLSFANE HORROR!*

A crack of lightning split the sky with a slithering flash of light. A woman in the crowd suddenly screamed.

"You can't let them out. They're dead. Why don't you let them rest in peace!"

Someone led her gently away as the coroner opened the doors wider. The first shock was over. Light streamed hungrily into the mausoleum, where it had not been for almost a century. Three caskets stood inside. The casket on the left bore the inscription "Suzanne." The coroner gently put his hand on the oakwood as if afraid of being burned. He lifted his eyes heavenward.

"God help me," he said.
And started to raise the lid. . . .

THE
OWLSFANE
HORROR

Duffy Stein

A DELL BOOK

Published by
Dell Publishing Co., Inc.
1 Dag Hammarskjold Plaza
New York, New York 10017

Dell ® TM 681510, Dell Publishing Co., Inc.

ISBN: 0-440-16781-7

Printed in the United States of America

First printing—December 1981

For my parents, Estelle and Marty

ACKNOWLEDGMENTS

My thanks and gratitude extend without limitation to: Bob and Hourig Sahagian and their family, who opened up their lives and home to so many of us. Helen Barrett, my friend and agent, whose help and guidance over the years we have worked together have proved invaluable to the writing of this and future books. Lillian Cominsky, who spent hours providing psychological insight into a very troubled character. Debra Schneider, who willingly cut her weekends short so this novel could take final form. And finally, Linda Grey, my editor, who guided me from idea to novel. This book exists because of her faith and assistance.

AUTHOR'S NOTE

THE OWLSFANE HORROR is a work of fiction. The town of Owlsfane, Vermont, is fictitious, but the Wallford House exists. It has been written about under its rightful name in its rightful town in *The New York Times* Sunday Travel section.

The ski house next door also exists. It is the one I belonged to for a number of years. All of my characters, however, exist only in my imagination and on these pages. Any similarities to any people from within the walls of the ski house or the borders of Owlsfane or neighboring towns is purely coincidental and unintended.

The events in this book did not take place. But they could have.

Synchronicity: An unexpected parallelism between psychic and physical events.

—Jung

PROLOGUE

OWLSFANE, VERMONT, 1880

Suzanne breathed and woke up.

A heavy, labored breathing, as if a giant weight were positioned on her chest. She strained against the pain and fought to fill her lungs with air.

She opened her eyes, but there was only darkness; a blackness that was tactile, a silence that could have been cut. No hint of light, no breath of sound.

She was not in her bedroom; she knew that intuitively. Even at night there would be the faint sliver of light sneaking in from under the door, creaks from the house, whimpers from the horses in the stable across the cobbled path.

There was nothing.

Except cold. An unreal, brittle cold that had settled within her. Her teeth began to chatter, the sound echoing loudly in her ears.

She was confused and tried to sit. Her head brushed against something solid. She reached above her and felt a low ceiling inches away. Her hands shot out to the sides, frantically hitting against the wood that surrounded her.

Then she coughed, but the sound frozen deep within her throat never emerged.

The heart of the nineteen-year-old girl turned stone-cold, and she knew.

All around her were walls. Her stomach fluttered with the gut-grabbing, sinking feeling of total isolation, of one who knows she is inside her own coffin.

She stifled a scream and strained with her arms above her, testing the lid and sensing it move. Three attempts later it was up, and she was sitting.

Her chest was in knots, her breathing tight. She gasped for air.

It was night. The mausoleum let in no light. The blackness buzzed loudly in her inner ear, dizzying her. She was exhausted. She knew she had one chance.

She threw herself out of the coffin and onto the floor.

She did not have the strength to stand, and started to crawl for the door.

Her arm reached out above her to push on the handle that opened the door outward. But she could not reach it and her fingers dug into the door with a rasping sound, breaking the skin and drawing blood. Again and again she clawed at the door, thrusting her shivering body up towards the handle. More desperately. More feverishly. Her remaining strength was ebbing quickly. Each time she sank back again, her fingernails leaving bloody scratchmarks down to the floor.

With a final upward push she grasped the handle and tried to force open the door, but she was too weak, and her fingers slipped slowly, painfully, from the handle to the floor of the mausoleum. She could try no more.

She screamed; the hollow sound reverberated from the walls of the tomb. Someone would pass by; someone would hear. But no one heard; the sound was swallowed by the blowing winds and snowstorm outside.

She screamed again—a last long wailing cry—before

her throat tightened and blocked off the sound. Her mouth was open, yet nothing more emerged.

Final tears froze on the face of the beautiful young girl they had buried alive.

BOOK I

Eben

CHAPTER I

The Buick turned off I-91 at Exit 4 in Vermont, turned left at the intersection, and headed northwest on Route 93. The ski rack, suctioned and strapped to the rain gutters on the roof, secured a pair of brand-new top-of-the-line-model Olin Mark IV skis, wind-tunnel dragging as the car buffeted the night gusts.

Snow was flurrying. Squalls were predicted, and already the blacktop road sported a thin cushion of snow. Away from the headlights and reflectors of the highway, the car plunged deeper into the Vermont blackness. It was nearing midnight and there were only a few other cars on the road, mostly skiers heading north for the Christmas week. An occasional truck on the Boston-Burlington-Montreal run passed them in the opposite direction, Christmas-tree-red-and-green flashers wildly blinking warning. On eye level with the approaching headlights, the driver was momentarily blinded, but managed to hold the wheel steady, the car straight.

David Thomas blinked twice to reaccustom himself to the night black after the sudden onslaught of the headlights. Dark, with piercing eyes, raven-black hair, and a well-grown mustache edging downward toward his strong, square chin, he looked every bit the stereotypical skier. He glanced up through the windshield to make certain the skis were securely positioned on the rack, an annoying nervous habit brought on by New York City paranoia. Satisfied they hadn't accidentally slipped off or been removed by ghostly hands, he reached out with his right hand to encircle the left of his sleeping passenger. Trailing a finger in between hers with a light circular motion, he gently prodded her out of her doze.

Sandy Horne shifted, trying to find a comfortable position, head leaning back against the neck rest, elbow propped on the door handle. As her eyes opened she let out a vigorous if inelegant yawn. A *Guinness Book of World Records* yawn. She flexed her shoulders and recaptured her left hand, stretching. Two or three more short yawns escaped her throat before she recentered herself with ladylike dignity, hands folded demurely over her seatbelt buckle.

David stared at her, incredulous, before breaking into gales of laughter.

"Are you through?" was all he could spit out.

"I guess I just wasn't cut out for long-distance traveling," Sandy said, finding his hand on the seat between them. The long dark hair, parted in the center, that framed her oval face was moist with condensation where it had been resting against the passenger window. Errant strands of hair lay across her right cheek, slightly curved nose, and over her soft-blue almond-shaped eyes, and she flipped them back in place with the tip of her index finger. She was dressed in a tight-fitting beige quilted down ski parka with matching pants.

"That so?" David asked in his best Bogart. "Well, shtick with me, baby, and that's all you'll be doing." He had been making this trip every other winter weekend for the last five seasons. The five-hour drive almost felt like commuting.

They entered the town of Framingham and slowed to the posted thirty-five-miles-per-hour speed limit.

"We can be married by the Greenwich toll collector," David added with a wink. "It'll only cost us a quarter."

"You definitely are my kind of romantic," Sandy said, and then sweetly batted her eyelashes. "And I'll let you go on the honeymoon with the Greenwich toll collector too."

They had met at work.

Sandy, twenty-two, less than a year out of Syracuse with a master's in journalism, had landed an assistant editorship at *New York* magazine by putting together the best list (out of over six hundred applicants) of "the articles I would buy if given an assistant editorship at *New York* magazine." So far they hadn't let her buy any of them.

She was assigned cubicle 21. Her roommate was senior editor David Thomas, twenty-seven. It was attraction. It was instant. A sexual thing from the outset. It became love during a Sunday matinee revival performance of *Oklahoma!* Lunch and the tickets had taken the last of their money except for some change needed for the bus fare back to David's apartment.

During the intermission Sandy had given her two remaining quarters to the woman who handed out the towels in the rest room of the Palace Theatre because nobody else was putting anything into the plate. It was the walk home that changed the relationship. David delighted in it and swore they had invented the emotion. They were engaged three months later—at *his* insistence, she was pleased to report. He was not going to let this good-hearted, good-natured wonderful person get away from him. He had waited too long for someone like her. They were now in the process of deciding which studio apartment to keep while on the lookout for an affordable one-bedroom. They both felt they had outgrown Castro convertibles and wall units that concealed platform beds.

For David it was the end of the Friday bar scene

and the Hamptons summers, which was not all that great a concession: he had had visions of becoming a professional single. But his compromising ended with the singles' beaches. Winter was his time. Sandy was going to learn how to ski.

Learn to ski, she had muttered to herself more than once when packing the night before. David had told her to be certain to dress warmly, and there she was, folding every sweater she owned into the suitcase, a "better safe than sorry" expression plastered across her face. She had packed enough clothing for an arctic excursion, let alone a week in the Vermont mountains. But she had resigned herself to skiing—it came with the territory. It was a shame, though, that it had to go ahead and actually snow!

Suddenly something made her stop packing. There was a butterfly hollowness in her stomach. Something was bothering her, although she couldn't define what it was. Odd. Instinctively she had looked about her. There was nothing there, no one in the room. It was a strange passing feeling that needled at her from within, nothing she could put her finger on.

She fought the prickly feeling, wondered what it was that was making her sensitive (*and to what*), chalked it up to her fear of having to ski down a mountain, finished her packing (it had taken two suitcases to get it all in), and here she was.

She let go of David's hand, reached into her Vuitton handbag, and pulled out a pack of cigarettes. (She had a lot to learn. Who brings Vuitton handbags on a skiing trip?) She offered the package to David.

"No thanks," he said. "It cuts down on my wind."

Sandy reached for the cigarette lighter in the dashboard. "You're serious about this skiing business, aren't you?"

"Sure. I swear off smoking from Christmas through Memorial Day. Ski better that way."

She shook her head. "I still don't believe it, but I guess it can't do you any harm."

The car shot past a "resume speed limit" sign. David resumed the speed limit.

"Turn on the radio," he said. "See if you can get a weather report."

Sandy opened the car window. The blowing snow danced in. She quickly rolled the window back up.

"*I* can give you the weather report," she said. "It's snowing."

"Inches. Inches. Helluva difference between two and nine."

"*I'll* say," Sandy said purposefully.

"I was talking snow."

"I wasn't, Macho," she answered innocently, and blew a ring of smoke in his direction.

"Try for a local station. See if you can pick up Glendon. The way it's coming down now it could last the night and dump two or three feet on the mountain."

"Is that good?" Sandy asked with mock innocence.

Her sarcasm was lost on him.

"Outasight skiing," he answered, already envisioning the splendors the next day would hold.

Sandy fiddled with the radio dial but could only pick up static; the storm and surrounding mountains masked the reception. She gave up.

"Somehow I just can't share your passion for cold weather," she said, zipping her parka up to her neck. She folded her arms across her chest and huddled into herself as a cold wind blew in through a tear in the window rubber.

"First timers never do. But you will tomorrow. Coasting down the mountain. Real powder under your feet—"

"Visions of sugarplums dancing in my head?" She fluttered her eyelids and smiled sweetly. Butter would melt in her mouth.

David shot her an "I'll ignore that" look. "We're going for the first run. I'll wake you at six."

"A.M.?"

"Of course. Beat the crowds that way."

"At six A.M. I'm just rolling over."

"Not up here. Where's your hale and hearty spirit?"

"I think I left it on the Triborough Bridge." She threw her arms out in a shrug. "Oh, what the hell. I'm here to learn how to ski—the things one does for love." She furrowed her forehead. "This *is* love, isn't it? It better be. But next year it's the Caribbean."

"Deal," David said, smiling. "And only because it is."

"Hmmm?"

"Love, that is."

For a die-hard skier to waste even one precious winter moment on a beach, something had to be up. He glanced into her inviting eyes before turning back to watch the road.

Something was.

They were driving into the storm now, the road covered by a thick blanket of snow. David alternated between high and low beams, trying for better visibility. His hands gripped the steering wheel tightly to prevent the car from skidding.

A rush of wind entered the car and David jammed the window tightly shut. They were passing through the town of High Falls, completely silent, the crossroads gas station closed, its windows opaque. Sandy stared out the car window past the swirling snow into the white evergreened yards of ramshackle old wooden houses, framed in shadows from the town's streetlights. The night was heavy, silent, cold, and black. A country night.

"There is nothing," Sandy said in surprise and fascination. "You'd think *somebody* would be watching the *Tonight Show.*"

"If you think this is desolate," David said with a

smile, "you're never going to believe Owlsfane. It's got a population of about a hundred."

Sandy laughed. "There are more people on one floor of my apartment building."

David nosed the car across a narrow truss bridge that spanned a nearly frozen stream.

The gentle, intimate hills of Owlsfane, the foothills of the southern Vermont ski areas, were just visible now as dark, amorphous shapes rising up on both sides of the valley, low-hanging branches framing the road. An apple orchard, asleep for the winter, reared back into the darkness from the stream that paralleled the road, its grassy banks snow-covered. Swamp maples grew out of a diamond-shaped lake on the other side of the road. Landmarks. They were nearing home.

Sandy shifted in place, leaned her head sideways against the back of the seat, and played with the ends of David's hair, curling it between and around her fingers. His breath quickened slightly as he glanced in the rearview mirror.

"It's so eerie to look behind you and see absolutely nothing. Blackness. The Long Island Expressway should be like this going out to the Hamptons."

Sandy turned around to see. "I guess you're just a little old country boy at heart," she said.

"And body." David winked. "I perform better without city distractions, you know."

"Oh? Not afraid anything *that* strenuous is going to cut down on your wind, are you?"

David laughed. "I never said I was that much of a skiing fanatic. Smoking is one thing."

He paused uneasily, nervously clearing his throat. Sandy knew that sound.

"Okay," she said. "What is it you don't really want to—but have to—tell me? A couple of *New York* magazine editors won't be good enough for the house?"

"Drawbacks," he said simply.

"Drawbacks?" she asked.

"Now that you can't turn around and go home, there may be a couple of, well, drawbacks to the house I may have neglected to mention."

"You *may* have neglected to mention? Over all these months we've known each other, with you jabbering away about the house?"

"Slip of the mind," he said.

"Like for instance?" she asked, eyebrows up.

He cleared his throat.

"It's usually pretty crowded over Christmas week. We'll probably have to spend a couple of nights dormitory style."

"Boys in one room, girls in the other?"

"Something like that."

"Bunk beds too, I bet."

David nodded.

"Marvelous. What else?"

"No smoking above the first floor." He hesitated.

"I can live with that. Barely." She thought a moment. "No smoking, no sex. My wind'll be as strong as yours. Just what I wanted, a strong wind."

"The nearest fire department's about an hour away. If a house starts to burn in Owlsfane, the whole neighborhood turns out to watch. You'd think they'd organize a volunteer fire brigade or something." He broke off, shrugging. "What's the difference? The water pressure's not strong enough anyway."

"You're also trying to tell me—in your own elegant, articulate way, that there's no shower water," she offered.

"Of course there's shower water," he said almost defensively.

"Thank you."

"But not necessarily hot."

She smiled sweetly.

David cleared his throat.

"Go ahead," Sandy said. "What else?"

"One last drawback, which doesn't have to be a drawback. It depends on how you look at it."

"You're babbling. Just spit it out."

"The house next door." He paused.

"Yeah—?"

"It's haunted."

"Haunted? Like in ghosts and spirits and zombies and things?"

"Like in *real* ghosts and spirits and zombies and things."

"I wouldn't call that a drawback," she said, blowing a smoke ring. "I think it sounds like fun."

They passed the Owlsfane road sign, which was almost obscured by the snow. David slowed the car as they approached the ski house.

A real haunted house, Sandy mused. It did sound like fun at that.

CHAPTER II

Left directional signal on out of force of habit—there were no other cars in sight—David maneuvered the Buick carefully into the driveway over the small mound of snow created by passing snowplows that was already beginning to ice over through melting and refreezing. He deftly avoided the driveway ruts and angled between a station wagon and a VW bus. A half-dozen other cars were positioned along the driveway, with the choice spot in front of the kitchen steps reserved for Bob Kanon, the owner of the house.

He carefully unloaded his brand-new Olins from the rack on top of the car, pulled the suitcases from the trunk, handed Sandy hers, and juggling skis, boots, and valises, half stumbled across the driveway toward the kitchen stairs, Sandy in tow.

He stopped for a second, rested his boots on the ground next to him, and stared upward at the swirling snow. He opened his mouth and let several slightly salty flakes settle on his tongue. They melted instantly. He had Sandy do the same. First snow always tasted good. He pointed with his suitcase up the road about three hundred feet, where a house was silhouetted against the night.

"There it is," he said, a hint of triumph creeping into his voice.

"What?"

"The haunted house. The Wallford place. The big one. See it?"

Sandy turned and looked. The only streetlamp in Owlsfane stood near the house, illuminating it eerily in a tentative frozen half-light. It was framed haughtily against the pitch-black sky and reflected back from a side window the weak yellow-orange light cast upon it. It was an old house—cold in appearance, foreboding, taller than it was square, defying entry—aristocratic, three stories high with a spire roof. But what caught Sandy's eye were the vertical iron bars on the windows of one room on the second floor.

David pointed across the road.

"And there, my dear, the Owlsfane cemetery. Final resting place for all skiers who forget to bend their knees."

"I'll remember that." Sandy looked across at the lonely country cemetery. The light from the streetlamp was cast upon it, although it seemed as if the graveyard were trying to shrink away from the flat yellow glare. It would not take too much imagination, she thought, to conjure up ghosts rising from the shadowed and silent graves.

Suddenly she gasped. There was movement in the cemetery. Ghosts? "David, look!" she cried. She grabbed his arm.

David looked and started to laugh. Sandy looked more closely and dropped his arm. Not ghosts. Children! They looked to be about eleven or twelve.

"Oh, you," she said, and took a swing at him. He ducked out of the way, his suitcases falling to the ground.

Two children were having a snowball fight in the cemetery, darting in and out of the shadows, using the headstones as shields, racing around the Wallford mausoleum.

"Kids from the house," David said. "Everybody ends up in that cemetery sooner or later."

"Later for me, please."

David pointed out the children. "That's Scott. He belongs to Bob and Pauline Kanon, the owners of the house. The girl is Judy. She's Tom's daughter—the shrink I told you about? Those kids have been friends and rivals for as many years as I've been coming to the house."

"What kind of rivals?"

"The usual boy/girl stuff. You know: 'I can do anything better than you.' I guess that'll peak pretty soon. Then nature will take over and they'll probably be very attracted to each other."

"Like we are?" Sandy asked.

"I would hope a little more so," David answered, ducking out of the way again.

"Why are they in the cemetery?" Sandy asked, a bit uneasy. A graveyard at midnight didn't strike her as an ideal place for play.

David shrugged. "Why not? They've always played there. Hell, I've played there myself." He lowered his voice mysteriously. "Eben Wallford hasn't gotten any of us yet."

Sandy shook her head. "David, you're such an infant."

He laughed. "We do snowdances there all the time. No harm."

"Perhaps. But it still seems a little sacrilegious to me."

She stared for another second at the Wallford mausoleum, a hulking structure, square-shaped, bold, sixteen feet high and long, half as many wide. It towered over the other graves on a sloping high ground. In front of it was the weather-beaten stone figure of a bearded old man, bent slightly at the waist, leaning in pleadingly toward the door, almost appearing to be listening for sounds from within. An out-of-control snowball splattered against the back of the figure's head.

Sandy gasped, half expecting the lifelike, life-sized statue to turn in angry response.

Suddenly from behind them the kitchen door opened violently. They jumped. David whirled around to see silhouetted in the light of the doorway the short, stocky frame of Bob Kanon.

"Bob, you S.O.B.," he said. "You just scared the hell out of us."

"You think Wallford's the only ghost in the neighborhood? Get in here before I freeze my ass off."

Not needing a second invitation, they struggled up the snow-covered steps, stamping the excess off their boots. David threw a fake punch at Bob, but was careful not to connect. At forty-five Bob had kept up his shape and strength. While he lacked height, with his blacksmith's arms and muscular tree-trunk legs, he was sometimes referred to as Little Sasquatch. He skied every weekend of the season as well as during his vacation.

As for the off-season, members of the house had sworn thay had caught him lifting buses for fun.

David deposited the skis on the railing inside the closed-in vestibule and entered the kitchen. It was a modern rebuilt kitchen in an old rural farmhouse, which Bob had reconstructed himself. There were several ovens, ranges (gas and electric), refrigerators, freezers, and, it seemed, miles and miles of counter space. Sandy guessed they had the room to feed seven thousand. A servants' staircase led upstairs behind a half-closed door decorated with ski posters. There was another door, tightly shut, which Sandy suspected led down to the cellar.

"How was the drive up?" Bob asked.

"A snap," David said.

"Endless," Sandy sighed simultaneously.

Bob and David exchanged knowing glances.

"The uninitiated," David said, pointing a thumb at

Sandy. "Give me a little time with her and she'll be taking the trip up here during the off-season just for dinner."

"That," Sandy said with a broad smile, "is unlikely at best."

On a corner of the counter a trayful of steaming mugs greeted them.

"Hey. That's more like it. What's that?"

"Broken skis," Bob said. "My own secret concoction of hot apple cider, cinnamon sticks, and assorted liquor." With a twinkle he added, "Mostly assorted liquor."

"I'm glad they're not called broken *legs,*" Sandy said, and gratefully accepted the mug. David warmed his hands on the steamed outside of his mug as Sandy sipped the hot liquid.

"When you're dressed for it, you almost forget how cold it can get out there," David exclaimed, transferring the new warmth of his hands to his red, cold face.

Bob's face clouded.

"Yes," he agreed soberly. "We've been up here all week and it's not been a good one."

"What happened?"

"The ski patrol found a kid on the mountain. He must have gotten separated from his friends, found himself on an advanced run, and thought he could make it down. Probably a beginner."

David nodded solemnly, already suspecting the rest of the story.

"He went off the trail—this is only speculation—hit his head on something. Was knocked out cold. The patrols searched all the easy runs where the kid would have been—*should* have been. They used torches as well as the snow-making lights. Nothing. They found him the next morning, under the main chair on the steepest part of the mountain. He had frozen to death."

"My God!" Sandy gasped.

"The whole search team must have been riding the chair above him all night long. You learn respect for Vermont cold," he said with deadly seriousness. "Minus ten degrees, stark naked, you'd last about thirty seconds. Although they do say that freezing to death is one of the more pleasant ways to go. Almost euphoric."

"Thanks," Sandy said, shuddering, holding up her hand in a "no thanks" gesture. "I'll take your word for it."

She finished her broken ski. They stood in silence for a second until David broke the mood.

"Well," he said with some cheer, "I guess there'll be no skinny dipping in the pond then."

Fresh drinks in hand, they followed Bob into the living room, where the rest of the house members were sitting in a semicircle around a crackling fire. New wood was piled up adjacent to a fireplace that sported a row of hanging socks and stockings—some serving as Christmas decorations, others drying out from a day of skiing. A few backgammon and chess games were in progress.

A floor-to-ceiling tinseled blinking Christmas tree warmed the room. It stood off to the side and far enough from the fire to be out of danger from any jumping sparks.

A large overstuffed patchwork couch, re-upholstered eight times over, several caved-in Morris chairs, mats, and thick sandpapered tree stumps were filled with bodies, relaxing after the Friday-night drive up or recuperating from a day of downhill shushing. An oval hooked rug directly in front of the fireplace held a pockmarked coffee table wtih bowls of peanuts and home-popped corn. Hands were reaching in from all directions and scooping up. Strains of Bach's haunting Little Fugue in G Minor enveloped the room.

The house was unlike any Sandy had ever seen. Originally built in the early 1770s, it had been expanded, with rooms added on as families grew larger.

Bob and Pauline had converted the four large rooms
on the first floor into living and dining rooms to comfortably accommodate the ski house members. Sandy
marveled at the width of the original exterior walls,
visible where they had been broken through to open
into an added room—fourteen inches of white oak,
brick, clapboard, and wood paneling. A fortress compared to the thin plaster of her Manhattan apartment.
The rooms were all connected by sliding wood-paneled
doors, which disappeared into the walls when opened.
A room with a Ping-Pong table opened off the kitchen.

The house was filled with antiques: a mother-of-pearl
iron-front grandfather clock sat stoically ticking in the
corner, a silent observer of all that happened in the
house. A crank-handled Victrola stood next to the
front door with a recording of "Dixie" ready to play
in high-pitched splendor.

Italian marble fireplaces with brick fronts were in
each of the four rooms. On the dining-room mantel,
tiny glass figurines of skiers in motion danced around
wooden pinecones. Above the fireplace, a collection of
weather vanes was on display. They dated back to the
early eighteenth century: a Canada goose in flight,
black, sleek, with linear elegance and downpointing
wings; a free-flowing serpent, shaped from one piece of
wood, and a mallard duck with a two-foot wingspan
mounted at a downward-swooping angle.

Above the living-room mantel, stretching elegantly
upward to the high ceiling, was an exquisite gilded
swan-necked lyre-shaped looking glass of antique
beauty and graceful design.

Dominating the living room and separating it from
the dining area was a squared staircase with a hand-
carved newel post. It doubled back upon itself as it
climbed steeply to the second-floor bedrooms. Sitting
atop the lower banister was a two-foot cast-iron statue
of a Spanish conquistador, a torch lit by a twenty-watt

electric bulb in his triumphantly extended right arm. A Burger King chef's hat was propped at a rakish angle on its head.

Sandy was marveling at the statue.

"We call him Christopher," Bob said.

"It's fantastic." She ran her hand up and down the cold iron.

"It was here when we bought the place. We like to think he guards the bedrooms upstairs."

"Do they need guarding?" Sandy asked.

Bob winked mysteriously to indicate he was deliberately ducking the question. He took her hand and led her into the room with David following. "Come. Meet everybody. Guys—David and Sandy."

A dark-haired man of about thirty hauled himself out of a Morris chair and went to clasp David's hand.

"Hey, I heard you had gone and gotten engaged. Is this the unlucky—er, lucky—girl?"

"You got it," Sandy grinned.

David smiled. "His name's Stan."

"Really great to meet you," Stan said with a broad grin. "Any fiancée of David's is a fiancée of ours." He raised his eyebrows seductively. "With all the fringe benefits. Right, fellas?"

Behind him two friends shouted approval. Stan turned around to introduce them. "That's Ron and the horny one over there is Craig."

"I'll make certain to watch out for Craig," Sandy said, smiling.

David stepped surely next to Sandy, putting his arm protectively around her waist, staking his claim. He grinned. "No, *I'll* watch out for Craig." Then he saw a tall girl sitting in the corner working on needlepoint. "Ricky—how are you?"

"Really good," she said. "Up for another year."

"I thought your boyfriend was transferred to the coast."

Ricky shrugged, smiling weakly. "He was. I wasn't."

"It's great to have you back," David said. He turned to Sandy to explain. "Her boyfriend dragged her up skiing last year for the first time."

"There's a lot of that going around," Sandy growled under her breath to David, jabbing him in the ribs with her index finger. David winced.

"Never expected to see you back without him, Ricky," David said.

"Found I liked skiing," Ricky said, shrugging. She addressed Sandy. "This your first time up?"

Sandy nodded. "How can you tell?"

"The absolute terror behind your eyes. I was like you last year. Maybe even worse." She eyed David suspiciously. "Let me give you one word of advice about this clown. Don't let him bully you around out there tomorrow. If he's anything like Hal was, he'll expect you to be an expert in one day."

Stan put his arm around David's shoulders. "David, my friend." His voice was sad. "While I envy you your choice of fiancée, let me just say this to you. We were out on the slopes today and the number of good-looking girls out there this year must total in the millions. No— I'm being too conservative: the *billions!* If you're willing to trade all those unattached foxes for—" He indicated Sandy as David chimed in.

"In a minute."

"I would too," Stan agreed. "But hey, can I get to use all your good opening lines?"

"Whatever was mine is yours," David said grandly.

"What kind of opening lines?" Sandy asked, interested.

Stan furrowed his brow and thought for a moment. "Really creative ones like: 'You come here often?' Or the old standby: 'Boy, the snow was good today!' "

From across the room Ron called out, "Not to mention 'What's a nice girl like you doing in a cast like that?' "

Everyone groaned. Ricky tossed a throw pillow at him.

A small sandy-haired girl of six peered out from behind the arm of the couch. Sandy smiled warmly.

"And who's this?"

"My youngest," Bob said. He looked down at the girl. "Cynthia, say hello to David and Sandy."

"Hi." The voice was small, uncertain.

"She's a little shy. Give her a day or two and she'll warm up to you."

"She's very pretty," Sandy said cheerily. Cynthia blushed, embarrassed, and tried to hide behind her mother's skirts.

"And my wife," Bob said, tipping an imaginary hat toward Pauline.

She was a stunning blond, full-busted woman of forty. She smiled at Sandy and then pointed to Cynthia.

"She's tired," she said in a whisper. "She skied really hard today. Outlasted me." She gave her daughter a little push on the small of her back. "Hey—up to bed, okay? I'll be up in a few minutes to tuck you in."

"Okay, Mommy."

"Say goodnight to everyone."

Having to address the room, Cynthia mumbled a "Good night," then darted up the stairs.

"She skis already?" Sandy asked with genuine surprise.

Bob nodded. "Both kids started to ski at just about the same time they started to walk. At eleven Scott is a strong advanced skier."

"I think I'm getting a late start," Sandy said. She suddenly had an idea. "David, why don't I wait until my next life and I'll start younger. I promise."

David opened his arms to the room. "Don't you just love her?" he beamed. "You have to love her."

Craig growled low. "Is that an observation or an invitation?"

Sandy turned back to the conquistador. "This is a great statue," she commented.

Pauline smiled. "You should see old Chris on New Year's Eve." She gave the conquistador an affectionate pat on the rump. "We tinsel him up and stick a noise-maker in his mouth. He's probably worth something, but by now he's become a member of the house. We're going to teach him to ski."

"This house must have cost a fortune," Sandy said.

"Actually we picked it up quite cheaply," Bob said.

"But that's only because the Wallford house next door is haunted," David added. "Real estate broker saw a couple of suckers coming and unloaded a white elephant. Nobody in his right mind would buy this place. But," he added, "nobody ever said Bob was in his right mind."

"Is it really haunted?" Sandy asked, looking at David, a smug smile on her face.

Bob answered cryptically. "I'll get to that later, my dear. On the stroke of one."

Almost as if on cue, the grandfather clock chimed once.

David laughed and hummed eight bars of spooky music. "Oh, no. It's going to be another 'Welcome to Owlsfane, here's the Wallford story before going to bed' routine." He went into a hard sales pitch. "Guaranteed to keep you awake in bed, wondering, worrying, dreaming, screaming, or double your money back. And if you buy tonight, yours free of charge, a guided tour through the Wallford mausoleum. The number in Jersey is Bigelow—"

One of the house members, Gail Landberg, got up, holding up her hand in front of her.

"Hold it, Bob. I refuse to hear that story again. Last year I had nightmares for a week. I'll go and get the kids. If we're getting up early tomorrow, they should be in bed."

"Don't you mind their playing in the cemetery?" Sandy asked.

"What could happen in a cemetery?" Gail asked. Then, smiling sheepishly: "I'll go get them." Everyone laughed.

A man lifted himself painfully out of one of the Morris chairs. He was slightly paunchy, more than slightly balding, with fine golden hair and a nose a little too large for his small round face. He pulled down his red Ski-tique turtleneck from where it had crept slowly up his back from the too comfortable chair. All around him there was scrambling as the easy chair was vacated.

"There's the shrink I told you about," David said to Sandy. "Tom Landberg. If he treats his patients the way he skis, it's a wonder he makes a living."

Tom reached over and grasped Sandy's hand. "Don't believe a word he says. David's had it in for me ever since I diagnosed him as being anal-retentive."

Sandy laughed and turned to David. "I like him."

David winked slyly at her. "Two inches. And I don't mean snow."

Tom shook his head and turned to his wife. "Before this banter makes me lose control and I turn into the other half of my schizophrenic self, can I give you some help rounding up the kids?"

"No. Thanks. You stay for the story. I'll let you play the heavy tomorrow night."

Not having to be told again, Tom immediately resumed his slouch. He smiled apologetically at those who had stood ready to pounce on the soft chair.

Bob waited until Gail had left the room and the record had shut off.

"Kill the lights, will you, Dave," he said in a voice that reeked of mystery. "Ghost stories are always best told by the light of a fire."

The games stopped as David turned off all but the

light offered by the conquistador. The half-glow from the fire cast heavy shadows around the room and across expectant faces. There was silence except for the ever present ticktock of the grandfather clock and the crackling of escaping sparks in the fireplace.

Bob paused before beginning. He had told this story a dozen times before to new ski members each year; his routine and timing had been perfected. When all was quiet he began.

"This story is supposed to be true." He shrugged noncommittally. "You can make up your own minds whether to believe it or not. It was written up in *The New York Times* Travel section. That might lend it some believability, or it might not. . . ."

He took a breath.

"Eben Wallford built the house next door in the mid eighteen hundreds—1860, 1865. He was incredibly wealthy, especially by Owlsfane standards—owned the lumber mill up in Bartsbury that employed a good many of the townspeople, and a lot of land. He lived in the house with his wife and daughter.

"He led an extraordinarily unfortunate life, though. During the winter of 1880, his daughter, Suzanne, a beautiful young girl of nineteen, was out in back of the house, a little way up beyond our barn. The stream had not fully frozen over, and she slipped and fell into the icy water. Caught pneumonia. And died." He paused heavily to let his words hit home. "A tragedy for any family, but for Eben Wallford perhaps doubly so. The family had always been fiercely close, and Eben was very struck by her death. The daughter was interred in the mausoleum that Eben had built for the three of them.

"Less than six months later, his wife took ill. Also pneumonia. Also died. Once again they held the funeral services in the church across the road, as they had for Suzanne. After the very abbreviated services—a few words, the Lord's prayer; that was all Eben could take—the procession began. The casket exited first, followed by the mourners. They picked their way down the church steps, and through the gate leading to the cemetery.

"The mausoleum loomed before them as they approached it from the side. Its unbroken profile was stark, foreboding, yet strangely peaceful and inviting. The final resting place. Beside it, in the half-acre cemetery, were the other graves. Tiny headstones seemed to stand at attention out of respect for the newly dead."

A practiced showman, Bob let his voice drop, so that those in the room had to lean forward to catch his words. And, he noted with pride, lean they did.

"The procession stopped in front of the mausoleum. The minister waited for those at the end of the line to fill in the gaps toward the front. The people fanned out in a half-moon down the slope toward the road, spilling out across it. A crack of lightning and a peal of thunder split the air. The mourners stepped out from under the trees and looked nervously upward, hoping for a speedy finish to the services so they might safely return home. The minister shuddered before moving toward the door of the mausoleum.

"He spoke in a loud voice, so that he could be heard above the pelting rain. 'Think of this not as the door to death,' he said, 'but rather the door to eternal life.'

"Three neighbors stepped forward and began to swing open the mighty bronze doors. The first person to see and fully comprehend was a woman near the front of the line of mourners. She screamed and fainted. The sight carried to the end of the line as everyone simultaneously pushed forward to see. 'It's the devil,' yelled one of the older men, and turned on his heel.

"Eben Wallford could not move. His friend Simon Stoneham lowered his end of the casket to the ground, forcing the other pallbearers to do the same. Eben had no choice but to follow; his eyes, though, never left the mausoleum's door. The casket on the ground, Simon crossed quickly to his friend to shield him from the sight, supporting his shoulders and covering his eyes.

"On the muddy path the casket lay forgotten as those who remained at the gravesite stared in frozen silence, waiting for direction from the minister. The minister, eyes heavenward, was praying silently.

"On the inside door of the mausoleum, dried, blood-ied nail marks ran to the floor, and lying on the floor, face filled with terror, mouth open, tongue hanging out in dry finality, was the partially decomposed body of Eben Wallford's daughter, Suzanne."

His half-second pause seemed interminable.

"She had been buried alive."

Sandy gasped. "Dear God!"

"She was too weak to push open the heavy doors and of course died eventually anyway, but everyone knew she had been put in the mausoleum while still living. And the sight of her nail marks running the length of the door, her mouth open wide in a silent scream, was too much for Eben Wallford. He withdrew into himself and began to punish himself. He carried with him to his death, not long afterward, the tremendous guilt of the premature burial and his belief that he had killed his daughter."

The fire leapt high. The ashes stirred as a log broke in two and fell inward into the inferno, gray-and-black-speckled soot swirling and resettling. Bob saw Sandy looking at him, an intent, almost spellbound concentration on her face as he continued.

"It wasn't his fault. The doctor had pronounced Suzanne dead. But still Eben Wallford took it all on himself. And the poor, tortured soul then had to live with this guilt." He stopped himself. "Correction: *chose* to live with this guilt."

Bob raised an eyebrow, nodding his head solemnly, "And torture himself he did. He abandoned his business and with few exceptions, would neither see nor talk to anyone. He became a prisoner of his own house and a prisoner of his own mind. Through his desperate, intense guilt, he created a hell for himself on Earth.

"He started to spend long periods of time standing by the doors of the mausoleum, his ear pressed against them, listening. Listening for the slightest sound to indicate that perhaps his wife and dear daughter, whom he loved to his very core, were in there, alive, and trying to get out. The statue outside the mausoleum is a statue of Wallford—listening."

Sandy fidgeted. A strange, disturbing feeling flashed over her beyond the superficial shock of the ghost story. It wasn't defined. It was nothing she could put her finger on. Just a ripple of concern. It was odd. This whole thing had happened a century before, yet there was this bizarre, disquieting, transient feeling almost like a shadow passing over her. As if it had some meaning in *her* life.

She reached for David's hand, curling her fingers tightly in his, letting his presence warm her. She said nothing. She looked sideways at him. His face was impassive. He was lazily absorbed in the familiar story, absentmindedly swirling a finger in a Scotch and soda on the floor beside him.

She shook her head as if to banish the fleeting strangeness. Suddenly the feeling was gone.

"Who cares for the statue and the mausoleum?" one of the new members asked.

"The Stonehams," Bob said. "They live in the house almost directly behind us. Very old, very simple, very believing people. The descendants of Simon Stoneham, who was Wallford's friend, attorney, and executor of his estate. In fact, Simon virtually took over Wallford's business and personal care until his death less than a year later.

"The bulk of the estate money ran out years ago, but Simon's descendants still dutifully clean and care for the statue and house.

"Why do they do it?" he asked rhetorically. "Clean a

house where no one has lived for a hundred years? I don't know. Maybe they're trying to keep it up to protect its resale value, but I don't think so. They're elderly, have no children, and I don't even know whom they've willed their own property to. Probably the town." He shrugged. "Josiah Stoneham has lived in his house from birth, and I imagine he's very content."

"Loyalty?" Sandy suggested.

"Perhaps," Bob said. "To his great grandfather and his great grandfather's dear friend. Maybe respect." He looked into the fire, making certain he did not make eye contact with anyone in the room and then coldly shuddered. "Fear, maybe. When the Stonehams die, I don't know what will happen."

Bob paused as a passing car's headlights panned the room, twin spotlights in a horror play. He had his audience. The silence could be felt, touched. Those who knew the story would spoil none of it for the newcomers.

The gnawing feeling started again. Sandy tried to force it from her thoughts. A cold pounding that struggled to possess her mind. Perhaps it was just the unease of knowing she would be skiing down a mountain the next day that was unsettling her. Unsettling her? *Hell—terrifying* her. But that wasn't it. There was something more. There was the slightest bit of—*something*— in this story. Familiarity? No. She hadn't read the *Times* article, not that she remembered. Nor had she heard the name Wallford before. Empathy. That might be it. Almost an unnatural, unwarranted feeling of identification with the dead Eben Wallford. But that she could not justify to herself. Or understand. She cleared her head as Bob continued in a sepulchral voice.

"Mealtimes had always been important for the Wallford family. It was the time for them to be together to catch up on gossip or news from the town and mill. After Suzanne died, Eben and his wife frequently ate in silence, staring at each other from opposite ends of the dining table. Suzanne's place, though, was always set, her plate heaped high with food, as if she were just late in coming down to dinner and was expected momentarily.

"But all of this is really only the background of the story."

Bob sipped from a can of beer he was holding in his hand; every eye in the room watched him swallow.

"Eben Wallford was a very religious, very God-fearing man. Obsessed with a belief in the afterlife. Part of the reason, I imagine, for erecting such a kingly mausoleum. When he wasn't listening at the mausoleum door—something really tragic in itself—he was making every attempt to contact his family in the hereafter. Trying to cover all the bases, if you will. If they weren't alive in there, then they were somewhere else, and he was going to talk to them in either case. Although, I gather from my research, he appears to have been unsuccessful. Less than a year after his family's deaths, he too died."

Bob took a breath as a passing snowplow shattered the silence in the room.

"Now, Wallford was certain that they would all somehow return and be together again. Return to the house where they had been happiest. And when they came back, he felt they would be reunited at the table where they had spent so much time together. So he wanted to make certain there would be food there for them to eat. He left a provision in his will whereby servants would stay on in the house to maintain it. Each day they would prepare dinner for the three of them—Wallford, his wife, and daughter. So in case they returned that night, the food would be there."

A loud sigh was heard from Craig, who was standing with his arm draped around the conquistador. Bob fought to hold back a grin.

"So a family moved in. Each day they set the table, cooked and laid out the food, and then went to their quarters upstairs. In the morning they came down, and of course the food would not havé been eaten. They'd reheat it and eat it themselves. Then they'd go about their chores and cook the meal for that day. This went on for several years. The servants were obviously quite happy. The estate money was there and they were eating well."

Bob's eyes widened and his voice took on a mysterious lilt.

"But one morning they came down and found that some of the food on one of the plates had been eaten. Not completely. But they could tell someone had been there."

"They returned—?" one of the members asked.

Bob put up a restraining hand.

"Whether it really was the Wallfords who had returned or just neighborhood kids who had broken in, we don't know. But the servants were convinced that the Wallfords had come back and didn't want to stay on in that house any longer.

"I can't say I question that," he commented with a sly grin that David knew helped the story. A member of the house for five years, he had heard the ghost story at least a half-dozen times but never lost his fascination with it. Whether it was all true, or local legend, or pure bullshit, he didn't know. Nor did he care, because the story worked. The look on Sandy's face confirmed that.

He drew his attention back as Bob continued.

"Simon Stoneham, who was still alive, persuaded them to stay on as housekeepers. They agreed, but refused to remain in the house after dark. Their routine was pretty much the same—clean the house, cook the meal, set the table, lay out the food. Only now, instead of going upstairs to bed, they would lock the house and leave, taking home the previous day's uneaten food. So they were still doing all right."

"Incredible," someone sighed.

"This went on for a period of time. But one morning, when they unlocked the door and came into the house, they saw that the food had once more been partaken of. A thorough search of the house revealed no locks had been opened and no windows broken. The conclusion? Who knows?

"Again, neighborhood kids might have been able to find a way in and out without destroying anything—"

"That's a pretty long way to go for a joke," Sandy said.

"It is," Bob agreed. "And that's why the people around here believe it was indeed Eben Wallford who had returned."

He took a long sip of beer.

"After that, the servants quit—naturally. And Stoneham couldn't find anyone else to take their place. Naturally. The estate money was running low by now anyway. There was just enough in reserve for upkeep and taxes. So Simon locked up the house for good. However, he did put some pieces of hard cake out on the table for them. Just in case . . ."

He paused.

"After the servants quit for the second time and the house was fully locked, strange—if I may use that word—occurrences started. Lights were seen blinking on and off from time to time in Wallford's bedroom. Smoke came out of the chimney. Who knows whether it really was Wallford or a funny reflection from the streetlamp or a practical joker—although why go through that kind of bother in the slim hope someone might see you? But no one around here was taking any chances. Bars were placed on the windows of his room to keep whatever might be in there, in there."

Sandy shuddered inwardly, as from a chill on a cool day. The bars! She had noticed them when she first saw the house. She knew she had to learn more.

"To this day, the Stonehams change the cake periodically. They don't talk much about it. Just do it from time to time during one of their sweeps through the house. The people of Owlsfane and Bartsbury keep up the grounds.

"However," Bob said, holding up a finger in punctuation, "people believe that Wallford alone has come back. His family, not. The lights have appeared only in his room, the food disappeared only from his plate. It seems likely that his wife and daughter never returned, and that if Eben Wallford did come back to his house from the grave, he remains in there alone, still a guilty and tortured soul who has not found his eternal peace."

"How tragic," Sandy said, and for another half second tried to escape from her mounting unease.

"Has any of the cake ever been eaten?" she asked.

"The Stonehams don't talk." Bob answered with a smile and shrug that indicated he was telling all he knew. "So your guess is as good as mine."

Sandy suddenly felt as if something were boring through her mind, from the inside out. It wasn't a headache, more like a hand drill going through tissues and cells. It came—and then it was gone.

"I picked up a hitchhiker once," Bob continued. "An older man from North Bartsbury, which is up the road several miles. I told him I was coming as far as here and would drop him off. As I let him off in front of the house, I looked back at him as he continued up the road and I saw him walking up the *center* of Route 93. He would not walk either in front of the cemetery on the one side of the road, or in front of the Wallford house on the other. A lot of people around here do that. Day or night. Out of respect again. Or fear."

Someone turned to Tom Landberg, the psychiatrist.

"Can people really believe something like this, Tom?"

Tom nodded. "When the story is spoon-fed with first solids, you grow up with it. You grow up never walking past the house because whatever is in there is going to reach out and get you. And your children grow up the same."

"In other words, you believe," Bob finished. "And I would say that many around here truly believe. Others just go along out of habit." He flip-flopped his hand. "And even if you're not certain whether to believe or not, it's easier to go along than—" A sly smile overtook his face. "Risk the consequences."

A log crackled and sputtered in the fireplace, falling inward. Several people jumped.

"Perfect timing," Bob said as he put his arms out in a shrug. " 'Cause dat's all folks."

"Have you ever been inside the house?" Sandy asked.

Pauline answered her. "We've snuck in a couple of times. The kids found an unlocked cellar window and created a way in for us. We threw a Halloween party there once. The house has no electricity so the whole thing was done by candlelight. A little spooky, I hasten to add."

"Did anything unusual happen?" Sandy pressed.

"No." Pauline smiled. "And I guess we weren't disappointed either."

"So you really don't believe the house is haunted," Sandy asked with a cryptic glance at David.

Bob answered slyly. "Who knows?"

"The Shadow do," David said, and they all laughed.

Bob got up. "I don't know about you guys, but if we're going to try to catch that first run, I'm going to bed. Last one up, please put out the fire."

"Good idea," Pauline said. "I think I'll join you. Folks—drinks on the house for the last time this season."

They had started up the stairs as Gail Landberg came running in from the kitchen.

"Tom. Bob. The kids. I can't find them."

"They were in the cemetery a half hour ago," Bob said. "Grab your coats and let's look."

"They wouldn't be playing down by the river, would they?" Gail asked nervously.

Her husband answered. "No. They know not to. But we'd better look anyway."

Slipping on their parkas they ran for the door.

CHAPTER III

Bob led them out of the house. Knowing the area, he took control and handed out the search assignments: Tom and his group were directed to the wooded backyard of the ski house, which sloped downward toward the partially frozen stream; Pauline was to cover the road running north toward the truss bridge and on into the center of town; Gail, the cemetery and churchyard, where the children were last seen; and Bob, David, and Sandy, the Wallford house. They fanned out in four directions, loudly calling the children's names.

Bob flashlighted the way through the plowed parking area off to the side of the ski house and on into the unpacked snowbanks that stretched from his property line up the slightly graded incline to the Wallford acres next door. The snow was falling heavily, windswept swirls surrounding them as they trudged through the knee-deep accumulation of winter fall. The strong-beamed light broke the path in front of them, but was quickly swallowed up by the dark snow-blown moonless night. The streetlamp was flickering, more dark than light, affording them no light in the snowfield far from the road.

From all around they heard the echoing sounds of adult voices calling the names of the children, bouncing eerily off the surrounding mountains and returning in reverberatory waves. Sandy was surprised at how far her voice carried, even in the wind, and was at first embarrassed by it.

The light from the ski house grew dimmer as they edged further and further onto the Wallford property. The house was still in the distance. The darkness of the night hung thickly over them.

"Watch your step," Bob cautioned. "The ground is all frozen, but there are probably dips and depressions everywhere. No sense in turning an ankle in a hollow. Won't help your skiing any tomorrow."

"I don't think *anything* will," Sandy said in response, but then turned her attention back to the missing children.

Bob whipped the flashlight in front of him in a semi-circular arc, checking for children's footprints. But except for small, rounded animal paw prints, theirs were the only testimony to a presence in the virgin snowfield.

A deer stood suspended not ten feet from where they walked, stunned by the light. Eyes wide with terror, nose twitching, the petrified animal refused to move from the blinding beam of the light. The deer was frozen in time and motion. Sandy had never seen a deer in the wild, the Central Park Zoo having been her sole encounter with nature. Bob flicked the flashlight on and off rapidly several times in succession. The strobe effect freed the deer from its transfixed state. In a second it had disappeared.

They were now far from the other search parties. Only an occasional voice properly caught by the wind carried back to them as they neared the haunting outline of the Wallford house. The only other sound was the squishing of their boots as they broke through the surface of the snow. They had intensified their own cries for the children, calling out their names, when, at the back of the Wallford house, the flashlight picked up two sets of footprints coming from the opposite side of the house and leading to a cellar window.

"They're here all right," Bob said with relief. "I'm going to find them and kill them."

"No, don't do that," Sandy said. "They're only playing."

David tossed a snowball at Sandy, which hit her knit hat and flaked off into a million pieces, the powder too dry to make the ball an effective weapon. "Leave them alone. They just wanted to explore the haunted house, that's all."

A moan was heard from inside. A strangling sound of rope on throat.

"They're hurt," Sandy gasped.

Bob whipped the flashlight around toward the window.

The snow covering the basement window had been pushed aside and stamped down, the window propped open with a rotting board pulled from the undersupport of the side veranda.

Bob knelt by the window and directed the light through the opening.

Screams from inside.

The three of them jumped back as, suddenly, framed by the flashlight, two badly scarred, grotesque creatures appeared, mouths open wide and howling at them in a frightening wail.

Sandy put her hand to her mouth and stifled a scream. David lost his balance and fell backward into the snow.

But just as quickly as the faces had appeared in the window, they disappeared, to be replaced by the mask-less giggling sounds of children's laughter. The laughter of children who have bested adults.

Knowing they had been spooked, David caught his breath and turned to Bob. "You hold them, *I'll* kill them."

"Deal," Bob answered as he stuck the flashlight into the window and fanned it from side to side, trying to catch the children's whereabouts in the pitch-black basement.

"Okay kids. Joke's over. Come on out." There was a tinge of annoyance to his voice.

The masks were handed out first, and then Bob and David helped lift the two eleven-year-olds out through the window.

The glee of the previous moment's surprise vanished at Bob's frown as Scott Kanon and Judy Landberg stood sheepishly, their heads lowered, waiting for the inevitable lecture.

Bob's face was stern. "Now what was this all about?" he asked.

His son shrugged.

"Scott?" Bob asked sharply.

"I don't know. We thought it would be fun. I guess it wasn't such a hot idea after all." He leaned over to Judy. "I told you it was a dumb idea and we'd get in trouble."

Judy's answer was confident. "We're not in any trouble."

Sandy swallowed a smile. She liked the self-assurance of this girl.

Bob looked down at the children. "I don't know about you, Judy, but Scott certainly is. Do you two have any idea of the danger you put yourselves into climbing down into that cellar? Who knows what you could have bumped into in the darkness!"

Scott held back the tears that threatened. "We never moved from this spot by the window. I swear it."

"Well, at least you have *some* common sense. But you never thought about the fright you gave us all. Or our having to come out in the middle of the night looking for you."

"No." His voice was small.

"No. I didn't think so. Tell me this: If we hadn't

come looking for you, how long would you have stayed down in that cellar? Until you froze?"

Judy's smile was angelic. "But we knew you'd come looking for us. You love us."

Her words and impish face deflated Bob. "Go on, back to the house. Both of you. I think we're going to have to have a little talk later. Maybe a day off from skiing might make you think twice the next time you want to have some fun."

With a flat palm on their backsides he sent them scurrying around the front of the Wallford house, out to the road, and back to the ski house. It was only then that the three adults dared laugh.

"Those two," Bob said. "I have to admit they got us, though."

"Another case successfully solved, Mr. Holmes," David said, saluting. "And now I suggest we return to Baker Street, shoot up with a little opium, and retire for the evening."

"Smashing idea," Bob said. "Let's go back out around the front. The traveling will be a little easier going along the road."

Sandy shuddered involuntarily.

The feeling that had crept coldly up on her during the ghost story was starting again, stronger now. She shook her head violently from side to side, but she could not escape the unmistakable magnetic pull that was drawing her to this house. *This man.*

She craned her neck and looked up at the house—stark, severe, brooding. A grim black reminder of all of the unhappiness in a house built of joy and love. And she felt drawn by it. Drawn *to* it. Was it the house or the man, Wallford, that attracted her so? She didn't know.

David and Bob were following the path taken by the children. They had already reached the corner of the house. Sandy remained behind.

"Wait!"

The men stopped. Turned around.

"Aren't you coming, my dear?" Bob asked, gallantly offering her his arm. "Perhaps later you'll let me spirit you out of the women's dorm—a prehistoric creation at best—and into a little special room I have fashioned for myself on the third floor. For nefarious reasons known only to me and a select few."

"Only to him," David echoed.

"I want to go inside," Sandy said, pointing to the Wallford house.

Bob assumed a hurt expression. "This is certainly the first time my masculine charms have taken second place to the rather questionable appeal of a hundred-year-old ghost."

How could she tell them? She didn't want them to think she was crazy. She suppressed a smile. Do normal people hear the siren call of a house that's been closed for a hundred years?

"I've never been in a haunted house before." Sandy shrugged, as her voice grew smaller. An angelic, impish grin appeared on her snow-powdered face. "At midnight." And smaller, more innocent still: "In the middle of a storm."

David and Bob looked at each other and then at Sandy, a "you're kidding" expression shared by the men.

"All well and good," David finally said, convinced of the joke. "And now's no time to start. Come on back to the house. If you're in the mood to be haunted, I'll read you 'The Monkey's Paw.'"

"It was okay for the kids to explore the house," Sandy protested. "You just said so."

"Kids don't know better," David said. "I do." He knew his answer was weak and he felt a bit foolish.

"What I said to the kids goes for you too," Bob said seriously. "I don't know what kind of junk is down in there. There's no telling what you could walk into."

"Or *who*," David said with a trill to his voice.

"Just for a minute," she half pouted. "It was written up in the *Times*."

She could not tell for certain if there was a pounding in her ears.

"So was World War II," David said.

She put her hands on her hips defiantly. "There might be a story for the Magazine, and as long as I came up here to go skiing with you, you could at least—" She stopped, realizing how silly and juvenile she sounded. She was almost ready to give up the whole thing. Instead, she heard herself say, "Bob, give me the flashlight and I'll see you back at the ski house in a little while. I'm going in."

"Sandy, you're crazy," David said.

"*I* don't give up cigarettes for six months."

"Come back with us and I'll chain-smoke for you."

Stalemated.

David put out his hand for the flashlight. Smiling, Bob silently passed it to him.

"Ah, wedded bliss," he smirked, and disappeared into the blackness at the side of the house.

"Lead the way," David said, resigned.

Josiah Stoneham stirred from sleep. Something was wrong.

His eyes darted furtively to and fro in the dark of the room. The only sound was the even, steady breathing of his wife, dead asleep next to him. It was pitch-black. He squinted toward the luminescent dial of the digital alarm clock, blinded momentarily by the concentration of light. He closed his eyes tightly and looked away, afterimages of orange-and-pink numerals flashing before him, then fading. He opened his eyes again and squinted at the clockface. He discerned the time, 1:35, and flipped on a soft lamp next to his bed. He never woke up in the middle of the night.

Despite his flannel pajamas and the heavy patch-

work quilt pulled close to his neck, he was cold. The
house attracted drafts. Towels were stuffed into the
window cracks to prevent the seepage of winter air
inside, but the stream of warm air that blew cautiously
up through the metal floor vents next to the door did
little to combat the cold that the Vermonters could
never fully escape. As if God were forcing the people
to be hearty and endure. Or killing them for their
failure.

Another blanket lay draped over a straight-back
chair in the corner of the room. Two steps on the cold
tile floor and he'd be able to grab the blanket, two steps
back and he'd have it over him. Two seconds of discomfort for a nighttime of warmth.

Yet something was keeping him in his bed. A
toss-up.

No. He would nestle in next to his wife. He was
chilled but held captive in his bed by feelings of alarm.

As he turned off the lamp he remembered.

The afterimage of his dream reappeared before his
closed eyes. Although he knew it was less a dream than
a memory. A memory of a long time ago when he was
only a boy.

The memory of the girl.

Somehow, for some reason, the girl had gone into
the Wallford house. She was no more than twenty, and
Josiah no longer remembered her name. She was in the
daughter's room—Suzanne's room—on the second
floor when Josiah, a child of thirteen, passing by, had
seen her from outside. He had stopped in curious surprise as he looked up and saw her strange posture. But
his amusement turned quickly to horror as he realized
she was not pretending. Her mouth was open and
twisted downward in a strangled death cry; her eyes
bulged wide in terror; her arms were outstretched above
her, as if she were trying to climb to the top of the
closed window, her fingers bent and stiff, as if she were
scratching at the window glass—no, more than that—

clawing at it, in a desperate frenzy to escape whatever was behind her in the room.

Suddenly flames spiraled around her, licking at the top of the window.

Josiah fought his fear and raced into the house.

Her screams of terror filled the mansion. The strong acrid odor of burning flesh assaulted him as he reached the top of the stairs. He pushed open the door to the bedroom and stared in horror at what he was witnessing. It was a scene from Dante. The girl was screaming. Flames licked at her, and still she was trying to claw her way through the window. He ran to her, threw her on the floor, and smothered her with a quilt until the fire was out. Her skin was charred red and black. Her arms fought viciously against him, seeing, he was certain, something or someone standing where he stood. He restrained her and wrapped her gently in a sheet. The poor girl never ceased her screams from the pain of the fire and the terrible vision.

They came for her and quietly took her away.

Josiah knew she had gone mad. She never regained her sanity. She had been institutionalized.

What had happened in that bedroom? No one knew.

What had set her on fire? Why had she been clawing at the window as if possessed? No one ever knew, for the girl never spoke again. She was forever lost in a soundless, sightless boxed-in coffin of a world.

Josiah shuddered to himself and closed his eyes, trying to banish the picture of the burning outstretched arms, an image he would carry with him to his death. But still he saw the girl as she had been that day—her arms reaching higher and higher up the window glass, trying to escape from the tomb she must have seen herself in.

Like Suzanne, when they had buried her alive.

With Sandy directing the flashlight, David grabbed hold of the upper rim of the window and hoisted himself into the basement. Balancing the flashlight in his parka pocket, he lowered Sandy next to him.

He aimed the light around the room. They were able to make out the shadowed shapes of rusty tools and broken furniture. Needle-sharp spokes of straw brushed against his face. A dirty fan-back rattan chair was turned upside down, resting on its arms, perched precariously on a rotted chest of drawers, one of which hung open and downward at a severe angle as if a breath might knock it clattering to the floor. Brightly colored painted animals of pink and white had once decorated the dresser, but the peeled, flaking remains of the design divulged the long period of nonuse and disrepair.

"His daughter's," David whispered, and his voice hung heavily. He trailed the flashlight along the decaying splintered surface. "He must have had it brought down here after she died."

From above came the low moaning sound of a floorboard creaking, the house crying under its own weight as it settled. Startled, David jumped back, his arm brushing against another arm. He gasped and whipped the flashlight around. A dressmaker's mannequin teetered back and forth on its metal base. It came dangerously close to falling into a stone-faced cast-iron winged griffin, the size of a large dog. Its blazing eagle eyes were colored in with enamel, which caught the light and flared backward in deep penetration.

When it all connected, David exhaled in relief. Steadying himself with an exaggerated hand over his heart, he also steadied the mannequin and nodded respectfully to the iron creature. He aimed the flashlight away from his face, but Sandy was still able to make out the rounded corners of a grin.

"Talk about susceptibility," she sighed.

"Come on," he whispered. "Let's get the hell out of here."

"Why are you whispering?" Sandy asked. "There's no one here."

"We don't know that for a fact."

"We'll find out," she said with an offhand smile.

"I don't want to find out," David spat out between clenched teeth.

Sandy grabbed the flashlight. The feeling of strangeness still persisted. At the far corner of the cellar, a staircase led up to the first floor.

"I thought you had all been in here before."

"*All,*" David said. "The key word to that sentence is *all.*"

"Just up the stairs, Fosdick, and then we'll tuck you into bed where the boogeyman can't get you."

David's response was a whistling exhalation. The things one did for love.

Flashlight leading the way, they maneuvered around the cluttered junk in the cellar to the foot of the stairs.

"At least we know now who the intrepid one is in this relationship," Sandy sighed.

"And we also know who the commonsensical one is," David said.

"*Non*sensical," Sandy answered smugly. Tentatively, she put her foot on the first step, which groaned under her weight. She felt a slight give from underneath and carefully shifted her balance before determining that the step would support her.

"Be careful. These steps might be rotted away after all this time and neglect."

"All of a sudden you're a contractor," David answered wryly, and followed her up, one creaking step at a time, to the first floor. Their mittens were black from the dirt of the handrail. Shining the flashlight behind them, they saw suspended dust particles dance downward through the disturbing beam of light.

The house settled beneath them again.

"He knows we're here," David said, only half joking.

His eyes darted back and forth, looking for some other sign of life in this supposedly dead house.

Sandy reached out to the doorknob. Her touch was tentative, as if she were afraid of receiving a charge through the metal. Nothing.

David silently hoped that the door would be locked. He wasn't really afraid, he kept telling himself. Yet there were just too many damned stories about the house . . . the lights . . . the chimney smoke . . . the reactions of the locals.

Suddenly he felt sorry about even suspecting the Wallford story was bullshit.

Oh, please let it be locked, please let it be locked.

The door opened easily—

Shit.

—creaking on its rusty hinges.

We have no business being here.

"You are out of your mind," he hissed.

"Oh, David, I've always been adventuresome," Sandy said, peering through the doorway. "I used to explore caves when I was a kid."

"Was that before or after reading Tom Sawyer?"

They stepped out into a thinly carpeted hallway that appeared to run the length of the house. A rear door leading outside stood to their right. At the other end of the long corridor were the double paneled glass front doors ever so slightly illuminated by the streetlamp outside.

David casually tried the rear door.

Locked.

Terrific, he thought.

He peered down the corridor, as if he truly expected Frankenstein's monster to appear at any moment through one of the windows. Or at the very least, a bat.

"And I'm paid up for a full membership this year," he sighed out loud.

Sandy looked at him sideways. "Come on, chicken-shit," she said, smiling. "This is all material for my novel."

"All of a sudden you're Ernest Hemingway?"

"Stephen King."

"Terrific," he muttered, taking in the hallway and sighing under his breath. Then, suddenly noticing: "Hey—don't leave me here alone!" He raced down the hallway to catch up with her.

With David following closely (a reversal that didn't escape him), Sandy led the way down the corridor toward the entrance hall, one side of which opened to the drawing room, the other to the dining room. Paralleling the long hallway, a staircase led to the second floor; the same threadbare carpet that covered the corridor snaked its way up the staircase to the murky blackness above. Water-stained peeling wallpaper surrounded them—a faded, graying floral-patterned yellow, some of it hanging in strips at the corners. David bent a brittle piece backward, tearing it from the wall, then ran it through his fingers, feeling it disintegrate as he balled it between his fingers and crumbled it to the floor.

The house was cold; colder than it was outside. Heatless, it trapped the frigid air that seeped in through unrepaired cracks in the wall. The wall itself served as a sponge for the cold, from early November until late spring. Even then the dampness never left it. A musty smell permeated the house. It reminded him of mold, a black patch. The smell and feel of sickness, a cancer eating away at the house inside and out; physically as well as—he couldn't quite put his finger on the word—spiritually? Yes. Exactly. A radioactive half-life of decay. That was what he smelled: decay. Spiritual as well as temporal decay.

The house sighed again beneath them. David wondered why after more than a century of settling it still creaked, as though the house were trying to escape from itself, to free itself of—what? The years? Was it a groan, not of a settling foundation, but of age? The creaking of aged, old bones, ready to give up the ghost? Wry choice of words, he thought. And yet the sudden thought flashed by that there was something preventing the house from resting in peace. Unfinished business?

Ahead of him Sandy stepped on a loose floorboard, which cried out to them with a sound of pain.

The sound startled her. She jumped back and stumbled. She grabbed at the wall for support. The flashlight clattered to the floor, illuminating the cracked molding between floor and wall. Its thin-lined beam lit a path down the corridor toward the front door.

"Susceptible," she said, bending down to retrieve the flashlight. "We all are. Very."

"It's trying to tell us we're not welcome," David whispered, and then added: "Why do I get the feeling a special effects crew is planning something dastardly for us right now?"

They entered the dining room, where sliding wood paneled doors like those in the ski house stood half open. David tried to push the doors open wide (*to make a fast getaway easier?*), but he couldn't budge the warped wood and decided uneasily that the house didn't want to help him plan his escape routes.

A tulipwood china cupboard stretched the length of one wall, its shelves displaying a collection of colored glass pitchers, decanters, compotes, and goblets standing at attention, all dust-free. Care had obviously been taken in arranging the treasures symmetrically with thought to style, color, and line. The flashlight skimmed over the burnished oakwood dining-room table, a single leaf inserted in order to seat eight comfortably. Bunched up at the head of the table and furthest from the entranceway, three complete place settings—china, silverware, and crystal—were spotlighted in the narrow beam. In the middle of the huge table was a centerpiece, an oval silver tray of very hard, very dry cakes.

"Hey, want to freak them out?" Sandy asked.

"Sandy, don't touch that cake," David warned.

"I won't. Adventuresome, yes. Sacrilegious, no."

She looked dolefully around the room. Her flashlight beam jumped from object to object. It outlined each eerily in turn, slashing through the heavy darkness, marking, and moving on.

They stood silently for a moment. David became aware of the loudness of his breathing. His breath clouded, misting as it surfaced into the cold air of the room. Sandy held the flashlight up, illuminating all at once, but for only a second, the joys and sadness of what had once been Eben Wallford's dining room.

"This is where he wanted his family to come back and be together," she said.

"Fine. Let them," David answered. "Only I would rather not be here when they do. Have you seen enough? Can we go now?"

Perhaps the pull was coming from the second floor.

"I want to go upstairs," she said firmly.

"Sandy, no!"

"David, don't live a cliché. Just because we're in a supposedly haunted house doesn't mean ghosts are coming out of the walls."

"I've had enough!" he said. "Susceptibility. You just acknowledged it. You go up there, you're liable to think you see something, trip, and hurt yourself. What is this fascination you have with this place anyway?"

"My susceptibility," she lied. "Maybe it's time I overcame it."

"You pick the strangest time for self-help," David answered, annoyed.

"So I'm illogical, then. Sue me." She regretted her flippancy, but the feeling was illogical. It was almost as if she were out of touch with her own emotions.

"This is breaking and entering," David sputtered. "We can be arrested."

"Who's going to press charges? You're being ridiculous."

"I'm being intelligent."

"Intelligent people don't believe in ghosts."

He raised his voice. "I'm not going to play word games with you in the middle of the House on Haunted Hill. If you're so locked into going upstairs, we can come back tomorrow in the daylight."

She hesitated, but it was now beyond her.

"And lose all this mood? Forget it. Now or never, baby."

She angled herself toward the sliding doors.

"I am not going up there and neither are you!"

"Try and stop me."

It had become a game. She made a break for the stairs, darting away before David knew what was happening. He took off after her, but without the benefit of the flashlight he ran into a chair and went sprawling over its back onto the floor. He called loudly after her, but she was already up the stairs and out of his control. As if she were ever in it. . . .

Sandy heard the fall from above and David calling to her, but as long as there was no cry of pain she knew he was not hurt. Just a quick look; that's all she would take, and then indeed she would get the hell out of there.

Why? she wondered. This was not like her. Because it's there? Was that it? Maybe. Now she really didn't know. She had come this far—was that reason enough? No.

What was the bonding she felt to this place?

It was black in the second floor hallway. The stairs opened up on the back of the house where the streetlamps didn't penetrate. She flashed the light around the hallway, illuminating the narrow corridor leading rearward to a blackened, shaded window.

She was able to make out five doors—two to the
left, two to the right, and one behind her leading to the
room over the front entranceway. It was this closed
door that blocked out the light from the streetlamp
below, holding the corridor in blackness. A staircase
behind her led higher still, to the third, and attic, floor.
She turned and moved toward the fifth door.

*The feeling slithered from deep within her. It was
something coldly intuitive that told her this was where
she had to go.*

It was the door that led to the front bedroom, *his*
bedroom, the windows of which she remembered seeing
barred over when they had first arrived in Owlsfane,
little more than an hour before. So much had happened
in that one hour.

One quick look. That's all she'd take.

The same yellowed, patterned wallpaper as on the
first floor led down the corridor to the front bedroom.
Even new, the pattern and color would have been de-
pressing to her. The peeling paint of the attic staircase
was in harmony with the general disrepair of the house;
the only exception had been the collection of cared-for
glassware. If the outer supports were anything like the
inside of the house, it was surprising that the house was
still standing. She laughed nervously. There she was, as
David had said, thinking like a contractor and an archi-
tect. Not to mention a fatalist.

Suddenly she discerned a curious odor, one that she
could not at first place. She inhaled sharply. It was far
away: faint, as if coming from a distance, or lingering,
as if lost in time. It was the residual slightly pungent
odor of burned flesh. She wrinkled her nose. Briefly she
wondered where the smell was coming from, but the
thought quickly passed as she stood silently, hesitantly,
in front of the closed bedroom door.

One quick look.

Curiosity. Idiotic curiosity.

But it was more than that and she knew it. She sensed it with her nostrils; she felt it with the feathery hairs on the back of her neck.

She remembered being scared stiff in the caves she had explored as a kid.

She tenatively touched the doorknob to Eben Wallford's bedroom—

—*Curiosity killed the cat.*

—almost as if afraid of an electrical charge

—*That was a dumb thought.*

—turned the knob

—*Am I really susceptible? Illogical? Intrepid?*

From below, David started up the stairs, calling her name.

—and entered.

The room was cold. An unnatural cold, much colder than the hall. A cold that could almost be seen; cut. It penetrated Sandy's layers of clothing, immediately chilling her. A shiver involuntarily shot up her spine and settled tightly in her neck. Her body stiffened.

The bedroom door closed slowly behind her, creaking on rusty hinges, barring her escape.

She had been called to this room and now it had her.

The streetlamp faintly illuminated the bedroom with a dim, shadowy yellow-orange light.

A gaslight fixture hung from the wall to the side of a lace-canopied four-poster bed. The bed was made up, a quilted coverlet tucked into place. A shirt was folded neatly on top of a bureau. A large wing chair sat in the corner by the window, facing out, positioned so a person sitting in the chair could look out at the mausoleum across the road. Dry pitch pine and scraps of scrub oak filled the woodbox next to the fireplace, and dusty yellowed newspaper was stacked to the side. Over the fireplace a large white sheet covered a picture. The fireplace was silent and dead.

She walked further into the room, drawn by an unseen power.

The wall opposite was stenciled with light-brown quarter fans. When they caught the beam of her flashlight it gave the effect of fans waving, hiding faces of modest ladies on a summer's day a long time ago.

A long time ago! That was what she felt in this room: the decay of age. The icy chill of death.

She silently breathed in the room as if to say *I'm here. What do you want?*

Once the thought was uttered, the moment hung suspended; yet she had the knowledge that something was about to happen, like the split second of waiting for the roar of the thunderclap after the lightning bolt has raced across the sky.

A moment of silence. Then it happened.

The uneasy feeling first pricked at her. Then grabbed her.

She was not alone in this room.

Someone was in here with her!

Her teeth began to chatter. From cold? Or from fear.

She was frightened and wanted to turn, to run from the room, but she couldn't.

Something was forcing her to be there.

Not alone in the room! No!

Her lips moved. *Who's there?* But the words remained thoughts. Her mouth was open, but fear, *or something,* had suddenly stolen her voice. Her mouth grew dry. She tasted her own breath, sour with fear. With difficulty she swallowed. She tongued her lips and slowly looked around.

Nothing. The room was silent.

But the clammy feeling grew, walking over her, overpowering her. Yet she could see no one there.

Why did she ever come into this room? Her brain tightened as she fought to remember. A confused knot grew in her forehead. But she couldn't remember. She was there. That was all she knew.

I'm here. What do you want?

Her breathing grew loud. She was aware of her chest heaving. Her skin prickled.

The flashlight grew heavy. Her hand shook.

There was definitely someone in the room. She could smell it.

Someone alive. Yet not alive.

Someone long dead. A hundred years long dead. A thousand.

But here!

The crawling sensation of being watched.

More than watched. Scrutinized. Devoured. From head to toe.

There was someone unseen there in the cold darkness peering at her. Sizing her up. She felt eyes on her, traveling up and down her body, stroking her. She could see nothing, yet she knew they were there.

A sound. Creaking. She did not know where it came from.

The flashlight beam jumped spastically around the room in desperate search, trying to see *who, where.*

Again she wanted to turn, to run; needed to escape, but her feet, cemented to the floor, refused to obey; would not respond to her commands. Her mind was not hers.

A cry escaped her lips.

She could do nothing. She started to sweat.

There was the cold terror of helplessness.

Then suddenly it happened.

Out of the corner of her eye, out of the icy blackness, she first sensed it, then saw it: movement. First a passing shadow, then the dim outline of a man behind her.

She whipped her flashlight around and caught only the briefest glimpse. But it registered.

He was old.

His hair and beard were gray.

His arms were outstretched in front of him.
And he was moving toward her.
Was he going to kill her? her mind shrieked.
It was her last thought before everything went blank.

Josiah Stoneham woke again. His eyes opened and
he stared into the pitch-black room. Unexplainable
feelings snaked through his head. Something was indeed very wrong.

The first time it was the disturbing memory that had
caused him to rise from sleep. Now it was something
more. An inner sense honed by time was attuned to the
Wallford house. The sounds of movement rolled past
him. Eben's presence felt strong. Even tactile. It was
enough to wake him from sleep. Twice, when he never
woke up in the midddle of the night.

Eben's presence in the house would walk for all time,
fed by a sadness and guilt that would not let go. Eben
would never give up the house he had so loved and
then grown to hate. What had caused him to wake and
walk tonight? Josiah remembered. It was Christmas-
time, the anniversary of Eben's death, when he might be
expected to awaken.

But one becomes confused and frightened by the
thoughts and sounds of the night. Josiah's eyes grew
heavy and drifted closed, and sleep once again began
to overtake him. He fell into a restive trance, wondering
if he would remember, come morning, the lost and perhaps foolish memories of a dark midnight awakening.

CHAPTER IV

The cold air brought her around. They were outside. David was slapping Sandy, repeating her name, yelling at her. Her eyes were transparent, her gaze transfixed, her expression foreign and frightening. Slowly she blinked, responding to his force and persistence. She looked at him, remembered, and fell into his arms. She burst into tears and buried her face in his neck as if to hide. With reassuring strength he embraced her, supporting her.

"It's over," he said softly, although he was not certain what he was referring to. He was just relieved that she was indeed back with him. He had been terrified by her blank expression and trancelike state. "It's over," he repeated with finality, and tightened his hold on her, perhaps more to reassure himself. "Let's go on back to the house."

For moments she couldn't move, and he continued to hold her, enveloping her in a net of security and safety. Slowly he lifted her chin so he could look into her eyes, and wiped the freezing tears from her cheeks.

"It's over," he said once more, and started down the road back toward the ski house, supporting her every step, wondering what in the hell had happened.

He had raced up the stairs, only moments behind
her. He had gone into the front bedroom and there he
had seen her, arms hanging limply at her sides, the
beam from the flashlight a motionless circle on the
floor.

"There you are," he had said from behind. "I've had
to search every goddamned room in this goddamned
house looking for you!"

Then he had noticed that something was wrong. She
had not turned to him; did not move. Her posture in
the dim quarter light was rigid, unnaturally so. He
touched her shoulder, turned her around, and looked
closely at her.

Her eyes were blank, staring ahead, zombielike.

No recognition. No response.

"Jesus!" he had said, and had shaken her. She had
continued to look out, unseeing. It was no gag.

He had led her outside into the cold air. Now, as
they walked back to the ski house he listened in horror
to what she was trying to tell him.

Sandy's parka was draped sloppily over the back of
one of the dining-room chairs. Pauline entered from the
kitchen with a brandy. Sandy took it, held it tightly
between two still-quivering hands, and lifted it to her
mouth to sip. Around her were David, Bob, and Tom.
David had a reassuring hand on her knee. The sliding
doors were closed to the others. David didn't want any
of them to see Sandy when she was vulnerable and
frightened. Tom had asked if he could stay; perhaps he
could help. The psychiatrist straddled a chair off to the
side, leaning on its back, watching Sandy closely.

"The door closed behind me," Sandy said. Her voice
was calm, forcibly steady. The cold air and brandy
were helping. She sipped again before continuing, the
fierce, warming liquid renewing her strength. "For a
split second there was nothing. Then I sensed someone;

felt someone watching me. Then I saw him: Eben
Wallford!"

Bob and David exchanged surreptitious glances.

"How do you know it was Eben Wallford?" David
asked.

"David, who else would it be?" Sandy flared.

Tom never took his eyes from Sandy. Pauline stood
behind her and stroked her hair.

"And then what?" Bob asked softly.

"Then David was slapping my face. Outside. It still
hurts." She smiled, rubbing her cheek.

"You don't remember walking back down the stairs
or through the cellar?"

She shook her head. "No."

"Climbing out through the window?"

"Nothing."

David took the glass from her hands and put it on
the dining table. "She was spaced," he said. "Blank. I
shined the flashlight directly into her eyes."

Sandy looked from Bob to Tom, confused. "I didn't
even know he was there." She took David's hand and
squeezed it. She was afraid to let go, as if doing so
might throw her back to where she had been.

"It was almost as if she had left her body," David
observed.

Tom put up a restraining hand. "Wait one minute!
Let's not just say things here with no substantiation.
People don't just leave their bodies."

"Then where was she?" David asked flatly. "She ran
up to the second floor like a she-demon and I had to
practically carry her down."

He smiled at Sandy. "Incidentally, you should think
about losing some weight if I have to go dragging you
around like that."

Sandy looked at him, a smile breaking across her
face. "Who are you? The Seven Santinis?" She play-
fully tried to break his grip. Sensing the increased tension against his fingertips, he held on more tightly, but

relaxed inwardly. With her humor restored, he knew Sandy was back.

"You know," Sandy said slowly, suddenly realizing, "I'm the first person on my block ever to have seen a ghost." Her eyes were wide. "That's an accomplishment of sorts, don't you think?"

Tom leaned in over the back of his chair, shifting his weight forward, resting his chin on his folded arms. "What exactly did you see?" he asked softly. All attention was suddenly on him.

"A ghost?" she asked weakly, uncertainly, with a half-smile of confusion on her face. She looked questioningly toward David. "At least I think I did."

And then another possibility hit home. She looked from one to the other, a momentary flash of panic across her face. "I'm not crazy! I didn't hallucinate the whole thing!"

"Talk," Tom said in a whisper that hung heavily over the room.

And she did, telling them all that had happened, including the magnetic pull that had drawn her to the house, the room. No one moved until she was finished, each lost in thoughts of his own.

David felt cold helplessness creep over him. His palms leaked water.

"Why didn't you say something?" he asked in a voice tinged with undefined anger and fear. He looked toward Tom with a vague uncertainty that didn't spell "worry" exactly—rather, scattered confusion.

Like when he was seven years old and his family moved to a new apartment in Queens. The school was only one block from his new house, across one street. The first lunch hour, he stood on the corner in utter befuddlement, unable to remember *which street to cross, which block to walk*. He was lost, yet he wasn't. It was that same feeling he was experiencing now.

"Perhaps if we knew about this strange attraction you had to the house we could have stopped you." His

voice trailed off foolishly, hesitantly. "Or something."
A half-scowl of apprehension lined his face.

Sandy's hands were in front of her, palms open in
exasperation. "David, how could I have told you there
was a mysterious force pulling me to a haunted house?
You would have called for a wagon."

David smiled sheepishly. She was right. "Maybe," he
conceded.

Another thought flashed suddenly. "But maybe we
would have—" and was just as suddenly dismissed. He
broke off. "I don't know." He turned to the psychiatrist. "Tom—?"

"It's over now," Tom said in a voice that was
strangely hypnotic and strongly reassuring. In that moment David knew how he talked to his patients, and
why they got better. "It was exciting and unusual, but
I think now we should send Sandy up to bed."

Hearing what Tom was saying, David kept silent. It
was obvious the psychiatrist did not wish to dwell on
what had happened.

"Sandy, if we're all getting up in a couple of hours,
I think you can use the sleep." He tapped her knee
twice in a gesture that sang, *Off to bed with you now,
lassie.*

"I think you're right," Sandy agreed. "And it was
unusual." Her voice quivered and rose. "Exciting—?
I don't know."

"I'll tuck you in up there," David said, and started
to lead her from the room. Pauline stopped him.

"You know the rules, David," she said sternly, but
with a suppressed smile. "No men in female bedrooms."
The tentative smile played across the corner of her lips,
then broke full.

David was momentarily thoughtful.

"I remember back in Junior High School," he said,
"I was reported one lunch hour and brought to the
principal's office for kissing my girl friend in the cafeteria. Somehow this feels exactly like ninth grade all

over again, without the algebra. But—" he said, leaning in to Pauline, a worldly gleam in his eye, "I don't care, because I'm not afraid of the principal anymore."

He cradled Sandy protectively and kissed her. She held tightly to him for the strength that passed almost wavelike between them.

"You'll be all right?" he asked in a whisper. He stroked her hair gently.

She nodded. "I think so."

"I'll be right down the hall if you need anything."

"I'm even closer," Pauline said. "Next room over. Give a scream or a bang on the wall and I'll be there."

She took Sandy from David. "Come on. I'll get you settled."

Sandy turned and faced the others in the room. "I feel like a total jackass. I'm sorry." She tried to shrug it all off with a smile. "*I'm* what David's marrying."

Tom returned the smile. "I wondered how someone so anal-retentive did so well.

David grimaced wryly. "The last time Tom cooked dinner up here, believe me, we *all* wished we were anal-retentive."

Everyone laughed as Pauline walked Sandy up the stairs.

The living room was empty; everyone had gone upstairs to bed.

The fire was dying, the wood consumed, a dull-red Phoenix glow rising out of the gray ashes and unburned splinters of wood scattered beyond range of the flames. When they entered the room, Bob moved to poke at the embers, scattering the ashes to extinguish the fire, almost as if trying to beat the last remaining flames to death. Tom poured from a bottle of Scotch that was hidden under the bar. He lifted the bottle toward David, who nodded, and reached under the counter for a third glass.

"What do you think?" David asked.

"I think," Tom answered, bringing them each their glasses and lifting his own, "that we should all chip in next year to buy this clown some good liquor. A dollar thirty-nine a fifth is not my idea of party booze."

"You're right," David said. "But that wasn't what I meant."

Tom frowned. "I didn't think it was. But I was hoping."

"Did she see a ghost?" David asked, then shuddered involuntarily. He felt as if someone had screeched chalk against a blackboard.

Tom swallowed some of the Scotch. "You'd probably make a good psychiatrist, David. You're very direct. The first question I ask my patients on their first visit is 'Why are you here?' You get more out of a direct question than by trying to work around something."

"Then how about answering my direct question," David asked.

"People do see ghosts," Tom equivocated.

"Goddamn it!" David exploded. "I don't care about people. Did *she* see one? Sandy's a completely normal, rational human being—as sane as any of us are. Tonight she comes up here, hears a spooky story, gets strange feelings, and presto! sees ghosts. For Chrissakes, Tom. Does it all add up? I'm going to marry her!"

With slow care and his eyes on the glass he was holding, Tom answered: "There is no way of knowing for certain. At least not now. Even though Sandy says she never knew herself to be psychic, she probably possesses some psychic abilities that never had the opportunity or cause to appear before. Although whether Eben Wallford is stalking the house tonight and came through to her, or if she just picked up a long-tarrying telepathic impression . . ." He trailed off, shrugging. "Who knows?"

David felt the tension flow from him. His legs felt

rubbery and he grasped the back of the Morris chair. "Why the trance, Tom? Why the spaced look?"

"Nothing supernatural about that. She may have had a shock reaction. You don't walk into a bedroom expecting to see a dead person. Hysteria, maybe, as a result of the shock. Partial, temporary paralysis. Even perhaps a hypnotic state of sorts."

"Nothing to worry about, then?" David asked. "Straight?"

"Straight," the psychiatrist answered, knowing he was about to lie. "Nothing to worry about."

David took Bob's arm. "I want you to walk me upstairs, because if I leave you two down here without me, I'm going to be wondering what you're talking about."

"David, you have my word," Tom said. "Any other verbal analysis I do will include you."

"What about your thought process?" David asked.

"That's private."

"And that's what worries me the most."

Tom held up a restraining hand to lighten the mood. "Before you go upstairs, let me give you one theory of ghostly appearance to fall asleep over. Some feel that apparitions get their manifesting energy from the living. Possibly sexual energy. Ghosts may just appear as the result of untapped sexual energy. Although," he smirked, "I don't think there's that much untapped sexual energy around here."

Bob stifled a grin as David answered. "A week up there in those bunks and, believe me, there's gonna be a whole lot of untapped sexual energy around this place."

Tom laughed as David and Bob disappeared upstairs.

He poured himself two last fingers and relaxed.

The house was quietly settled above him as he sat staring into the now cold fire. Welcome silence surrounded him. He was able to think. He put his feet up on the coffee table in front of him, scattered potato chips blasted to crumbs by the weight of his heels, and rested his head on the faded fabric.

He knew that so much of what is called "the supernatural" has its origins in what might be called psychologically normal. He, himself, always tried to look for natural causes for what seemed to be unnatural phenomena. If Sandy's ghostly vision was not a psychic impression or retrocognition of a man long dead, then why was she hallucinating ghosts? And why now?

There was importance to the strange pull she had experienced. Was it really a psychic summons? Or was it something else? Perhaps a seepage of some repressed matter long buried in her subconscious, suddenly triggered free.

A powerful defense mechanism, repression, where we bury what might be too painful or harmful to live with.

To ghost . . . or not to ghost . . . he thought as he switched off the light and walked upstairs to bed.

He hoped it wasn't going to be a busman's holiday.

As he rounded the landing he saw Bob rushing into the women's dorm room and heard excited voices from inside. He took the remaining steps two at a time and charged into the room. The light was on and the women were climbing out of their beds. Instinctively he rubbed his hands together. It was then that he noticed what was wrong. The room was freezing. It felt as if a net of cold air had suddenly and ferociously been dropped over the bedroom. The women were pulling on their robes and wrapping themselves in blankets. Ricky slipped on her ski parka.

"What is it?" he asked Bob as David and the other men emptied out of their room and crossed the hallway.

"Jesus!" Stan exclaimed, and darted back to his room for a sweater.

"I don't know." Puzzled, Bob went to the two windows and pulled up the shades. Neither window was open. No draft was coming in through the frame or sash.

"I'm cold, Mommy," Cynthia cried. Pauline crossed to her and sat next to her on the bed. She held her in her arms so the blankets wrapped tightly around the little girl.

"Where's it coming from, Bob?" she asked.

Bob shook his head. He looked into the fireplace. It was never used, but somehow the flue might have sprung open. It had not. He walked to the closet and swung the door open. Flipping on the light, he checked to see if the trapdoor to the attic had somehow opened. He tightened his lips. No. All was in order. The room should not be as cold as it was.

He stepped out into the hallway. The web of cold extended throughout the second floor of the house but was decidedly stronger in the women's dorm room. The window at the end of the hallway was shut tightly. No cold air leaked in.

Stan came out of his bedroom, a white turtleneck sweater pulled partway over his head. He tugged it down snugly into place. Bob pointed back to the men's bedroom. "Check the windows in there, will you, Stan? And in the johns."

Stan nodded and trotted off. Although Bob didn't expect they'd find the answer in the other rooms.

Sandy pulled on her woolen socks. A strange prickly feeling settled over her as the veil of cold tightened about her. She was nervous and her hands trembled. Gooseflesh crawled on her arms. Something told her this night would never end. She looked up suddenly, surprised at the frightening thought that coursed through her: *he had followed her into the ski house!*

"It's Eben," she whispered, unaware that the thought had escaped into words until the room grew suddenly quiet around her.

David was at her side. "Don't be ridiculous," he said softly.

She smiled weakly, embarrassed. "I am being ridiculous, aren't I?"

"I think so," Tom said firmly. He looked toward Bob, who was standing in the center of the room, his hands on his hips. He stared upward at the ceiling, hoping an answer would miraculously appear from midair.

"I just don't know," Bob said, shrugging. "The radiator isn't cold, but it's not exactly pumping out gobs of hot air either. I'll check the heating system in the morning." But he knew it wasn't the heating system; the cold was too sudden and intense. It was something else. A leak from somewhere. A hole—

"Nothing," Stan said, appearing in the doorway.

Judy Landberg searched the room as if trying to discern something the others could not. "It's got to be a ghost," she said with eleven-year-old certainty. Her lips were pursed and she was nodding. "I have no other explanation."

Tom put his finger to his lips, indicating to his daughter that she should remain quiet. "I don't think anybody's asking you to come up with one, Judy."

"It makes sense," she answered petulantly, convinced she was correct. "Spirits pull the energy from the air so they can appear and the room gets colder."

Scott scoffed at her. "Well, where's your spirit, then? I don't see him anywhere." He broke into a broad "so there" grin.

Judy didn't have an answer. Clearly there was no ghost visible in the room. Although she knew it had to be so, she had no tangible proof. She remained quiet. Scott knew he was on top. "There're no such things as ghosts," he pressed, in a voice intended to put an end to the discussion.

Cynthia raised her head from Pauline's lap. "Is there a ghost, Mommy?" Her voice was loud and shaky, her eyes wide with fright. She sank into the security of the woolen blankets and her mother's softness.

"Of course not," Pauline answered. "You heard Scott. There're no such things as ghosts."

"That's right," Bob said to his daughter in the controlled voice she had come to trust. She knew her father knew everything.

"You'll find out," Judy said to Scott with a degree of knowing satisfaction. She turned away from him, silently praying the ghost would appear and prove her correct.

Tom raised his voice to Judy. He didn't want Cynthia any more frightened than she was. "No more ghost talk, okay?" His words were strong and metered carefully, all for Cynthia's benefit: "There is no ghost!"

"Right," Scott echoed. "No ghost."

"That's enough," Bob said. "I'll find the source of the cold, I promise. For now, I suggest we all get some extra blankets."

"Good idea," Pauline said. The diversion would give Cynthia a chance to calm down. She went to the closet and started to pull blankets down from the top shelf.

When suddenly the coldness passed, as quickly as it had come, more than one of them wondered if they had imagined the whole thing. The room was warmer, back to the temperature it had been before. All looked from one to the other. Sandy felt the strange feeling pass.

It was Stan who spoke first. "Bob, when you tell a ghost story, you certainly go for authenticity."

Cynthia started to cry. "She brought the ghost back with her!" Her voice quavered with accusation and her whole body shook. "He was in the house and now he's gone."

Pauline stroked her daughter's head. "Quiet, baby," she said softly. "It's all right. There's no ghost. We'll find whatever it was. There's no reason to be afraid."

Sandy felt the child's eyes on her. She knew that logically she was not the cause of what had just happened, but how can you speak logically to a frightened six-year-old? Cynthia was staring at her with suspicion and blame.

The house members stood idly around as if waiting for something more to happen. Soon they realized the show was over. Layers of clothing started to come off. David looked at Sandy and shrugged broadly. Whatever it was, it was gone.

"Hey—would you look at this," Bob said suddenly, trying to end the episode on an up note. "I didn't notice it before when we found the kids at the Wallford house because it was dark and they had their ski hats on, but—" He motioned to Sandy. "Come over here. Stand next to Judy."

Everyone looked.

"See!" Bob said. "Look at them. Same hair—color and style. And same eyes: almond-shaped. Wouldn't you say?" He peered closely into each girl's eyes. "Color?"

Judy's were more green to Sandy's blue. Bob shrugged. "Can't have it all."

Judy and Sandy looked at each other. Bob was right. Their hair and eyes were similar.

Sandy smiled. "Maybe we were sisters in a former life."

Judy shrugged. "Could be."

From the doorway Craig called into the room. "Hey, David, when you sneak back in here later on, make sure you crawl into the right bed. One is definitely jailbait."

Pauline smiled politely. "I'm sure there will be no sneaking back in here later." Then a little less certainly she asked, "Will there be?"

David just shrugged and grinned noncommittally.

Scott eyed Sandy up and down leeringly and commented, "They may have the same eyes and hair, but believe me, Sandy's got more of what a man likes."

"Don't be fresh," Pauline said, but she couldn't hide her grin.

"Yeah?" Judy shot back, looking down at herself in disappointment. "What do *you* know about what a man likes?"

Ricky shot her a thumbs up and she beamed.

"Enough to know you ain't got it," Scott topped her, blowing lightly on his fingers and rubbing them against his pajama top.

"Okay," Bob said, smiling. "I think we can break this up for now. I, for one, want to try to get a little sleep. Lots of good skiing tomorrow."

"I wouldn't know," Scott muttered, his punishment looming ahead of him.

The men started to drift out of the room. Tom and Bob walked together. Pauline stayed with her daughter, patting her to sleep.

"What do you really think, Tom?" Bob asked, so no one else could hear. "Taken with everything else tonight."

"There's no ghost, Bob," Tom said evenly. "Believe me, ghosts are rare enough. And it's a rarer ghost still who travels far from his location of death. No, I think what we have here is a girl with something she is repressing, and a hole somewhere that blows open and closed."

"I guess," Bob answered. "But a ghost certainly is the easiest explanation. Also the most exotic. I'd certainly be able to fill the house next year if I was able to advertise a ghost-in-residence." He sighed. "Ah, well, we'll start looking for gopher holes in the morning."

The house slowly quieted into sleep. Pauline, feeling her daughter had drifted off, got up and went to her own bedroom, where she settled in warmly next to Bob. Her feet were still cold and she let them play against his. Neither spoke. There was really nothing to say.

But Cynthia was not asleep. She tossed in her bed with frightening child's images of ghosts and demons flailing through her mind. She could not find a comfortable position; she could not fall asleep. The ghost had been there and she was frightened. But she knew her father would protect her; he always did.

CHAPTER V

Sandy lay in bed under two heavy woolen blankets. Her eyes slowly became accustomed to the darkness of the room. The door to the hallway was open a crack and a thin beam of light trickled in, angled away from her. The house was breathing easily. The sounds of sleep filled her ears: covers twisting, pillows scrunching, the heavy breathing of restful sleep. Lying on her back, she stretched, trying consciously to relax. She really didn't want to think anymore. She extended her arms upward and grasped the metal springs of the top bunk above; then, afraid of waking Gail Landberg, she quickly lowered them and folded them across her breasts, fingers crisscrossed in a flattened steeple. She breathed deeply to try to bring on the rhythm of sleep, and tried to blank her mind, but she was unsuccessful. She could not reach back to any conscious memory to explain what had happened tonight. She never knew herself to be so affected by the power of suggestion, but then, like your heartbeat, that wasn't something you really thought about.

She reviewed the facts: she had just heard the Wallford story, felt a spring-coil tug to the house, was in the house, the house was dark, her brain was churning on

overdrive—and bingo! A ghost! A mind's-eye ghost?
No. That would have put the whole episode in her
imagination. She was not going to accept hallucination
as the answer. She didn't imagine the vision. He was
there. He was real!

And—she sniffed the darkness wide-eyed—he was
in the room with her. There was no mistaking the very
real—or rather, she thought wryly, *unreal*—cold that
had invaded the house. She wondered again if Eben
Wallford had indeed followed her back to the ski house.
She was frightened by the fantasy, yet half excited by it
as well. She snuggled deeper under the covers. Despite
the two heavy woolen blankets tucked tightly under her
chin she shivered involuntarily.

What was happening?

A faint smell tickled her nose, almost like a wisp of
smoke. She sniffed the air, tentatively at first, and then
with deeper breaths. Yes, there was the smell: the same
smell she remembered from the Wallford house. Burning, smoldering flesh. Was it a lingering odor in her
nostrils? A memory triggered by her fear? Or was it
fresh? *What did he want?*

She drew the blanket tightly around her, as if its
physical closeness would ensure her safety. And sanity.

Faintly in the distance she heard the deep-toned
chime of the grandfather clock. She stretched once
more, rolled over onto her side, cradled her pillow as if
it had been David, and got ready to settle into sleep.

David. She needed him. She felt so damned strange
sleeping without him; she had not done so for months.
She realized she was used to him. To his feel, warmth,
taste. His smell and touch. She really needed him tonight. She didn't want to go through this herself.

Psychic impressions. Although she had no memories
of being at all psychic. If she had been, she probably
would have done better at school. Maybe this was her
first experience—then watch out—Dial-a-Psychic!

The disquieting feeling passed through her again, refusing to relinquish its shifty hold. An eerie, lightning flash of strangeness.

And with that she drifted into sleep.

She felt cold. Freezing cold. She was outside in the snow, in the cemetery across the road. Wet snow struck her body, dousing her, caking her in white. She hunched herself up, arms clasped in front of her as she fought for warmth.

She heard a voice: Bob's. *"You learn respect for the cold here,"* it warned, as if in accusation. *"Minus ten degrees, stark naked, you'd last about thirty seconds."*

The intense cold burned her skin. There was a sensation of fire pain. She looked at herself. It was not the cold that was scalding her, it was fire. Her arms were on fire. She was burning! Flames billowed up around her, charring her skin, blackening it.

There was an intuitive sense of punishment. There was reason for the pain.

She screamed for help, her calls becoming more shrill, more pronounced, more frantic, as the fire ate away at her.

Suddenly she saw a man appear from among the headstones. An old man with gray hair and beard. Eben Wallford! His eyes were intense, as if burning through her, feeding the fire.

She reached out to him, seeking help. Please, would he put out the flames that exploded around her. Her hands touched him, imploring.

She felt him push her.

What was he doing?

His push was harder, more insistent.

What was he doing?

She was standing in front of the Wallford mausoleum. The statue of Eben Wallford was pushing her. The door to the mausoleum was opening.

He was pushing her into the mausoleum!

She fought against him, desperately swinging her burning arms, screaming frantically.

David sat at the side of her bed, fighting off her arms, which were waving wildly, spastically, trying to claw at his face. He grabbed her by the wrists, restraining her, as her eyes opened.

At first she saw him: Eben Wallford! Then she blinked and she knew. Her cries for help faded as she rose from sleep and realized where she was. Her eyes darted back and forth across his face in bewilderment as David gently, reassuringly stroked her arm from shoulder to hand. She was all right, she would be all right, he kept repeating over and over again. His touch brought her around. She buried her face in his lap and sobbed. He softly patted her head until she stopped crying.

She raised her head and looked at him. He smiled.

She was home. She was safe.

"You okay?" he finally asked.

She shook her head in relief and embarrassment. "I really am making a spectacle of myself."

"No," he said. "You're not. You're all right." Her eyes were glazed, distant. To look into them was to look through them.

She held on to him for warmth and support, letting his strength revive her once again. The vivid, horrifying dream remained with her; not like so many other dreams or nightmares that came terrifyingly, then disappeared tracelessly: fleeting, vague half-memories. She did not, for the most part, remember her dreams. Nor her nightmares. In fact, as she thought back, she very distinctly did not recall her dreams upon awakening. This one, however, clung; she was still able to experience the intense cold, the push into the mausoleum, and the strange burning pain so out of place in her frigid hell. Yet somehow it wasn't, and that made her shiver anew.

It was as if her mind were forcing her to remember.
She was trembling.

"I was on fire, David," she said, grasping at him, digging her fingers into his flesh, almost as if trying to convince herself that he was real, corporeal. Mortal. "I was burning to death." She shuddered, breaking off.

David held her. "It was a dream. Nothing else."

She started to say more; *wanted* to say more. To tell him the dream *was* something else; *vision* perhaps, to be more accurate. Eben Wallford burning her, pushing her into the mausoleum, trying to bury her alive.

But the overhead light in the room was on, the globeless bare bulb burning harshly. A half-dozen pairs of eyes peered curiously at her.

"What time is it?" she asked softly, suddenly hideously self-conscious. She squinted from the glare of the light.

"A little past four. You want to go back to sleep?"

She did. Yet she was afraid of what lay waiting for her. Power of suggestion, all right. Jesus! What was it? Was her mind going? *What?*

She really wanted to be held. Rocked. A need she hadn't had since she was a child. She remembered being rocked by her father—a fleeting, instantaneous image of her father flashed before her—although she couldn't remember why he had rocked her. But even now she could feel his strong arms encircling her protectively, comfortingly. She wanted to be held and rocked by David. Downstairs. Away from the people and by the warmth of the fire, but she knew the fire was long cold and that David was tired and eager to rest for the day of skiing that was now only hours away.

"I'll sleep now," she said quietly, although the thought of it frightened her.

"Can I make you a cup of chocolate?" Pauline asked. She stood worriedly behind David, red-sashed woolen robe pulled around her body. "It might relax you."

Sandy smiled feebly, embarrassed. "I'm fine. Really.

Thanks." She had made an absolute spectacle of herself. How could she face these people? It was only a nightmare, for Christ's sake. She addressed the others in the room. "My apologies."

David was still holding her, stroking her forehead, wiping the tears that were drying on her face. She was fine now, but she didn't want him to stop.

"Helluva night, isn't it?" she whispered to him, smiling stupidly, ashamed at her reaction to a dream. Fears and chills faded as reality breathed more strongly around her.

He smiled back at her.

"I'll sit with you for a while until you fall back to sleep." He gestured to Pauline that all was under control. The light was turned off. The occupants of the room settled slowly back to sleep. Sandy relaxed as she felt the light, tingling pressure of David's touch.

She thought once again of her father. Strange. He had been dead for five years. It was just that something reminded her of him, although she couldn't quite determine what. Perhaps it was only a reaction to her fear and a memory of her father once holding her during a storm.

The thought passed quickly, though, as she continued to concentrate on the hands that were rippling over her body. David's touch was arousing and she wanted him. Her hand under her nightgown moved downward and played across her body. David noticed, leaned over, and quietly kissed her. She knew he was also excited. He pushed the covers aside, and breaking the ski house rules, climbed into bed and made silent, soothing love to her.

David made certain that Sandy was asleep before gingerly climbing out of the bed. His bare feet missed his thong slippers and landed on the icy tiled floor. He scrunched his toes up under him to minimize the area of foot in contact with the cold floor, and stifled a yelp, as he felt frantically for his slippers. He tucked Sandy's covers tightly under the mattress, imprisoning her so she could not push free again. His eyes, adjusted to the quarter-light of the room, took her in; she lay motionless, save her constant, even breathing, in peaceful sleep.

David returned to his room across the hall and pulled himself into his upper bunk.

He was worried.

Two episodes tonight. Sandy was not prone to nightmares, nor to suggestion, nor, of course, to hallucination. He really had to accept, in fact needed to accept, the possibility that something existed in the Wallford house, although many of the members had been inside for nothing more than a spooky evening of mock-haunted fun.

They had held a blast of a Halloween party there a few years ago, attended by all the regulars of the previous several years. There had been no skiing that weekend, but the Saturday night party had been well worth the drive north, even at eighty-seven cents a gallon. The invitations Bob and Pauline had sent out had been on yellowed, aged, almost brittle paper, with scattered reddish-brown spots he took to be imitation blood. "Eben Wallford and family request your presence at a Halloween Party." The careful fountain-penned archaic script had provided details as to time and, he remembered, smiling, place.

And it had been fun. Bob had rigged skeletons that popped out when the coat closet was opened, startling each new arrival in turn; each, then, keeping the secret from the one to follow, and then all howling in laughter as the spooking continued. They sat in a circle on the drawing-room floor, in dim candlelight. The shades were drawn tightly so that no light escaped. That would have truly freaked out the neighbors or attracted the attention of a passing state trooper. They took turns telling ghost stories, each more eerie than the one before.

They had decided to explore the house at the haunting hour of twelve. Nobody had been upstairs to the second floor yet, and no one was eager to be first. They all climbed up—*together*. After the candlelit circle, no one was going to venture upstairs alone. There had been precisely thirteen guests present, a coven. Bob had planned his party well.

They had opened all the doors and poked around in the upstairs rooms. They had been very careful not to disturb or remove anything, and explored the third floor and attic as well.

Absolutely nothing had happened.

And with thirteen of them there, they certainly had enough psychic energy to conjure up a dozen ghosts. But no ghost appeared, and as Pauline had remarked, no one seemed overly disappointed. They had decided the ghost was shy and fearful of crowds. To test this theory Bob had offered a free weekend to anyone bold enough to spend the night alone in the Wallford house. Not surprisingly, he had no takers.

That had been it. They had spent the next day enjoying the last of the fall foliage, the way only a New England turning could be—kingly displays of reds and oranges, rust and burnt umber, leaves dying in a brilliance of color, each differently hued. One final burst of individuality.

David lay on his back, hands clasped at the back of his neck. His own indefinable strangeness, a fleeting feeling of unease, passed over him like an invisible black veil. He cast a surreptitious look at the door, half expecting Eben Wallford to be walking up the stairs outside. He had to peek at the house, if only to convince himself it was still there and had not moved closer down the road. Completely irrational, he acknowledged.

The snow had stopped, the storm had moved off. He stared across the wide expanse at the Wallford house, silent, dead black, almost defiant. A few stars were in evidence through breaks in the fast-drifting clouds. No cars traveled the road at this late hour, and he could almost reach out and touch the heavy silence outdoors. Although, he had to concede, it was all completely normal and there was nothing taunting about it.

He blinked. He thought he saw something out of the corner of his eye. Was that a light in Wallford's window? He blinked again, but the flickering light in the window of the room behind the bars was gone.

To keep whatever was in there, in there.

He realized with relief and exasperation that it was only the streetlight that was flickering, a loose or dying bulb. Power of suggestion, he thought ruefully. We are really all susceptible.

He crawled under the covers and fell into a dreamless sleep.

Across the hall in the women's dorm Sandy stirred briefly from sleep. A cold hand had brushed against hers. Her eyelids fluttered but did not open. David, she smiled, as she snuggled into the moist warmth of her pillow. He was always there when she needed him.

Moments later it was Cynthia who felt the coldness on her and instantly came awake. The cold was like a shock, a zing of electricity. She felt a cruel burning sensation on her face. Someone had stroked her cheek with a touch as cold as ice. Her eyes shot open wide. She saw only the hint of a shadow, a disappearing gray shadow.

She wanted her mother. Her father had failed her.

He had let the ghost get her.

She opened her mouth and screamed.

The overhead light was snapped on as Pauline hurried into the room, closing her robe around her. Bob was right behind. Pauline went to her daughter. The little girl's face was white with fright. Pauline cradled the girl in her arms, rocking her back and forth.

"It's all right, Cindy," she purred. "All right."

The rest of the room was silent.

"The ghost, Mommy. It was the ghost." Cynthia's voice was small and almost swallowed by the sobs.

"There. There." Pauline patted her daughter's face.

"He touched me. He——" She stopped, saw the others looking at her, and threw herself into her mother's lap. "I saw him," she cried.

"It was only a dream, honey," Pauline said softly as she lightly stroked her face. "Only a dream."

"I saw him. He touched me."

Sandy looked at the little girl. Her eyes were wide with sadness and pity. She shared the child's fear.

It was then that Sandy realized David was not next to her on the bed. But he had been there. In a moment of confusion, panic seized her. He had been there! In bed with her right before Cynthia awoke. But then she relaxed. He must have jumped off the bed so he wouldn't get caught. Yes——that was it.

Bob came in and knelt beside Cynthia's bed. He looked up at Pauline, who shrugged helplessly. Unconsciously she shifted her glance across the room to Sandy, a twinge of accusation in her eyes, and then, embarrassed, she looked away. Sandy looked down at the floor. She knew what Pauline was thinking.

Bob touched his daughter. He gently lifted her head from his wife's lap. The little girl fought him. She wanted her mother.

"Cindy," he said softly. "It was all a dream. Now you know that, don't you?"

Cynthia looked at her father. His face was so strong, his eyes reassuring.

But it wasn't a dream!

She touched her face. The burning feeling was gone. She reached out to her father and encircled him with her arms. He hugged her tightly and stood up, lifting her.

"It was a dream, baby. Just a silly old dream that frightened you so. And you remember what we said about dreams, don't you?"

Cynthia nodded.

"What?"

"That they can't hurt me," Cynthia answered in a small voice.

"That's right," Bob said. "They can't hurt you."

He laid her down on the bed. "Now, are you ready to go to sleep again?"

She nodded.

"Good. But if you want, you can come and sleep with Mommy and me. Do you want that?"

She hesitated. She did want that. But she was a big girl, in first grade. And big girls in first grade didn't still sleep with their parents. Even after bad dreams.

"No."

"All right. You stay here. But we're really close if you change your mind. You just crawl into bed with us if you want. Okay?"

"Okay," she answered.

"Okay. Now we're all going to forget about ghosts and bad dreams and go back to sleep and dream about happy things. It's almost tomorrow, and we're in for a really good day of skiing."

If we ever get there, he thought.

"Good night, Daddy," the little girl said without conviction. She turned from them and pressed her face into the pillow.

Pauline kissed her cheek. "Good night, honey."

She and Bob left the room, flipping off the light.

But Cynthia was far from sleep. She lay awake in her bed, looking at shapes in the darkness, watching for movement. She tensed against the ghostly coldness. It would be some time before she would fall asleep.

Sandy lay awake as well, eyes searching the room. Something told her that it was just beginning.

BOOK II

Sandy

CHAPTER VI

Owlsfane lived by Ben Franklin's adage of early to bed and early to rise. The town stirred with first light. On the tiny farms off the main road the cows had to be milked, eggs gathered in, and feed spread around for grazing animals. In the All-Fresh cheese factory, white-capped early-shift workers were already sifting through curds and whey, elbow-deep in troughs the size of Ping-Pong tables, and the finished wheels of cheese from the days before were cooling, stored on long shelves waiting to be wrapped in meshed cloth for boxing.

Those who worked the mountain had to punch in early to man lift towers or concessions, rental shops, and ticket booths. The clerks in the local shops and attendants in gas stations were preparing for the morning onslaught of tourists out to make the desperate most of their precious vacation time, or to serve neighbors who had awakened early because that is what they have done all their lives. Farm people, country people, small-town people, creatures of habit all, even in the winter, when morning cold tempts you to remain in bed until the deceitful warmth of noon.

On lovely wintry days like this one, when the sun

rises full and strong, you can watch the needle of the
thermometer affixed to your back porch point to below
zero in the dark of predawn and then rapidly rise thirty
or forty degrees in the full glow of direct sunlight.

But it all doesn't make much matter. Because if
you've lived in Vermont all your life, you will live there
the rest of it, and you will continue to rise with the sun,
or before, as do your parents in Bartsbury, and not be
bothered by cold air or low-slung clouds or threatening
skies or whipping snows. You just throw on another
hole-worn sweater under your black-and-red checked
mackinaw, pull your earflaps tighter over your head,
take the gloves off the mantel, where they've been
warming for you all night, and step outside and breathe
in a lungful of air. For nowhere on earth is the air
cleaner or life better, even if you've just lost your job
when the G.E. factory moved to Rutland ninety miles
away and you didn't want to make the trip every morning. You would just continue to go to Cal's in the eve-
nings and nurse your beers and know that things would
have to improve. Because—well, because they had to.

Josiah Stoneham was already dressed. He was wash-
ing and listening to the familiar morning sounds downstairs: the ringing echo of aluminum on formica as his
wife readied the pan for frying, the crisp sizzle of fresh
butter, the crackle of eggs splattering in the skillet, and
the stuttering burps of perking coffee. His juice was
waiting on the table as he entered the kitchen. As he
did every morning, he lowered the white bread into the
toaster—four slices, two for each of them.

He checked his boots, which were flopped casually
on the rubber mat next to the side door, and was
pleased to see they had dried. They would not be cold
and damp when he slipped them on. Not that he had
far to walk: only from his door, down the road, across
the truss bridge, and on into the main street of Owlsfane—called "93" after the county highway—where he

would open the grocery store. It was no more than a quarter mile, which got the blood coursing the way it should. He was already dreading his late closing tonight as last-minute shoppers hurriedly filled their holiday orders, and he hoped he wouldn't have to make any evening deliveries up the hilly road to some of the old people of South Pittsfield. Lately the truck hadn't been starting well and had been sluggish going up the hills, and he was worried about getting stuck. He'd have Ray at the garage look at it right after the holiday.

In the safe light of the morning sun the uneasiness that had disturbed his sleep seemed distant, a residual hollow sound like the echo one thinks one hears after a siren scream or church-bell peal fades almost to silence. Perhaps it was just a buzzing reminder that they had not been in the house for many weeks.

A buzzing reminder from within him.

Yes, that was it and nothing more, he tried to convince himself, although intuitively he felt otherwise. Something had awakened Eben Wallford; something had disturbed him and caused him to walk. And Eben had awakened Josiah, the man who took care of him, the man who brought him food. His friend.

For three generations the Stonehams had taken care of Eben and his house. Josiah felt a twinge of guilt knowing no one would do so after he and his wife had gone. They never had any children—not that they hadn't tried, God knew. It just wasn't meant to be. The Stoneham line would end with him and, presumably, so would the care of Eben. Josiah was the executor of the Wallford estate. In his own will, he had left both their houses to the town for the town to do with them what they would. Hopefully Owlsfane would continue to care for Eben the way Josiah had, and his father and grandfather before him. But Josiah would not worry about any of that now. His responsibility ended with his death. He would die with his conscience clear; he was at peace with himself.

With a chime of its bell, the toaster spit up its bread just as his wife carried in the two plates of steaming eggs, unbroken yolks quivering and staring at him. With his fork Josiah stabbed the eyes and combined the running yellow and white before mixing in his toast.

He wanted to check on the house today to quell any lingering feelings, but he would not have the time. Tomorrow. He needed to make certain that everything was set for the holiday. They would both go—he and his wife—because he remembered her saying she had some things she wanted to do there. And it was best they go tomorrow, because the day after was Christmas, and that meant early-morning church and then people stopping by to visit.

He glanced out the window and looked at the lineup of cars next to the ski house. He frowned. Didn't like it. Too many people coming and going at all hours. Arriving late at night, doors slamming, lights burning. The people used to park in the churchyard, as it was always plowed in winter; the state plows took care of that. But the townspeople had taken a vote and the locals didn't want the cars parked there. Even during the week when there were no services. Wasn't right. No reason was given to Bob Kanon, but no reason had to be. It was their church and it wasn't right, that's all.

He did know what the reason was, though he would never articulate it: resentment, the viral kind that grows fierce and hard over the years and gnaws and feeds on itself as it spirals stronger and becomes mistrust. Toward the winter people, as they're called, the vacationers, the ski house people. Those with the money to do what they wished, with no struggle. Those who didn't have to worry about the G.E. plant's moving to Rutland.

He had heard what others had done to the winter people. Not in Owlsfane. Not here. But not far away either. In other areas in the state, sugar was thrown into gas tanks to stall and damage engines; others refused to sell gas to cars with out-of-state plates. (*What's that? Gas you need? Sorry. All out. Iran, you know. Howdy, Jack, come on 'round back, we'll see what we got. So long now, good trip back to New York.*) The economy, though, depended on the transients; the damn fools should know that. The winter people who came and played and left. And ate. And slept. And bought the phony, overpriced antiques and seven-pound wheels of cheese and buckets of maple sugar and gift candies. Damn fools.

Stoneham didn't like the ski house people. He would be cordial to them (*Mr. Kanon, Mrs. Kanon; nod and wave and smile*). But it stopped there. He didn't go to their house socially, nor they to his. It just wasn't done. He lived here. They may have owned the house next to Eben, which was their right, but they didn't really belong and never would. They were winter people. Strangers.

Josiah scratched his white stubbly beard. He'd shave the next evening for the holiday. That would hold him for a couple of days. He ran his hand through his hair, finding the part and patting it down. Still had it all. Pushing seventy and still had it. The Stoneham men turned white as the snow that surrounded the house an honest five months of the year. He glanced up at the family pictures hanging on the wall. Three prior generations of Stoneham men had lived in that house, all with full heads of paste-white hair—his father, grandfather, and great grandfather, Simon.

His eyes were still strong, thank God. Never needed glasses. Dark eyes, well worked over the years of squinting from the sun's reflecting off the snow. Wrinkles fanned out from his eyes—crow's feet, some called them, and tried to hide them. He didn't. Wrinkles were from age and honest work.

He smiled at his wife who sat across the table from him mopping up the last of her eggs with a second slice of toast. They'd clean the dishes and leave together to open the store. The shelves needed stocking. The cans had arrived late last night; the truck had been delayed. He'd sort the stock and price the items. His wife would prepare the water for the take-out coffee. It was mostly a local business—Owlsfane, Bartsbury, South Pittsfield, and the farms. Travelers didn't much stop there. And those who knew the area at all would pass on through. If they wanted coffee and a quick bite, it was the Dunkin' Donuts in Glendon. Those who didn't probably wouldn't be there anyway. But it was all right. The local business was good. The new mall in Glendon would hurt, and he'd have to consider lowering his prices; but that was six months away, so he had enough time before he had to worry.

Josiah chewed on a last piece of toast and watched the ski house people come out of the house and start their cars. Great clouds of gray exhaust belched into the air. He once again cursed the damned city people and their irreverence. All that shouting and hollering on the Sabbath; carrying those skis in and out while God-fearing people were driving up to Sunday services. That might be okay in New York or wherever they were from. But not here. Not in Owlsfane. People kept the Sabbath in Owlsfane. They didn't go to work and they didn't go up to the mountain skiing. They didn't park in the churchyard during the week unless they had business in the church. And their children didn't play in the graveyard. Oh, yes. He had seen those ski house children playing on the hallowed ground of the cemetery—*his* cemetery, where his parents and grandparents were buried—walking all over their graves, disturbing the dead. Sacrilegious, that was; spitting in the face of all that was holy.

Can't do that, he thought, shaking his head slowly back and forth. *Can't do that without bringing up something to stop 'em.* They'd get theirs, the city people. One day something would come along to take care of them, that he knew.

He got up from the table; his wife was removing the plates and cups. Too much to do this morning. After closing, they would trim the tree. The balls had been taken down from the closet, the tinsel new-bought. He prayed it would be a good Christmas. He just hoped his truck wouldn't die on him.

CHAPTER VII

The noise of Pauline's clogs on the bare wooden floor outside her door woke Sandy. Ricky was already up, pulling on her long underwear and heavy bulky-knit sweater. Judy was still asleep in her bunk across the room; she wasn't going skiing today, so there was no reason to get up early. Like Scott, she had been grounded. Cynthia was not in her bunk.

There were feet shuffling outside in the hallway as the other house members made their way to and from the bathrooms at the rear of the hall. Laughter and tingling excitement filled the air as boasts of greatness and hoped-for accomplishments wafted in from the men's dorm. Today, on her first day of skiing, about all Sandy had was delusions of adequacy.

Gail's feet dangled over the side of the upper bunk, swaying back and forth in front of Sandy's face as she negotiated the jump to the floor. The thudded landing was anything but graceful, and Gail turned sheepishly to Sandy.

"That's about how well I ski too," she said laughing. Then her voice changed as she remembered. "You all right?" she asked.

"Yes. Thanks," Sandy said, rolling her eyes in embarrassed disbelief at what she had put everyone through several hours before. She was really more concerned for Cynthia and looked around for her, but the six-year-old was not in the room.

"Good," Gail said, and then dropped it. She looked over toward her daughter. Judy's left foot stuck out from under the gray army blanket that was bunched up under her chin. Gail crossed the room and covered her daughter's foot. Judy stirred slightly but did not awaken. "Got to get to the john before the line gets too long," she said. She grabbed her robe and wrapped herself in it. "You'd better get a move on too. Knowing David, if his isn't the first car out of the parking lot, there's going to be all hell to pay."

"Got it," Sandy said, grateful that Gail was not about to make further comments about what had happened during the night.

She rolled off her side, and it was then that she became aware of the dull pain in her right arm; a million tiny fiery pinpricks almost leading to numbness. As if her arm had been shot full of buckshot. Or, she thought ruefully, remembering her dream: as if it had been thrust into fire. She must have slept on it, she thought. She started to massage the pain away, surprised to discover her skin was dry and chapped. She'd have to remember to put some cream on it to combat the dry air in the ski house.

She got on the bathroom line with Ricky, Stan, and Craig, and waited her turn.

"How are you feeling?" Ricky asked. "That must have been a whopper of a nightmare."

"It was," Sandy said, trying to smile warmly. She didn't want to talk about it, but she knew it was inevitable. She thought about the whopper that Cynthia must have experienced and knew it would have to be rougher on the six-year-old. And if *she* was still a bit shaky, she could only imagine what the little girl was feeling this morning.

Ricky winked conspiratorially. "I've heard of girls doing some pretty crazy things to try to get out of going skiing with their boyfriends. But this ghost thing of yours really wins the award."

Sandy exhaled shortly. "Believe me, Ricky, when I tell you I sincerely wish it had all been a gag."

Ricky put her arm around Sandy's shoulder. "Hey, I know, okay? Anything I can do, just holler."

"Thanks."

Stan leaned over and whispered in her ear. "If you lose confidence in David up there on the mountain, I'll be there."

To which Craig huskily added, "If you lose confidence in David in bed, I'm right above him." Then quickly, with a smile: "In the upper bunk, I mean."

David stepped out of one of the johns. He made a striking appearance in his jet-black ribbed ski pants and matching turtleneck. Not a pinch of unwanted flab covered his body, a perfectly unbroken profile. Sandy took note that the other guys in the bathroom line did some gut sucking as David's sleek figure passed by.

He pecked Sandy on the cheek and looked into her eyes. He took her hands full in his and squeezed them in silent recall of their lovemaking, and in the reassurance that he was always there.

"See you downstairs for breakfast," he said.

She watched him jump the stairs three at a time and shuffled forward in line as Stan ducked into a john.

Ricky leaned over and whispered in her ear. "You realize, don't you, that you're going to be talked about around here for years. You're famous."

Sandy knew. She was "the girl who saw the ghost," as in *Did you hear about the girl who saw the ghost?*

She smiled, knowing Ricky meant well.

She didn't want to be famous. She wanted to be like the others. To turn back the clock to *before.*

* * *

Sandy entered the kitchen. David met her at the archway balancing two plates of scrambled eggs and bacon, a slice of buttered toast dangling from his mouth. With a nod of his head and a flapping wave of the bread, he was able to communicate to Sandy to grab the piece of toast and started chewing. It was getting late.

"David, I've only been up for—" She checked her watch. "Eleven minutes. Give me a second to start breathing."

David put down the plates on one of the dining-room tables, and grabbing a butter knife as a cigar, crouched and Groucho'd, "If you haven't been breathing for eleven minutes, I think you'd *better* start."

"That was weak, David."

The eyebrows went up and down twice.

"If you haven't been breathing for a *week,* you should be dead."

Sandy looked out the window. It was cold and crisp as only a Vermont morning can be. The rising sun was inching higher in the sky, a ball of flaring yellow and white. All the residue of the previous night's storm had burned away except, of course, for ten inches of sparkling deep powder.

Snow was everywhere: completely covering the parked cars, piled delicately on branches, and exploding off in free-fall as a burst of wind shook the trees. The woodpile outside the kitchen door was entirely snowed under, an occasional log poking through as if trying to breathe. The plows were out in force, sparks flying ferociously as the metal blades came in fiery contact with the asphalt, thunderously propelling the snow onto the roadbanks with no thought at all for the blocked-in driveways. As if reading her mind, David muttered assurance.

"Don't worry. We're just going to barrel right on through. Haven't been stopped by snowdrifts yet."

Her look was withering. "Believe me, David. I wasn't worried."

A set of windshield wipers scattered dry crystals of snow from a car window as an engine started up outside.

"Thank the good Lord for that," David said, looking up from his plate. "All we need is one car, and if there's any trouble we can always jump-start the others. Sometimes the mornings are so cold, nobody's car starts and we all end up sitting around here until it warms up. Sometimes as late as nine o'clock."

"Heavens!" Sandy exclaimed as if shocked. "That's almost the time normal people on vacation are getting up."

"Wry comment noted," David said. "And ignored."

Gray coughing fumes sputtered out of the rear of a Volkswagen, melting and discoloring the snow beneath the exhaust pipe.

"It almost seems a sacrilege to run an engine in country air like this," Sandy said wistfully as the wind shifted and started to blow the noxious cloud in the direction of the house. She looked past the row of cars toward the untamed wooded areas in the back. A scene of pure picture-postcard Vermont: snow clinging to the bark of trees on the side where the wind had piled it, some gentle boughs hanging low from the extra weight of the crystals. The red barn off to the side of the house with its white crossed-bar doors and hayloft window was just so incredibly—*rural* to her city eyes. And to top it off, the snow was pure white. Not dogged yellow or slushed, tire-splattered brown as it was in New York. She didn't think the brown and gray muck even dared to show itself in the entire state.

She forced her eyes upward to look at the Wallford house. Somehow it didn't seem so ominous in the daylight, but then haunted houses rarely did. She took her first good look at it in sunlight. The sun caressed it softly, in innocence. It was indeed an imposing structure, situated as it was on the high sloping ground, as if by design, commanding attention and demanding homage from those who passed by.

But it was still only a house. An empty house at that. Eben Wallford's face flashed fresh in her mind.

What did he want from her?

She was confused, frightened, unable to define her feelings: the draw she felt. She wondered briefly if it was better not to know.

"Eat," David ordered, pointing to her plate and swallowing a mouthful of his own eggs. "This stuff ain't elegant, but it's satisfying."

"You know I never eat breakfast," Sandy said.

"Up here you do. And a big one. Everyone does. We don't break for lunch until at least one o'clock, and depending on the conditions, sometimes we don't even bother, then."

All around them the house members were carrying plates heaped high with waffles, French toast, or scrambled eggs. They beat a continuous path to the coffee urn that was percolating happily on the sideboard. Sandy never drank coffee and sipped instead from a cup of tea that sat steaming in front of her. The aromas engulfed her, and picking up a fork, she stared at her plateful of runny, lukewarm eggs. "When in Rome . . ." she sighed, and went at it as David got up to get another order of waffles.

Tom Landberg passed by, heading for the other dining room, juggling two plates, for himself and Gail. He pulled up next to Sandy, resting the plates on the table. He appeared at a loss for words. Sandy decided to help him out.

"I'm feeling better," she said easily. "Nightmares are over, I promise."

"Good," Tom said, smiling. His outward appearance belied his inner concern. "And if you ever find you need me—for anything—I'm here."

"Deal," she said, flashing a grin and extending her

hand. Tom looked her square in the eye and then reached down and scooped up the two plates.

Sandy felt eyes upon her and turned around. Cynthia was peering at her from behind the kitchen door.

Cynthia did not take her eyes from Sandy. As she and her mother passed near her, Cynthia hid behind her mother's legs. She was frightened by this girl—the girl who had brought the ghost into the house.

Pauline, sensing what was needed, put her daughter's plate on the table across from Sandy.

"Why don't you sit here and eat?" she asked.

Cynthia shook her head back and forth. She didn't want to be near Sandy.

Sandy tried to smile warmly and extended her hand. But still the little girl hung back. It wasn't shyness as it had been last night; it was fear.

"Come on. I won't bite."

Cynthia tugged at Pauline's ski clothes. "I don't like her, Mommy. I'm afraid."

"There's no reason to be afraid, honey. She's a nice girl."

"She's a bad person. Make her go away, Mommy."

Sandy sadly dropped her hand.

Pauline smiled apologetically. "I think we'll need a little time," she said to Sandy. Sandy nodded gently.

"Make her go away," the little girl pressed.

Pauline picked up her daughter's plate and started into the other dining room.

"Now you know I can't do that, honey. Sandy's a guest here. Our guest. And we're all to treat her like a guest. Like we do with everybody. All right?"

Cynthia didn't answer. She turned slowly around and stole a glance at Sandy, who tried to put on a cheery face. The child turned quickly away and sat at a table with her back to Sandy. She didn't like this girl, the one the ghost wanted. She didn't like her one bit. And she didn't want her in the house. Her young instincts were screaming a warning. As long as that girl was in the ski house, none of them was safe from the ghost.

Sandy turned back to her breakfast. Pauline was right. There'd be enough time later to make friends with the little girl.

She finished eating the eggs; her gaze returned to the Wallford House. Despite the anguish it had caused her last night, there was still something alluring about it. Something strangely friendly and inviting, almost exuding a curious beckoning light that attracted but frightened her at the same time.

The pull to the house was still there.

But was it the house? Or was it the man?

A chill spiraled upward from within her. She remembered her fear, but the urge to go back was stronger.

David returned with a second helping of waffles, threw his left leg over the back of the chair, and climbed on.

A swell of cold air burst into the room as Bob, dressed in an Antarctic-style fur-hooded full-length parka, clomped in from the outside. He stamped snow off his heavy boots on the rug mat that separated the kitchen from the other rooms.

"Cold front came down following the storm," he said, flapping his arms and blowing on his ungloved hands to warm up. The zippered parka hood lay unused behind him and his ears were beet-red, tingling from the cold.

"What's the temperature?" Sandy asked.

"Minus nine." He held up a hand to silence her. "And promising to warm to thirty. Once the sun gets its ass in gear we're in for some unbelievable weather today. There's not a cloud in the sky. You couldn't ask for a more glorious first day on the slopes. Don't get spoiled, though. You don't see days like this too often."

"Ever," David said, coming up for air. "Ten inches

of fresh snow and good sun." He looked at Sandy's empty plate. "You ready yet? Time to get moving."

"Minus nine?" she asked weakly, wondering if she should refill her plate. By the time she finished her second helping perhaps the temperature would have warmed to minus five. "Why would anybody purposely go out when it's minus nine?"

"Ah," Bob sighed. "The uninitiated."

"If she'd just move her ass, I'd initiate her," David growled.

Sandy caught some of the snowflakes still settling at Bob's feet and watched them disappear through her warm fingers, wetting them. "Wasn't it Scarlett O'Hara who once said, 'I'll never be cold again'?"

David grabbed the butter knife again and went into his imitation. "Close, but no cigar." Then, looking at what he held in his hand, he crouched lower and added, "I was right; this is no cigar."

Sandy sat for a moment more, her gaze drifting toward the Wallford house.

"You're both going to think I'm insane," she said slowly, suddenly wondering if she was. "More than insane. But I want to go back into that house now that it's light."

David and Bob exchanged glances.

"No!" The word came from both simultaneously.

"David, I have to," she said with assertion.

"What are you trying for? Strike three?"

"I don't know what I'm trying for, but I have to go back into that room and see what's there. Maybe just to see if I'm crazy or not."

Bob was worried. "Sandy, I don't think you should."

"Bob, something got to me last night, and I'd be more afraid *not* going back there. I've got to conquer whatever it is that conquered me—a ghost, hallucination, vision, psychic impression—whatever. Understand it. I'm not going to do that by running away from it."

"What do you hope to accomplish by going in there?"

"I don't know," she said, shrugging.

Find out why he wanted me there.

"You go in there, you see nothing. What then?"

"I don't know," she repeated. "It'll be over, I guess. That's what I'll have accomplished. I know myself. If I let it—and I put 'it' in quotes—get the best of me, I'm going to be afraid to go to sleep tonight." She smiled. "Then you're going to have to put up with me again as you did last night."

Bob did not return the smile. "What if you see something?"

"Then we'll know that Eben Wallford is walking around in there and I'll never go in again."

She tried harder to convince him to see her point of view. "Bob, I am not going to do anything stupid. Or heroic. I promise you. I just need to settle my own mind over this. And believe me, I am not going to let David leave my side for a minute."

"Let's go," David said, getting up and cradling her shoulder. He knew her well enough to know that no amount of logical debate was going to stop her from storming the house again. As much as he wanted to fight her, it would be pointless.

"Then we'll all go," Bob said, reaching for his parka.

"All?" David asked, smiling. He ran a mental count. "All thirteen of us?"

Bob laughed. "That would be a sight, wouldn't it? Thirteen of us marching up the road in single file, entering a house that has been closed up for a century. All right, you made your point. You don't need thirteen. You don't need three. Go. Nothing ever happens in the daylight anyway."

"Although," he added, looking at Sandy, "people also usually think a little more clearly in the daylight too. I don't see all that much clear thinking going on around here. But who am I to comment? Just the

land baron of this glorious estate. Go. See your ghosts."
And then addressing David: "I'll meet you at the Summit Lodge at one thirty. We'll take a run together."

"I'll be there," David said, his hands at his side drawing for an imaginary gun as if ready to do battle at the O.K. Corral. He turned to Sandy. "Ready?"

"Give me a minute. I just want to grab a second cup of tea. One doesn't brave minus nine on only one cup. May I?"

"Go ahead," David said. "I have to run upstairs and get my scarf anyway. Even for those of us who are used to it, minus nine is still a bit overwhelming."

He darted up the stairs as Sandy went into the empty kitchen.

As she put the water up to boil she wondered if she indeed *was* insane for wanting to go back into the Wallford house. Wouldn't she be better off just saying the hell with it and going with David up to the mountain? No—there was no denying what she was experiencing: a very real pull to that house. It almost felt as if in some way the house owned her. Or if somehow she belonged there and it was calling her home. Whether the feeling was coming from within her or projected from without, she didn't know. She had to go back there, though. She just hoped her return to the house would resolve her anguish.

She found the teabags under the kitchen counter, draped one over the edge of the cup, and reached for the kettle of boiling water. Minus nine—she ought to have her head examined. Out of the corner of her eye, through the kitchen window, she was able to see the Wallford house. *I'm coming,* she almost started to say.

It all happened in a fraction of a second. She was pouring the water into the cup when she felt it: an icy touch on the back of her neck. As if something cold had brushed against her and moved quickly on. Startled, she jerked the arm that held the kettle and spilled some of the boiling liquid onto her other hand. She screamed in surprise and pain, crashing the kettle to the counter-top and spilling more water. Bob, entering the kitchen, saw what had happened, grabbed Sandy, and pulled her outside. He jammed her hand into the soft snow piled at the kitchen steps. The coldness instantly removed the sting.

"There," he asked. "That better?"

"Yes," she said, staring oddly at her hand, turning it from front to back, looking for damage. The scalding was only minor, and Bob's quick thinking had lessened the discomfort considerably. "Thank you."

Someone or something had touched her. Her neck burned. She rubbed her hand over it.

But there had been no one else in the kitchen.

"What happened?" Bob asked as he brought her back into the house.

She had felt *something* on her neck. There was no doubt. An icy touch; a cold, feathery pressure.

She smiled weakly. "Just a little shaky, I guess." It would do her no good to tell anyone what she thought had happened. Because, she reasoned, it probably hadn't. There was no one else in the room. It was a draft, a fly, her imagination. No one had touched her because no one was there.

But, as David came downstairs and they started out of the house, she was still trying to convince herself.

There may not have been anyone else in the room, but someone or something had touched her neck, and that touch was frightening and cold.

CHAPTER VIII

Pulling on their parkas and boots, Sandy and David left by the kitchen door, clumping down the snow-covered stairs. It was nearly knee-deep and absolutely glorious.

Ron and Craig were helping to push Stan's car out of the snow-filled ruts, wheels spinning furiously, snow flying from underneath. But as there was no ice base under the new-fallen snow, traction was good and it was just a matter of pushing the car over the fender-deep snow out onto the plowed road.

Sandy felt ten years old again as she scooped up handfuls of snow to dump down David's neck.

The sun reflected brightly off the surface of the snow, tiny brilliant diamonds of dazzling white dancing before her eyes. She almost swooned from the display and had to flip her goggles down in front of her eyes. During the second hour of the trip up the previous night (God, that was ages ago), David told her what had happened the first year he had gone skiing. It had been a glittering spring day, with sun such as this, only with rays stronger and more direct. He had skied the whole day without goggles and had been badly sunburned, a deep tanning line running upward from the midpoint of his neck where his turtleneck shirt had folded down. He had also burned his eyelids and, he feared, his eyes. He had rushed to the emergency room of the Glendon hospital the next day to see what he had done to himself. Luckily a soothing ointment removed the sting. But he did receive a strong admonition from a young skiing doctor never to do it again. And he didn't. Whenever the sun was strong, the goggles were flipped in place.

They helped push Ricky's Ford Granada over the hump of snow that separated the driveway from Route 93. They waved good-bye to her and started up the road toward the Wallford house.

"You get to change your mind anytime now," David said. "I won't hold it against you. Believe me."

"Nope," Sandy said. There was at least no tension or arguing about what they were doing. David had accepted her need to clear her mind.

They chugged up the hill on the narrow shoulder of the road, David leading the way, Sandy following. Cars shot by in each direction, spewing sand and gravel out at them from under rear wheels, the sanding truck having just passed by.

It was cold indeed. Sandy thrust her mittened fingers deep into the pockets of her parka. He had made her buy these horrible-looking dark-gray down-filled mittens the day before. She had a favorite pair of red knit gloves with little cat faces that she loved to wear, but David had taken one look at them and guaranteed she would get frostbite within fifteen minutes of being on the mountain. The mittens provided freedom for her fingers to warm each other; the separated fingers of the knit gloves were an open invitation for the cold to do its worst. Damn it, she realized, he was right. Her fingers were warm. Her exposed face, though, was something else. Tiny needles of cold pricked her sharply as they walked into the wind.

She couldn't believe she was really there, sun-worshiping Sandy Horne in minus nine degrees. But in a relationship, one compromised and yielded to the wishes of the other. This compromise was hers. The son of a bitch owed her!

Suddenly David grabbed her arm and pulled her across the road, darting in front of a lumbering St. Johnsbury truck traveling north.

"What are you doing?"

"As long as we're here," he said, "we might as well take in the whole tour."

"What whole tour? What are you talking about?"

He pointed. They were standing in front of the cross-barred gate leading into the Owlsfane cemetery.

"Oh," she said with impish eyes. "That whole tour."

"Comes with the territory," David said, only half joking.

The gate was blocked by mounds of piled snow, and David was unable to swing it open. Instead of walking back down the road and entering the cemetery through the churchyard, David whisked the snow away from the top of the chest-high stone cemetery wall with a sweep of his glove. He gained a handhold on the dull smoothed stones on top and hoisted himself up, then helped Sandy up. They jumped together into the softness of the snowy ground on the other side of the wall. Evergreens cast shadows through the graveyard and they were able to remove the sun goggles, perching them high on their heads.

"What do you think?" he asked, arms stretched out expansively.

"It's a cemetery," she answered.

"It dates back to Colonial days. Probably the late sixteen hundreds."

There were hundreds of tiny sagging tombstones in the two-acre plot, some standing shoulder to shoulder in ordered rows, others in random or haphazard patterns, as if the organized array had been an afterthought. Many were almost completely covered by the snow, held suspended as they had been for two hundred winters, with only the very tops of these smaller ones visible. Others, the taller ones, stood starkly, defiantly above the drifts. Most of the stones were of clay or slate; a few made of quarried marble, indicated the burial of some of Owlsfane's wealthier citizens.

"You know," David continued, surveying the cemetery, "I think there are more dead people in Owlsfane than living people today."

Sandy laughed shortly. "You don't say. I've already met one of them."

She looked at the artwork that adorned many of the early tombstones, designed by local stonecutters: etchings of skeletons, hourglasses with dripping sands, Father Time figures with scythes, and scenes of the resurrection. The haunting allure and horror of the death's-head mask topped many of the headstones, griffin wings flying out in regal span to the sides, all leaving no doubt in the minds of passersby about the certainty of death.

"This is true American art," Sandy said. "It's sinful that these stones should be in such disrepair."

David nodded. "We'll drive home through Bennington next week and I'll show you a really old Colonial cemetery. There are some marvelous inscriptions on some of the stones. The town has kept up the graveyard, removing lichens that cover the lettering, and restoring some of the older stones."

Sandy looked around the graveyard, the quiet only broken by the whine of cars passing on the road outside. Strangely, the sound did not disturb the peace that reigned within the shadowed, tree-lined walls.

"Why did they put the cemetery right in the middle of town?" she asked. "It's ghoulish to have to pass by the graveyard every day."

"Most New England cemeteries are attached to the churches. Death was not a horror to the first settlers up here. It was a very real fact of life. They were very religious people, the Puritans, and they shared a strong belief in life after death, where they would be reunited with those who had died earlier. A lot of them, believe it or not, used to hang around the cemetery before or after the town meetings that were held in the church."

"I guess that was before bingo," Sandy half quipped. Suddenly she felt like an intruder in the quiet holiness of the churchyard. She was walking on graves and the thought chilled her from within.

"It was a relatively common practice of the people to visit the cemetery frequently," David was saying. And then he commented sadly, "As bizarre as it might sound, they did it because they never knew who was going to be next."

His words unnerved her. She stood up. "Let's go, David."

"One stop first," he said. "At the mausoleum."

She flashed him a grin. "Somehow I knew that was coming."

"Whole tour, hon," he said.

He thumbed up the road toward the Wallford mansion. "You're the one running into the spook house. Not me. Although I'll be right at your side—through conscription, I hasten to point out, and not through choice. I just want to show you what you're up against."

She shot him a wry smile. "Lead the way, Pizarro, and let's check out the mausoleum."

They picked their way among the headstones that stretched in front of them, up the hill to the mausoleum. The deep snow made their progress slow, and Sandy wondered how centuries before people were buried in winters like this. She imagined the family members and neighbors struggling for hours, first to clear the snow away from the plot and then to break through the frozen ground.

She was glad she didn't live two hundred years ago; she would have made a rotten colonist.

They approached the mausoleum from the side. The cemetery followed the contour of the road and the mausoleum stood at the apex, as Wallford would have it, directly across from the house, on a hill that sloped downward to the church and ski house on the one side, and in the other direction to a tiny run-down farm.

Sandy reached out tentatively to run her hand up and down the cold stone.

"They're all in here, huh?" she asked, patting the wall confidently.

David, missing her point, nodded affirmatively.

"*All* of them?" she emphasized, smiling.

"Oh," David said, knowing where the question was heading. "Physically, yes. Spiritually, we don't really know yet, do we?" A wise, fish-eyed look appeared on his face.

They walked around to the front, up the snow-covered steps to where the sculpted stone statue of Eben Wallford stood, hunched over, knees slightly bent. The gray stone figure was bespeckled with snow, accenting the age and despair visible in his face and frozen eyes. For a slow count of ten Sandy took in the face—with calm recognition—and then let her eyes run up and down the cloaked figure before returning to the old, lined face. The likeness of the man was familiar to her. It was the face of the apparition and the dream of the night before, the face of the man who had tried to push her into the mausoleum. She nodded grimly to herself. Somehow, she was not surprised and perhaps would have been disappointed otherwise.

On the other hand, she knew she had seen the statue when they had first arrived at the house. Although it had been too dark to really absorb the features, had the passing glance at the figure clicked in her unconscious and manifested itself later in the house and then in her dream? She didn't know what answer she was hoping for.

There was sorrow in the face of the old man leaning

toward the mausoleum door, his ear almost pressing
against it. Listening. Listening for sounds from inside
to indicate there was still life. How truly sad, Sandy
thought, and once again, despite her fear, felt an unexplainable closeness to this man. She fought off tears
that had begun to form. The man held a hat in his hand
as he respectfully bowed and listened at the door.
Angels played across the black doors as if to indicate
the pleasant peaceful sleep of the dead and not the dis-
quiet that must be inside. She fingered the brass ring
handles, making no attempt to pull on them for fear
of opening the Pandora's box—unless, she thought ruefully, it already had been opened.

A car was approaching from below. Exposed to
view from the roadway, they ducked behind the statue
lest they be seen by someone from one of the neighboring towns. David wondered if their sudden motion
might have given the impression that the statue was
alive. The thought made him smile.

"Seen enough?" he asked.

She nodded.

"Want to skip the house?" he asked hopefully.

"No. I still want to go in there."

She took her mitten off and touched the coldness of
the statue, quickly pulling her hand back. The feel of it
chilled her beyond the iciness of the day and the coldness of the stone. Gooseflesh crawled over her body.

"Shall we, then?" David asked, and took her hand,
which she gratefully gave him, and led her down the
steps.

They crossed the road and rounded the Wallford
house to work their way in once again through the cellar window. The snow was still stamped down from the
night before, and David thought there really wasn't anything particularly scary about this strange, odd-shaped
old house in broad daylight. But then he thought of the

expression "famous last words" and smiled wryly to himself.

"Care to lead?" he asked her. "There was no holding you back last night."

"I've matured a lot since then," Sandy answered. "I'm older, you know."

"You're right. Time to trade you in for a younger model." As Sandy swung at him, David ducked into the cellar window and pulled his fiancée down beside him.

Despite the brilliance of the sun, the cellar was heavily shadowed, although far from black. Filtered light streamed in obliquely through clear gaps in the half-dozen or so dirt-streaked windows to the back and one side of the house. Ambitious rays fought to break through windows covered over with fallen and drifted snow on the side that had faced the wind during the storm, and the veranda support in front of the house allowed little seepage of light through its close-standing wooden supports. Most of the light entered through the window they had used, propped open and cleared of snow by the children last night. David realized he had forgotten to close it in his rush to get Sandy out, and promised to remind himself, upon leaving, to remove all evidence of their two visits inside. That included disturbing nothing within the house and pushing snow back up against the window to cover their entry. He did not expect any of the locals to be wandering in back of the house (nor in front, for that matter, as he re-called Bob's incident with the hitchhiker), but he did not know if the Stonehams had any set routine for their inspection and cleaning of the house, though the dust particles that danced in front of them were a good indi-cation that they never got down to the basement.

The cellar objects were at least partially discernible now. David, bolder in the light of day, felt a little fool-ish over his squeamish actions of the previous night.

He patted the eagle head of the griffin, although at arm's length, half jokingly for Sandy's benefit and half perhaps to reassure the winged guardian of the cellar that they came in peace, albeit in disrespect.

Yet his internal alarm was turned on, already scouting and sniffing the air for danger. But he would show none of this fear to Sandy, who perhaps was the intrepid one in the relationship. He'd change that, though, he thought with a smile. He'd whip her ass on the ski slopes.

He waved casually to the mannequin he had knocked over and then ran his hands sensuously up and down its sleek, slender body.

"What are you doing?" Sandy asked, an amused look crossing her face.

"Jealous?" he asked, smirking.

"No. Just amazed that you'd prefer her to me."

David eyed her up and down, comparing her to the silent, shapely mannequin.

"It would take me an hour to get all those clothes off you." He pointed to the mannequin. "This one's ready to go."

Sandy pondered his comment. "A," she said. "If you do prefer her to me, she's yours. I'll step away. Plenty of guys back at the ski house would be glad to hear I'm free. And B," she finished seductively, in a sultry whisper, "I've got that hour."

"Do you?" David asked, a wide grin on his face. "You'd freeze to death before I got past the third layer of what you've got on there."

She waved her arms to keep him from continuing, laughed, and lowered her voice to sound masculine, to echo words from before: "To the uninitiated, two sweaters, a flannel shirt, and two pairs of long underwear under this parka are just fine for minus nine promising to warm to thirty."

"In today's sun you're going to sweat like a water buffalo like that," he said.

"I'll take my chances. I can always take some of it off. It's easier than putting it on. On top of that dumb mountain four hundred thousand feet in the air, they don't have any clothing boutiques."

"It's four thousand feet," he answered patiently. "Mt. Everest is only twenty-nine thousand."

"Thank you, Marco Polo," she said. "Trust me. I know my body chemistry a little better than you do." She caught him grinning at her. "Maybe *only* a little better," she added hastily.

He grabbed her and hugged her, feigning difficulty in getting his arms around the many layers of clothing. After a few aborted attempts his lips met hers.

"If this doesn't wake Wallford," he said, "nothing will."

She crinkled her nose and smiled at him. Her eyes sparkled and danced.

"I am crazy about you, you know that," he whispered. It was a statement more than a question.

She nodded. "You risked getting thrown out of the dumb ski house with that little four thirty A.M. panty raid."

"That was just physical," he said, dismissing it.

"That was *needed,*" she said appreciatively.

"And that is also why," he said, turning serious, "I don't want anything to happen to you. Which is why I want to get out of here and never look at or think about this place again."

She felt the house in her spine, her neck, her head.

"Just this one look. That's all I want. And then I promise."

"Okay," he sighed. "Then let's make it snappy. This place gives me the genuine creeps."

She held on to him a moment longer and pecked him gently on the cheek. "Thanks," she said simply.

They moved further away from the light of the open window. There were still pockets of darkness in the room. As David led Sandy through the cluttered cellar to the staircase, he avoided these corners, remaining on guard as if something or someone might suddenly vault out of the blackness at them. Last night had been an unknown; today, however, they were forewarned. There was the possibility that something still inhabited the house.

Sandy, though, was in no rush. She wanted to stop and admire. She ran her hand up and down the back of a rotting bronze-stenciled Hitchcock chair. She tested the chair gingerly and decided it was too weak to support her.

"You could have one hell of a garage sale down here," she said.

"Perhaps," David growled, exhaling in exasperation. "But I don't want to stand around and make small talk with you at eight o'clock in the morning in the middle of the Mummy's Tomb." He looked around uneasily. "Why do I get the feeling Vincent Price is going to show at any second?"

"Hey," she reminded him. "I'm the one with the dreams, remember? If anyone should be scared sense-less around here, it should be me."

"Up the stairs," he pointed. "A quick look and then out." He felt so damned uncomfortable about being in the house and wanted to be out of there as soon as possible. He wasn't a shrink—or a para-shrink—but as so brief a visit the previous night had caused Sandy so much trouble, a second visit, even in daylight, might compound it. If indeed the unseen presence of Wallford was in the house, latching on to Sandy, he didn't want to give it that much more of a chance to discern her reentry and come through again. But he didn't voice his fears to Sandy. She was too obstinate. It might cause her to spend even more time here, daring the ghost to show again.

He led the way up the stairs, again testing each in turn to see if it would support them. The handrail was loose and wobbled back and forth, sending up clouds of choking dust. David was afraid it would topple to the cellar floor at any moment, with a clattering noise loud enough to wake all the ghosts in the Owlsfane cemetery across the road. But it held.

Sun illuminated the first-floor hallway, streaming in through all the spanking-clean windows: a yellow-white path leading down the corridor from front to rear, that almost warmed the house in spirit, if not in actual temperature. He felt a little more easy. If anything should happen, help was only out the door and down the road.

The front door? It suddenly occurred to him that he should have used it last night to get Sandy out of the house. But the night mind, confused and fearful, works differently, and he hadn't thought of it then.

"Whoever dusts this place does a hell of a job," he said. "My mother's windows aren't this clean."

In the sunlight the house was old New England, although as David had noticed the previous night, it was damp, excessively so, and cold. The cold air hung suspended; it didn't move. He could detect no draft, all the windows were sealed shut.

Damp and musty. The house felt unused, forgotten. The faint lingering odor of disinfectant masked what he knew lay underneath: the cancerous wasting-away. The house didn't seem appreciative of guests. It felt to David that the entire structure wanted to be left to live and die according to its own timetable, to settle, to breathe, to decay undisturbed. They were intruding, and he hoped the house was forgiving. Last night it did not appear to be, and he dreaded Sandy's having a recurrence of the visions.

He was basing his fears on nothing concrete, he knew. Just chilling, slithering instinct. Like not walking down a dark street. But for all his worries, the house could be just an abandoned, yet cared for, white elephant.

The cake was untouched on the dining-room table.

"He was up there last night," Sandy said. "But I guess he didn't come down to eat."

"Hypotheses, Sandy." David corrected her. "You're presupposing he was *there*—" David's finger pointed up to the second floor—"and not *there*." His finger pressed lightly against her temple.

"Of course," she echoed dryly, and then added thoughtfully, "I'm crazy or possessed. Either way I lose."

"Shall we head up?" he asked, motioning to the second floor.

"In a second." She crossed to the cupboard and opened one of its glass doors. "I just want to see some of these marvelous old things."

David exploded, "Sandy, come on!" His tone was disapproving, and laced with fear. "We have no business being here. I don't want to get caught and explain to the state police what we're doing. It wouldn't be all that easy, you know. I just want to go upstairs with you— because you feel you have to—and then get out of here. We shouldn't have been here last night; look what happened. And I don't want to spend one more minute here than we have to. If you want to see old things we can go antiquing after skiing today or else all day tomorrow, I don't care. But for now let's do what we came to do and get out!"

His intensity unnerved her. He was right. She didn't want to dally in the house either. She closed the glass door, relatching it.

They climbed together to the second floor, David leading the way, holding on to her hand. She trailed one step behind him. David felt his heart beating faster as nervousness set in, and he slowed his pace as they neared the top.

"I feel ridiculous, sneaking around like this," he whispered, still fearful of disturbing the undead.

"Of course. That's your defense mechanism at work." Sandy gulped. "Mine too."

"Look at us," he said disgustedly. "Like we're walking the last mile." In that moment he suddenly wished all thirteen members of the ski house were in single file behind them. Or better yet, in front of them.

Sun burst in through the rear window on the second floor, a welcome beacon as they reached the top of the stairs. Or was it meant as a decoy? David wondered. A trap? He turned down the hall toward the front bedroom. Sandy held back.

"I want to see Suzanne's room first," she said.

"Sandy!" he yelled, as if in torment, and then lowered his voice to a hoarse whisper. "Why are you doing this to me? To yourself?"

"One quick look," she bristled. "I don't want to move in."

"One quick look," he sighed. He couldn't win.

She led him down the hallway to the rear door on the left. He turned the knob. The pink-and-white girl's bedroom opened to them, white lace curtains covering the two catty-corner windows. They stepped into the room; the door closed behind them. It looked as if the girl were just outside playing, as though she might return at any time.

Dolls were everywhere. Costumed dolls of muslin and yarn dating back to early Colonial times leaned against the rose-colored floral coverlet, their backs propped against the beaded head-pillows. Indian dolls with carved wooden heads and buckskin costumes sat atop a stenciled side table next to the bed. At the foot was a hand-fashioned doll's cradle in which lay a Negro doll of papier-mâché wearing a starched ruffled party dress. Cradled in the fists of the doll was a recorder, the fipple mouth touching the lips of the doll as if being played.

"All so beautiful," Sandy gasped, momentarily envious of the dead girl's collection. "And the horses!"

A stable of sculpted horses' heads was bracketed onto the walls. A pink speckled rocking horse, with a smooth, rounded saw-tooth mane and leather saddle, sat in the corner ready to buck.

"She had been riding the day she fell into the water," David commented. "She tied the horse to a tree and went walking down by the stream. She fell in, soaking herself. If she hadn't taken the time to bring the horse back to the barn and feed him before changing out of her wet clothes, she might never have gotten the pneumonia." He stopped himself. "And this all happened over a hundred years ago, okay?"

Sandy gave the wooden horse a push, sending it tilting back and forth on its rockers. She noticed a small pinewood Noah's Ark behind, partially hidden by the base of the horse, with a dozen pairs of hand-carved, exquisitely detailed wooden animals. Sandy knelt down to look more closely at the tiny toys.

"It seems to me," she said softly, rolling a zebra in her palm, "that Suzanne may have had no friends. Her animals, her dolls, her playthings, were the only playmates she had."

"I wouldn't know," David said, and then suddenly stopped, a knot tightening in the back of his neck. "Sandy, how did you know to come to this room?" he asked.

She looked at him blankly, not understanding what he was getting at. "I don't know."

"You said you wanted to come to Suzanne's room and you came here."

She shrugged. "Yes. So?"

"You weren't in this room last night," he pressed.

"No. Just Wallford's."

"Lucky guess you just came down here?" he asked uneasily.

She thought for a second. "I don't know. I just felt this would be her room, so I came here. I could have been wrong. This could have been the john."

"But you weren't wrong," he said evenly, a chill playing across his back.

"Nope," she agreed, lips pursed. She had given it no thought; had just known intuitively that this was Suzanne's room. And now didn't know how she had known. Granted there were only four doors to choose from. A one-in-four probability. Twenty-five percent. She had picked the right one.

She shrugged it off. Maybe she was psychic.

David walked back to the door and opened it. It squealed loudly and he winced at the noise. He took off his ski hat, whipped it under him in a circular flourish, and bowed low from the waist. His accent was that of an English gentleman. "Shall we get the hell out of here, my dear?"

"Yes," Sandy said, smiling, and making a brief curtsy. "I've seen enough."

David stepped out of the room and into the hallway. He held the door open for her. She crossed the threshold, but something prickly made her turn back to the room for a last look.

For only the briefest of moments she perceived an image. Her mouth opened wide in surprise. She blinked and the image was gone.

She had seen a girl standing at the window. Her back was to the door. Her arms reached high above her head. And the worst of it was, she was on fire.

Sandy gasped audibly. Did she really see what she thought she did? She felt herself go and roughly grabbed David's arm to prevent herself from falling.

David turned, alarmed. "What is it?"

She shook her head to clear it. "I don't know. I thought I saw—"

He overrode her. "Saw what?" His voice was sharp.

"I don't know." Confusion lit her face. "A girl. At the window."

She pointed into the room. David looked. There was nothing. No one.

"She's not there now."

They stepped back into the room, David taking it in

in a 360-degree arc. Sandy bit the fleshy part of her hand
between her thumb and index finger. "I saw only her
back, but her arms were outstretched above her. Like
this." She stretched full, her arms over her head, her
fingers bent into stiffened claws. Her voice grew
weaker. "And she was on fire."

"Fire?" David said. The word was uttered blankly,
in disbelief.

She nodded shortly. "That's what I saw. Or at least
what I thought I saw." She muttered to herself, "And
I thought I had smelled burning flesh. . . ."

David led her from the room. She held the door
open with the flat of her hand as if not wanting to leave.

"Sandy, let's get out of here," he said gently.
"Please." He tried to take her elbow and guide her
toward the stairs. She pulled free from him.

"No," she said strongly. "I have to go into his bedroom."

David bristled. "Sandy, you're seeing people in this
house when there are no people."

Her hands moved to her hips, but there was no fight
in her voice; it was matter of fact. "You promised me
a look."

David thought quickly. He knew it would be easier
to give her her way. One quick look and then they'd be
out of there.

"Right," he answered tightly. "I did." He reached behind her for the doorknob and started to pull the bedroom door closed. "Let's get it over with."

Her hand eased its pressure on the open door and
she let him close it. She took one last look behind her
into the room. Nothing.

But there *was* a girl; she knew that. And she was on
fire. Unconsciously she rubbed the dry patch on her
arm. She remembered the horrible burning of her nightmare only hours before.

They silently crossed the second floor hallway and
stood outside Eben Wallford's bedroom.

Sandy looked at the bedroom door and suddenly all that she had experienced the night before came flooding back: the coldness, the crawling terror, the inability to move, the dead man reaching out toward her. Her heart started to race and her skin grew clammy. She knew she should turn and leave and never look back.

David watched her, aware of what she was thinking, hoping she would change her mind. She didn't. Swallowing tightly and clearing her throat nervously, she nodded to David, who reached out for the ornate brass knob.

He tried to make light of the moment.

"As the Cowardly Lion once safely said, 'I do believe in ghosts, I do believe in ghosts, I do believe in ghosts.' "

Standing in the hallway, he slowly pushed open the door into the room. They peered in.

"Nothing!" Sandy said, in exclamation, her voice strong.

David felt silly, and all of a sudden a little more certain; the flood of reassurance that comes with relief. "Of course not," he said confidently. "Ghosts don't come out in daylight."

"You didn't feel that way downstairs, Macho," she replied smugly. She too suddenly felt much more at ease, seeing that the room was empty. "Let's take a closer look."

She entered the room first, David following.

"One thing I remember from last night is the door closing behind me."

The door, warped and tilted, started to close, creaking on its hinges. Without turning, Sandy thumbed at the closed door. "Like that."

David turned, defenses suddenly working overtime. He called out to the unseen spirit, "Clichéd. Definitely clichéd. Come on, you can be more inventive than that, ghost." He turned back to Sandy and said, "It's empty. Let's go."

"David, wait a second," she said, ruffled. "I need to walk around for a moment, all right?"

"All right."

In a sweeping glance Sandy took in the room and tried to compare it to what she remembered from last night. It was the same—the bed, the coverlet, the wing chair. She crossed the room and sat in the large old chair, as she knew he must have sat, *must still sit,* looking out at the mausoleum.

The sun played teasingly across the mausoleum beneath her.

She closed her eyes as if to will a vision on, but nothing came. Suddenly feeling a little uneasy, she jumped out of the chair.

She turned and faced David, who was watching her. He had not moved from the spot by the door. She held her hands out in a lost gesture.

"I honestly don't know what I expected to find here."

"I can't help you," David said. "Except to suggest we leave and forget it."

She looked out at the mausoleum once again. Snow spray, picked up by the breeze, flew in circular wisps off the roof. She stared at the statue, half expecting it to look back at her. He had stood there, ear pressed against the cold stone, listening for sounds of life. She wondered if she would encounter any signs of life if she remained in that room. Or anything else, for that matter.

David was moving. He was at the fireplace staring upward at the sheet that covered a painting. He was breaking a promise he had made to himself to disturb nothing in the house.

"He must have covered a family portrait after his wife and daughter died. I want to see what he looked like," he said. "All these years of listening to the story and I've never known."

I know what he looks like, Sandy thought. *I've seen him twice.* She wanted to tell him not to remove the sheet, that she didn't need additional confirmation, that she had indeed seen Eben Wallford. But she knew she wanted that confirmation. It was more exotic to go home and tell everyone she had seen a ghost than reporting that she had had psychotic hallucinations while on vacation.

David reached for a corner of the sheet. He started to pull on it. A thread snagged on a burr on the wood frame. He tossed the corner of the sheet up and over, freeing it. The sheet fell in a pile in front of them as they both looked up at the portrait. Their gazes fell first on Wallford—distinguished-looking, dressed in black, full head of gray, beard cropped and styled, less gray than Sandy had known it. But it was he. There was no mistaking or denying it. Her eyes met those in the picture—*were drawn to them*. For a moment she could not shift her gaze from his.

It was then that David saw it; Sandy a half moment later.

"Omigod," he gasped.

Sandy saw and nodded in understanding.

She was standing in front of the fireplace, six feet back from the portrait. It was as though a motion picture camera had zoomed up and in for a close-up. The image of the girl in the picture, Eben Wallford's daughter, Suzanne, bore a striking resemblance to Sandy. Sandy stared at her own likeness in the portrait, as if she were looking into the lyre-shaped mirror of the ski house.

All David could do was whistle shortly. In his head a warning call blasted as loudly as a factory whistle.

Sandy spoke first, trying to dismiss it.

"Plenty of girls look like that. Like me." She looked from Suzanne to Eben to Suzanne. Looking for clues. Looking to make sense.

"Perhaps," David answered slowly. "But *she* was buried alive."

CHAPTER IX

The whining groan of the ski-lift motor assailed their ears as they inched forward on the line. The snakelike cattle corrals were backed up with seemingly endless numbers of people spilling out in half-moons beyond the ropes, waiting for their turn to enter the line. David was not alone in his desire to get an early start this morning. It was a thought collectively shared, it appeared, by about nine million other skiers.

By the time they arrived at the mountain, the main parking areas were filled and they were forced to leave their car in a plowed field off to the side of the winter condominiums. They raced to the rental shop just in time to secure the last pair of boots the shop had to offer. Sandy complained slightly of toe pinching. David scanned the empty boot bins and told her it was normal; she'd get used to it.

Now they were on line for the chair lift, Sandy trying to maintain her balance and propel herself through the line on three-foot training skis, half holding on to the wooden posts and separating ropes of the corral, half dragged by an impatient David.

"This is not going to work, David," she protested and grabbed the arm of the person ahead of her to keep from falling, almost pulling the two of them down.

"It will if you would just stand over your skis and stop letting them skid out from under you," David growled. He let a safe distance grow between them and the twosome in front before guiding Sandy around a 180-degree bend in the corral.

"That was not what I was referring to. I was talking about us. You and me. You teaching me to ski." She practically hissed at him, between clenched teeth that were threatening to chatter.

"I can teach you how to ski," he muttered.

"You can't even teach me how to stand!" she exclaimed, exasperated. "Every time I try to walk on these things they're moving out to the side, under me, every which way except forward. Like they had a mind of their own." She noticed a couple on the other side of the rope listening, enjoying the confrontation, and she stuck her tongue out at them. An incredibly adult thing to do, she realized, but here was her fiancée trying to kill her!

"Let me off this line and I'll go into the ski school and sign up for lessons, which I should have done in the first place. That will work out fine for both of us. You'll ski the day without interruption, I'll remain whole, and we can go on loving each other."

"The fun is skiing together," David said, raising his voice in an angry arc. "And we came here to have fun. I didn't drag you up here just to trundle you off to some ski school. Besides, we're almost up to the chair lift. You can't go back around the fences. We'll try it once. If it doesn't work out, you have my blessings to go sign up for lessons."

"Once," she repeated, looking up the hill and sighing. She couldn't even see the top. The chairs curved slightly to the right and disappeared over a ridge. "The one trip could take us all day."

She stared up at the wide-open slope. Tiny figures

sailed over the ridge in graceful motion and shot elegantly down the hill, traversing the slope in symmetrical half circles, shooting up sprays of soft snow behind
them as they executed a particularly finely carved turn.
Others shot clumsily over the ridge, in awkward acro-
batic maneuvers calculated to maintain their balance
and avoid disaster.

You've really got to be an idiot to do this, Sandy
thought. Getting up at six o'clock in the morning to
join rush-hour traffic all for the purpose of sliding down
a wet mountain. Perhaps she was missing something.
Maybe there was more to this thing than she was seeing. Maybe once she got up there . . .

David was talking to her. They were nearing the head
of the lift line and he was pointing to the fifth couple
in front of them.

"Watch how they get on the chair," he said. "They
slide from the line onto the track, the chair comes
whipping around behind them, they turn to the outside,
grab the pole with their hands, and simply sit down.
The chair then whisks you up and away. Simple, no?"

She watched. The couple did exactly what David had
said and were breezed high into the air.

"Watch again." He nudged her as the next couple
approached the track. This pair wasn't as lucky. The
girl on the outside lost her balance in what looked like
speeded-up slow motion and was nicked by the chair
in the back of the knee. She went sprawling out un-
gracefully in front of the lift, the attendant quickly shutting off the machinery so the chair would not pass over
her and hit her in the head.

"Oops," David said sheepishly, trying to make light
of the mishap. "You win some, you lose some."

Sandy's return glance of icy blue told him his humor
hadn't succeeded. "It's probably her first day," he said.

"It's *my* first day," Sandy flared. "Or did you forget
I wasn't Suzy Chapstick."

*   *   *

Gasoline fumes wafted in their direction from the chugging motor. It was the first foul smell she had encountered since leaving the parking lot. The whole feel of the mountain was pine-tree fresh; the air enticingly pinprick-crisp, so ruddy cold it almost hurt, but warmed by the insistent winter sun, a brilliant ball of flaring white and gold. The sky was a blue Sandy had never seen before.

Then it was their turn. The sound of the machine was loud: a cranking, whooshing sound echoing all around her. So loud she couldn't hear David's commands. She looked behind her, saw the chair darting around the corner like a whip ride at an amusement park. She felt pressure on the backs of her legs, and suddenly she was seated. David pulled the safety bar down in front of them. Her feet lifted off the ground, and the chair rocked gently back and forth on its solitary hinge. They were airborne.

"Hey, open your eyes," he said. "We've made it."

The safety bar held them securely in place.

"Now I know what Amelia Earhart felt like," she said.

The cable strained above them, whining softly as it went over and through the pulley wheels of the support towers, an intermittent *ker-chug, ker-chug* as it entered and left the bracketed tower. The chair rose and fell in sine-curve order between the lift towers. Far ahead and above her she saw the top of the mountain, its white cap silhouetted against the deep blue of the low-hanging sky. Other peaks stood off in the distance: a ridge of high, jutting rocks and evergreens pointed heavenward, severely outlined against the intense sky.

Snow capped the trees, piled heavily and thickly on branches, creating giant snow statues, creaturelike with wide, extended arms. The chair lift edged up the side of the slope, and Sandy could almost reach out with her ski pole and scatter the flakes of snow delicately balanced on boughs. In many places others before her had done so, and the green-white contrast was sharp; the individual needles, bespeckled with white, glistened in the sun. The snow below her was dazzling to the eyes, like a million pinpoint mirrors, multifaceted diamond-like reflective surfaces all in radiant sparkle.

She realized she was enjoying the ride. The nature. The freshness.

Through a break in the trees she saw tracks coming straight to the edge of the ski slope and then doubling back into the forest as if the animal—a raccoon, by the size of the prints—had thought better of crossing the heavily trafficked ski slope and decided to take its chances back in the woods. She hoped the poor animal had enough to eat for the winter. The blanket of snow must have covered the earth a yard deep.

The chair bounced and swayed as it pulled closer to the top. Despite the serenity that surrounded her, she felt her inner tension growing, her fear mounting, as she realized that very soon she would have to ski. The butterflies hit her stomach as it churned against itself.

The big breakfast David had insisted she have was in danger of coming back up.

With conscious effort she kept it down and with trepidation watched the skiers beneath her.

Damn it: If that little four-year-old in the striped parka can come charging fearlessly down the mountain, then I can!

The only thing she had to fear was fear itself.

That was horseshit and she knew it.

Besides, four-year-olds didn't have that far to fall.

They had not talked much in the car driving up to the mountain.

Each had been filled with unspoken thoughts after seeing the portrait, the resemblance. They had kept their impressions and fears to themselves.

David, Sandy knew, had been more disturbed than

she, and wanted to talk. She had silenced him, though, as they climbed back out of the Wallford cellar, carefully closing the window and repacking snow to hide their tracks. She suddenly remembered they had not re-covered the portrait.

They stopped for gas in Glendon. David stood grumbling off to the side as the price gauge turned at ten times the rate of the gas being pumped into his car.

It was when they had pulled out of the service station, twenty-two dollars poorer, that David's mind began to wander back to every horror movie he had ever sat through. The coincidence unnerved him.

"Sandy—" he said.

She cut him off. "David, there is nothing in that picture that can be of harm."

As if the floodgates had been opened, David snapped back at her, "Damn it, Sandy. That's *you* in that portrait."

"No," she said evenly. "It's Suzanne. Of a hundred years ago."

"Don't dismiss it so quickly. Enough people in Owlsfane believe that something spooky is going on in that house. You confirmed that yourself last night. Twice. And again, just a few minutes ago. For all we know, Eben Wallford's spirit might just be walking around the place: eating food, turning on lights where there is no electricity, smoking cigars, I don't know what else."

"Doing crossword puzzles?" she offered.

He shot her a look. "You'll have to admit that what happened to you last night is just a little suspect."

"A little," she conceded.

"You saw a ghost!" he almost screamed in her ear. "And a girl on fire. And there's the dream. And a freezing-cold room. And a portrait that is just too damned close to pass as coincidence. What more do you want—a written program?"

"David!" she said with exasperation.

But he wasn't stopping. "So what do we have? A kook, Wallford, so preoccupied with life after death he has servants come in to whip up a posthumous picnic, a girl burning at a windowsill, and a daughter who looks exactly like you whom the kook just happened to bury alive." He sat back and waited for her to comment.

"Good alliteration," she said.

"What?" he asked blankly. Did he miss something?

"Posthumous picnic. I like that."

"You're taking none of this seriously," he said.

She turned full in her seat to face him.

"And aren't you making too much of it? Yes, I saw something. And yes, I had a nightmare. And yes, the room was cold. And yes, there is a portrait. But if you don't mind, I just don't want to talk about it anymore. Please. The whole thing is silly. Okay?"

He shook his head.

"Okay?" she repeated, more loudly.

"Okay," he said, tight-lipped, and turned his attention back to the road. He knew, of course, that he would not let it drop. It was too disturbing, and while he would not admit it to her, it scared the hell out of him.

Sandy also knew the whole thing wasn't silly, but she didn't know what to do about it, short of leaving Owlsfane and ruining the week of skiing, which she wasn't about to do. Perhaps if she ignored it, it would go away.

It was then that the image of the burning girl came back to her.

Her heart fluttered with the realization; the jigsaw pieces came together in her memory. There was something that was oddly familiar about the burning girl. She had only seen the image for a fraction of a second, but it was still enough to know. It was her hair. It reminded her somewhat of Suzanne's hair in the portrait.

But then her realization grew stronger still: it was her own hair as well. She took off her ski hat and ran her hand through it: the long dark hair, parted in the center.

She wondered what it all meant—if anything.

The top of the mountain was within grasp, only a half-dozen lift towers away. It was colder up here and the wind had picked up somewhat, stinging their faces and sending swirling waves of snow aloft.

Sandy's teeth started to chatter and her body shivered involuntarily. David draped his right arm around her, drawing her closer to him, as if pressing themselves together would generate more heat.

The mountain dropped off sharply to the right as it contoured eastward, a steep fall of expert slope that opened to a twenty-five-mile uninterrupted view. Evergreens and mountaintops stretched out far below them, nature at its most primeval, awe-inspiring best. Sandy's intake of breath bespoke her feelings. She could not take her eyes from the wintry scene sprawled out below her.

David too looked. Even though he had been on this ride a hundred times (after the fifth year, who still counted?), it was a vision that still humbled him. On a clear day they could see almost forever, it seemed, and forever was a snow-topped wilderness of greens, blues, and sloping whites.

He was worried. His mind clouded over with concern for Sandy. He glanced over at her, specks of snow dusting her red, flushed cheeks. A wave of love passed over him.

"What is happening is real," he said, perhaps only half out loud, but when she looked questioningly at him, he repeated, "Real life and not fiction."

"You're talking about it," she said with the slightest tinge of annoyance, but she wasn't silencing him.

"I keep thinking it's almost as if there's this giant master plan with you in the center of it."

"Giant master plan?" she asked with a smile. "Isn't that a bit psychopathic?"

"A bit," he admitted wryly. "But things appear to be—can I say—*too* planned. Too organized. Too ordered. First the vision last night, then the dream, today the portrait."

"I admit things appear to be stacked on top of each other, but—" She shrugged in a "What can we do about it?" gesture.

"I keep on wondering why I removed the sheet from the portrait. It makes no sense for me to have done that. We'd really be suspecting nothing now. But I had to go ahead and create a major worry for both of us."

"You didn't," she said. "If you hadn't lifted the sheet, I think maybe I would have. To check out what Eben Wallford looked like. To see if he was the same man I saw last night."

"And?" David asked, already knowing the answer.

"And," she answered, "things are stacked on top of each other."

There was a moment of silence between them. David was annoyed at himself. He had gone into the house promising to touch nothing. Had Sandy made a move for the sheet, he probably would have stopped her. A cold wave shot through him. Were they *supposed* to see it? He wondered, worried, and then as if by heavenly insight it hit him.

"Sandy, this may sound crazy. Okay?"

She looked at him sideways. "Okay."

"Crazy," he repeated in emphasis, holding up a hand.

"Yeah. Right. Crazy."

"Piecing together what we have, and given the similarities—the *strong* similarities," he corrected himself, "between you and Suzanne, I think it's possible that Wallford, if he still is bopping around in that house, really might have gotten through to you last night, thinking, I don't know—thinking you were his daughter come home."

Sandy stared straight ahead and her answer was flat. "His daughter is dead, David. I'm not dead."

That's easily arranged, David thought in a flash, and then banished the horrifying nibble from his mind.

"You knew where her room was," he said.

She opened her hands wide so that she almost dropped her ski poles. "You're building a case for something. What?"

"For all we know," David said slowly, "you may just be the reincarnation of his dead daughter." There. He'd said it.

Sandy listened. For a split second she thought of her dream and of Eben Wallford's pushing her into the mausoleum, as if he had wanted to bury her alive. Then she spoke. "David, I have just one question for you."

"What?"

"How do we get off this thing?"

The chair in front had just unloaded its passengers. Sandy watched as one of the pair skied down the unloading ramp and fell flat on her ass.

CHAPTER X

Judy was tired of throwing snowballs at Scott. Left alone since early that morning when everyone went skiing, they had done nothing else since ten o'clock. Her arm was tired and she was bored. The game had lost all its fun as it swung into the third hour. As they played in the fresh snow of the Owlsfane cemetery, the full impact of their punishment hit home: they were missing one hell of a terrific day at the mountain. Ah, well, Judy thought as she mounted her last and final attack of the day, the snow would still be there tomorrow. She just hoped the soft top surface wouldn't be all skied away.

She waved her arm to end the game and stepped out from behind the headstone she was using as cover. A snowball splattered against her face.

"That's enough, Scott!" she bellowed. "I waved that I was quitting."

"Can't quit," he called back as he launched another ball of snow at her. It fell short.

Judy dived behind the headstone.

"Why can't I quit?"

"Because we have nothing else to do."

She had to admit he was right. It was too perfect a

day to be indoors, and there'd be enough time for that anyway in the afternoon when the sun started its decent and the temperature dropped. Then there would be Monopoly and backgammon.

Outdoors, though, there was little else to occupy them. There was nothing to see in Owlsfane, they were not allowed in the woods behind the ski house where the property sloped downward toward the river, and they already knew every inch of the cemetery.

There was, however, always the Wallford house. . . .

Curiosity spiraled upward from Judy's stomach.

She stared across the road at it. The house was silent, yet intimidating. Almost defiant. Daring her to cross the road and approach it.

A snowball flew past her.

She had never really thought much about the house one way or another. It was always just there, that was all. They had played in the cemetery, around the mausoleum, had circled the Wallford house, and last night had even been *inside* the Wallford house. Not far, granted, but inside nonetheless.

But today, somehow there was a difference.

So much had happened. The girl, Sandy, had gone into the house and had seen the ghost. And the ghost was in the ski house too. Despite what the others thought. She wasn't buying that dream stuff. The house was cold, and then the ghost touched Cynthia. She just wished that the six-year-old could have articulated her sensations better. What she had seen, felt.

There was a ghost. Judy was certain of it.

And today she felt she could almost sense movement within the house.

Her curiosity mounted.

She stepped out from behind the protective headstone once more, waving both arms high over her head, dodging the last of Scott's snowballs.

When he saw she wasn't doing much to resist, the game was no longer fun and he stopped.

"What's up?"

"Let's take a look around the Wallford place."

Scott was immediately uncertain. "Why?"

She echoed his statement of a moment before. "Because we have nothing else to do."

"Right," he answered. "But why do we have to do that?"

"Oh, I don't know," she said wistfully. "Maybe we'll get to see the ghost."

Scott exhaled. They had covered this already. "There're no such things as ghosts."

"Fine," she said. "So you shouldn't mind exploring around the house, then."

He shrugged. "Guess not."

"Come on."

She led the way down the slope of the cemetery to the road. They waited as several cars and a Greyhound bus aimed toward Burlington sped past them and then raced across the road to the Wallford house.

Judy was the first one up the porch steps; Scott dragged behind.

There was a space between the window shade and the inside sill and Judy knelt down next to one of the front windows. She shielded her eyes with an open palm, squinted to escape the glare, and tried to see into the living room. She could make out a padded couch and heavy New England Morris chairs. There was no life within.

Yet something still told her: something was in there.

"You want to go in?" she asked casually. She was game.

"No," he said with certainty. "I don't want to go in. We got burned last night for going in." But that wasn't the real reason, he knew; he was afraid.

"Well, there's no one around to see us."

"I'm not going."

Judy shrugged. "Probably won't see anything anyway. Ghosts never come out in daylight."

"Right," Scott readily agreed.

Judy walked around the veranda to a side window and peered into the dining room. She looked at the goblets and decanters standing at attention in the cupboard, at the dining-room table set with plates and silver as if the family were about to come to dinner. She was flushed with anticipation, fully expecting to see the ghost of Eben Wallford sit down at the table and eat. Scott flopped down on the porch steps and started to bunch snow between his legs, writing his name in the undisturbed snow beside him.

So he wasn't with her when she screamed.

It was a cry of surprise. She had felt something touch her. Someone behind her. An icy finger. A breath of cold well beyond the chill of the day. She whirled around: nothing. By then Scott had rounded the corner of the house and was beside her.

"Did you see anything, Scott?" Her voice was raised, excited.

"No. What?" He was caught up in her frenzy but didn't know why.

Judy spun around 360 degrees.

"He was just here."

"Who?"

"The ghost. Eben Wallford. He touched me."

Scott opened his arms. "Where? I don't see him."

"He's not here anymore. But I tell you. He touched me."

Scott snorted. "Yeah. Right." His voice had a sarcastic edge. "But he's not here anymore."

"I felt him," she protested, her voice cracking. "He touched my neck. It was a cold, icy touch." She rubbed the back of her neck to show him the exact spot. Scott watched, unimpressed. She thought a moment before adding, "The touch of the dead."

"You sound like Chiller Theater," Scott scoffed. "You wanted to feel him, that's all. You already had it

in your mind he's in there, so you just proved to yourself he was."

She put her hands on her hips and stared at him petulantly. "Now what makes you think I had it in my mind
he's in there?"

"You just did," Scott said, shrugging. "I don't know
why, but you did. Probably imagined the whole thing."

"Didn't," Judy said, her voice challenging. "I was
looking in the window and felt the cold on my neck."
She ran her hand across her neck again. "It almost feels
like it's burning."

Scott looked up at the eaves under the veranda roof.
He was checking for dripping snow melting in the sun.
Drops of cold water could have landed on her, causing
the icy sensation. But there was nothing. The air was
cold enough to prevent the melting. He shrugged and
dismissed it. He still didn't believe in ghosts. Judy had
imagined the whole thing.

"Let's go back to the house," he said.

Judy nodded. She was a little unnerved by the ghostly
touch, but excitement tingled up and down her spine.
She knew she'd be back.

It was when they were walking down the front path
and away from the house that a slithering, creeping
feeling from within her made her turn around.

There was nothing. No one.

But when she inhaled sharply for an instant she
smelled it—a weak, distant odor of something charred,
something black and burned.

The ghost was in the house, that she knew; and the
sensation of heat and cold that still burned her neck,
and the flip-flopping feeling within her told her he had
just tried to contact her.

She did not know why it was, but there was no denying the needling twinge she felt; the spiny urge to return
to this house and go inside.

CHAPTER XI

Three hours after David and Sandy started their run down the mountain, they were back in the lodge, nursing a hot chocolate in the cafeteria. Not exactly something you would call the Guiness people about, David thought, but an honest start nonetheless.

"So?" he asked, eyebrows up, when they were settled in.

"So what?" Sandy answered evasively. She swallowed a mouthful of cocoa.

He drummed his fingers on the table. He wasn't going to let her get him. "The skiing?" he asked with detached interest.

"Ohhhh," she answered magnanimously, shaking her head up and down as if she finally understood integral calculus. "That's what you were referring to."

David rolled his eyes. "That's what I was referring to."

She looked across the cafeteria. "Look, David. Racers. They're all wearing those cute little bibs."

"You're never going to tell me, are you?"

"I'm only kidding," she said. "I . . . um . . . liked it."

His eyes widened and a smile broke out. "In spite of yourself?" he asked.

She held up a cautious hand. "I choose to reserve final judgment."

"Let's go up again. Help you to decide." He reached for his parka on the chair next to him. The snow conditions were too perfect to waste time indoors.

She waved him off. "I've had it for a while. I'm going to sit here, thaw myself above freezing on either scale—Fahrenheit or centigrade—consume my weight in hot chocolate, and maybe if I regain the strength and warmth and courage, brave it again."

He slumped back into the chair, a little-boy look of disappointment crossing his face.

"But," she continued, "I want to sign up for a group lesson and I don't want you to stop me. I've wasted enough of your time today."

As he put up his hand to silence her, she added: "And don't tell me I haven't. The little kid in the green stripes passed us five times while I was getting down. And if he could do five runs in that time, you could have done at least . . . two." She started to laugh.

"At least," he agreed.

"Besides, you're supposed to meet Bob about now, aren't you?"

"I forgot!" David exclaimed. "What time is it?"

"A little after one."

"I told him I'd meet him at the summit at one thirty."

"I know." She beamed. "That's part of the reason you're marrying me. I keep your calendar straight."

"Come up with me. We'll ski down together. Bob has a way of attracting half the house around him. Last year twenty of us commandeered the Bunny Buster slope.

She shook her head. "Not now. I'm bushed." She glanced up at the clock behind the ski school desk. "I think I'll try for a two o'clock lesson. And I promise you've got me all day tomorrow. Unless, of course, I become too good for you and don't want to waste *my* day."

David buttoned his parka and slipped on his mittens. "You sure you don't mind skiing alone?"

"There'll be fifteen people in the class."

"Yeah, I know," he said, a dumb, cat-getting-loose-near-the-fish-tank grin on his face. "Just don't meet anyone."

"Get out of here," she said, laughing. "Who else am I going to meet who takes me to haunted houses?"

"I'll meet you at four," he said. "They have a folk-singer here who's quite good."

"Done," she said, waving good-bye. "You and me and whoever I pick up in the class."

He leaned over, kissed her, and then looked deeply into her eyes. "I'm crazy about you," he said.

She smiled in return. "I'll bet you say that to all the Bunny Busters."

She watched him leave the cafeteria. There was a spring to his step and she knew he was excited about the afternoon of skiing. Good, she thought. They had each done what was expected of them. He, the gallant bit, giving up his own time to teach her to ski; she, acting as the willing, albeit terrified, maiden. And it had all worked out well. She went back to her hot chocolate, draining the styrofoam cup and tonguing the inside rim. She sat back in her chair and smiled broadly—for no other reason except that she loved David so very much. And this skiing business, really the last hurdle, had now been successfully jumped.

She did have to admit he was right. In spite of herself she really found she was enjoying this sport. Although she would never tell that to David, of course. She did need some leverage. She had no intention of becoming a fanatic like him, and every intention of holding him to the Caribbean bargain made on the trip up. It was a fair trade-off, she reasoned. He got skiing and Sandy; she got a trip to the Islands.

But for now—oh, how she ached. She glanced up at the clock. She had a good half hour before she'd have to drag herself over to where the ski school classes met. She'd use every second of it to rest her very tired and angry muscles.

She sat straight up in the chair and let her eyes drift slowly shut and her breathing ease. It was a relaxing technique she often used. Her rigid posture prevented her from falling asleep (the way she felt now she didn't think she'd ever get up again), but her closed eyes gave her wonderful moments of stolen rest. Her eyelids fluttered and she defocused the Babel of background noise that buzzed past her. As so often happened when she was relaxing this way, she let her mind drift off into a half-asleep/half-awake state, where thoughts could trip unrestrained in front of her closed eyes.

She saw the ocean.

There were waves on a sandy white beach. A child was playing on the beach, building a sandcastle . . .

She felt her head start to nod and with a jerking motion forced herself upright.

The ocean waves entered from a thousand different directions and washed away the barrier walls of the sandcastle. . . .

Get away from here!

She heard the girl's voice clearly and distinctly. It came in a hoarse whisper, as if the speaker were afraid of being overheard. Her eyes sprang open and she looked around. The background din became focused and she heard conversation. There were people at the next table and people behind her. The cafeteria was crowded, but no one was talking to her; no one was paying her any attention. Yet she knew she hadn't imagined the voice. Maybe it was someone passing by.

But when she played it back she realized that it was not a passerby. The voice she had heard sounded as if it had come not from outside her, but from within.

Get away from here. . . . Those were the words.

Terrific, she thought ruefully. Not only was she see-ing ghosts, now she was hearing voices.

But this was not a ghostly voice; it couldn't have been. It must have been her own instincts, more fright-ened by events than Sandy knew herself to be, whis-pering a warning in her half-conscious state. Well, she thought with a smile, there had been plenty of times in the past when she hadn't listened to herself and her instincts. This time would be no exception. This week was important to David, important to them both, and she was not going to blow it!

She didn't want to close her eyes again, telling her-self that she was not really afraid of the invisible voice of warning, but rather her few remaining minutes would be better put to use if she splashed cold water on her face and got psyched for the ski lesson.

Lifting herself painfully out of the chair, she crossed the cafeteria and pushed open the swinging doors to the ladies' room. The heavy clump-clumping of ski boots echoed loudly around her on the white tiled floor.

She threw water on her face and raised her head to look at herself in the mirror, oblivious to all others in the rest room.

The fire appeared to come from behind her head, slowly reaching her, touching her, kissing her face, bathing her in flame, shooting upward. She stood mo-tionless, staring into the mirror, watching the flames lap at her face.

She thought she felt someone touch her shoulder, but she could only stare at the fire that threatened to con-sume her. The touch again, harder pressure on her right shoulder. She watched in horror as her skin reddened and charred and bubbled.

Someone *was* shaking her. There was a voice.

"Hey—where are you?"

She shook her head violently from side to side. Her eyes opened fully. The flames were gone. *There were no flames.*

Ricky stood beside her.

"Hey—?"

Sandy smiled weakly, still shaken from the vision in the mirror. She peered closely into the glass. No flames. No burning. Just the concerned face of Ricky and her own—flushed and tired.

Jesus!

"Are you okay?"

No. She wasn't. She really wasn't.

"I don't think I can handle much more of this, Ricky."

Ricky smiled broadly. "Nah. You'll get used to the skiing. I promise."

The skiing? What was she talking about? Sandy wondered. Then it clicked. "Oh, I didn't mean the skiing. . . ." She trailed off. What *did* she mean? Damn it! She really had to clear her head.

Ricky nodded. She understood. "The ghost thing still getting to you?"

Sandy smiled, chagrined. At that moment she thought she would have settled for "the ghost thing." What was happening to her? She was seeing things, hearing things. Was she losing her mind?

She briefly wondered if she should tell Ricky about the portrait, the vision, everything. No. She didn't know this girl at all. It was easier to drop the whole thing. She was tired, that was it, and her mind had gotten away from her. First the voice, then the vision. What a hyperactive imagination and tired body could manufacture for itself!

"I sent David off by himself for some honest skiing time," she said, smiling weakly, changing the subject. "He earned it, good little Boy Scout that he was."

"He's not giving you a hard time, then is he?" Ricky asked.

"No," Sandy answered. "He isn't." If anything, she thought to herself, it was she who was giving David the hard time. And she firmly resolved she would knock it off then and there!

With giant herringbone steps David raced up the incline to the chair lift. One fifteen. If the line wasn't too long he'd be able to make it to the top of the lift in time to meet Bob at one thirty for—*ugh,* another lunch. He hoped Bob was finished so he could just make a pit stop and head out for the afternoon. They could easily cover most of the mountain in the three remaining hours of daylight. They would ski their brains out.

He didn't mind skiing with Sandy, of course. It was just that it wasn't really *skiing*. It was more *ski ten feet, make two instructional turns, have her watch, watch her ski down to where he was, and pick her up when she fell.*

He did have to admit, though, that after the first third of the hill she really wasn't falling all that often. In fact, for the first run ever, she was doing pretty damned well. And he had been good to her up there: never yelled, as exasperating as it sometimes got, gave her encouragement, and complimented her when she had done well. Come spring, he decided, after she had mastered skiing, he would stick a tennis racket in her hand, get her a Central Park permit, and see if he could formulate a perfect existence for himself.

They had thought about a wedding in June. He would consult a *Farmers' Almanac* to pick a rainy Sunday so the ceremony would not interfere with any outdoor activities. Although, he reasoned, he'd still be able to squeeze in an hour of indoor tennis in the morning, before. . . .

The ride up the mountain was fifteen minutes, and he welcomed it now. There was no better place to think than the isolation of a chair lift, when the mountain below was lunchtime-quiet and there was no seatmate with whom to engage in idle small talk. Stretching out across the length of the chair, head thrown back and eyes closed, he realized he was alone for the first time since they had come up the night before.

He loved her.

A strong "Singing In The Rain" type of love for perhaps the first time in his life. It was her first, as well. A genuine love and not the dependence it would have been so easy for her to fall into.

Her life had not been easy. Both her parents were dead. Her father's sister had looked after her through the end of college; an older woman who perhaps smothered her too much in overcompensation and forced the break. They had never reconciled before her death.

She had been difficult to get close to, as if fighting off the relationship, *any* relationship. He had pressed, she had retreated. His initial intensity had overwhelmed her, unnerved her. She was afraid of becoming involved. Finally he had discovered the proper pace, and it had worked.

He knew she needed her space, and he gave it. He also knew she needed to be held. As she had last night. And he was there.

She had watched her mother drown when she was twelve, and he tried to empathize with the horror. She was there on the sand as it happened, and saw her mother's body pulled out of the water. She and her father had become close after that—very close—until his death in a car accident five years later.

She never really liked to talk about her father. It was as if a strange, fleeting fear would pass over her, even to the point of a visible flash behind her eyes and an almost imperceptible pulling away whenever she mentioned him. She couldn't explain it. The feeling was alien and she admitted it. They had been close, yet she felt so damned uncomfortable about him.

During one of their first dinners, when they were exchanging vital statistics, he saw immediately that this was one she did not wish to share. As if there were something holding her back, preventing her from talking freely. But nothing she could put her finger on or define. Consequently he had never pressed.

He could only try to understand the painful memories she must have relived, the shock of losing the second parent. They had told her she had been helped from the crash that killed him and had escaped with only minor burns, yet she had no recollection of it. Also very understandable; a repression of the horrid event. The rare times the incident was ever mentioned she would dismiss it lightly, claiming she had nine lives, like a cat, and was then working on her third. A queer remark, he realized. Her third. Why not her second? She didn't know why she had said it. Nor was it something he had ever given any further thought to. He wondered why it had popped uninvited into his mind right now.

He did know one thing: if she indeed had nine lives, he wasn't about to give one of them away to Eben Wallford.

She must have been right when she said something in that house had gotten to her. He wasn't going to give it another chance to get her again. They shouldn't stay in the ski house that night. It was just too close to the Wallford house. Whatever it was had invaded the privacy of her dreams.

CHAPTER XII

Tom and Bob were finishing lunch as David came inside. He stamped snow from his boots and tried to warm up from the cold ride up the mountain. Despite the brilliance of the sun, the day had remained cold. He grabbed a cup of coffee from the express line and pulled up a chair next to them.

"I didn't want to stop," he said, sipping the coffee and squeezing his hands tightly together to get the blood thawed and circulating again. The coffee burned his lips. "But it's just too damned cold to run right out again. How's your day been?"

They compared notes. David listened with envy as Tom told him he'd been the first to float down the virgin snowfield of the advanced slope.

As if reading David's mind—not to mention the wide-eyed, open-mouthed stare that betrayed him—Tom tempered his own fun by commenting, "It was all for a good cause, David. Believe me, she's worth it."

"I know. But why couldn't the conditions have been rotten. It wouldn't hurt so much."

They all laughed, and then David sobered.

He told them about the picture in the Wallford bedroom and the burning girl that Sandy had seen.

Bob emitted a low whistle of surprise. "You're kidding?" he said blankly, as if asking David to confirm the joke.

Fighting a feeling of foolishness, David voiced his reincarnation theory.

"How is she?" asked Tom.

"All right. I give her a lot of credit. I think she's dealing with it quite well. She even told me to butt out. Not that she meant it or that I'm going to." He pointed to the slope outside the window. "It takes a hell of a lot of concentration to get out there and do what she did today. Even in the best of moods. I think she's doing a good job keeping it out of her mind." He paused and looked from one to the other. "What do you make of it?"

Tom opened his hands in a shrug and offered, tight-lipped: "About the portrait? A strong coincidence?"

David shook his head. "Can't buy it," he answered softly.

Bob agreed. "By itself, maybe. It would even be amusing. We'd probably all traipse up to the bedroom to look at it, pull out a Polaroid, and have Sandy stand in front of it." His voice dropped and became more serious. "Taken with everything else, I'm at a loss."

They sat in silence for a long moment as the lunch-time sounds of the lodge swelled around them, each trying to draw some rationale from the air. David watched the psychiatrist. If anybody had an explanation, it would certainly be Tom.

Tom finally exhaled. He knew the others were looking toward him. Most people did. It had taken him several years to finally feel comfortable in the godlike role others gave him.

He looked past David and Bob. He appeared distant, as if he were trying to think out loud, trying to make some logical sense of what they all knew. He didn't have an answer, nor would he pretend to. He would

never diagnose, or even comment, without substantiation. He would rather be cautious than wrong.

"What about the burning girl, Tom?" David asked.
"Another ghost?"

"I don't know," Tom answered softly.

"Hallucination?"

Tom chose not to answer directly. Rather, he said:
"A hallucination or vision can fulfill a need of a particular individual." He shrugged, letting his words hang.

David quickly answered. "Sandy has no need to see
ghosts or girls on fire." He looked to Bob for support.
Then his voice choked. "Tom, you really don't think
Sandy has been seeing actual ghosts, do you?"

"I don't know, David," Tom said flatly. "It's indeed
possible, I'll say that. The house does come with a
story. I'd rather she were seeing real ghosts than having
hallucinations, you know that. So until we have confirmation one way or the other, let us say that Sandy has
been seeing ghosts. However it might be helpful,
David," he said, "if you could find out for me what was
in her nightmare last night. *I* don't want to ask her."

"I understand."

"But don't be obvious about it. Try to draw it from
her so as not to alarm."

David leaned forward across the table. "But what has
any of this got to do with the portrait?" He noticed his
voice was getting loud and he checked himself. "*That* is
real. Perhaps the only undeniably real thing we have!"

"David, I honestly don't know."

David fell back into his chair.

Tom honestly didn't know. He also questioned why he
was getting involved. This was his vacation. Sandy was
not his patient, nor his problem. But David was his
friend, and right now he had trouble. And that was why.

They had met at the ski house. Tom, a half-dozen
years older than David, had a young daughter he was
just starting out on skis, and a fledgling practice. David
had just gotten his first editorial assistant's job on a

trade magazine. Despite their age and life-style differences, they clicked. They became, and remained, good friends in Vermont and back home as well. They skied, played tennis, and sailed together. And they were able to talk. That was something Tom knew was unusual in even the best of friendships. Especially when one of the friends was a psychiatrist.

Tom would not let his friend flounder alone. Although he knew they were straddling the line between friendship and profession.

The portrait confused him as well. He'd have to look at it. Sandy too, a little more closely, although subtly. Something was happening—her dream and second vision confirmed that, although he didn't know how or where the portrait fitted in. He knew they'd be looking to him more and more for guidance. He could not refuse the help.

David's lips were tight, his eyes frightened. "You'll be honest with me, Tom?"

"Completely," Tom said. "Even when I don't have an answer. And right now I don't."

He felt a twinge of guilt. He was not being entirely truthful with David even now. He was being a doctor rather than a friend, but the situation called for it. He knew that David strongly suspected that the visions might have been something other than ghosts, and that would have pointed to a problem Sandy had. Had Sandy been his patient in a more formalized setting, it might have been different. What they didn't need, he knew, was a psychiatrist to generate alarm. He tried to cure problems, not cause them.

David was still staring at him intently, as if waiting for something more. But Tom had nothing more. He smiled warmly to break the tension of the moment. "Shall we hit the slopes, gentlemen?"

Bob and David grabbed their parkas and with Tom headed out into the cold.

CHAPTER XIII

The First Annual Christmas Week Backgammon Tournament was off to a glowing start. Game boards were set up around the living room and the cutthroat elimination play was under way. The sounds of tossed dice, scraping checkers, and an occasional shout and groan filled the ski house as each member vied for the first prize—a free weekend at the house, on the house. Bob was trying his damnedest to come in first in order to avoid actually having to award the prize.

David and Sandy were not in the ski house.

A string of bad dice rolls brought Judy up short very quickly in her first match, and her name was crossed off the Peg-Board. She extended her hand to Ricky, the victor, who took it graciously. Scott, still in his match with Craig, grinned broadly at her defeat and thumbed his nose at her, waving his fingers in the air. She pushed her chin toward him in silent defiant response and picked up her paperback.

She commandeered a chair next to the fire, threw her feet comfortably over one of the arms, and sank deeply into its softness. She tried to read but could not concentrate on the book. Her mind kept drifting.

Something was pulling her attention from the book, fighting for her thoughts.

Something was jabbing at her from within. Sparring with her mind.

Bob was defeated in his match with Stan, which dashed his hopes of saving the weekend prize. He knelt down next to the fire, added a half-dozen small logs in pyramid fashion, and watched the fire burst into new life.

The crackling in the fireplace captured Judy's attention. Grateful for the diversion, she put the book down on her lap to watch the fire. She peered into it, quickly losing herself in the wavy pattern of the rising flames.

Something was forcing her to look at the fire.

Something from within her.

Something strong.

The fire held her mesmerized. She no longer heard the sounds of play in the room. She concentrated on the eerie dancing glow of the rising flames. Her mind wandered unchecked; her thoughts were not under her control.

It was as if she were being forced to imagine what it would be like to walk into the fire, *to be on fire,* to let the heat scorch her skin and blacken it; what it would be like to burn to the bone, to be incinerated.

She did not know where the frightening thoughts were coming from. But they were not hers; *that* she knew.

There was a smell lodged deep inside her nostrils: the searing smell left hovering in the air after a branding iron has made its mark.

She could not pull herself from the vision. She saw herself as flames swirled about her, billowing up and around her head. Fire exploded from her nostrils and mouth. Judy saw her face for only an instant before it was completely engulfed by the inferno, reduced to a formless black pulp.

Ron's voice broke through. His triumphant "I won!" brought her back to the room.

Everything was as it had been before, yet the smell lingered in her memory: the almost familiar tight, pungent odor of charred flesh.

Then she noticed that something else was different.

She was no longer seated in the chair. She was standing in front of the fireplace. The tips of her fingers were reaching for the flames; her hands were inches from the fire. She looked at them uncomprehendingly for a suspended moment and instinctively drew her arms back. She stared at her hands, turning them from front to back, and then looked at the fire with wide-eyed confusion.

She did not remember how she got there.

Her eyes darted cautiously from the fire and she looked around the room, hoping someone would come to her and ask her what was wrong. But no one seemed to notice anything wrong with her. She was warming herself by the fire. That was all.

Judy stepped back, away from the fire. She stared at it uncertainly, a little fearfully. She reached behind her for the arms of the chair and lowered herself into it again.

She looked at the fire, her head tilted with suspicion. Nothing seemed wrong. Nothing was out of place. The others were folding the backgammon sets, putting them away, and getting ready to go upstairs.

Detached, she watched the motion in the rest of the room.

But try as she could, she could not remember having moved from the chair.

They were sitting in the Red Barn Restaurant.

David had explained to Sandy why he didn't want to return to the ski house that night. She had scoffed, called him an alarmist, said she didn't want to spend sixty dollars of *their* money, but in the end acknowledged he might be right. Besides, in a motel she wouldn't be sharing a bunk with Gail Landberg. She needed David next to her that night; too much had happened during the day. She could already envision his warmth and strength as he held her. And when he asked, she told him about the nightmare she'd had, surprised that she remembered the dream so vividly; she never really remembered her dreams, even immediately upon awakening.

But she did not tell him of the vision in the mirror or about the voice she heard.

After dinner they went dancing. The disco was loud, crowded, and Sandy lost herself to the flash of the lights and the pulse of the bass.

They registered at the motel as husband and wife. Sandy realized they were indeed beginning to act—and look—like a married couple. Their room was on the second floor at the end of a long corridor. Sandy fell appreciatively onto the bed.

"I feel like a beached whale," she sighed, trying to disappear into the softness of the mattress. Arms and legs flopped to the side, she vowed: "I am never getting up again. I don't think I've ever been this tired before."

David started to unzip her parka. "Let me help you off with those nineteen layers of clothing."

"Leave them on. I'll die warm."

David managed to pry off several of the top layers, and pulled off his own parka and ski sweater.

"A hot shower and you'll be good as new," he offered.

"Let me take a nap first," she groaned. "A fourteen-hour nap. Better, a fourteen-year nap. Rip Van Winkle knew how to live."

He pulled her off the bed and herded her in the direction of the bathroom, arms at her side, a dead weight, her feet shuffling painfully against the deep brown carpeting.

"I don't have the strength to turn the water on.

They're going to find me here in the spring." She turned to him, begging. "Don't make me do this again. Please don't make me do this again."

He had to laugh. She was so funny: hair plastered across her face and flattened from the snug hat she'd worn the entire day, stomach bulging from the lumpy flannel shirt she had on. Her mutterings brought him back as he struggled to get her into the bathroom.

"I'll never be cold again."

If she'd had the strength to lift her fist it would have been waving in the air. "I'll never ski again! You owe me for this, you son of a—"

The bathroom door slammed in his face. Moments later he heard the curative sounds of running water. He smiled, knowing the shower would pick her up just fine. He eyed the bed and slipped off his pants. He'd just stretch out until she she finished. . . .

David awoke. Sandy was leaning over him, kissing him softly.

"Poor baby," she sighed. He couldn't tell if it was sarcasm or pity. "You needed a nap, didn't you?"

He reached up and encircled her in his arms, bringing her down to him. He breathed in her freshness.

"I must have fallen asleep for a minute," he said.

"Try an hour."

"That long?" He tried to raise himself up on his elbows. She blocked his way.

"Do you have anywhere you really have to go?" she asked.

His eyes found hers, twinkling in anticipation. Her tongue ran softly over her lips. *Well, half the fun of skiing was the she-ing.*

"No," he said. "There isn't anywhere I really have to go."

He pulled her to him. His hand found the light-switch and flipped it off. Their lovemaking continued until exhaustion took hold and both settled into sleep. Sandy skipped her usual cigarette and the pillow talk they both enjoyed, to give in to her very tired, sore, and stiffened muscles. She would kill for a tube of Ben-Gay, she thought, although now, snuggled next to the warmth of David, skiing didn't seem all that awful.

The dreaming began again.

It was a winter night, a long time ago.

Eben Wallford lay dying, a guilty soul that could not find peace. Sandy watched Eben Wallford shudder and breathe his last.

There was a blinding white light, starting as a small distant dot, becoming an ever expanding corona of light until it filled Sandy's entire vision; a thousand suns burning as one, yet gentle on the eye, and Sandy did not have to turn away. Into the midst of this light, growing from nothing, from afar, came the hollow, lined, lifeless face of Eben Wallford.

Sandy knew she was seeing Eben after his death.

The white faded and turned to gray, the dull gray of an old black-and-white movie played on a badly tuned television. An oppressive, disturbing murkiness that swirled and clung. Eben Wallford's face was sad, brow wrinkled and furrowed in apparent search; the troubled, lost look of a soul that did not know where it was or where it was to go. As he had listened at the mausoleum door in life, so he seemed to be searching in death, powerless, bewildered almost to the point of terror.

Panic and confusion lined his face as his sharp eyes darted about, trying to grasp what he could not see, trying to understand, trying to contact, trying to escape problems unresolvable. A lost hopelessness of time and place; the suspension of understanding and knowledge.

Sandy knew he was suspended between the two states of existence—the physical world, and the next world, where his family was and where he desperately wanted to be.

But he wasn't with them; he was lost.

Their eyes locked once more, and Eben's face relaxed. A beckoning hand extended out to her from the dull-gray backlight. The face implored her to grasp it. She hesitated. She was curious; she was drawn. She wanted to help him, to go with him; but frightened, she held back and would not take the hand.

Despair and terror glinted in his eyes as if in sudden realization of his doom: to stand calling, arm outstretched painfully forever. Never again to be with his wife and daughter.

Then the light faded away and the figure in front of her vanished.

But her dream continued; the scene changed.

She was at the beach; a child playing in the sand, building sandcastles.

A breeze flew off the water, carrying the scream. Sandy looked up with alarm. Far away, almost on the horizon, two arms waved furiously out of the water and a woman disappeared from view, drawn under by the ocean. A man ran into the water, thrashing furiously to try to reach the woman who was drifting further away.

Then the man came out of the water and walked slowly past the child, past Sandy. The man had lost his wife to the sea. Sandy's mother had drowned.

The scene changed yet again.

The downhill ski slope lay in front of her, fresh snow packed as softly as a woven mat. She was skiing well: bending her knees, leaning her body downhill, planting her poles.

The trail flattened and narrowed, a halo of trees formed an archway above her. The sun burned through the trees, rays filtering through and catching her eyes with flashes of light. Twigs and broken boughs lay across the trail, polka-dotted with emerald and dying brown needles of evergreen. Suddenly the corridor of trees ended and the trail opened wide in front of her.

The slope dropped off. She picked up speed. She saw herself heading toward a lift-tower pole. She glanced off a mound of snow with an icy crown. She tried to correct her mistake, but missed a turn. She could not get her uphill ski around in time to allow her to traverse the mountain slope in the opposite direction and slow herself down. It was almost as if the skis were frozen to the snow, magnetically attracted and held, unresponsive to her commands.

She was pointing straight down the hill, in the fall line.

She moved down the ever steepening slope at faster and faster speeds. She hurtled out of control.

The sky was upside down and suddenly she was outside herself. She watched her body cartwheel down the mountain. Her skis spun behind her. She came to rest on her right side, landing on her arm, which lay bent beneath her at an awkward angle.

She stirred out of sleep, reality and unreality jockeying for position before her slowly opening eyes. Then wakefulness hit her.

Yet she was unable to move. The horror of her skiing fall lurked full in her consciousness, not drifting from view as she prayed it would. It eclipsed all else.

Her arm hurt again. It was the same tingling numbness that she had awakened with that morning. Kneading the spot of pain with her fingers, she thought back to the dream; less through her own desire, more because it sucked her mercilessly in.

The strange surreal familiarity of the ocean scene made her wonder. Her mother's drowning. She knew she had dreamed it before, but could not recall the time or place.

But she recalled so few of her dreams.

Then she realized: her dreams of Eben Wallford—her *nightmares*—were continuing even miles from the haunted house. She could not escape them by running away.

It was as if he followed her wherever she went.

She would not tell David of her dream; she didn't want to alarm him. She lay in bed with her eyes open, listening to the gentle sounds of David's soft sleep. The terror-struck face of the dead Eben Wallford danced in front of her; she was unable to banish the vision. She swallowed and choked back her fear. Sleep was not her friend, but her body ached for it, demanded it, and she allowed herself to give in.

The ski house was silent. The heavy sounds of nighttime breathing rose from the women's dorm when Cynthia came up from sleep. The blankets were pulled up protectively under her chin, the scratchy wool irritating her tender skin. Her throat was dry and she had to go to the bathroom, but an undefined feeling of warning kept her locked in the security of the bed. Her eyes slowly opened.

A thin band of yellow hall light snaked in from where the door was not fully closed. Around her, the huddled, sleeping forms of the others rose rhythmically. An escaping whistle from a sleeper across the room broke the air and Cynthia followed the sound.

It was then that she understood her instincts to remain in the bed.

A figure was in the room, only barely discernible in the dim light. The little girl watched it as it moved slowly and methodically from bed to bed, in and out of the shadows. It was a man's figure and it looked as if he were checking on the people in the room. An old man. Hunched over.

Who was he? she wondered. And why was he checking on them? Why wasn't it her father or Tom who was looking in on the sleeping women? She didn't remember ever seeing this man before.

Then she knew who he was and she froze.

She watched the man through half-opened eyes.

The man stood over Judy for a long moment, looking at her, before moving silently on.

He was looking for someone, she realized. But who?

Her throat scratched and tickled and her bladder was full, but natural caution and instinct did not allow her to move even a muscle as she watched the man stare into the sleeping face of Judy's mother, Gail.

Looking . . .

The room felt suddenly chillier, as if a cloud of cold had settled over it. As it had felt the night before. Cynthia turned up her nose. What was that odd smell? It was nothing pleasant.

When the man turned away from the empty bunk across the room and looked her way, Cynthia's stomach quivered and she suddenly knew.

Who he was looking for.

He was looking for the girl. The girl who brought him into the house the night before. But she wasn't here tonight!

Her fear mounted: Who else would he take?

The smell grew stronger. She tried to close her nostrils to block the smell. She thought of burning leaves in the fall, but knew that wasn't fully right. The odor had no prior place in her young memory.

The ghost turned toward her. Her eyes widened. Her skin grew cold. Her throat locked, her heart skipped. She felt her bladder begin to empty. She closed her eyes tightly, but then opened them a slit so she could see. She was too afraid to scream. She strained against herself so she would not wet the sheets.

He approached her bed. She shrank smaller under the covers, fearful of his icy, evil touch. Fearful of what else he would do to her. Perhaps he wouldn't see her! She was small. He could pass her by.

The man's feet made no noise as he crossed the room. He stood by her bed and looked at Ricky in the bunk above.

Cynthia was suddenly aware of her breathing. It sounded like a rush of wind through a deep canyon. She knew he heard her as well.

He started to bend down to her.

The ghost! He wanted *her!*

She swallowed tightly and her eyes bulged.

Their eyes met.

The ghost reached out to her. His hand hovered over her face. She could see right through it, to his burning eyes above. He touched her. It was like wearing a mask of ice.

She jammed her eyes shut, opened her mouth, and forced the sound from deep within her. Past throat muscles that had tightly closed. Through lips dry and cracked and caked wtih fear.

When she stopped screaming the ghost was gone, the overhead light was on, and the room was awake.

Gail stood next to her and quickly yielded to Pauline, who scooped up her daughter in her arms and once again brought her tightly to her.

"The ghost!" Cynthia cried. "He was here again." Tears streamed from her eyes.

"My poor baby," Pauline sighed. She held Cynthia's head, gently patting it with one hand, wiping her face with the other.

Bob was beside her. His voice was soft.

"Another dream, honey?"

"It wasn't a dream," Cynthia protested loudly. "He was here. I saw him. He put his hand over my face. It was so cold."

Cold!

Judy, awake in her bed, was alert, listening to Cynthia describe her encounter with the ghost. Cynthia had felt the cold touch too, the same as she. Damn! Why couldn't she have seen him. It was *her* he wanted to contact anyway, not Cynthia. She started to speak, but closed her mouth. She calculated that nothing good could come of her admission of having explored the Wallford house. Scott stood in the doorway. She shot him a silencing look, but Scott didn't need to be told. At least now there were no doubts in her mind that there *was* a ghost. And there couldn't be any doubts in Scott's either.

Bob turned to the others. "Did anybody else see anything?"

They looked from one to the other. It was Gail who answered for them all.

"Nothing, Bob." Her hands were open in a shrug. "But we didn't wake up until after she started to scream."

Cynthia was quieting down. Pauline stroked her head.

When the girl stopped crying, Bob lifted her up.

"Come on. Let's go into our room, okay?"

Cynthia nodded weakly.

"It was a dream, Cindy. Only a dream."

"It was not a dream," she said to her father as he carried her out of the room.

The others watched them leave. They shook their heads, shrugged silently, and turned back to sleep. There was nothing else to do.

Bob and Pauline put their daughter between them on the bed, pressing her with their warmth.

Bob stroked her arms. Her breathing eased.

He spoke softly, taking her in deeply with his eyes.

"It was a dream, honey. Just another dream. That's all. There is no ghost. Certainly not in this house."

She looked at him wide-eyed. She so wanted to believe him, yet she knew what she saw.

What she thought she saw.

"You're perfectly safe in this house. Mommy and Daddy are here and we'll protect you. No harm will come to you. You know that, don't you?"

"Yes."

"Perhaps you'd like to go home? Maybe the dreams will stop there. Would you like that?"

Cynthia shook her head. She liked to ski.

"No."

"Okay. But you'll sleep with us tonight. And tomorrow night if you want. And let's see if we can get these nasty dreams to stop." He smiled warmly. It was the face she knew and trusted. "What do you say?"

A smile broke through on her face. She nodded vigorously. She felt safe. In the warm protection of her parents' bed nothing bad would happen to her; she was sure of that. The ghost or the dreams or whatever it was could not touch her here. She turned on her stomach and, exhausted, moved quickly toward sleep.

But suddenly her smile faded. Her last thought before losing herself to sleep was about the girl—the one who had brought the ghost into the house. This was all her fault.

Bob and Pauline looked at their daughter and then each other, communicating with their eyes. They'd watch Cynthia closely, and if need be they would take her home. Maybe the dreams would stop in the familiarity of her bed at home.

In the women's dorm Judy was awake. She was making plans to go into the Wallford house the next night. After dinner. When their parents thought she and Scott were outside playing. Well, they would be outside playing—technically—but they'd also be exploring the inside of the Wallford house. They would find the ghost and prove to the others that there was one.

She shuddered with anticipation and fell off to sleep with the tingling fantasy of confronting the ghost.

To what end? She didn't know. Just a needling feeling from within that somehow she had to. That somehow, for some reason, he was drawing her to him.

And she had to go.

CHAPTER XIV

Sandy opened her eyes.

If she dreamed any more that night, she did not remember.

They awoke at seven thirty as the first rays of sun began to peek through the heavy drawn curtains. Sandy stirred first and stretched, flexing her shoulders, then moving downward to her legs. Especially her legs. She ached all over and felt like hell. As if she couldn't possibly ever get enough sleep. She closed her eyes again and tried to will herself back to sleep, but almost instinctively, it seemed, David was awake beside her, engulfing her with his arms. She breathed in pain and emitted a long muscle-ached moan. Even her hair hurt.

She rubbed the arm that had pained her from her dream. Her skin was dry and itchy. She wasn't certain, but it felt rougher than it had the day before. Damn! She had forgotten to use the moisturizing cream.

David stretched beside her, trying to work out the stiffness in his cramped leg muscles. He always felt like this the second day of skiing. As if he had died. He didn't want to get up. The sun caught him in the eyes and he closed them to escape the glint. He was in no

rush to move from the warmth of the bed, and had no
desire to assume a vertical position. Ever.

His hand lazily stroked Sandy's body and he felt hers
on him. It was an awakening ritual for both before a
word would pass between them. Her left hand lightly
traced lazy circles on his body and he felt himself
grow. The circles became larger, heavier, and then instinctively more concentrated as his pleasure mounted.
She nuzzled his ear as he spread her legs and found the
moistness between them. With eyes still tightly closed,
he raised himself up. Their bodies met. Tension flowed
from each of them and they relaxed, David's arm
crooked at the elbow underneath her neck, his hand
lightly stroking her face, her lips buried in his neck.
Her arm held his stomach, her fingers playing across
his chest.

In spite of his desire to make the most of the week,
he allowed himself to drift off to sleep, realizing with
his last thoughts that he was indeed making the most
of it.

Sandy, beside him, needing no encouragement, abandoned herself to sleep once again.

It was easier than trying to think or remember.

Bob was sitting alone at one of the dining-room
tables when Tom walked over, balancing a cup of
coffee and his breakfast plate of waffles and eggs.

"Care for company?" he asked.

"Sure." Bob motioned to the seat next to him.

Tom sat and reached for the syrup. "How's Cynthia?" he asked.

"Better. It took her a little time to come down from
that dream. She was quite shaken by it."

Tom nodded. "Being touched by a ghost, yes, I
would say. Kids that age can experience some really
fierce nightmares. You and Pauline did the right thing—
sitting with her until she was calmed. She'll grow out of
it soon enough." He smiled. "I did."

Bob raised his eyebrows. "You suffered from night-mares when you were a child?"

"The worst. I would wake up unable to breathe or move, screaming my bloody head off. Cynthia's seems mild compared to some of mine. It got so that I was even afraid to go to sleep." He laughed shortly. "Perhaps my desire to become a psychiatrist has its seeds in those horrible nights."

"What do we do?"

Tom furrowed his brows, indicating that there was no real problem. "Just wait it out. The events of the last several days have been disturbing to her, and that undoubtedly has been the triggering force for her dreams. There may be more. But she'll outgrow them soon enough."

"That's a relief," Bob said.

"However," Tom said, raising his finger. "I think it's about time the two of us took a look in that house."

Bob led the way to the back of the Wallford house and he and Tom climbed in through the cellar window. Allergic to dust, Tom coughed and sneezed his way across the basement and up the stairs to the main floor.

Bob gave him a quick tour of the downstairs, where he marveled at the collection of antiques scattered around the house. If he were Josiah Stoneham, he would open the place as a museum or at least sell off the valuables the house contained. They were certainly not doing anyone any good where they were, in the empty house.

But he had to smile to himself. As much as he believed there was nothing in there, they still didn't know for certain if the house was indeed empty.

They were there to look at the portrait.

There was a pall of gloom over the house—something Tom could sense, even smell. His senses seemed attuned to more than he could see, and it made his fine

hairs bristle. Unmistakably there was something there—
the feel of evil?—something not quite defined, and Tom
couldn't be certain if it was anything more than imagination. He felt it in his stomach too, which twitched
coldly, in his very being. But not in his reason, which
dictated logic, not emotion.

The power of suggestion. Even he was not immune.

They climbed the stairs to the second floor and
turned toward the front of the house. He wanted to be
able to say with a degree of certainty that the strangeness had increased, that it had gotten colder, the air
heavier, from a spirit presence, but he could not. He
knew he was looking for it now; it was in his mind.

The door to Wallford's bedroom was closed. Tom
sensed the air, flaring his nostrils, seeking confirmation.
None was to come, but at that moment he knew that
whatever force, internal or external, had drawn Sandy
into that room in the dark of night, was a force to be
contended with. Unless powerfully driven, he knew that
he, for one, would not have come.

Bob pushed the door open, holding it ajar with his
foot so that it would not swing closed on its hinges.

The sheet lay in a crumpled heap on the floor in
front of the fireplace, where David had let it fall. Above
the fireplace they saw the portrait. Silently they looked
at it. There was no exaggeration in what David had
said. Sandy was indeed a physical double of the dead
Suzanne.

It was then that they heard the noise.

It came from below and assaulted their ears like a
gunshot at night. A moment frozen in time. Another
intruder in the closed house. The rough slam of a glass
paneled door, then the rattle of resettling glass. Bob
strained his ears to hear more, crossing a finger over his
lips, motioning for silence.

Bob was still supporting the door with his foot. The
spring release mechanism was rusty and the squeal
would betray their presence upstairs.

There were footsteps below them, crossing the house, down the main hallway toward the rear door. Heavy footsteps. Footsteps with knowledge and purpose; not tentative, not exploring. Footsteps at home.

Then they discerned a second pair of footsteps. A lighter footfall of someone smaller, stepping gingerly on spots of squeaking board. They groaned under the weight and presence of the new visitors, the whining sound of old, rotting wood sighing in protest, imploring to be left alone.

The voices began, and Bob recognized them: the soft, cracking voice of the woman; the gruff, graveled voice of the man. The Stonehams.

"I want to make certain the kitchen is clean," the woman said.

The kitchen door squealed open and the light footfall disappeared. They listened, immobile, as the heavy step of Josiah walked beneath them in inspection, in and out of every room. Bob silently prayed they would not come up the stairs.

Josiah's voice, calling to his wife through the closed kitchen door, carried upstairs. "Did you bring him any of the Christmas cake?"

"Yes. I left it for him."

The woman's footsteps joined those of her husband in the front of the house. Bob knew they were at the base of the stairs and unconsciously held his breath. Even his racing, thumping heart sounded loud. Any noise from them now would be heard below. They'd never be able to explain their presence in the house.

"We'd better go," Mrs. Stoneham said. "All seems in order." The waver in her voice betrayed her nervousness at being in the house.

Bob flashed a hopeful look to Tom as they heard the woman move toward the door, then changed expression when Josiah asked, "Did you clean upstairs?"

There was a pause before the uncertain voice answered. "For Thanksgiving. Yes." The voice grew stronger. "It should still be clean. I don't have to do any more."

Then the front door opened and closed. They were outside the house. The residual rattle faded to silence. From the bedroom window Tom watched them walk up the road. It was only then that they dared to move.

"Let's get out of here before they decide to come back," Tom said. He was utterly amazed at what had just taken place.

Bob shook his head in agreement and led the way downstairs. He knew they had intruded on something very private, very spiritual, and perhaps very sacred. He prayed there would be no repercussions, but he couldn't imagine any.

He brought up the rear, following Tom down the steps. As they rounded the stairs toward the cellar door, he turned around and glanced back up, half expecting to see someone, some*thing*—an outline, a shadow, a presence—watching them leave.

There would be no Halloween party in the house next year.

The day was once again cloudless. The air was warmed by an unbroken sea of sun, the sky the calming blue of a deep, motionless spring pool. A warming air mass was coming in from the south, and David was nervous about a thaw. A refreezing overnight when the temperature dropped could ice up the mountain and make the skiing slippery and dangerous.

The chair-lift wait was a short one, and they were airborne once again. By now, her fourth trip up the mountain, Sandy felt like an old pro and ready to conquer the world.

But suddenly, in a black wisp, the dreams came back to her again. As did the feelings, stronger now. The strangeness, the pull, the queer attraction she felt to the Wallford house, seized her anew. A cause and effect, but she was uncertain as to which followed which. She still felt confused, trapped by an uncertainty that would not yield to understanding.

Twice in a row he had appeared to her in dreams. And twice in a row the dreams seemed more than dreams.

It was almost as if he had been waiting for her.

No! Oh, no! She wouldn't think that.

Coincidence. It was coincidence, she stated to herself with finality. Coincidence and her reaction to a ghost story, an apparition, a portrait. Single elements. Interrelated, but not organized, not purposefully projected as David had suggested.

The ghost was real! And the dreams were hers alone. Not put there by any other entity.

And that was that!

David had not mentioned the Wallford ghost again. Driving up to the mountain, he had asked her how she was and she had said fine and they had both dropped the subject. She had slept soundly, she said, and he had smiled.

And she would sleep soundly and dreamlessly, back in the ski house. And if not? If not, they were only dreams; she was in no danger. Dreams she could deal with and perhaps come to understand eventually.

Yet, no matter how she tried, she was drawn back to the thought she wanted to bury. Her mind was forcing her to consider the other possibility. What if indeed she *had* been singled out. *What if he* had *been waiting for her?*

Then, so be it. She would take the dreams as they came to her. But she would tell none of them to David.

She had waited too long for him.

She would do nothing to jeopardize their life together.

She was all her father had left.

Her mother was dead, and it was the two of them, alone. From the time he had scooped her up in his

arms, a child of twelve, and carried her screaming from
the beach, not comprehending the magnitude of the
tragedy, they had almost been as one.

They could communicate without speaking, it
seemed, and he had held on to her, as if afraid to lose
her as he had his wife. Ironic, she thought; she had lost
him.

He had not remarried. They were inseparable, father
and daughter.

And then he had died.

For five years she did not let herself become close
with anyone.

Until David.

The bond of father-daughter was replaced by another, perhaps stronger. Odd. For the first time in her
months of knowing and loving David, she wondered if
her father approved.

It was the way the small plane entered her line of
sight from the left, poking into the blue above her, that
triggered her memory and brought it back. The plane,
a small flag-colored twin-engine Cessna, angled downward, east to the Rutland airport. Banked for the approach turn, the plane seemed to skim the purple-white
mountain ridge and disappear into the next valley, the
whining sound quickly becoming absorbed by the wind.
The plane was almost an unwelcome visitor into the sea
of serenity about her.

And so it also was on that day.

In a sudden burst she saw what she had not seen in
five years. She saw it all in one sweeping motion-picture
long shot: at her feet, the pile of dirt, underlayers of
soft earth exposed to the glint of the sun for perhaps
the first time since creation. The hole between her and
the piled dirt a bottomless pit of unspeakable meaning
and horror. She remembered walking to the edge and
staring down, swooning, and losing her foothold. But

grabbed and hand-held by those around and gently led backward from the mouth of the pit. In the background lazed the men with shovels, caked mud on their heavy workboots, as they leaned against the dirt-splattered pickup truck with the wooden side boards and open back. *She could even see the knotholes in the side planks of the truck.* And then the lowering of the casket; her father's final resting place.

Fragmented recall.

The doctor had told her she could attend the funeral, but the morning of the day she had remained in the hospital bed. Dressed. She had dressed the night before, and except for her shoes she was ready. Her arm was still bandaged from the burns and she remembered the pain.

But she had not gotten out of bed. The nurse had come in and opened the floor-to-ceiling louvered blinds and the brilliance of the sunlight had found its mark, catching her square in the eye.

But she had not moved from the bed. As if not to go would be not to have to acknowledge, and all would be as it had been. In a flash the events would be erased, as if they hadn't happened. One of those times when one feels that just by wishing something away it would be gone.

The light and the shuffle of rubber-soled shoes on the spotless tiled floor woke her. The nurse stood over her, eclipsing the sun, with pitying eyes, as if sharing her vision that not to go would make everything right itself again. But she had spoken.

"Aren't you going to the funeral?" she had asked, and in a flood the tears had come anew.

She was pulled back to the edge of the grave as the casket was lowered. The conspicuous silence of the cemetery engulfed her. Leafless branches, caught by the breeze, swayed soundlessly back and forth. The cry of the cemetery birds waiting to swoop for worms in the upturned earth was the only sound, save the grunting of the pall bearers as they lowered her father into the shadowed blackness of his burial hole.

It was then that the plane had loudly entered, its droning whine shattering the silence and solemnity of the scene.

For Sandy, the plane was a daring intruder, a mocking, terrifying reminder that life would go on. Although she was alone.

She had not remembered this, try as she might. It had been blocked. And now it was back in frightening Technicolor vividness that made her reach out to remember more.

"Look! Pauline!"

David had grabbed her arm and was pointing beneath them. Schussing expertly under their chair, ski pole waving in greeting, was Pauline, orange and black parka hunched forward in her very distinctive, albeit unusual, style of skiing, the upper part of her body bent almost parallel to the ground, more like a bicycle racer than a skier. But she never fell. David had never seen Pauline fall. And if it worked for her, why comment?

Sandy was brought back. They were nearing the top of the lift and in moments she would be skiing again.

She was doing well: good up-down motion, good bend of the knees (she was surprised they actually were able to bend), good pole planting in one-two in front of her. They had already covered twice the distance they had yesterday and she still felt strong. Urging David to pick another trail, as she had tired of this familiar one, she felt she could do anything. She now knew why David had called skiing a mind-cleansing experience. She really could think of nothing else except survival as she picked her way down the mountain slope.

The flat connecting trail brought them to another section of mountain, another chair. Still a beginner's area, but the trails were narrower, forcing skiers to make their interconnected turns faster, with less width for runouts than she had been used to. They stood at the base of the chair, David pointing upward, offering her a bail-out. But she was feeling good. If it proved too difficult, she could always slip-slide her way down, as she'd been taught in class yesterday, head back to the main base area, and take her afternoon lesson. And if it didn't prove too difficult? Well, in that case, she thought blithely, it was the expert run next.

The chair angled into the wind and the secluded warmth of the previous lift was suddenly replaced by stinging needles. David told her not to worry, they would be heading down the other side of the mountain where it was warmer.

A combination of fate and circumstance led her to where they were going.

They were halfway down, David in the lead, when she felt something was wrong. But it shouldn't be. Her second day of skiing was smooth-motion perfect.

It was the formation of the trees above her, the way they grew over the trail, which had narrowed considerably as well as flattened out to the gentlest of slopes. There was an isolation to this trail, an isolation from other trails and from the sky as well. The overgrowth of trees engulfed her, the sun only peeking its way through the thick, defiant branches, scattering wavy shadows on the snow beneath her as the branches responded to the force of the wind. A rug of broken pine needles lay at her feet and she picked around them.

But the fun ended as the realization grew.

The trail opened in front of her, widening and steepening *as it had last night in her dream.*

She had been here before. She had seen all of this. And with a sinking feeling she knew what was inevitably to happen.

Both David and her instructor had taught her one basic element of ski-slope survival. If she ever found herself out of control, she should simply sit down on the snow. This would prevent a damaging spill worsened by momentum.

The lift tower loomed before her: tall, red, snow-splattered. She tried to sit in place, but couldn't. She hurtled forward faster, yielding to what she could not control. She heard David yell to her from below to stop, to sit, to slow, to turn. A mogul lay directly in her path—a mound of snow formed by the continuous passage of hundreds of skiers all turning in the same spot, which others could use to turn on or jump from. She was coming toward it at a bad angle. She would have to shift her direction uphill to avoid it. Below it was a drop-off.

She glanced off the top of it, and the sudden weight-lessness of her skis at the very tip caused a change in her downhill direction. She was angled straight down the fall line, out of control. Despite David's admonitions to turn, to fall, she could not coordinate mind and skis.

It was all happening as it had in the dream of last night.

As her right ski caught an inner edge and left the ground, she started to fall.

CHAPTER XV

It was almost as if a clarion call had gone out to the members of the ski house that one of their own was in trouble. The first-aid room was SRO as the word was passed on the mountain, from chair lift to slope and back again.

Nothing was broken. She had landed on her right shoulder and had the wind knocked out of her. It was just a sprain; the X rays were negative. A few days rest and she could be back on the slopes once more. If she wanted to, David thought, worriedly. This injury would not do much to enhance her enjoyment of the sport.

It was like horseback riding. If you didn't get right back out there . . .

Now Sandy lay in her bunk. The midafternoon house was quiet around her, the others were still at the mountain. There was a throb in her shoulder, but it was dulled from the pills. Maybe skiing just wasn't her thing and she should hang up the old poles.

But it was more than that. She had dreamed the fall. Just as it had happened. Every damned pine needle in place, it seemed, and that scared hell out of her.

She drifted off into sleep and awoke several hours later as the house came alive with returning skiers. She opened her eyes slowly and saw David perched at the edge of the bed watching her.

"I am lousing up your vacation, aren't I?" she asked, as she wiped the sleep from her eyes.

"No," he said softly, and stroked her forehead. It was hot under the blankets and she was sweating. Her eyes searched his face, looking for some sign. Of what, she didn't know. The last forty-eight hours had been hell for her. A quiet, nonskiing day tomorrow would do wonders. It might even bring her back to normal.

"You're wounded," he said, smiling at her.

"If I were a horse, you'd shoot me."

He lightly rubbed her shoulder blades. "Horses don't have wings."

"Horses also don't ski," she smirked. "What time is it?"

"They're setting up for happy hour. Think you can make it downstairs?"

"Of course." She smiled wanly. "Give everybody a chance to look at me."

"Nobody's going to look at you. Other people in the house have hurt themselves. If anything, you'll find yourself at the center of some pretty concerned attention."

"It's not just the fall, David. It's everything."

He matched her look and started to protest. She put up a hand to stop him and forced a half-smile. "Don't, David. No matter what you were going to say, don't. You've got to admit that I've made a lousy first impression here. Dale Carnegie wouldn't be proud. You can't change the fact that to all of them I appear to be"—she hesitated—"different? crazy?"

"That's all in your head," he answered. "And if you want to keep it there, you will. And *then* you'll really begin having problems. You listen to me and cut out that 'different' crap. Okay?"

She answered in a small voice. "Okay."

"Good."

She thought a moment. "Is Tom back from the mountain yet? I want to talk to him." She wanted to know why the dream was so damned accurate.

David nodded and left the room. As she was pulling on a sweater Cynthia came into the room. She was back from the mountain. The little girl looked at Sandy and froze. Sandy didn't move either. She had heard about the second nightmare the girl had had, and from her previous outburst knew what Cynthia was thinking: that somehow she was responsible.

She wanted desperately to calm her, to tell her she was not the cause of her nightmares, but she didn't know what to say. Nothing seemed to make sense. Besides, she didn't think the girl would listen to anything she said.

And for all Sandy knew, she probably was somehow responsible for the nightmares.

Cynthia swallowed tightly and looked warily at Sandy. She was here. The girl who brought the ghost into the house. She wasn't here last night. Why had she come back? Then she considered that it might be good that she had come back. If the ghost wanted this girl and she was there then, everyone else was safe. *She* was safe. But Cynthia wasn't certain if it was good or bad that Sandy was back in the ski house. All she knew was that she was afraid of her.

From the stairway landing Pauline was calling her daughter. Cynthia did not respond. Sandy heard Pauline call the girl's name again and answered for her.

"Up here."

Moments later Pauline was in the room with them. She first saw Sandy and then her daughter, across the room, motionless. In a flash she assessed the situation. Cynthia ran to her mother. Sandy sadly shook her head. This was not the way to make friends with a child's mother—terrifying the child.

But Sandy tried.

"I was just getting changed to go downstairs. I understand from David that happy hour is better than ever."

Pauline smiled tightly. She spoke pleasantly, but Sandy caught an edge to her voice. She felt decidedly uncomfortable in the other woman's house.

"Feeling better?" Pauline asked.

Sandy tried to smile warmly.

"Yes. Thank you. It wasn't a bad fall." Unconsciously she rubbed her shoulder, looking for sympathy from Pauline.

"I'm sorry it happened almost your first time out."

"Thank you."

Silence. There was strain.

"I hope it won't sour you on skiing," Pauline said. She had her arm protectively around Cynthia's shoulder, slowly easing her daughter's head toward her.

"No." Sandy put on a smile and tried to make it convincing. "I'll be out for a couple of days and then right back up there." She put a twirl into her voice and tried to sound cheerful.

"That's good," Pauline said.

They stood awkwardly for a moment.

"Well," Pauline finally said, trying to fill the vacuum, "I was coming up to help Cynthia change, but we can let you finish up first, okay?" Without waiting for a response, Pauline was already ushering Cynthia out of the room.

Sandy wanted to call after her, to ask her to stay, and perhaps they could all try to work this thing out together. She was really okay, she really was, and meant nobody any harm. But it just seemed easier to let Pauline and Cynthia leave her alone in the room. For now, she would lie low, go her separate way from Cynthia, steer clear of Pauline, just be one of the house, and hope that within a few days they would all be on speaking terms again. If it was up to her alone, she would clear out of the house. But it wasn't up to her—she was doing all this for David. This was his ski house and these were his friends and she would be damned before she would come between them or cause him to leave.

Besides, she really *did* want to stay.

David met her at the landing and offered her his arm. She felt everyone's eyes on her as she walked down the stairs.

The other members looked up from their tortilla chips, pickle slices, and fondue, more so, it seemed to her, than if she were just anyone else coming down (*limping* down) to happy hour. With her bad arm she waved to them, and it was then that someone started clapping, a motion soon to be picked up by the others in the room; a warm, welcoming round of applause for one of the group who had been injured.

David nudged her. "Traditional."

"Why didn't you tell me?"

"And spoil the surprise? Never."

As they rounded the landing, she looked out over the smiling faces and felt as if she were a general reviewing the troops.

The applause broke, and Bob got up from his wing chair, which was closest to the fire. He reached out to assist her gallantly down the final steps and smiled broadly.

"We really should buy a record of 'Hail to the Chief' to play during moments such as these." They all laughed and returned to their games or conversations. Sandy felt better; she was indeed one of them.

As if from nowhere a glass of white wine appeared, and Sandy took it gratefully, downing half in one gulp.

"Good," she acknowledged.

"Vintage Poughkeepsie, New York," Bob said. "November. A good season, if I recall."

Tom joined them and led a toast to her speedy return to the slopes.

Sandy turned to the psychiatrist. "Tom, I want to talk to you."

"Of course," he said. "Why don't you step into my office." He took her arm and led her toward the dining room.

David hung back. "Am I welcome?"

For a half second Sandy hesitated. She didn't want him to overhear. She didn't want him to worry, but David would resent the exclusion, worry all the more, and find out later anyway. She couldn't leave him out.

"I think that could be arranged," she said, trying for a joke. The words were light, but they sounded stiff and almost caught in her throat. She realized she was opening up more and more to the psychiatrist, as well as to her fiancé. And perhaps even to herself. *She remembered the funeral of her father.*

Tom closed the sliding doors to block the living-room noise and they pulled up chairs at the head of the table. Sandy folded her hands prayerlike in front of her. She told them about the funeral, about the dream, about her mother's drowning, with the vague, uncomfortable familiarity she had experienced. And she told them about the foreshadowing of the accident.

"It seemed everything was exactly as in the dream. The trail, the lift tower, the configuration of the trees." She broke off, her throat suddenly dry and constricted, her voice foreign. "And then I fell."

Tom listened intently. She needed explanation, assurance. But if she were looking for quick answers, it would not be all that easy. Nor was this the time or place for him to probe.

"Well, we've already established you might be a bit psychic," he offered easily. "People do have precognitive visions of disasters: planes crashing, ships sinking. Then they change their reservations and are spared." He let his voice soften and his eyes warm. "But perhaps it was something else, Sandy."

"What?" she questioned.

He hesitated and then prodded gently. "Perhaps you wanted to fall."

Her eyes widened like saucers. "I didn't, Tom—I—" She broke off, flustered, thrown by the question. She looked toward David, a curious expression on her face. "I didn't—"

Neither the time nor the place. Tom let it drop. But he knew he had planted a seed. "I had a precognitive dream once. We all have them from time to time. Woke up one morning dreaming of someone named Silverbach. I didn't know anyone named Silverbach, but the dream was so insistent and the name stuck so after waking that I remembered it. Damned if before the day was out a new patient didn't call me." He smiled broadly. "Name was Silverbach." He shrugged comfortingly and touched her shoulder. "It happens."

But inwardly he frowned. This wasn't Silverbach. Especially when he recalled later that he had been told previously that someone named Silverbach was going to call. His dream was less precognition than an unconscious reminder. He doubted there was any psychic connection to her fall. What he silently wondered was *why* she wanted to fall; why she wanted to hurt herself.

Scott ate slowly. Judy stared at him from her seat at the head of the table, watching his teeth grind every last mouthful to disintegration. Her eyes screamed at him across the table: *Move it! I want to go now!* She had hardly touched her food; she was chafing to get out of there. Finally she couldn't stand it anymore. Exasperation took over.

"Scott, that's your fourth portion of mashed potatoes. If you eat any more we'll be able to ski down your stomach!"

From the foot of the table, Cynthia giggled.

Mouth full, Scott shrugged. "I'm hungry. Sue me."

Judy's icy expression shot back: *Bull! You're chicken and you know it!*

Dessert was ice cream and she anguished through Scott's two helpings of chocolate fudge. She rolled her

eyes as he managed to dribble some onto his white ski
sweater. Finally he was finished and she was able to
drag him—the last one—from the table. They piled
their dishes in the sink and Judy raced to the bedroom
for her ski parka.

Jumping the stairs two at a time, she ran head first
into her father's chest.

"Whoa," Tom said. "Where's the fire?"

"No fire," she said casually. "Me and Scott are going
out."

"Scott and I are going out," he corrected.

"You coming too?" Judy smiled, and then jabbed a
finger into her father's belt. "Gotcha."

"Dress warmly if you're going to be rolling around
in the snow."

"Okay."

"Don't stay out too late."

"Okay."

"And stay out of the Wallford house."

Gulp.

"Okay," Judy smiled, itching to get away from him
before she gave herself away. *How did he know?* She
dismissed the thought. Somehow parents always knew.

She trotted back down the stairs, zipping her parka
and pulling a knit hat down over her ears.

Scott joined her in the kitchen vestibule, grabbed
flashlights from the porch for each of them, and together the two eleven-year-olds headed out into the
Vermont night. It was windless and not too cold, and
Judy whipped off her hat and shoved it into her pocket.
Her long dark hair cascaded over her shoulders. With
the tip of her index finger she flipped a few strands back
into place so that they lay on their side of the center
part.

They turned out of the driveway and started up the
road toward the Wallford house. To the left of them
the Owlsfane cemetery lay silent and shadowed. For
years they had fearlessly played among the graves, but

somehow tonight, the dimly lit cemetery seemed eerier than on any of the other nights. As if the frozen headstones knew what they were planning. It would be a long time before he would play in the cemetery again, Scott vowed, suddenly cold beyond the chill of the evening.

As the house loomed high in front of them, Scott felt the fourth portion of mashed potatoes rise to his throat, and he fought the feeling of inky trepidation that washed over him.

There are no such things as ghosts, no such things as ghosts, no such things . . . he kept repeating to himself over and over. But he was still looking for a way out.

His thought escaped: "My father's right. There's so much junk down there we can trip over."

"Not chickening out, are you?" Judy asked pleasantly, making him feel about nine inches tall.

"No." Although he wished that he could. And suddenly he knew why he was so nervous. What if there *were* such things as ghosts, and what if the ghost of Eben Wallford were waiting for them right now?

But what could he do to them?

The answer came swift and sure, an instantaneous printout: *Scare the hell out of them!* That's what he could do.

They stole glances at the mausoleum on their left. Illuminated by the streetlamp, it stood starkly tall against the black night. It seemed oddly calm, deceptively innocent, sealing the unknown behind its closed doors. Only days before the stone statue of Eben Wallford had been a structure to play hide-and-seek behind; now the statue seemed to follow their progress up to the house. He knows we're coming, Scott thought.

No such things as ghosts. No such things . . .

"What is it with you and this house?" he asked in a tinny voice as they rounded the corner and headed toward the back and the cellar window.

Judy shrugged shortly. "Curiosity, I guess."

But it was much more than that. Curiosity goes into the house in daylight and casually pokes around; obsession walks at night in prescribed search.

Throughout the day the strange, thorny feeling had continued to nip at her bedevilingly. Like a tune that was playing over and over inside of her, exhausting her to capitulation, one from which she could not pull herself free.

> I want to see the ghost,
> I want to see the ghost.
> Hi ho the derry ooo—
> *I'm going to see the ghost!*

The urge persisted: she had to go into the house and see what was there. It was like craving hotdogs, but different: like having an idea, an exciting idea, and carrying it around all day in fantasy form, relishing it, honing it, becoming more and more obsessed by it to the point of distraction.

Like the time she was going to write a review book on seventh grade math. She had helped two classmates learn to factor polynomials. The calculations had come as a breeze to her, but somehow the others couldn't grasp it. She had explained it away in the simplest of terms, and like a revelation they had learned from her. She became high from the tutoring experience. So all that afternoon she carried with her the exciting notion that *she* was going to write a study guide on seventh grade math.

The fantasy blossomed: every seventh grader in the country would read her book. It would become an indispensable manual. She'd be the youngest author in the world and receive public acclaim as well as financial success. She'd be on Merv Griffin! The fantasy was pleasing—more than pleasing: *consuming,* and she had spent her day living it, distracted from all else, carving sentences, sketching cover art, accepting awards—all in her head. However, that night when she sat down at her desk with a clean sheet of paper, a sharpened pencil, high ideals, and the scent of success, her fantasy suddenly and ferociously went bust. She could not do it. She could not write the book.

She had played the fantasy game all that day. She'd go into the house and prove the existence of the ghost. To Scott. To her father. To everyone. She really didn't know why, but somehow it seemed important; the urge had needled her relentlessly.

Like craving hot dogs, she had to go in. . . .

But this fantasy was rapidly going bust as well. Doubts were growing, fears becoming dominant. As they stood in front of the cellar window, she held back. Queasy. Uncertain.

"What's the matter?" Scott asked. Instinct told him not to bait her.

Judy hesitated. She grabbed on to the upper rim of the window and stared down into the penetrating blackness of the Wallford basement. She prepared to let herself down inside as they had done only days before when they had played the joke on their parents. She aimed her flashlight inside and stiffened, not knowing what might be silhouetted in the darkness. The last time it had been a game; now suddenly the rules had changed. She knew that something was in the house. What she didn't know was whether it could harm. The bubble was bursting. Came the sudden discovery that the hot dog could never taste as good as the fantasy teased; the discovery that she could not write a book; the discovery that the fear that walked on her skin was stronger than the urge to go inside the house.

She looked at Scott. A pity she had come on so strong that afternoon. She had gone after his masculinity, charging that he was afraid to go into the house while she was not, shaming him into coming with her. She could not now admit her fear.

Scott held his breath in tentative anticipation that she would break down. He couldn't be first. Men couldn't be afraid. If she were going into the house, so would he.

Stalemate. Pride was the victor.

Judy gave him her flashlight and crouched low to drop to the cellar floor.

"Let's go," she said simply, and jumped in. Scott inhaled sharply, handed her the two flashlights, and slid down next to her.

The heavy blackness of the cellar immediately engulfed them. The flashlights broke a narrow path in front of them as they inched their way in half steps through the cellar to the staircase on the other side. Behind them the house quickly closed in like a tight-fitting web. The darkness was strangling. Scott led the way. Judy huddled close by him, clawing at his back. They walked as one, their senses switched to overdrive, ready to discern the slightest sound, smell, or movement. There was a buzzing sensation in Judy's ears, as if the cold silence of the house were pulsating with sound of its own. Her throat was dry, a flour-and-water taste in her mouth. Her neck muscles were tense to the point of spasm. Her palms were sweaty in the heavy down mittens.

Like the study guide that would make her famous, *it had seemed like a good idea at the time.*

Scott aimed the flashlight beam up and down the steps leading to the first floor. His hand quivered, scrambling the thin beam of light. This was the last chance to bail out. He spoke the first words since they had entered the cellar.

"You're sure?" he asked. His voice was toneless and unnatural. There was a queer gummy taste in his mouth like what remains on the teeth after the dentist has cleaned them.

Judy nodded. Having come this far, they were already halfway there.

But her thoughts were mush, curiosity and fear equally balanced. Terror of the unknown easily tipped the scales. She assumed Scott felt the same way, his pasty face was a giveaway. She no longer knew if she wanted to see anything in this old house. In fact she was sure she did not, and offered a silent prayer for the ghost to remain invisible. But she could not admit her fear to Scott; they had to go upstairs.

They started up the steps, the rotting wood creaking under them like the whining sound of a trapdoor somewhere close by being inched open.

They stood in front of the doorway at the top of the stairs. Scott turned his flashlight toward Judy's face and caught her tentative nod. He hunched forward and slowly elbowed the door open a sliver, pushing the flashlight through. He expected to be met by a chalk-white face, piercing, burning eyes; or a sheeted ghost, body stiff and bound, or mummified with outstretched arms. A ghost who likes to eat children. He swallowed tightly, forcing the saliva down through straining neck muscles. What can ghosts actually do to people? he wondered. In horror movies they did terrible things. But what of real-life ghosts?

No such things as ghosts, no such things as ghosts, no such things . . .

They probably did terrible things too.

They snuck through the cellar door into the first floor hallway.

"Where?" he whispered heavily. This was *her* show.

Judy shrugged, tight-shouldered. She had no idea. She pointed forward with her flashlight. Ahead was as good a direction as any.

The floorboards whined beneath them in a tethered growl and the children froze. Scott exhaled round-mouthed into a misty white cloud that hung in the air before disintegrating. He couldn't remember ever having been as frightened as he was now. He thought of vampires.

Judy hung on to his arm so they would not be separated. She almost pulled him down. She was rapidly throwing away her intrepid demeanor. Scott had some gratification that at least he was apparently the braver of the two. Just apparently: he was on the rim of cracking too. But he should be the bolder one. After all, he was the male.

But his rush of masculine bravery lasted only a fraction of a second as the parlor and dining rooms opened up on either side of them, their monster furniture poised to pounce and devour. His stomach trembled and threatened to turn upside down as it did on the first downhill track at the Adventureland roller coaster.

No such things as ghosts. Nothing here that can hurt me.

Judy sucked in her breath shortly. She had seen—imagined?—movement in the silent, dark room. She whipped her flashlight through the dining room, tracing light patterns on the glass-covered cupboard and among the heavy pieces of dining furniture. A zillion places for a ghost to hide.

Her eyes were frozen wide. Her heart hung in her throat, beating at twice the normal rate. She felt a pounding in her temples, an exploding confusion in her chest. Her breathing was heavy and rasping, audible to both of them.

Her nostrils closed suddenly to keep out the noxious smell: something was burning.

There would be no going further; her feet would not allow it.

"Let's get out of here," she whispered heavily to Scott.

"Why?" he asked brightly. "Things are just getting good." And then all pretenses dropped. "You don't have to say that again." At least she had broken first. He indicated the front door ahead of them. "There."

Judy nodded and they walked down the hallway toward the glass paneled door, trying to make their exit

seem nonchalant. A sharp groaning split the air. They
dove for the door. Scott grabbed the doorknob and
yanked: locked. He aimed the flashlight toward the
keyhole.

It was then that Judy sensed something behind her.
At the same time, Scott felt the rough touch on his
shoulder. Their cries were swallowed by the loud rumble of a passing flatbed truck outside.

CHAPTER XVI

The house members were lounging in the living room as Bob passed out songsheets for Christmas caroling. He had hinted all throughout dinner that he might have a new story for them for later.

Gail poured the eggnog and Sandy found herself in a backgammon game with David. She was beaten very quickly and very badly; her concentration was just not on the game.

Why had she wanted to fall? How curious . . .

Pauline sat down at the piano to start the round of carols, and Sandy threw herself heartily into the singing, leading the chorus of the twelve days of Christmas. She avoided all eye contact with Pauline.

The lights of the Christmas tree twinkled on and off warmly and the glow of the fire filled the room. Then Bob again assumed center stage.

He cleared his throat and the room became hushed in expectation.

David nuzzled Sandy's neck. His touch was tingling. "Would you rather not listen to the story?" he whispered.

"I'm all right," she answered. "Just keep up what you're doing back there."

David smiled and led her to one of the couches, where they both perched in anticipation.

"Not so much a story tonight," Bob started. The room groaned. "But," he said, holding his hand in a peace-making gesture and winking conspiratorially, "something to think about."

He paused a second as the grumblings settled down. "Enough people have asked me about this, and I think it deserves a public answer and then your own speculation.

"All of the old members have been down in the cellar. That's where we store the skis during the week and at the season's end. There's a workshop down there for sharpening edges and waxing bottoms and filling gaps." He addressed himself to the new members. "There's also the boiler, the hot-water system, pipes galore, and a broken snowblower I've been promising to fix for the last seventeen years. The cellar isn't heated and pretty much assumes the temperature of the outside, so we can store food down there as well.

"What is also down there," he continued ominously, "is a wall."

"A wall?" David questioned.

"One of many that supports this house."

"Thank you."

"We bought the house several years ago, as most of you know, from a real estate agent who was hesitant to sell it to us—to anyone—because of our friend next door. But we wanted it and took it anyway. Upon stumping through the house, we came across this wall down in the cellar. Really, a portion of a wall. It appears to be a rather sloppy bricking job, with the bricks out of line and not flush with the rest of the wall on that side. Almost as if," he said, with a lilt of fear creeping into his voice, "it had been bricked over very hastily with no care except to finish the job, *and keep whatever is in there, in there.*

"There is a room behind it, we know that, because

of the way the rest of the cellar is laid out. But we don't know what is in the room behind that section of wall.

"Or," he said in a voice that dripped with the threat of blood, "who."

"Dum de dum dum," Ron sang.

"And we don't know why it was bricked over in such a hurry. The real estate agent didn't know, and none of my research into this house or the neighborhood has turned up anything."

"Why don't we drill through it?" Gail asked.

"I won't allow it," Bob said. "Not so much for the sake of my telling you this story. I have enough stories; you know that. I admit quite openly to being afraid to find out. The room was bricked over, I am certain, for a very good reason. Let it stay bricked over. I, for one, don't want to find out what is behind that wall. There is enough spookiness in this area without having to go looking for it in our own house.

"You are all free to speculate on what might be down there. You are also all free to sleep next to the wall, but I would bring my long johns, because it gets awfully cold down there."

He got up from the chair. "And with that, I am going to tiptoe into the kitchen where I happen to know there is a last plate of ice cream hidden that I am going to commandeer for myself before any of the kids discover there is still some left."

He gave Cynthia a tweak on the nose and then asked from the doorway, "Hey—speaking of the kids, where are they?"

Scott craned his neck to the limit. In the beam of light behind him there were skeleton fingers digging deep into his flesh. He tried to make a run from the firm hand that was tightly clasping his shoulder, but he could not pull free. Judy wasn't being held, but she couldn't get her feet to move. She was frozen in fear, exhausted, and her throat was sore from the screaming.

Scott tried to think fast, his eyes darting rapidly about him. If only he could break loose, he knew the way out: back down the hall, through the door, down the steps. . . . He'd grab Judy by the hand and pull her from this terrible house, away from the ghost that had him. But as if reading his mind, the clawlike hand dug deeper, penetrating many layers of clothing, pinning his shoulder in a viselike grip. He could not break from the powerful handhold. He started to scream again. Someone might hear him. That set Judy off again as as well.

"Shut up!" a deep voice growled. The hand shook Scott roughly and turned him around. Then he knew.

It was not a ghost that had captured them. It was a man. Scott and Judy stood facing him, their bodies heaving from cold and fear, trying to catch their breaths. They stared into the harsh, hot glow of a flashlight beam only inches from their faces. They had briefly caught a glimpse of the man before being blinded by the light. His hair was white and full, his face stubbled and sunken. His eyes were burning fiercely. They knew who he was; they had seen him before.

"What are you doing here? What do you want?" Josiah's hand was still holding Scott's shoulder firmly. He shook the boy again as if he were trying to shake snow off a garment. Scott balled his fists and lashed out wildly, but Stoneham sidestepped, and with one quick motion let go of Scott's shoulder and grabbed tightly on to both of his wrists, holding him securely in place.

It was Judy who recovered first. This was not a ghost. There was no ghostly danger. She tried to find her voice, lost somewhere deep within her. It felt as though her mouth were frozen shut by the cold.

"We—we came to see the ghost, Mr. Stoneham," she finally stuttered. Her voice sounded hollow and so alien to her that she wondered if it were really hers. She tried to shield her eyes from the burning light. When she looked away she saw colored circles against the blackness. It reminded her of having her picture taken with a flashcube.

The man's voice was loud and angry. "What ghost? Who told you there was a ghost here?" Judy detected a shaky note of fear in the voice as well. "There is no ghost!"

"We heard the stories and—"

Josiah cut her off. "Don't you ever come here. This is private property." His voice boomed. "How did you get in? The door is always locked."

Judy could only spit out the answer. "Through the cellar window. We came in through the basement."

"Who are you? Where are you from?" The questions came in rapid fire, each word punctuated with a shake of Scott's arms.

"From Bob Kanon's ski house. Next door. Sandy came in here the other night and saw him—Eben Wallford!" Her eyes were wide and Judy knew she was babbling uncontrollably, but she could not shut herself off. "And we wanted to see him too, to prove to the others there was a ghost."

Josiah let go of Scott, who rubbed his wrists.

"What's this? Who's Sandy?" Suddenly something began to make sense.

Finally free, Scott was able to find his voice. "A new member of the ski house. She came here and saw him—!"

The old man stood sternly over him. His face was colder and uglier than it had been before. "Tell me what Sandy saw."

As the children tried to piece together the story from what little they knew, Josiah found himself only half listening. He began to understand the feelings he had had. The girl, Sandy, had come into the house. She had disturbed Eben and caused him to stir, and that was what Josiah had sensed the night he had twice awakened.

Josiah fetched a key from a deep pocket in his mackinaw. He used his flashlight to find the keyhole, opened the door, and roughly pushed the children out.

"I'm taking you home," he said gruffly. "And don't try to run away from me, because it will be worse for you if you do."

Neither child moved. They believed this man and what he said. They sensed he was angry enough to make good any threats to hurt them.

Josiah shoved the flashlight into his pocket and snapped it shut. He took each child by the arm, holding them securely by the fleshy part of the underside between elbow and shoulder, and walked them back down the road to the Kanon ski house. His steps were twice as large as the children's. They had to run to keep up.

The ring of the front doorbell was unusual. All of the members and any deliveries came in through the kitchen door. Bob was more than surprised to see Josiah Stoneham standing there, practically thrusting the children at him through the opening.

"How dare you people come around here and go into Eben's house like you owned it!" There was a croaking sound to his voice. He was so angry, his face quivered.

"Mr. Stoneham—" Bob began.

"You've no right to be there," Josiah continued loudly. His eyes were wide, and anger flared from deep within them.

Other house members started to gather.

Judy and Scott saw their mothers in the room and ran to them, burying their faces in the familiar warmth. Each mother stroked her child's head, still uncertain what had happened, but unnerved nonetheless by the intensity of Josiah's tone.

"City people," he spit out, as if the very words produced a bad taste. "Think you can come around here and do what you want. Go into Eben's house. Steal things."

Bob tried to silence him. "Whoa—please calm down, Josiah." He turned to his son. "Scott, were you in the Wallford house?"

Scott freed himself from his mother long enough to nod. The expression on his father's face told him he was in very definite trouble.

"Did you take anything?"

"No, sir."

"Disturb anything?"

"No."

"Judy?"

"No. We just wanted to see—"

Bob cut her off. "That's enough." He turned back to Stoneham and tempered his voice. "Josiah, I apologize for the children's having gone into Eben's house. It was very wrong of them and they will be punished severely." He hoped his softer tone and threats of punishment would calm the man. Stoneham looked as if his anger could trigger a stroke. His eyes bulged wide, his neck veins throbbed.

But Josiah did not want to be calmed. He looked past Bob into the room.

"Who's Sandy?" His voice was gravelly.

Sandy stepped out from next to David. "I am."

David curled his fingers in hers, preventing her from going closer to the man.

Josiah shook a bony finger at her. "I'm warning you." He addressed the room. "I'm warning all of you. Stay out of Eben's house. That's no place for any of you. You don't know about the things that go on in that house! I'm boarding up that cellar window so none of you can ever get in. And if I catch you in that house again, I'll get the sheriff after you and close this place down!"

"I assure you, Josiah, it will not happen again," Bob

started to say, the words coming out in a tumble. But the old man was having no more talk. Having said his piece, he had already turned on his heel and was partway down the snowy steps.

Bob watched him go and then slammed the door shut. The room was chilled by the intrusion of cold air. He turned to face the children, who groped protectively for their mothers. Gail helped Judy off with her parka. Scott could not face his father. The last ten minutes had been the worst of his life: the next ten did not promise to be much better. He was still quaking: from the cold, from the fear of being in the house and thinking the ghost had gotten them, from the angry shaking and yelling done by Josiah, and now from the fear of what was still to come. But at least he knew he was safe again. No matter what his father did to him, it couldn't be as bad as anything else that had happened tonight.

The house members began drifting away, embarrassed for Bob for what he had to do. David helped Sandy up the stairs to the bedroom. Her shoulder was throbbing and she needed her rest.

Bob and Tom took their children from their wives. Neither had seen Bob so angry before. They went into the dining room and slid the door shut. Bob's half-eaten bowl of ice cream sat melting on the table.

The children were silent. They knew they were in for it. They'd had no business being in the house.

"You were told not to go into the Wallford house," Bob began. His voice was calm, and for a fraction of a second Scott felt it wasn't going to be as bad as he thought it might. His father would hold on to him and hug him free from his fear; tell him he was glad he was all right, that there had been no damage done, that he had not been hurt or gotten by the ghost; that the stern voice had just been for the benefit of the old man. But then Scott realized that neither his father nor Dr. Landberg knew of the fear he and Judy had experienced inside the house. For all they knew, it had been just another game.

"I guess one day off from skiing wasn't enough for you," Bob continued. "You seem to want more. Is that right?"

Scott hung his head. "No, sir."

"But still you went back into the house."

"Yes."

"Why?"

Scott hesitated. He bit his lip. How could he tell his father he went with Judy so she wouldn't think he was chicken.

Judy picked it up. "I was curious. I wanted to prove to all of you there was a ghost." Her voice grew smaller. "I was afraid, though, and asked Scott to come with me."

"And did you prove there was a ghost?" Tom asked his daughter.

Her voice was smaller still. "No."

"No," Tom repeated. "You know, if this had been the first time, perhaps I wouldn't be so angry. Kids your age are supposed to be curious about things like haunted houses. But this wasn't the first time. The other night we warned you about going into the house. We said you could have gotten hurt, that something could have happened. So you knew better. Didn't you?"

"Yes."

"And you went anyway?"

Judy knew her father's tone. She would not be getting off easily. "Yes."

"Well, I suggest we listen to what Bob has to say. Whatever punishment he suggests for Scott, I think I'll go along with."

Bob looked at the children. He was angry. Curiosity or not, they might have gotten themselves hurt tonight. Or even arrested. But what they did manage to do was break an already strained and distant relationship he had with Josiah Stoneham. He knew Josiah didn't like them, but he still looked after the ski house during the week when nobody was up there—if only for the good of the neighborhood, to make certain it was not burned, vandalized, or looted. Bob did not expect Josiah to continue to do this.

"I want to ski this week," he said quietly, "as does Tom. Neither of us wants to spend our vacation week keeping you two out of trouble. So we're all going to ski this holiday week as if nothing had happened; but Scott, that's it for the season. You'd better make the most of this Christmas week, because after New Year's you can hang up your skis until next year."

Judy glanced searchingly at her father.

"That goes for me too," Tom said firmly. "Now promise me again you'll never go back into that house."

"I promise," she said weakly.

"Scott?" Bob asked.

"Yes, sir. I promise."

Scott glanced over at Judy. She had really done it to him this time, getting him into trouble the way she had, lousing up the whole rest of the winter. Especially this one, when he was on the verge of becoming an expert skier. But then he realized that, no, she hadn't gotten him into trouble; he had done it to himself. He should have known better than to go into the house when he didn't want to. And if she was going to call him a chicken, she would have called him a chicken. But he'd still be able to go clucking down the mountain. The price was awfully high, but Scott knew he had learned an important lesson.

Judy was disappointed. Even after all of that, she had still not gotten to see the ghost. But still she felt him inside her, calling her to him.

CHAPTER XVII

Sandy was the first in her dorm room to head up to bed and David accompanied her in. She dressed in her flannel nightclothes, and David made certain there was an extra blanket handy in case she got cold. As he pulled the covers up to her neck he kissed her.

"We can always go back to the motel if you want."

She shook her head. "Not necessary. I'm fine. Fine? I'm exhausted, stiff, in pain, can't move my shoulder, and I'm an absolute physical and nervous wreck."

"But other than that?"

"Other than that, get out of here and let me sleep." She didn't want to mention her encounter with Pauline. If Pauline had said nothing more to either of them that whole long night, she was probably safe, off the hook for at least a little while. She had bought some time.

Until Cynthia's next nightmare. . . .

Sandy prayed it would not be that night or anytime soon.

She looked at David petulantly. "I thought I told you to get out of here."

But David didn't move. Nor did she really want him to. She ran her fingers up and down his leg, almost tugging at his pants. She was unwilling to let him go. "David," she said softly.

"Yes?"

"What did Josiah Stoneham mean when he said we don't know about the things that go on in that house?"

David shook his head. "Probably nothing. It was nothing more than the superstitious ramblings of an old man. You saw how irrational he was."

"I guess."

Inwardly, though, David wondered. Was there more here that they didn't know about? More here than Tom suspected?

Sandy took hold of his fingers, entwining hers in his. "I feel responsible for those kids, David, and for that man's being here."

"Don't be. You had nothing to do with any of that."

"They went into the house because *I* was in the house," she protested. "Presumably to see the same things"—her voice trailed off, but she finished—"that I did."

"We don't know that," David said. "Remember, they were in the house the first night too. Before you. They just went back in again. If anything, they're responsible for *your* having been in the house."

She shook her head. "No. I would have wanted to go in anyway. And I would have. Even if I had to drag you from here, or, as I threatened, go myself."

With a slight nod David acknowledged that she was right.

Sandy looked deeply into his eyes. "I didn't want to fall today, David."

"I know."

"Why did Tom suggest that?"

"I don't know," he answered, and he really didn't. "Tell you what. I'll stay with you tomorrow. We can go look at antiques, take a ride over to Woodstock, maybe see Queechee Falls. Something. Anything."

"You're going skiing, David," she said strongly. "I don't need a baby sitter, okay?"

"I wouldn't be your baby sitter. I just want to spend the day with you."

"There'll be plenty of days you can spend with me. I want to solo it tomorrow. I need to. Please. Just trust me and let me be."

Her father's funeral flashed into her mind. What else was there for her to remember?

David looked down at her. He always gave in to what she wanted, especially when she needed room to breathe. He suddenly saw them twenty years in the future, long married, Sandy wanting a fur coat or something else outlandish and him buying it for her. For the mother of his children, nothing was too good. He'd give her the day to herself to let her do what she had to do and maybe everything would right itself. He hoped it would, but something told him there was more trouble ahead.

He kissed her goodnight and closed the door. Tired too, he went into his room, undressed, and quickly fell into a heavy sleep.

Pauline was half asleep when Bob climbed into bed next to her.

"How's Scott?" she asked.

"Still a little shaken. Although I don't know if it's more from the events of the evening or from the punishment I meted out."

"What were they doing in the house?"

Bob exhaled and shrugged. "I don't know. Judy got it into her head to see the ghost. Prove there really was one. Cynthia's dream triggered that one. Dragged poor Scott along with her. He never wanted to go." He paused and looked up at the ceiling. "Perhaps I was too rough on him. I guess I was just reacting to Josiah. He transferred his anger onto me or something."

"You were upset," Pauline observed.

"Only because Josiah was. Crazy old man. Takes that damn place too seriously. It's his life. I guess they were wrong to go poking around in there, but we've all done it. All the big folks, that is. I'd say that we're pretty lucky he didn't barge in on us the night of the Halloween party. Somehow I think that might have been a tougher one to explain away. Thirteen adults in trick-or-treat costumes."

Pauline smiled and propped herself up on one arm. "You feel lousy about yelling at Scott, don't you?" she said.

"I most definitely do," Bob said. "I'm going to talk to Tom tomorrow and see if there's a way we can rescind the punishment. Still," he continued, "they've got to learn the importance of keeping a promise. But I think I'll save the heavy guns for when it really counts. When they're teenagers. Something's bound to come up to make me want to punish him good."

Pauline kissed him. "You know, in my book, you're Father of the Year."

He returned the kiss. "In mine too."

They were silent for a moment. Pauline put her hands under her head and stared upward, her eyes open. Finally she spoke.

"Cynthia is terrified of Sandy," she said softly.

"Why?"

"She blames Sandy for her nightmares. I found her and Cynthia together tonight. Cynthia was frightened just being around her. She thinks Sandy is responsible for bringing the ghost of Eben Wallford into the house. What can we do, Bob?"

Bob shook his head. "I don't see how we can do anything. Or if we should do anything. Sandy's a guest here. I can't ask her to leave just because Cindy is having nightmares. We'll have to talk to Cynthia some more. Tell her there's no ghost in the house and that nightmares are natural and can't hurt her. She'll have to get over it, as well as her fear of Sandy.

"And she *will*," he added pointedly. "Kids have very short memories."

"I guess," Pauline said, exhaling. She knew her husband was right, and perhaps she had been a little hard on Sandy with her coldness. Rationally, she knew that Cynthia's nightmares were her own and Sandy had nothing to do with them. But she was still the triggering force. . . . So much was now happening in the house; there had been *nothing* until Sandy had gotten there.

She turned to Bob.

"Let me ask you one question, O Father of the Year."

A smile. "Ask away."

"Where'd you get that wall business from?"

A bigger smile. "Made it up. Effective, huh?"

"Effective as hell. I just left a half-dozen people down there trying to figure out what—or *who*—" she chirped mockingly, "is down there. When are you going to grow up? Or better yet, write a novel so we can put some of these stories to good use."

She pecked him goodnight and then asked, "Why *do* you think those bricks are out of line with the rest of the wall?"

Bob didn't answer. He had already drifted off to sleep.

CHAPTER XVIII

Sandy heard the hoarse, muffled sound of the recorder as it strained in tuneless song. It was a distant sound, disturbing her sleep yet strangely appealing, the Pied Piper inviting in soft, calming play. The practicing of a child, soothing to a mother's ears, warmly beckoning her to come closer and listen. It sounded as if it were coming from downstairs. That was odd. She didn't know of anyone in the house playing a recorder. And if there was, why hadn't it been played during the caroling? Was the child embarrassed? She wanted to see who it was, to tell the child not to be self-conscious about the playing, that it was good.

She threw off her covers and got out of the bed. Around her, the others in the room were lost to sleep. Why didn't they also hear the music? Why weren't they also going down to hear the playing of the child? She shook the girl in the next bunk, Ricky. Nothing. No response to her touch; as if she were dead. The same with Gail above her. She was confused. Why were they not waking?

It didn't matter. The recorder was playing just for her, drawing her to it with soft sounds. She slid open the door to the upstairs hallway and the music grew louder, almost physical to the touch, and she went toward it. Down the stairs to the first floor. She was losing the light of the upper hallway but instinctively knew her way among the living rooms. The fire was out; the room was cold, and she wished she had taken her comforter with her. She stood torn. She wanted to go back upstairs to bed, yet she wanted too to follow the music that kept calling to her.

But where was it coming from?

She felt as if she were playing the hot-and-cold game she had played as a child. When looking for a lost object, if she moved closer to it she was told she was getting warmer, getting warmer, getting hot, until hottest, when she would find it. When moving away she would be getting colder and colder. So it was with the music of the recorder. A change in the texture of the notes, in pitch, in inviting intensity, as she moved among the first floor rooms in search.

The second living room? No. **Getting colder . . .** getting colder.

The weather vanes above the mantel seemed to spring to life, each pointing downward in a different direction, as if to mislead. She smiled. She was enjoying the hide-and-seek game.

Where was the child?

The music grew louder as she entered the kitchen. That was it. The child was in the kitchen. But where? Behind the counter? In the giant cupboard? Outside in the vestibule?

No. Nowhere.

She had been everywhere, yet still the music persisted. A door stood at the side of the kitchen. She had not gone through the door, yet she knew it led to the cellar. That was it. The child was behind the door, waiting for her to open it, and would jump out at her in surprise. Just as the children had done with the funny masks. She smiled, pleased with herself that she had figured it out, and reached out to take the door-knob, pull the door toward her in triumphant surprise, and hug the child playing the alluring music.

There was no one there, yet the music was at its loudest. *Getting warmer.* The child was down below the wooden steps in the cellar. He could be nowhere else. She had searched the rest of the house and here the music was at its greatest volume. Didn't anyone else hear?

She grabbed on to the wooden handrail and started to walk down the steps. *Getting warmer.*

The cellar was cold, bone-chilling beyond the cold of the mountain, and her flannel nightgown was not protection enough. She hesitated. If only someone else were with her. But it was as if she were held captive, a prisoner of the music, magnetically drawn to what lay below her, powerless to break the hold it had on her. But she didn't want to. The music was soft to her ears.

She continued, her footfall light on the plankboard wooden steps, yet each one squeaked in eerie response to the additional weight.

The music led her to the far wall, where it abruptly stopped. How odd. She looked around her and heard herself call out to the sudden darkness of the cellar. *Play! Continue to play!* She needed to hear the music that had attracted her so.

But then she pulled back in horror and tragic understanding. She knew why the music had stopped. It had served its purpose. She was there.

HOT.

She wanted to turn, to run back up the stairs. It was a mistake. She didn't want to come down here. She shouldn't be here. She had gone too far. She wanted to go back. She called out to her father to help her with the sudden sinking, sickening realization that there was no turning back. She had been driven here; had indeed brought herself here. Willingly. Lulled and drawn by the false peace the music had promised, by the release it had offered. And here she was, and here she would remain for all time.

The red bricks of the wall melted away before her eyes to a vast nothingness that stretched endlessly before her, an endless tunnel that drew her in mercilessly, engulfing her, surrounding her, sucking her forward.

Her feet left the ground as she was propelled head first horizontally through the tunnel, as if in flight; concentric black circles and elliptical arches opening up in front of her. A blinding light captured her, gouging her eyes with a white brilliance she had never before experienced, to the point of unimaginable burning pain, as if concentrated acid had been poured into her eyes. Even closing her eyelids tightly did not bring relief from the heat or dazzling penetration of the light; it was as if she had no eyes and had been ordered to see what she was to see. Yet despite the effulgence of the light, it was the light of darkness that surrounded her—*this she knew*—and at once she also knew that her mistake was irreparable.

And still she moved forward under a power not her own.

Demon hands reached out and tugged at her body, poking, prodding, pointing to her as if she were one of them. Faceless masks appeared before her, like formless creatures that seemed to guide her way at speeds she had never before experienced or imagined. Elongated, puffy, arthritic fingers came out of the light to seize her neck. She twisted from their grasp, kicking with her legs as if they were rudders to change her direction and avoid the strangling fingers. Devil birds of raven-black with the harsh squawk of the forever-damned paralleled her in flight, pecking at her with razor-edged beaks that slashed at her flesh.

Then came the faces. Witches' masks with pointed

noses crowned with bumps and boils. Snorting fire for breath, with eyes that brimmed with the pain of doom. Cracked doll-heads with unseeing, bulging eyes forever open wide in a last vision of terror, blood dripping from noses and ears, heads bobbing back and forth as limply as jack-in-the-boxes. Grotesque masks with ever changing faces contorted in desperation; and black, faceless spirits, like victims of intense and fatal burnings. Guardian griffins with wings of fire and manes of Midas-gold lapped at her, their snakelike tongues licking at her body, turning her corkscrew-spinning in their hungered frenzy. A burning wetness covered her body as she realized instinctively that this was just the beginning. It wouldn't be long before she became one of them.

There was noise. Louder and louder, as a cacophony of sound assaulted her ears. The lilting joy of the recorder became the disharmony of a symphony off-key, a mile-high speaker system blasting the discordant Babel noise of clanking steel, bellowing winds, roaring jungle animals, and calls of warring demon birds. All at once and together. And louder and louder. She took her fingers away from her eyes and covered her ears, but from out of the blackness they were ripped from her hands.

Then the light gave way to grayness, and then to black, a thickness about her she could reach out and touch. And feel. Individual particles of dark, holding her suspended as if in gelatin; a slow-motion murky movement to her body as she tried to escape the sticky substance that held her captive. And she cried out for the burning light and the horrid faces, because now she could no longer see and it was worse. Because still they came, and breathed, and touched. Electrical charges jumping from unseen amorphous bodies to hers as they taunted her. And she cried out for rescue, for mercy, for understanding, for forgiveness; she hadn't meant it to be this way, she hadn't meant to go after the peace offered by the music. Then her prayer was answered.

She was back in the light with the creatures of hell, and without a word she knew she too was a creature of hell.

She awoke, too terrified to move, too terrified even to cry out, residual arms and hands and hook-nosed faces disappearing in the soft dark of the bedroom. She had been sleeping, she told herself. Dreaming. But it was more than a dream. It was a dream steeped in experience, memory, of having been. And too fraught with terror to think anymore, she felt the hands of sleep come for her again. She fought them off; she didn't want to sleep. It was the unspeakable that waited for her in the dreamdepths. Still, she fell backward into sleep once more.

And once again she stood before the mouth of hell, watching it slowly dissolve in front of her to the awesome blackness harbored beyond, and the peaceless, ceaseless torture of the lost. She felt the pull into the darkness of the pit, but held her ground. She was not going in. She was not giving in. With a grit of her teeth and a solid grasp of the concrete floor, she readied herself for the fight of her life, for the only fight of meaning, for the salvation of her soul.

From the mouth of the tunnel the gray outline of a face appeared, at first formless, then taking on recognizable features. The gray hair, the mottled brown beard, the deep-set burning, tortured eyes.

Eben Wallford reached out to take her hand, to lead her forever forward into the pit of despair. His hand clasped around hers, a fierce grip for one as old as he, a viselike hold on her that made her faint. And then he began to pull.

No. She would not go with him. She knew where he wanted to lead her and she would not follow. He had played on her attraction to him, her uncertainties. Now he was reaching out to her, forcefully pulling her toward him, to take her to inescapable low regions. But she would not go. She would fight with the final strength she had and summon all the angelic forces to help her in her final battle. She dug into the ground and held her position. The strain on her arm was unbearable; the pain horrible. She almost gave up the tug-of-war to be free of the misery.

And then Eben Wallford, with hardly a strain or effort, began to win, and she watched her arm disappear into the blackness in front of her. Perspiration poured from her as she tensed her body and with a final effort fought to break free.

And then suddenly, at the moment of her greatest distress, she was released.

The pull on her arm was gone. She fell backward onto the floor of the cellar. The face of Eben Wallford dissolved from her sight. The wall reformed as she watched, the bricks again back where they had been.

She had survived.

With horror she looked down at her arm, the arm that had been pulled into the tunnel, and she saw the fate she had escaped. Her arm was charred red; black, burnt skin smoldering, oozing pus, dry and painful to the touch; elephantlike wrinkles on her once soft, flesh-pink arm.

She awoke, again with the pain she had experienced before, now certain where it came from. Her shoulder ached badly.

Rubbing her arm, her eyes wide with the terror of recall, she once again had a moment of *déjà vu*. The burnt arm, the pit of hell. She had experienced both. In another time, perhaps; she didn't know. But she knew she had been there before. She begged God not to let her return again.

BOOK III

Suzanne

CHAPTER XIX

A tuneless melody, playing dully, faintly, in her inner ear, drew Sandy from sleep; the distant music didn't stop once her eyes were open. She carried the tinny blur with her into full wakefulness. She tried to shake it off, until she realized it was not some inner devil-call, but rather something from the stereo downstairs.

She was in the safety of daylight once more. The horrors of the dream world could not reach her here. Without thinking, she moved to rub her right arm and shoulder, then stopped and let the throbbing continue. She would rather it pain her than acknowledge it.

The room was empty. Outside in the hallway there was only an occasional shuffle of slippered feet. She checked the clock by her bed. It was after ten, and she supposed most people had already left for the mountain.

The bedroom door slipped open on its runners and David entered, fully dressed in his ski clothes. She smiled at him from the bed, and seeing she was awake, he went to her.

She reached up and encircled him with her arms. He kissed her and their tongues met.

"What are you still doing here?" she asked.

"I wasn't just going to leave you here," he answered.

"Then why didn't you wake me to say good-bye? You've missed half the day already."

"There'll be other days."

"Now you're making me feel guilty," she pouted.

His eyes locked on hers and took her full in. "Just stop that, will you. You're saying things you can't and shouldn't believe."

She didn't answer She knew she couldn't have expected him just to leave her there. But that was indeed what she wanted.

"How was last night?" he asked.

She rubbed her shoulder and arm. "Lonely." She smiled.

He matched her smile, his dark eyes twinkling. "I know. But otherwise—?"

"I slept comfortably," she lied. Her voice cracked and betrayed her.

"Any dreams?"

She hesitated. She didn't want to tell him, but she didn't want to shoulder it all herself.

She nodded uneasily.

"Bad?" he asked.

"No," she said, too quickly. She couldn't face him. She looked away.

"Let me get Tom. He's still here. We were all waiting for you to wake up."

"David, please don't. I think if I'm just left all alone this will go away."

"That's not going to happen!" he said sharply, and wanted to take back the words as soon as they were out. Fear flashed in her eyes.

"Why do you say that?"

He shrugged and tried to dismiss it. "There's someone here who might be able to help you. I just want you to talk to him again."

"A shrink!" she challenged, immediately regretting her tone.

"A friend," he countered softly.

She pursed her lips and looked at him. "I'll talk to a friend," she said. "I've decided I don't want to be told I'm crazy."

"Nobody said you were."

"Everybody thinks I am." She dropped her eyes. "Including me." *I'm the girl who saw the ghost.*

David looked down at her and fought back the tears that threatened. She looked so helpless lying there, so vulnerable. He wanted to do anything he could to rescue her from the horrors she was living through, self-created or otherwise.

"Get dressed," he said suddenly. "We're going home."

"Back to New York?"

"This morning. Right now. I want to get you the hell away from this place."

As if from nowhere she thought of her father and remembered his funeral. She needed time to be alone, to think about it more. To remember more. To recall what somehow had been lost in tucked-away corners of her mind. If she just had this time alone, it would all come back.

"No," she said. "I don't want to go."

"You want to stay here until those dreams of yours finally do drive you crazy." It was more a statement than a question.

"You've been looking forward to this week for half a year, and I'm not going to spoil it for you." The words were weak, but she let them stand.

"Don't worry about me," he said. "We can ski closer to home. Hunter Mountain or Great Gorge. I'm not giving up skiing. Just Owlsfane." He got up from the edge of the bed. "I'm going to get Tom. You get dressed and we'll have a fast breakfast and split. Okay?"

"Tomorrow," she said. She wanted the day to herself without interruption, without conversation, to spend it with nothing but memory. Things were coming through, and somehow they were tied in with this place. To leave now might be to lose what she had begun to recall.

"Tonight," he offered as a compromise. "Before you sleep again. I don't want you up here at night."

If she could gather her thoughts before dark, that would be all right.

"We'll see," she said.

David put up a finger toward her. "Tonight."

"Tonight," she acquiesced.

"Good. Now I'll get Tom. I want you to tell him what you dreamed. It might help."

She watched him walk across the room, the outline of his ass temptingly seductive. He was right, she realized. They'd better get out of there tonight. The hellish dream of hours, or moments, before, lingered and terrified her.

She thought back to times before when she had been afraid: the bark of a vicious dog, the ominous appearance of two strangers in her path. And the resultant freezing of the stomach, the flip-flopping, the hollowness. The legs refusing to support, the allover goosebump sensation as fear took hold. The quickening of breath and the instinct to make oneself smaller. And the desire to be home in bed, small and fetal, face buried in the soft moistness of a down pillow.

And then the welcome relief when the false danger had passed. That was what she wanted now. But the fear persisted. Her body was tense, tingling; her brain on overtime, looking for escape routes. And here she was being offered one. David wanted to take her home. Common sense dictated that they go. Then. That very minute. Let someone else bring home the bags. Run to the car and bury herself in his strength until they were past the Wallford house and miles from Owlsfane. But something deeper than common sense forbade her to go. Gut-holding curiosity. And the need to know things about herself that a lost part of her had told her she shouldn't know. Now that she had access to that part, she knew she must take full advantage. Otherwise she might never be in touch with it again.

Although common sense was saying no.

When she talked with Tom she downplayed the dream, stating simply that she had seen Eben Wallford behind the cellar wall. It was a dream anyone could have had after hearing the story Bob had told the night before.

But she tripped over her words and fooled no one. Her eyes too gave her away: a shooting flash of fear tingeing the white, the way she didn't look them straight in the eye. Tom saw right through her masquerade to her terror beneath. He suspected there was more, but would not pull it from her. He supported David's desire to take her home. But then she forcefully, stubbornly told him her reasons for needing to stay, and he reluctantly agreed.

They would leave her there alone, provided she promised to be ready to head for New York at the end of the day. She also promised not to go out of the house, or down to the cellar. Or to nap, for fear of dreaming again without anyone to call upon.

And with that, David and Tom left her, each determined to have his fun on the mountain, each knowing he didn't stand a snowball's chance in hell.

Once alone, she did not think, because no thoughts would come. She stared at objects blankly, stupidly: the conquistador in regal splendor at the foot of the stairs, who was assigned to guard the bedrooms but failed miserably in his task; the crankhandle Victrola of an era of mechanical simplicity long gone; and finally her own reflection in the lyre-shaped mirror—the slightly faded yellow tint to the glass cheating her of her natural complexion, truthfully revealing how tired

and worn she really was. She felt drawn. She tried
fluffing her limp hair into place, but it was as if the
mirror were mocking her feeble attempts, as if the mirror were part of it all.

She trained her thoughts on her father and saw him
as he was in life. And then in death, as within her she
saw the lowering of the coffin, the scattering of earth,
the plane, the hospital room, and heard the words of the
nurse: *"Aren't you going to the funeral?"* But nothing
more. Perhaps the door to her memory was open only
a sliver, and that was as far as it would ever go, stuck
in place. Her needing this time alone was a sham; nothing would be gained from it.

The dream flashed, trying to surface; demon faces
threatened to appear, and she touched her arm, which
tingled as if it had fallen asleep. *The burnt arm, the
pit of hell. She had experienced both. In another time,
perhaps, another dimension.*

She felt her skin crawl, and vigorously rubbed her
hand up and down her arm to make it stop. She tried
to wipe her mind clear of the dream that was threatening to possess her, but it was like telling herself not to
think of pink elephants.

It was a mistake remaining in the house alone, and
now she had five hours to repent.

She felt like a teenager who dreams of her own
apartment, without parental controls, but who, once
there, regrets the move and thinks back to the times
she had with a family who loved her.

Nothing else came back to her, even when she assumed the silly standard thinking position, chin resting
on open palm, eyebrows tensed and furrowed as if a
hard stare would shake loose lost forgotten thoughts.
She laughed off the sudden urge she had to scratch her
head, but succumbed to pacing the silent house, as if
her movement would jar free buried thoughts that refused to come by themselves.

From behind a curtain in the living room she

watched the townspeople leaving the church across the road after Christmas services. She hadn't been to church in many, many years. An odd thought, but she wondered if she indeed needed divine intervention.

The morning began to drag, and her feet tired from walking from room to room, in circular pattern, around the first floor of the house: from living room to second living room, Ping-Pong room to kitchen (past the door she remembered so well) to the first dining room to the second dining room and back again to the living room. Once and again she made this round trip, and when she was fooled into believing a thought was taking hold she would stop, stand in place, and devote her entire being to concentration. And then, in failure, she would reverse her direction.

She decided she was hungry. Not exactly the hunger that comes from needing food; rather, the hunger that gnaws from boredom. For want of something better to do, eat. She pulled a platter of leftover ham and sliced turkey from the refrigerator, and taking this, with some potato salad from a vat in the outdoor vestibule, she sat down to pick at a meal she didn't want, and began to count the hours until David and the others would return.

She moved to the couch to read. Picking up an ancient edition of *Ski* magazine, full of dried glass-rings and coffee stains, she read about the new boots and bindings a half-dozen companies were manufacturing, as well as the best places to pick up men in Val d'Isère; from her photo, the writer looked like someone who would have no trouble picking up men in a monastery.

Tired, she sat at the piano and began idly to play songs from her past, letting her fingers trail lightly, lazily over the sticking, scratched keys. But she had never learned to play for her own gratification and was quickly bored.

Get away from here!

The voice was lost in the plinking sound of the off-key piano notes. She stopped her playing and immediately the room was embraced by a heavy silence. Not a car passed outside; not a burp came from the radiator or downstairs boiler. She strained against the silence to search for the voice, leaning forward over the piano, even though she had no idea from which direction it was coming. Nothing. But there was no mistaking it. She knew she had heard it. It was the same voice she had heard in the cafeteria at the mountain. The same voice and the same words. Voice and words of internal warning. *So what else is new?* she thought ruefully. And suddenly it was no longer important that she listen for the one voice. Her whole stay up there had been strange voices, distant memories. A buried lifetime slowly filtering back to her, with great difficulty, as if oozing through a heavy mesh filter, one painful drop at a time. Yes, she'd get away from there. Gladly. Nothing more was coming back to her.

Now they could leave. There was nothing magical or mysterious in the house that would draw memories from her. If they were to come, it would not be place that brought them out or forced thought. Tom knew that, but she'd had to find out for herself. It would be herself, and it would be time, or some triggering event, or merely a passing notion fleetingly taking hold, then leading to another itinerant thought and another. And that might do it. For amusement she tried to trace back her last thought patterns, but it was as confusing as trying to contemplate infinity.

She frowned.

Something was bothering her. Gnawing at her. As it had the first night, when she heard the story of Eben Wallford and his daughter and went oh-so-willingly—*too* willingly—into the haunted house.

The girl who saw the ghost.

She felt it physically, on her arms and legs, muscles tensely excited, nerves twitching, as controlling commands from somewhere else surged through her, as if an electrical current was charging through her body: the unmistakable pull to go down to the cellar.

Where she knew he *was.*

The pull was growing stronger than the fear. She could not understand it; yet she could not fight it.

Just one peek. What harm could there be? One fast look and her curiosity would be satisfied. No one would ever know.

She fought the growing urge, weakly, like a dieter tempting the fates by keeping a cheesecake in the refrigerator. She walked back and forth past the door a half dozen times. All to prove to herself she was strong-willed enough not to open the door and go down.

Yet something within her battling, confused mind, where surfacing emotions were at war with reason, was telling her that the answers she was seeking were to be found behind the dreaded door. And common sense took a back seat to the unrelenting stimulus. From her own mind, or drawn from without, she wasn't certain. But nothing could happen, she told herself in a voice she could almost hear. It was broad daylight, and nothing bad ever happens in the safe light of day. *That's true only in fiction,* commented that part of her mind she was choosing to block out. She ignored her own warning call.

She made one final pass through the house, from kitchen to dining rooms to living rooms, heart racing, pulse pounding, knowing she was making a mistake, unconsciously praying for an interruption, a reason not to return to—

The kitchen.

She paused in front of the cellar door. An innocent slab of knotty pinewood, behind which lay—what? The lady or the tiger? Answers, or terror, or both?

What the hell was she thinking about? It was only a cellar, and now she wanted to go down to prove to herself she was not afraid. To look at the cheesecake to prove she would not touch it. Forgetting her promises to David and Tom and giving unknown dangers no further thought, she breathed deeply and opened the door.

Familiarity swirled around her, rooted, and took hold.

It was as in her dream: the plankboard wooden steps leading downward into the semidarkness, the empty plastic milk containers stuffed into hollows formed by support beams, the rush of cold.

And still she continued.

She found the light switch and flipped it on, bathing the dark cellar in a dim light of dusty orange. Some sun seeped in through cracks in the wall, offering no more than a suggestion of daylight. Other than that, the windowless cellar ignored the clock.

The room was cold; icy tendrils stroked her body, and she remembered it as it was in her dream. Her parka was in the kitchen but she did not return for it.

It was silent, but a silence that comes from waiting for the unexpected, of dread moments before fears are borne out. The silence of a quiet park at twilight where light and dark hover indistinguishably, where deceitful shadows of haunting trees appear tentaclelike, branches reaching out like devil arms to engulf and consume.

The silence of an empty house.

A haunted cellar.

When suddenly the silence was broken by the click of a motor and the whining hum of the water heater turning itself on, singing through the cellar like a jackhammer on a city street.

Her stomach jumped toward her throat, but the familiar sound, with its base in reality, was welcome. With purpose, she walked down the steps, mind more a blank than conscious of fears, drawn to the wall that she knew lay beyond. To her left, abandoned skis and discarded boots lay in a random pattern. To her right was a workshop of wood tables; vises; a bench with rusty, dust-covered tools; boxes of binding parts; colored ski wax; and an expanse of metal files. Through an archway to a dark room beyond, where the light barely filtered, she saw the wall she had last seen in her dream, just as it had been, as if she had already been down there; and something deep within her, down to her very first intuitive brain cell, told her she already had.

Searching for a light switch, she flicked it on, and a cold shadowed fluorescent light hummed as if annoyed by the intrusion. It flickered slowly into operation, a dying tube refusing obstinately to glow to full strength, making the room appear more dark and overcast than before.

She stood before the wall that had drawn her so, staring with furrowed intensity, mesmerized by the pattern of brick and mortar interface, captured by the symmetrical patterns of black-striped reds and crisscrossing whites. Her eyes followed the cracks, tracing odd designs from the spaces between the bricks running to the ends of the wall unflush with the other, and doubling back.

She had no idea how long she stood; a moment, an hour, time frozen, nonexistent, in her hypnotic state.

And then she lost reality. She didn't know if she was asleep or awake. In a conscious state or a hypnotic trance. Or if she had even left her body.

All she knew was that she could not move. Her feet were cemented to the floor where she stood, her eyes riveted, unblinking, to the dread wall in front of her.

Then it happened.

As in the nightmare, the wall started to melt away to an inky black hole beyond, a blackness from which emanated no light, a mausoleum blackness. She found herself moving closer to the wall, feet responding to commands of unknown origin.

She tried to fight as she had in her dream. To pull herself away. To turn, to run, to shriek; but her body followed a mind not her own; and powerless to resist, she moved forward to the door of hell. She had premonitions of inescapable doom, and once again she had willingly gone.

She had sworn she would not go into the cellar.

There was a swirling movement ahead of her, as individual particles of thick, murky darkness seemed to flow together to form the oh-so-familiar pattern once again. The dead-gray face of Eben Wallford, with his sallow lost eyes and pained expression, reached out to her, to pull her to him.

Was she asleep? She'd promised she wouldn't sleep.

She saw her weightless arm move toward his as if in levitation. Closer and closer to his, until their fingers almost touched. Until—

—from her fear of hell she caused her own mind to snap!

With a shriek and one final burst of will, she wrenched herself from her frozen state.

She turned and dove for the steps. She jumped them two at a time, tripping on the splintered wood and regaining her balance with her hands on the stairs above. Afraid even to turn around lest he grab her once again with those hypnotizing eyes, she half ran, half stumbled, half crawled up the cellar stairs, and burst through the door, nearly tearing it free from its creaky hinges.

As she clutched the kitchen counter for relief and support, she breathed in sharp, shallow breaths to fill her aching lungs. Only then did she dare to turn back and see the innocent cellar door swing slowly closed behind her until only a sliver of blackness remained where the door did not fully mesh with the jamb. She broke from the counter and put on its latch, as if the flimsy metal clasp would hold back the hell she had escaped.

She had to get out of the house. She grabbed her

parka from the kitchen stool and slammed out into the sunny, chilly air.

They had just been going through the motions of skiing: taking easy, familiar trails by rote, neither enjoying himself. Now Tom and David were sitting on a chair that was limping up the hill. At the rate they were going, with the chair malfunctioning every half-dozen feet, dipping downward on a sagging, straining cable, and then springing high into the air, the cold ride up the mountain would be another half hour at least. David had once ridden up with a physicist when the chair had behaved in the same way. The scientist had used the time to calculate the stress on the metal cable that was needed to snap it from the support towers and send them plummeting. Nervously he had suggested they jump and take their chances from the fall, but David's common sense won, and they slowed safely to the top of the mountain. Today it was just cold, and David was envisioning the chair getting stuck and their having to evacuate everyone by use of rope ladders.

"I'm a psychiatrist first, David," Tom was saying. "And only after that, with my limited training and study—although *observation* may be a more apt word—in parapsychology, a believer in the so-called occult, and then only under certain circumstances.

He coughed into his gloves and sent up puffy white clouds of frozen breath. He leaned forward, balancing his arms on the safety bar. "What I want to do is try to take a lot of the spookiness out of this. So much of what we consider supernatural has its origins very strongly in what is really the psychological."

"You're not going to tell me there are no such things as ghosts?" David asked. "All the books, the verified hauntings, the Amityville Horror?"

"No. There is indeed enough evidence and literature to almost prove the existence of ghosts and ghostlike phenomena. Although Jung said it conversely and perhaps a little better—'we may doubt cases of spirit appearances, but we've never been able to prove a single instance of the *non*existence of spirits.' He believed that the unconscious can pick up telepathic impressions from the dead."

"As Sandy did," David suggested hopefully.

"No," Tom said, turning to him to make his point strongly. "In the vast majority of cases, the psychiatrist and even the parapsychologist will look for natural reasons or causes for seemingly unnatural phenomena. Only at the failure to find a natural explanation—in only the rarest of cases—can one honestly declare the possibility of a ghost or spirit. And even then, where it is probably better to err on the side of restraint, only hesitantly."

David looked at Tom evenly. "Then you don't really think we have a ghost here, do you?"

Tom shook his head from side to side. "I can't say for certain, but I think it's unlikely. When sudden dreams and visions seem to have their origins in the paranormal, I'd want to look for a reason for the visions, and the symbolism of the dream content, for possible repressed matter from the patient's past. We can't look at Sandy's seeing a ghost or a girl on fire in isolation. We have to consider everything that she's been through over the last several days as a whole."

"What about Cynthia, Tom? She was so very certain she saw a ghost in the bedroom."

"Cynthia is young, and susceptible to what has been happening. She was dreaming."

"She seemed so positive about what she saw."

"To the dreamer, dreams are real. They're happening." Tom continued hurriedly before David could say anything else. "And yes, the room got cold, and I have no explanation for it. But if we're going to dwell on the supernatural aspects of these occurrences, I think we're misdirecting our energies. Meanwhile,

Sandy is not receiving the—" Tom hesitated. He started to say "help," but changed in mid-thought and instead offered, *"looking after* she needs."

David nodded.

"I'm not saying," Tom went on, "that we can't at least keep one eye toward the paranormal. We've got to keep our options open. But I need to question why Sandy apparently wanted to fall on that slope yesterday. You know I brought that up last night."

David nodded. "She referred to it later as well."

"Did she offer anything?"

"No."

"I don't know her well enough yet to say anything that would be more than guesswork."

David shook his head tentatively; he understood.

Tom turned full face to him. "What would be helpful to me is to know more about Sandy. Anything you can tell me about her, even down to your impressions, will be a good starting point."

David nodded and began to talk. He told Tom of her parents' deaths and the hesitant way in which she spoke about her father. Tom listened. With what he already knew, or suspected, some things were beginning to make sense.

CHAPTER XX

Sandy stood in the safety of the open parking area, arms limply at her side, head thrown back, mouth open like a runner who had just finished a mile race. She took deep, calming breaths of fresh, cold air and let the sun wash over her.

She shoved her hands deep into the pockets of the parka and walked away from the ski house and out onto Route 93. She started to hum the "Twelve Days of Christmas," unable to shake the repetitious tune.

She did not realize where she was walking.

Why did she want to hurt herself?

She didn't! No reason!

What did he want from her? she screamed to herself.

Suddenly she stopped.

She was standing in front of the Wallford house.

She looked wildly around. The mausoleum stood tall on her left; the house was on her right. How had she gotten here? She had just been in the ski house yard. While her thoughts had occupied her, her feet had brought her here!

She looked up at the house, half protected by the glare of the sun. She thought she saw it beckon to her, and the shade of the second floor bedroom window seemed to wink at her.

She felt a cloudiness come over her and a sudden urgent need to go into the house. As if she were being willed in by thought alone.

She wanted to turn away from the house but she could not. There was something she could not fight, an internal force that had captured her being. Her mind was suddenly filled with thoughts of her father inside the house, calling to her.

And she had to get to him.

Hurrying up the front stairs, she entered the house.

As she passed under the archway into the dining room Eben Wallford looked up from his plate of turkey and yams and smiled.

She was home.

Wordlessly she watched the man fill her plate, but as she reached for the fork to lift the food to her mouth she suddenly snapped from her hypnotic state and stared horror-stricken at her surroundings.

She screamed, but the scream never escaped the century-old closed house.

Bolting from her chair, she vaulted for the door. She clawed at the knob, which slipped through her perspiring fingers. She kept gaping over her shoulder to see the man coming toward her. And when he appeared in the archway, napkin tucked neatly into his shirt collar, a puzzled look in his gray, sad eyes, she screamed once again in a desperate attempt to pull the door free from its rusty hinges. Her fingers dug into the wooden frame, splinters lodging under her nails. Blood and scratch-marks streaked to the floor. She fell to her knees in exhaustion against the door as if in prayer, her fore-head against the cold brass knob. Tears streamed down her cheeks. Then, breathless from fear, she stood and faced him. Her back was to the door, like a cat about to spring. Her shoulders heaved spasmodically. Her eyes darted in search of escape.

"Let me out of here," she whispered between clenched teeth. Her eyes traveled past him to the windows beyond. Then, almost as if afraid even to voice the words, she said, *"I am not your daughter."*

The man did not move. With a questioning look he held out his hand to her in the frightening gesture Sandy recognized from the cellar. She bolted. Rushing past him, she jammed her leg into one of the dining-room chairs. She caught herself before pitching forward and she lunged for the window. She strained against it with all the strength she was able to muster, but she could not budge the frame that had been painted closed a century before. She turned to face Eben Wallford. *What did he want from her?* She thought she knew. All of the happenings of the last seventy-two hours cascaded through her terrified mind.

"My God!" she half cried to herself, trying to make some rational sense out of what she was seeing—a table laden with hundred-year-old food and the lifelike ghost of a man long buried.

And in less time than it takes a thought to form, advance, and be recognized, she wondered why her own mind was letting her live through this. Why it didn't snap and leave her in idiotic and apathetic peace.

The man walked toward her, straight from the reel of a horror movie, almost with kaleidoscopic slow-motion stop-action. She blinked tightly to try to will the image away.

"Your daughter is dead!" she cried, in a voice she didn't recognize as her own, a voice summoned from primal depths.

She broke away from the window, keeping the long table between them.

"Suzanne—I didn't know. I swear."

They circled the table, the man perhaps more fearful than Sandy, as if he only had one chance and this was it. He reached out to her, his arms in supplication, the dread of the universe and eternity on his tired, drawn face.

"They told me you were dead. I believed them."

Her voice started small, no more than a swallowed whisper—

"No—"

—building from deep within, becoming garbled and lost in ever tightening vocal cords—

"No—"

—in the fierce, fist-pounding frustration of one who stutters, escaping air at battle with breathless intake—

"No—"

Her body was arched. The veins in her neck were huge and taut, her breath coming in spurts, until a scream shook her body.

"No!!"

She broke for the stairs, taking them two at a time, emerging at the top in the familiar upstairs hallway. In that one instant she could not separate dream from reality and did not know which was which. She looked behind her and saw the aged, ageless man start to mount the stairs, one heavy step at a time, eyes turned down lest he miss a step and trip.

At the end of the hallway she pushed open the door and burst into Suzanne's room. Immediately the sickening odor of burned, rotten flesh clogged her nostrils. The odor was not far away, as it had been the first time; it was not residual. It was there, and it was strong.

She saw the girl at the window, her arms at full extension above her in vain attempt to escape. Flames leapt from her hands and head, lapping at the ceiling, blackening it. The girl turned. Sandy gasped. Where there should have been a face there was nothing but a soft mass of oozing black pulp. Fire sprung from sockets where there once had been eyes. The flames snaked across the room toward Sandy, now frozen in terror in the doorway. The fire slowly curled into a twisting hand, separating into long red outstretched fingers. Sandy stood hypnotized in front of them as they beckoned to her. She felt the warmth of the flames on her.

She raced from the room. Her mouth was open but no sound came out. Eben Wallford was still climbing the stairs, one painful step at a time. She could not get down past him. She crossed the hallway and entered his bedroom. She went to the window. She would have to jump from the window to the roof of the veranda below, and from there make her way to the ground. Perhaps a passing car would see her and stop.

None of this she thought consciously. Rather, the escape route appeared instantaneously before her like a blueprint or a page from a movie script that a photographic memory had recorded and now reproduced.

In a final burst of desperate strength she forced the window outward and saw close-up the bars that blocked her escape, bars put up to *keep whatever was in there, in there.*

By then he was in the room with her, outstretched hands trembling fitfully, face quivering.

"Suzanne," he moaned, as if in fierce, final desperation. His whole body shook. He kept on repeating the one word in a crying voice louder and louder, until it reverberated painfully in her ears, so loudly that it threatened to shake the house loose from its foundation.

There was no other way out except past the hunched figure blocking the doorway, and she steeled herself as if preparing to jump into icy water.

Without giving her mind the time to stop her, she made a beeline for the door, arm and shoulder in taut readiness like a football player's to knock aside or tackle the old man. As she neared him, she tensed herself . . . and went falling to the floor in the hallway.

She had connected with nothing solid! She had gone right through him!

The apparition turned, the absence of a corporeal

body no less menacing, perhaps even more so, and she dove for the stairs, not remembering racing down them to the front door, which this time, without explanation or reason, opened easily to her grasping fingers.

The car radio was blasting rock and the beer was rolling freely. They were on vacation. Ten days away from BU to drink and ski and screw and get overall wasted. The posted speed limit on the curving Route 93 was thirty-five, but the roads were clear, dry, and holiday-empty, and the speedometer was edging higher. As they approached the top of the hill, the driver momentarily shifted his concentration to tune in the radio. It was his friend in the front seat who saw her and shouted, warning the driver to slow, to swerve, to stop; but he was fractionally too late.

Sandy never remembered seeing the car that hit her. Her next memory was a spinning red light, a siren call, and being lifted onto an ambulance stretcher. And a face in the upstairs bedroom: Eben Wallford, standing, looking out, his eyes dark and set, his expression hidden by the window bars. She closed her eyes to escape the stare of the old man who was torturing her so. Yet she could not dissolve the impression that still burned in her mind's eye.

Josiah Stoneham, interrupted from his Christmas dinner by the confusion and noise, leaned over her prone body. He was pushed aside by the ambulance attendants as they lifted the stretcher inside.

A state trooper was taking statements. The front-seat passenger, the one who had shouted the warning, was speaking excitedly. "She came running out of the house," he said, suddenly sobered. "It was like she was crazy. She wasn't looking where she was going. Ran right out in front of us. Jesus—! Will she be all right?"

Josiah heard the boy. Suddenly, something didn't make sense.

Running out of the house . . . That's what the boy had said.

But the house was locked! He always kept the front door locked. He had locked up the house when he had left with the children the night before. Suddenly his mind strained. Or had he? For a moment he stood confused, trying to remember. Had he locked up the house? The answer came easily: he must have locked it because he always did.

Fear and curiosity played against his spine and he had to wonder coldly: What did Eben want from her? Which triggered his memory and made him also ask: What did he want from the girl who was burned? And what was the connection?

He looked around him. The ambulance had sped off, heading northward toward Glendon and the area's hospital, its siren whining as it took the girl away. The state troopers were still there talking to the boys. Should he mention anything? No. He set his jaw. He would say nothing. Whatever had happened to her she deserved. She had been warned about going into the house. All of them had been warned. "Disrespectful city people," he spat out as he started back toward his house and his lunch.

Yet as Josiah opened his door to the sweet smell of fresh-baked apple pie floating in the air, he took one last glance up the road in the direction of the Wallford house and shivered. He wondered briefly—only briefly —if the girl was in any danger. Well, he reasoned as he closed the door, that was just not his problem. They had been warned.

CHAPTER XXI

David only left her bedside when Bob lightly grasped his shoulder and turned him around. It was late evening and visiting hours were ending. The hospital was settling into its nighttime routine. Their footsteps echoed loudly on the tiled corridor, and from behind the various doors the soft sounds of stirring patients were heard. In the dimly lit reception area, Pauline Kanon and Tom Landberg waited.

They went down the stairs and out into the cold night air. Only a half-dozen cars remained in the visitors' parking lot, and Tom walked toward his car as the others got into Bob's.

The silence lasted several minutes, then Bob broke it with words of puzzlement.

"I don't know what to say, David, except I'm so awfully sorry. We've all been in that house." He ended his words with a question mark that hung suspended in the air. "Nothing." He shrugged.

"We've always treated the house jokingly," Pauline added.

David bit his lower lip and almost drew blood. Faintly, very faintly in the distance he could make out the mountain lights as night crews readied snow guns and cats to pack the snow, break up clumps of ice, and flatten moguls. All would be as it had been. What had happened to Sandy would go unnoticed on the mountain. That was the true injustice, David thought. No one else would even care.

His words came slowly, as if the language were unfamiliar.

"Perhaps we've laughed about it for too long," he said, not talking directly to either of the Kanons, "and now he's paying us back."

"Stop it, David!" Bob said sharply in a voice that made Pauline gasp from the back seat. Bob flicked on the interior light and turned David full face to him. "Don't you blame us, and mostly, don't you blame yourself for what happened. I don't know what happened in that house. You don't know. Nobody does!"

David looked at him with bewilderment, as if trying to remember who he was. "She was in the house," he said finally, in a voice that defied comprehension, and suddenly Tom's words of only hours before were forgotten. "It's as if he were waiting for her."

Pauline touched him gently from behind. "You don't believe that, David."

David turned to her. "I don't know what to believe," he said blankly. "And right now, believing that Eben Wallford, someone who's been dead for a hundred years, lured her into his house, did God-knows-what to her, and then drove her out to be hit by a car, makes as much sense as anything else." He ran his hand through his hair, flattening it against his head. He breathed in deeply, tightly.

Bob started the car. "At least we can be thankful she wasn't hurt badly."

"Yes," David and Pauline concurred.

"She'll be out in a few days. Tomorrow even."

"And then I'll get her home," David said with finality. "Something I should have done days ago."

Bob pointed a finger at him. "If you start blaming

yourself like that, it's going to get to you and it's going to be worse. Do you hear me?"

David nodded. "Yeah."

Bob threw the car into gear and they left the hospital parking area. No one spoke. David was replaying in his mind the doctor's words:

"She's really not hurt all that badly—physically," he had said. "She was only grazed, and there were no broken bones. She was lucky."

"Lucky," David muttered.

"She was more traumatized than anything else. Which is normal. Although perhaps more in shock than is usual. I had to give her something to calm her down." He paused, but his silence was louder than his words. "She should sleep straight through until tomorrow. She was hysterical. She fought with the ambulance attendant—tried to climb out of the ambulance. As if she were desperate to get out, terrified of the confined space. Does she suffer from claustrophobia, do you know?"

David had been surprised. "No. Not that I know."

Desperate to get out. The words echoed in his mind. Not even Tom was able to offer anything. He didn't understand, and right now he wasn't even sure if he wanted to.

David closed his eyes and felt the renewed pounding in his temples. It had started when they had returned early from skiing to collect Sandy and head back to New York. The trooper was sitting outside. He had guessed that Sandy was a member of the ski house and was waiting until someone returned. He had told them then.

The headaches had come and gone as his tension mounted and receded, and now in the wake of the events of the day—no, the entire four days—it was as if the floodgates had opened. The pain swept through his head.

He threw his head back against the rest, closed his eyes and massaged his temples.

It still wasn't over.

It was the darkness that comes from the absence of any source of light. Not the misty grayness of a city night with headlights and streetlamps and randomly lit four-o'clock-in-the-morning waking windows to break the dark with patches of light. Rather, the blackness of a coal pit, the thick, murky, heavy blackness of the sea bottom, many fathoms deep, or a mausoleum sealed tight against a moonless night.

A sound slithered through the silence: a hesitant creaking, coming from a place where no one would expect sounds to form. Indeed, had a weak heart, or even a stalwart one, been within earshot, no doubt the mausoleum would have stood ready to receive one more.

Even within a dream, the sight and sound of the rising dead will terrify, because to the dreamer, everything has base in reality and all that unfolds appears tangible and concrete.

After a half-dozen false starts the heavy casket lid was painfully pushed upward, vertical on its hinges. The weakened figure inside fell backward onto her velvety cushion. And then as if bathed in an internal light source of her own, the girl, Suzanne, was able to sit up in what was to be her final resting place. The act of sitting exhausted her, yet seeing where she was spurred her on with a fear that the sleeping girl felt intuitively. She opened her mouth to call for help, but no sound would emerge.

It was cold, bone-chilling for those full of health, devastating for the girl who suffered the strains and pain of the pneumonia that had almost killed her.

She rolled herself out of the casket onto the cold floor. Too weak to stand, she dragged herself on arms and legs to the heavy mausoleum door. She started to shiver uncontrollably, her frail body losing its last vestiges of warmth as well as the strength to push open the door. Her hands reached upward and clawed in futile desperation at the closed door, as would a drowning person straining to hold head above water. The fear and doom of premature burial was on her pasty white face, and Sandy knew the girl was about to die—indeed, already had, a century past.

Sandy stood outside the mausoleum as she had in a dream once before. And in one time-freezing, breath-catching motion, the door swung open, the casket lid rose on creaking hinges, the skeleton of a girl sat easily up, the statue of Eben Wallford leaned over and pushed her inside, and the mausoleum door slammed shut behind her with a bang and an eternal echo.

With that she awoke, pulling herself from her drug-induced sleep to escape the horror that was so very real, so very vivid. And she loosed a scream of terror that woke the hospital and sent them running to her with further sedatives to send her back to the dream hell she was trying to escape.

They stood on the road outside the Wallford house, looking up at it—Tom, David, and Bob. The house seemed less foreboding, less mysterious. As if the fear had come from the unknown; and now the house stood open, exposed, ready to be conquered. It had done its worst.

In the warm sun, icicles dripped from the underside of the veranda and snow blew in wisps off the ledges and slanted roof. David rocked back and forth on his heels.

"Up until the other morning, Bob, I was quite happy to enjoy the stories as just—stories." He shrugged, "But now what do we do? Whom do we tell? What do we say?"

Tom turned to look at the mausoleum. In the bright golden sunlight there was nothing fearful or awesome about it except the word itself, which he rolled over in his mind.

"For starters," Bob said, "you'd probably have to explain what you were doing in there. What we were all doing in there."

David nodded through a tight half-smile. That in itself would be far from easy.

"Beyond that," Bob continued, "I don't know. Nothing. We don't do anything or tell anyone. We get Sandy back to New York."

"Yes," David agreed. "It's the proximity to this house." His voice tightened. "I really hate this place to get the better of us, but what's left to do? Burn it down?"

Bob shook his head. "You're probably safest leaving it alone. If Wallford *is* walking around in there, keep him there. Keep him contained." He looked toward Tom. "Don't you think?"

Tom wanted to shift their thinking away from the supernatural. He shook his head. "As you know, I think we should really look for a psychological cause for the visions. Perhaps something deep within her, something long forgotten, repressed, is seeping out to the surface symbolically through the Wallford story."

"I just can't buy that," David said. "What you're saying makes sense, Tom, but five days ago there was nothing wrong with her."

"David, listen to what she's been saying to us. She's remembering things about her father. The funeral of her father came back to her." Tom's eyes were intense. "Why did she ever lose it? What blocked it out? Look at the parallels! In both cases we have a father-daughter relationship." He ended on a rising inflection and his voice hung in the air. He opened his arms in a shrug. "There may even be other parallels—her fears of confinement? I'm not saying this is absolute, but it's a starting point."

"Tenuous," David said.

"But maybe more honest than saying a dead man is coming through to her and replaying scenes from his life." He lowered his voice. "The Wallford story is tragic. And there is a close-knit father-daughter story ending in tragedy and extreme guilt. David, what do you know about the death of Sandy's father?"

"Except that he died in a car accident, nothing."

"And up until yesterday, what did she really know?"

David answered slowly. "Nothing."

"But something is coming through to her. Perhaps triggered by hearing the story of the tortured soul. And perhaps that was powerful enough to allow something from her past to emerge. Something devastating enough to have made her repress it."

David tapped his foot on the ground and looked at it. "What do we do next?" he asked.

"Next," Tom answered, "we go to her and tell her we're going to help her because now perhaps we know where to begin."

Tom turned to leave, but David stopped him.

"Tom—? The portrait, Tom? How can repressed thoughts in Sandy's mind explain that?"

Tom hesitated and answered softly, almost inaudibly. "It can't."

The fire was out, the last dying embers struggling to remain alive. Charred wood and paper remains dusted the bottom of the fireplace in piles of gray and black. It was after two in the morning and the house was asleep. Judy sat alone in the living room, curled up in a corner of the couch, lost in a paperback thriller. For some reason, even after a day of hard skiing, she wasn't tired, her second wind having come at eleven.

The downstairs lights were switched off except for a lonely hundred-watt lamp under which she sat, eyes glued to the pages. The yellow bulb cast long shadows across the room, the furniture projected as black stains onto the ceiling and walls. The room was cold, and she

had pulled a blanket over her. Her knees were tucked
under her chin. The house was dead quiet except for
the ever present ticking of the grandfather clock.

She felt a prickliness on her neck. As if fingers, very
lightly, almost imperceptibly, had drummed across her.

Him.

She looked up from the book. Her eyes darted
rapidly about her, searching out the shadowy corners of
the room. But there was no one there. Except the unmistakable feeling that something had crept up on her.
The feeling was dark. Disturbing. Something was very
wrong. She was suddenly aware of how quiet the house
was. She listened to her own breathing and watched her
chest rise and fall. She could hear her heart beat. She let
her eyes travel slowly about the room. The ticking was
suddenly louder. Ominous. Beyond the archway the
dining room was black, as was the Ping-Pong room.
The blackness seemed to pulsate. The shadows of the
Christmas-tree branches darkening the wall behind her
loomed tall and grotesque with long, spidery arms. She
rubbed her hand over the back of her neck to remove
the crawling feeling that had slithered over her. She
swallowed tightly.

Very wrong.

She tried to ignore the prickly feeling and return to
the novel, but her eyes kept combing the room.
She sensed something behind her and quickly turned
around. There was nothing. She felt her skin rise, her
feathery hairs bristle. Outside, the wind whined through
the evergreens. She closed the book and put it on her
lap. She hunched herself forward as the feeling swept
over her again: the same itchy feeling that had sent her
into the Wallford house the other night, that had tickled
her into wanting to see the ghost and believing he had
made contact with her.

But somehow, this time the feeling was different. She
sensed that he was near and that he was looking for her
with a purpose.

This time it was not a game.

Her line of sight shifted; she was drawn suddenly to the fireplace; *was forced to look toward the fireplace.*

There was a strange new life to the fire. From weakly glowing embers, fresh flames were rising. It was not sudden; it was gradual, as if the embers had been stirred and paper and new wood slowly added. The fire rose in the hearth until it burned full.

Judy watched it. Odd as it was, there was still a comfort to this fire in the isolation and darkness of the room. The crackling of the sparks was welcome company.

The fire sucked her in. She began to lose herself in it, concentrating on the alluring pattern of the rising flames. Slender fingers of flame reached higher, with hypnotizing effect.

The paperback fell from her lap to the floor, where it remained. Judy was undisturbed by the sound—she did not hear it—and made no motion to retrieve the book.

She belonged to the fire.

Her breathing was steady, her eyes held by the appealing, relaxing, *commanding* flames. They beckoned for her to come.

She got up from the couch. The blanket fell to the floor beside her. She had to go to the fireplace.

She walked slowly toward it. Her arms were upraised in front of her like those of a sleepwalker. Or a zombie. When she was directly in front of the fireplace she stopped.

The flames had life. They shuddered and breathed.

They left the fireplace.

Long, twisting fingers of fire snaked outward. Judy was held by them, mesmerized by the movement, like a cobra transfixed by the slowly waving hand of the snakehandler.

The fire arched closer to her. Judy felt its nearness, its heat. She could not move. Her mouth was similarly affected; she could not even open it to scream. She was afraid the fire would enter her. Her mind was filled only with the flames; she could see nothing else.

The flames teased her, licked at her skin. The flesh on her arms grew hot and red. She tried to pull herself away from the flames that threatened to wrap themselves around her like lengths of burning red-orange twine, but she was unable to break free from the hypnotic hold the fire had over her.

Her skin was seared, red turning to black, flesh rough and blistering. She watched herself burn with a curious mixture of horror and detachment. She felt the pain, the burning. It was like beestings: thousands of tiny bees pumping gobs of venom into her skin. She felt the pain but it was almost as if it weren't hers. She could not immediately react to it. It was like the first split second after she put her hand or foot into extremely hot bath water to test it, when the brain is momentarily confused by the sudden heat and does not register the pain until an instant afterward, after it has already ordered the limb to pull away. It was this split second she was experiencing now, as a long, extended moment. She knew she was being burned, but the pain was not full.

She knew she was being burned, because her skin was smoking, blackening, seeming to peel from her body. And her nostrils were clogged with the sickening, pungent odor of herself. She sensed the skin on her face start to bubble and melt away.

Through the flames she saw him.

He was behind the flames, in the hearth.

He looked as she knew he would from the stories: old, gray, hunched over, his sunken eyes deep and penetrating, hypnotizing. The fire seemed to leap from his eyes. It was he who was burning her.

She could not speak, and sent up a silent plea to him as he watched her burn; *caused her to burn*. She screamed with her eyes and her mind. She was suffering.

Please. Would he let her be. Her arms plunged into the fire.

His mouth was set tight, in a hard, determined line. But as he watched her torment his eyes grew soft and wet.

It was at the exact moment when the burning pain began to fully register that Judy found her voice. As if whatever held her had suddenly released her. She screamed and cried for help.

Tom was the first down the stairs. He saw his daughter huddled in the corner of the couch. A blanket and a book were on the floor next to her. The fire was cold in the hearth.

This was what Tom took in visually in a single glance.

What he heard was his daughter screaming.

He scooped her up in his arms as the others started to gather at the top of the stairs. Gail pushed through to the front of the crowd and raced down the stairs.

"It's all right, honey. It's all right," Tom repeated over and over as he stroked the quivering girl from shoulder to hand. He was struck by the odd recognition of the words. Then he placed them. He sounded like Bob and Pauline trying to comfort Cynthia after she had seen the ghost.

"What is it, honey?" he asked in a controlled, even voice.

Judy spoke, but the words came out in a jumble. She was trying to say everything at once for fear of having her speech wrested from her again. "I saw him . . . the ghost . . . he tried to kill me . . . the fire burned me . . . it came at me—"

Only then did she realize that she was still sitting on the couch. She had never left the couch.

"You were dreaming, honey," Tom said quietly.

"No. It was not a dream," she said, with a fearful certainty.

From the second-floor landing Cynthia screamed shrilly. "The ghost was here again!"

Pauline pulled her daughter to her and hurried her back to their bedroom.

Tom pointed to the fireplace. He spoke softly. "The fire's dead, Judy."

"My arm! It burnt my arm! My face!" What was wrong with her father? Why didn't he see that her skin was burned?

Tom held her wrists tightly and pulled her arms out in front of her. "Where, honey? Where is it burned? Show me."

Judy looked down at her arms. The smooth flesh was unbroken. Initially it didn't register. Then her fingers formed a tense claw and her whole arm shook. "I don't know! But I saw it. I felt it. I smelled it. Why don't you believe me?" She could not remember ever having experienced such confusion.

Then she looked at the fire. The last pinpoints of dying light were popping and turning silent and cold. She looked quickly at herself again. Her skin was untouched. She ran her hands across her face. No burning. No odor.

"It was very real, wasn't it?" Tom asked her gently.

Judy nodded fiercely. Her eyes were wide.

"Well, you're back with us now and it's over. It was just a dream, like Cynthia's."

Judy shook her head. She had seen the ghost, she knew it. He had lured her to the fireplace and he had made the fire go to her. He had wanted to burn her. But there was absolutely no evidence; nothing at all. Nothing had changed from before except that her book was on the floor, where it must have landed when she had fallen asleep.

Fallen asleep.

Her father was right. He had to be. It was just a dream. A terrible, terrible dream unlike any she'd ever had.

No. Not all of it. The creepy feeling she'd experienced before the burning was not a dream. She had been awake then and she had felt it.

She closed her eyes.

No. There had been nothing there even then. Nothing had touched her neck. It was only the darkness she had felt. Just as there had been nothing to the ghostly touch she had felt at the Wallford house. Scott was right. She had wanted to sense his presence and so she had. Tonight as well. She clenched her fist tightly and looked at it. She needed to believe it was only a dream, because the reality of what had happened was too frightening. She had let the half-darkness and her own imagination build things that weren't there. Her father always said she had a creative mind. Boy, was she ever proving it on this vacation.

"Ready to go upstairs?" Gail asked her.

Judy looked at her mother and nodded. The dreams and the horror were over for the night. Somehow she felt she would sleep undisturbed.

Gail led her up the stairs, the others making way for them to pass.

Tom followed behind. He was confused and concerned. Judy was not subject to nightmares. But he knew she could have been affected by the nightmares experienced by Cynthia and Sandy.

Susceptibility.

There had been an extraordinary number of nightmares in the ski house. Taken in isolation, Judy's would have been one thing. As would Cynthia's, or Sandy's—in isolation. Together, though, Tom wondered. Was it merely coincidence? Merely susceptibility, one to the next? Or was it something more?

Something just didn't add up.

Like the portrait.

Upstairs, Pauline was having a difficult time calming Cynthia. Her daughter was almost out of control. She would not stop crying; would not be dissuaded from her fears that the ghost was in the ski house. It was Sandy who had brought the ghost into their house. He had gotten to Judy too. She knew it. He would not stop until he got them all.

Pauline looked at her husband, tight-lipped. She was angry. "I should know better," she said. "But nothing ever happened here until Sandy came into our lives and went into that goddamned house."

"That's right," Bob said calmly. "You do know better. Sandy has done nothing here."

Pauline did not respond. She wasn't buying Bob's words. She knew that somehow Sandy was indeed responsible for all that had happened.

She stroked her daughter's hair. With her face buried in her mother's nightgown, the little girl's sobs were muffled. Pauline would let her cry herself into exhaustion. Then she would sleep. Her little body shook. Pauline had never seen her daughter so frightened.

"Ghost or not," she said finally, "I think we'll have to take Cynthia away from here. I'll take her home in the morning."

Bob nodded. "I'd go with you, but we have a houseful of guests who need looking after."

"I know. We'll be all right." Pauline held her daughter at arm's length. "We'll go home in the morning, okay, honey? Whatever it is that's bothering you, we'll leave here."

Cynthia nodded weakly. Pauline led her to the bed, put her in the center, and wrapped her tightly in a blanket. She fell asleep immediately. Pauline knew that at some point they'd have to deal with getting her back to the ski house again. But they'd do that after the nightmares had ceased and after Sandy was no longer a member of the house.

As she thought of Sandy she found herself growing angry. Look what Sandy had done. She had affected everyone: Cynthia as well as Judy and Scott; she had disrupted the entire house. At least she wasn't around anymore, Pauline thought, satisfied. The ghost had taken care of her!

Suddenly Pauline was very ashamed of her thoughts.

Sandy was a victim, as was Cynthia. They were all victims, and she prayed it would all soon be over so things could get back to normal.

But what they were victims of, she didn't know.

It was late and the room was cold. Bob crawled into his side of the bed, Pauline hers. Pauline asked silent forgiveness for her thoughts about Sandy and wished the poor girl well.

Cynthia slept peacefully.

This time Judy knew she had dreamed and she woke up understanding.

He had appeared to her and told her: *before,* it had not been a dream. He could have burned her, but he hadn't.

She was not the one he wanted.

Yet something intuitive in her half-sleeping mind told Judy she was far from safe. He was in touch with her. Through her thoughts. He had drawn her into his house. He had lured her close to the fire. He had shown her he could burn her if he chose. He could do with her what he wished.

He needed something—this man, this ghost—and Judy knew she was vulnerable until he got it.

But she didn't know what he needed.

She fell back to sleep, and when she awoke in the morning she had only a hazy recollection of this ghostly visit and her brief flash of understanding. She glanced over at Cynthia's bed. It was empty, stripped, the blankets folded neatly at the foot. Pauline must have left with her little girl at first light.

Judy decided she would think of it as only another

distant dream. She would tell no one about it, for fear of their taking her home as they did Cynthia.

She would tell no one. And so they would all be unprepared for the time when *she* would be the one he wanted.

CHAPTER XXII

The hospital was coming awake. The kitchen was humming with breakfast being readied on trays; the emergency room was quiet and had remained so since early the previous evening, when Mrs. Banyas had been brought in by the state troopers after forgetting to take her medicine and collapsing on the bedroom floor, to be found by her son.

So incredibly different from Bellevue, Jill Josephson thought—here, where an emergency was the odd exception rather than the rule. An occasional car crash, an occasional leg break, an occasional Mrs. Banyas. But no stabbings, shootings, rapes, or blood. Hardly any, anyway, and rare enough so it was a big deal.

It was a different kind of life up here—skiing on her off days, tennis in the summer, all relatively hassle-free with breathable air and soothing quiet. Friends of hers wondered why she didn't go crazy from the isolation. She didn't. Why she didn't go into culture atrophy from the lack of museums or concert halls. Well, the last time she was in a museum was in fourth grade and she'd had to be there, and the last concert she attended was the Boston Pops, which had been held in the middle of nowhere, anyway; so she managed just fine, thank you very much. She felt she was even starting to think and talk like a native.

No. She'd never once regretted her move from New York to Glendon. Even if her husband had not started the real estate business on the mountain, she might have found the good life eventually anyway.

She checked her watch. The mountain would be opening for the day in about an hour. That meant in about two hours the first of the casualties would be wheeled in for X-raying, setting, and outfitting with casts and crutches. She'd gotten good, able to tell at a glance who had sustained fractures, or breaks, and who had only a torn or stretched ligament or tendon. The soft-tissue injuries were the worst, she thought, and when looking into the frightened eyes of an injured skier waiting for his X ray she so wanted to tell him a break might be better. Breaks healed in prescribed times, more or less; soft-tissue injuries went on forever, it seemed. Involuntarily she touched her right knee. It pained her in rain and humidity. Six months of rebuilding with stretching exercises and weight lifting. All the results of that goddamned idiotic momentary loss of concentration that had sent her cartwheeling. Was skiing worth it? She smiled to herself: yeah.

She had made it a practice since her early days of nursing that before leaving for home she would look in on the patients admitted into the hospital during her shift.

In the past eighteen hours, two from the emergency room had had to be admitted upstairs. There had been the concussion. Dumb schmuck. He was so getting off on looking good for people riding the chair above him that he'd skied head first into a lift tower. Well, the folks on the lift got their show, she thought glumly. Too bad the guy wasn't conscious long enough to notice.

Then there was the girl from the car accident, the one who had awakened with the frightening nightmare. Her injuries weren't bad; she'd be out in a day or so. A quick look in on her.

With the door to Sandy's room slightly ajar, something struck Jill Josephson as being wrong. She didn't quite know what it was. Cautiously she entered the room and then she saw it: the girl's arm was hanging limply over the edge of the bed. She moved closer to the sleeping Sandy, looked at her for an extended second with detached fascination and then horror, and shot from the room to find the resident on duty.

David arrived at the hospital before visiting hours, hoping to be with Sandy when she awoke. He was intercepted at the nurses' station and directed to Dr. Greenspan's office.

The doctor was finishing up a call when David entered, and he motioned him to sit in one of the chairs opposite the desk.

The office was Spartan, with a gray metal desk cluttered high with papers, folders, and medical magazines. A four-drawer file cabinet stood in one of the corners, the top drawer partially opened with a manila folder sticking out at an angle, marking a place. A bookcase covered the length of one of the walls, piled high with more magazines, scattered medical texts, and paperback best sellers. A lopsided paint-by-numbers farm scene of grazing cows on a green field covered a small portion of the hospital's off-white wall. An X ray viewing screen hung behind the doctor's low-back swivel chair. A plastic knee dominated the desk and a skeleton attached to a brace stood silently, as if in judgment. For a fraction of a second, David wondered if the guy had been a patient of Dr. Greenspan's.

"It's great being an orthopedist," Dr. Greenspan said, hanging up the phone and shifting his chair to face David. "We have the best toys."

David tried to force a smile to match the doctor's.

He was an older man, a Marcus Welby type with a little bit of the free spirit, as evidenced by his cavalier attitude toward his office furnishings and the Izod alligator sneaking through his lab coat.

"The nurse said you wanted to see me," he said, disarmed by the sparkle in the doctor's eyes. He unzipped his parka and slipped it off.

Dr. Greenspan nodded, but said nothing. The pause seemed interminable, as if the next words spoken might determine life or death. Indeed, in the doctor's office they might very well.

"She's still sleeping, David. I looked in on her."

"She's all right, isn't she?"

The doctor hesitated a fraction of a second that did not go unnoticed by David, before nodding affirmatively. "She's all right."

"What is it? Can I see her?" David eased cautiously from the chair.

"There is something," the doctor began, and David froze. "A complication."

"What?" His voice was sharp, accusatory.

"I know I said yesterday she'd be able to leave in a day or two. Even today."

"Yes—?" His confusion was visible.

Dr. Greenspan shook his head. "I don't think she should be released just yet."

David knew it was just his imagination, but for some reason he felt the skeleton take a step toward him. The small hairs on the back of his neck stood on end, a warning buzzer in his brain rang with a tinny whine. He fought for control.

"Why not?" He was perspiring. "I thought there was nothing wrong with her." For the first time in his life David felt truly frightened for somebody else.

"There wasn't. There isn't." The doctor took a breath before continuing, his palms out in front of him. "When Sandy was brought in after the accident her bruises were, for the most part, superficial. There was really little else besides scrapes and abrasions. In fact, she would have been released right away if not for her mental state."

"I know all about her mental state," David interrupted. "That's why I have to get her away from here."

"David, you've got to let me tell you what is happening to her." The doctor was intense, the smiling eyes of a moment before replaced with a sudden deep stare that silenced David immediately.

"She has developed a skin disorder on her right arm—"

"A skin—?"

"—where her skin is reddened," the doctor continued, ignoring David's interruption, "and covered with scales that are exfoliating—scaling, peeling from her body."

David looked at the doctor blankly, questioningly, and fought against the inner revulsion that suddenly threatened to consume him. What Greenspan was saying was not penetrating. *Her skin is peeling off?*

"She has bruises," he said, in a voice that refused to accept the cruel verbal joke the doctor was playing on him.

But the doctor wasn't playing trick or treat.

"Let me give you a few words about skin," Greenspan was saying. David was only half listening. "Very simply, there are two basic layers to the skin: the epidermis, or visible outer portion of the skin, made up of layers of covering cells which are constantly being shed as fresh ones are produced. Below that is the dermis, or true skin, which contains the nerve endings, blood vessels, follicles, and so on. The outer layer protects the inner layer. The skin usually regenerates in twelve to fourteen days. But in Sandy's case this process has been accelerated."

"Why?" David asked feebly.

"Right now we don't know. But don't take that to mean it's anything serious." He smiled. "There are dozens of different skin diseases, many overlapping with many similarities. If you got three dermatologists to look at the same symptoms, you might very well get three different diagnoses. Dermatology is not my area, so I called someone in to look at her. For now, until the testing is complete, we're labeling the disorder exfoliative dermatitis, which appears to be idiopathic in origin."

"Idiopathic?"

"Meaning we don't know where it has come from."

"It *just* appeared?" David asked, and felt himself grow smaller.

"It *just* appeared," Dr. Greenspan answered. "You saw her last night. She was fine. At midnight she was fine. Nothing. This morning one of our nurses found her and called the resident on duty. He called me. I called in Spinner. What he found most startling is the extent to which the condition has manifested itself in only a matter of hours."

He paused before continuing, looking past David to the silent skeleton beside the door. "Exfoliative dermatitis is a hodgepodge description encompassing a number of skin ailments. Psoriasis for one. Dr. Spinner, the dermatologist, will be taking a skin biopsy to test for a specific dermatosis and rule out or detect other skin diseases that also are characterized by scaling eruptions and erythema—the reddening that we see. Like seborrheic dermatitis or dermatitis mendicamentosa." He looked toward David, a comforting smile playing across his face. "Or other fancy words for rash."

"This is more than a rash, isn't it?" David asked flatly.

"I'm afraid so." They faced each other and the doctor continued. "The biopsy may tell us what it is. Then we can try to locate the origin. Perhaps it's just a severe allergic reaction to the starch we used on the sheets, some soap she used, or one of the tranquilizing drugs we administered to her when she came in. If need be, we can eventually do a blood or bone marrow study and a lymph node biopsy."

"That's to test for leukemia, isn't it?" David asked, startled.

"I would put it in slightly different terms," Dr. Greenspan answered. "To rule out the possibility of leukemia."

"Whatever," David agreed, grim faced.

"We're not rushing out to do these tests. Sixty percent of cases like this clear up as spontaneously as they appear. Most don't even require hospitalization. Spinner in no way thinks there's anything more serious behind it than an allergic reaction. We have every hope that once Sandy is isolated from anything that may have caused the reaction, she will improve spontaneously."

David covered his mouth with his hand and looked around the room. His blood felt frozen in his veins. He closed his eyes and then found words.

"What are you doing for her?"

"There are initial treatments that we would do for any number of skin disorders. Increase fluid intake, control the fever she has, give her no medication at all, and keep the skin moist through corticosteroids."

"Is there any danger?"

Greenspan pursed his lips. "Not really. There are always possible complications or outgrowths from something like this, but there's no point in talking about that right now. It would just be an academic exercise for me that would needlessly frighten you. I do not foresee any complications from the disease. But I will caution that idiopathic exfoliative dermatitis, if that is what she is evidencing, is unpredictable in nature."

"Meaning?"

"It could spread to other areas of her body, or it could clear up as quickly as it came on."

David draped his hands between his legs and clenched them together. "A few days ago, Doctor, we came up here to spend a week in Vermont. A broken leg or a fractured ankle during skiing, okay. I can understand that. Even laugh about it and take her home on crutches." He stopped short and shrugged, a confused look spreading across his face, like a first-grader trying to comprehend integral calculus. "This just doesn't make any sense, you know."

Greenspan nodded.

"Merry Christmas, right, Doctor?" He got up. "Can I see her now?"

Greenspan recalled what he had seen when the resident had pulled him into Sandy's room. Her arm was red, with wafer-thin scales falling freely from her.

"I'd rather you waited. She's sleeping." He started to say more but hesitated.

"What else, Doctor?"

"She awoke around midnight. Screaming."

"A nightmare?" David asked quickly.

"We don't know. Presumably. We sedated her, which perhaps aggravated the condition."

"She's been having nightmares," David stated matter-of-factly. Then he smiled to himself as he gave in to the tensions of the moment. "You see, Doctor, there's this haunted house . . ." The smile turned cold and tears of helplessness started to fall.

No. It was not over.

CHAPTER XXIII

From only a glance, the nurse on duty could not have known what was passing through the sleeping girl's mind. Her face looked at peace, not tight or contorted as perhaps it should when confronted with visions of the dead and dying. Perhaps her eyelids fluttered briefly; perhaps the corner of her nostril flared slightly. But that was all.

The nurse turned and walked into the brightly lit corridor as the wide hospital door closed silently on well-oiled hinges, plunging the room into shadowed grayness, leaving only a sliver of light from underneath, where it did not mesh with the floor.

For all intents and purposes the patient was sleeping soundly, and it was duly noted on her card as the nurse continued down the hall back to her station.

Sunlight streamed in through the windows of the Wallford parlor. Shadows splashed across the medallion-backed sofa that was upholstered in a pattern of grapes and leaves, and across the face of the girl who stood next to it.

The look on her face was intense, a picture of unbroken concentration, eyes staring at the sheet of music on the stand in front of her. The recorder's hoarse, soft music filled the room and filtered upward to the man resting in his Morris chair.

The girl finished her playing and looked up. She spoke.

Sandy had heard the voice before.

It was the voice of warning.

"Fight him," it said. *"Fight him. Fight him. Fight him. Don't let any part of you become part of me."*

It grew in loudness and intensity, becoming more desperate. A moan of pain and fear and trembling. A tortured voice one step removed from hopelessness, booming in her inner ear. The face of the girl contorted plaintively.

"Help me. Help him. Help yourself."

Then the voice suddenly stopped, as if a hand had been clamped over an open mouth or a telephone wire pulled from a wall. The scene dissolved; the girl disappeared. There was a momentary welcome silence, and Sandy thought she was being pulled from sleep.

Then just as suddenly she was thrust into the room with the dolls.

They were a silent jury: rag dolls, dolls of wood and rawhide, in clothes of cloth or silk, decorated with buttons of silver and coral. All were hushed, with saddened eyes and long expressions. The fine, high-pitched squeal of the rocking horse was a continuous whine as Eben nervously played it back and forth and watched his daughter lie tossing and moaning on the bed. The covers were drawn up close around her but she was still chilled, shivering uncontrollably. Her forehead was burning hot to the touch, and for two days Eben had sat, applying cold, wet towels in a vain attempt to break the fever. Her breathing was difficult and labored, with pains in her chest, as if a giant weight had been placed on her body.

Suzanne was dying.

The doctor stood to the side, speaking only with his

eyes to Eben across the bed. But Eben refused to accept, and dutifully replaced the towel in the tub of cold water, wrung out the excess, and placed the compress lightly on his daughter's forehead.

Hilda Wallford sat motionless in the corner, her hands in her lap, her fingers moving against each other in an idle, aimless twirl.

Suzanne looked up at her father, who she knew felt her pain, and their eyes met, for the last time. Eben swallowed, and held back his tears, trying to remain strong and give remnants of hope to the girl. Suzanne put her hand in his, grasping at his fingers with final, ebbing strength. And when she coughed it was weak and wet, with rust-colored sputum dribbling out of the corners of her mouth. She could barely inhale owing to the chest pains.

"Poppa, it hurts so when I breathe," she said through lips that hardly opened.

Eben squeezed her hand as the doctor looked silently on. He had done all he could.

Outside, the sky was low and gray. It had begun to snow, blanketing Owlsfane in a tomb of white. It was late afternoon and the doctor looked worriedly out of the window, wondering if he'd be able to get home before the snows piled up too deeply, but knowing he could not leave until . . .

The *clip-clopping* sound of horses' hooves filtered in from outdoors then faded, as a wagon made its way slowly along the isolated road.

Suzanne tried to speak, her mouth forming words which were not heard, the reddish saliva leaking from her mouth and down her chin, which Eben wiped with another towel.

"I love you, Poppa," she was finally able to say.

Her breathing sharpened with a final intake. Then it stopped. Silence hung in the room. The girl lay still.

Eben removed the cloth from his daughter's forehead, dipped it into the pan of water on the night table next to the bed, wrung it out, and was about to put it back on his daughter when the doctor's strong hand reached over the bed, grabbed his wrist tightly, and stopped him.

Their eyes locked, Eben not understanding, the doctor not releasing him.

"I'm sorry," the doctor said, and quietly pulled the towel from Eben's weakening grasp. It was then that he started to cry.

Sandy saw all of this from her surprising new vantage point above the bed of the dead girl, hovering, it seemed, just below the ceiling. It was an odd sensation of detachment, free-floating. Of being lighter than air.

But all the pain she had felt was now gone, and she breathed more easily, her chest lighter.

She watched the doctor draw the covers over the head of the girl and gently lead a transfixed Eben from the room. Hilda followed, shutting the door behind her.

Her last sensation before all around her became silent darkness was settling of the rocking horse to a neutral, silent position.

Then the darkness engulfed her and she sensed motion.

Intuitively she knew she was to share the death experience of the girl, Suzanne.

All at once the familiar long black tunnel was there.

As was the memory of the terror of where she was destined. She knew she could not gaze upon the demon figures again. She desperately tried to fight the inevitable propulsion by will alone.

Yet something was different.

This time a warmth surrounded her in the tunnel, a sweet rush of summer wind and a safe, womblike feeling. From the first moment of realization she knew that this journey would not be like the others. She relaxed.

In the distance there was a pinpoint of light. The light beckoned warmly to her. She felt herself propelled toward it.

As she drew near, the light grew larger and she sensed a godlike presence within.

All memories of pain ceased, and a wondrous immutable feeling seized pleasant hold of her.

She reached out toward the light, to meld, to become one with it, and as she did, a face formed in front of it. It was before the light, yet in no way blocking it. The face was part of the light. The face was the light.

Sandy was not afraid, for nothing in this sweet darkness or in the presence of this heavenly glow could be frightening or harmful. There was only tenderness and love.

The face took on features, and the features were recognizable to the sleeping girl. The image of her father stood before her, solid for only a second, less perhaps, or even more, in a time scheme other than earthly.

Then the face dissolved.

And as the face of her father disappeared, so did the light. It seemed to fade in intensity, but in a moment of intuitive time she knew the light was not growing dimmer. Rather, she was moving away from it, *was being pulled from it*. She was moving backward through the tunnel, farther and farther away from the divine light.

As the light faded from her view she once again felt hands on her body and the disappearance of all hope and the return of the pain.

If she had screamed she would not have known it, and she knew that no one, not even her God, would have heard or cared, for she was once again in the region of the forever damned.

There was first one and then more:

Distorted fish-eyed lens faces dripping blood and pus appeared before her again. Their faces were burned

*from eternal fires. Toothless mouths bit at her with
venomous tongues.*

Once again she knew she had been thrown into the
pits of hell.

*The creatures clung to her, tugging at her wtih fingers
of concentrated acid that made her wrench contortedly
from the pain. They ran their fiery hands up and down
her naked body as if in sexual assault, thrusting snakelike twisted penises of blood at her mouth, choking her
and blocking her cries.*

A rush of dry, hot wind blew past her with a roar,
stopping all vision and creating blackness.

From the blackness a voice spoke to her, a voice she
sensed more than heard, a low voice that almost wasn't
there.

"It isn't time," the voice told her, and she knew she
had heard those words before.

With that, all sensation stopped. In the distance she
once again saw the light fading from her view, growing dimmer and smaller and more distant as it eluded
her desperate grasp.

How she yearned to be one with the light and enjoy
its peace and leave all else behind. She did not want to
return to life! And in that one frozen moment of intuitive feeling, Sandy did not know if it was really herself
or the dead Suzanne who was coming back to life, as
Sandy knew she had in the mausoleum a hundred years
ago.

She fought to understand.

The clatter of a bedpan falling to the floor outside
her room jarred her from her sleep. In the first milli-
seconds after awakening, something in her mind explained it all.

She had returned from death; that she now knew.

The pleasant death of heavenly love experienced by
Suzanne—

—as well as the unspeakable horrors of her own,
lost to her in time and distance.

In the dim gray light of the curtained hospital room she looked down at her right arm, which lay free of the covers. The redness and scaling she had seen before seemed to mock her, and she pulled her eyes from it.

She lay in bed listening to the sounds of her own breathing, as if each breath meant another second of life, another second of distance between her and—

She began to shiver.

Then she glanced to her left and saw her other arm. She stared, *because it wasn't hers.*

The left arm was identical to the right.

Biting tightly on her lower lip, she squeezed the call buzzer, draped over the coffinlike guardrail of the hospital bed.

She did not know where first to train her half-awakened mind. To the harsh realities of the disease that was spreading like maggots across her body, or to the more terrifying dream of death.

Although, she suddenly realized, with a final body-wrenching shudder and a cold, cold fear like none she had ever experienced or imagined, she had no way of knowing if the dream of death had its seeds in a lost memory of some former life, or if it was, like the ski fall, precognitive of an eternal life yet to come.

Her mind numbed and gave way. She fainted, her hand tightly clutching the buzzer as if trying to grasp on to life and hope, her thumb firmly pressing down and alerting those in the station up the hall.

CHAPTER XXIV

It was late afternoon when David and Tom returned to the hospital.

Dr. Spinner introduced himself outside Sandy's room. He extended his arm to usher them down the hallway, and David sensed he was trying to bar their entrance to the room. He held back, but with a nod of his head and an indication of his hand, Spinner seemed insistent.

"Please. Let's have coffee. We can talk."

He started down the hallway, and Tom motioned that they should follow. Hesitantly, David complied.

Although he was a short man, Spinner's legs propelled him rapidly down the hospital corridor. The others had to break into a half trot to catch up. Spinner was built solidly. College football, David thought, sizing him up, as he turned sharply into the hospital cafeteria.

It was just before dinner hour, and while the cafeteria workers were readying their hot plates and jockeying trays of fruit cocktail and cottage cheese, the room itself was practically empty, and they moved quickly through the serving area.

The walls sported museum posters that did little to

raise the color level of the room above drabness. Ambience was not the attraction of this hospital cafeteria, David thought. Nor was the food, he considered, as he hurriedly took a sip of the bitter coffee.

They were silent until they sat at one of the long cream-colored tables in the corner.

"You've seen her already?" Spinner said, turning to David. It was more a confirmation than a question.

David nodded. "Early this morning. When she was sleeping."

Spinner took a sip of coffee and rolled the hot liquid over his tongue. "Then you saw her arm?"

The image flashed unchecked through David's mind. "Yes."

Spinner glanced over David's shoulder and out the window. The grounds lights had been turned on and fluorescent white broke through the grayness of cloudy twilight.

"The disease—the exfoliative dermatitis—has spread to her left arm as well," he said flatly, clinically.

David and Tom looked at each other and then away. Neither spoke. They waited for Spinner to continue.

"A couple of hours ago one of the nurses answered a call to her room. When she got there, Sandy was coming awake, her hand clutching the call button. The nurse noticed the spread of the disease and called me."

"You don't know why, do you?" Tom asked.

Spinner held his hands out in front of him in a gesture of uncertainty. "Where it came from? No. Why it's spreading? Also no. I don't." His mouth was set in a tight line, his eyes piercing and strong. "It may have been a reaction to the tranquilizers we gave her when she was admitted that first caused dermatitis medicamentosa—" He smiled apologetically. "That's a fancy term for 'drug eruption.' That, in turn, could have led to the exfoliative dermatitis. We have stopped giving her medications that may have been at fault." He turned to David. "She hasn't used anything on her body out of the ordinary that you know of, has she? Soaps? Deodorants? Solvents?"

David shook his head. "No. Just what she brought up here with her. What she's always used."

Spinner managed a half-smile. "I didn't think so. That would have made it too easy." He took another sip of coffee with obvious distaste. "The rapidness with which the disease has taken hold and spread is bewildering. Drug eruptions, yes. They will occur quickly. The scaling—the exfoliating—not as quickly, which makes it a little bewildering to me. But so much of dermatology is conjecture. In any event, we're administering systematic corticosteroids, which sometimes provide for spectacular improvement in fulminant exfoliative dermatitis. We're also dressing the skin, talcing it, and bathing it. It may clear up as spontaneously as it developed. That is what we always hope for."

Tom folded his hands in front of him and turned to David. "You don't mind if I talk, do you?"

"Of course not."

"Dr. Spinner," Tom said. "I'm a psychiatrist. Sandy is not my patient. She is David's fiancée. A friend. But I've been observing her over the last couple of days. She's been having nightmares and perhaps hallucinations."

David chilled at the word "observing." It sounded so clinical, so detached. Like looking at someone in a cage. Or under a microscope.

"Yes," Spinner answered. "David mentioned the nightmares to Greenspan this morning, and the nurses have suspected as much. The hallucinations I didn't know about."

Tom ran his hand through his hair, smoothing some of the long strands that hid his bald spot. He seemed to be choosing his words carefully.

"I suspect," he said slowly, "that all her dreams of late may have origins in matters long repressed, that have recently been triggered. There has also been a specific pattern to her dreams, and she has been saying things that indicate that she may be remembering events she has not recalled in a number of years."

He paused. Spinner was looking at him, absorbing. David's eyes were on his untouched cup of coffee. He was listening to Tom, but his eyes were focused on the blackness inside the cup.

"The disease—the scaling—came on quickly," Tom continued. "And like the disease, so much has come back to her so quickly. The funeral of her father, for instance, which she has not remembered or said anything to anybody about in five years. It is all just starting to come back to her."

As if a corner of her mind, locked away, has just mysteriously sprung open, David thought.

"We were going to take her home last night. Back to New York. Then, of course, there was the accident and the rest. My point is that since so much has come back to her so quickly, and the exfoliative dermatitis has spread so quickly, I will look for a connection."

"Connection?" Spinner asked.

"Do you think the disease could have been psychosomatically produced?"

Spinner shook his head. "Basically, what I look for when confronted with skin disorders are irritants—soaps, abrasive cleansers, allergens such as poison ivy, overexposure to sunlight, past history of a patient, drug eruptions." He rubbed his eyes. "It would definitely not be the norm, but I can't rule out your suggestion, either. Further testing may show something we've missed, but with luck the whole thing will clear up by then. Afterward you'll have to watch her, because recurrence is possible. Especially if it is determined that a specific drug or irritant caused the reaction."

"Can we see her now?" David asked.

Spinner nodded. "She's been calling for you."

As they got up, Spinner put his arm around David's

shoulder. "We're doing what we can, believe me. I don't think it's serious. Just disturbing and, of course, temporarily unsightly. It is also puzzling, as I mentioned, but I find myself saying that more times than I would like. I'm always available if you need me. We'll watch her, and I really do think you'll be surprised in a day or so."

Surprised, David thought glumly. That was indeed the word for it. Somehow skiing was no longer that important.

Spinner left them outside Sandy's door and continued down the hall. David stood uncertainly, with his hand resting on the doorknob as if frozen in place. Suddenly he wished there were another diversion to keep them from having to go into the room.

He shrugged at Tom. "What do I say to her?"

"Encouraging words," Tom answered with a smile.

"Thanks," David said ruefully. "That's being helpful."

"Do you want to see her alone? I can wait out here."

"No. If there have been more nightmares—and apparently there have been—I want you in there. Okay?"

"You got it," Tom said, and indicated to David that he should lead the way.

She was lying in bed, almost a stranger to the others, to herself. Her eyes were open, staring upward at the ceiling, idly tracing a hairline crack as it branched into rivulets. In the uncertain light of the hospital room it almost seemed as if the crack were slithering snakelike across the ceiling, holding her hypnotically as she followed its winding path.

When the door opened she turned to them. She sighed half to herself in relief and tried to look relaxed.

She couldn't pull it off, though, and turned away in shame. "Go away."

David and Tom moved closer. Tom went around the bed to the other side.

"Don't look at me," she said. "Please—"

David spoke softly to her. "Stop that, will you."

Sandy closed her eyes, as if her embarrassment would cease when she could no longer see the others. She recalled from somewhere that when men and women were put up naked for ridicule, men covered their genitals; women, their eyes.

"How are you feeling?" Tom asked.

"I itch like hell."

"Don't scratch," Tom said, and then laughed. "God, I sound like someone's mother."

"I've been warned," Sandy answered, opening her eyes, and the tension broke. "I have no pain. Just feel weak. I think I'm running a temperature. They take it every twenty minutes, it seems."

She suddenly looked very small and very frightened. David never remembered her ever looking as vulnerable as at this moment. The last days were clearly visible on her face. But for someone who had done nothing but sleep, she looked anything but rested. Drawn. Her eyes were tired and confused. She looked as if she didn't know if she wanted to face it all or run and hide.

But she didn't know where to go.

"What's happening to me?" she asked in a weak voice. It was a cry for help.

David looked toward Tom.

"The doctors don't know the reasons for the dermatitis. But they don't think it's serious. Maybe an allergic reaction to something." David noticed the hesitation in Tom's eyes, but he did not tell her what he might have suspected. "It'll clear up in a day or so. Hang in there."

"I look a mess, don't I?" She held up her arms in front of her, a look of cold disgust crossing her face. She dropped her arms and closed her eyes, throwing her head all the way back onto the pillow, practically burying herself in its softness. She looked as if she wanted to make herself invisible.

"I've seen you look better," David said with a smile.

There was a silence that hung cloudlike in the room. Tom broke it.

"You've had more dreams, haven't you?" he coaxed. She turned to him.

"Yes."

"Bad ones?"

She nodded strongly. "I've got to talk to you. I think I'm losing my mind."

Tom pulled up a chair and straddled it. David sat down at the edge of the bed, careful not to disturb her arms, which rested at her sides. He could not help but steal glances at the reddened skin and the patches of scaling yellow-white. He felt his own skin prickle and crawl. He tried to absorb it all in one look and turn away. He remembered the words of a teacher he once had a hundred and fifty years ago, or so it seemed. It was a human comment that dealt with voyeuristic curiosity and fascination with tragedy. *If you see a cripple coming toward you,* the teacher had said, *take one good long look, thank God it isn't you, and don't turn back.* David had just taken his long look, lined with fascination and horror. He fought off a sympathetic desire to scratch his own arm, which of course made it itch all the more, until he had to make a passing swipe at it.

Sandy caught him and exhaled a little nervous laugh. Then she turned somber. "I'm afraid to sleep," she said.

Tom nodded solemnly.

"There's more."

"I know," Tom said. "You were in the house."

"Yes."

"Why?"

She knew she felt guilty, but couldn't explain the feeling. It passed through her in awkward, uncertain waves, and she recalled the promises she had made. It was only a day, but she felt as if time had rushed by her at the speed of light. She had been through so damned much. She swallowed. "I can't tell you why. I don't know why." She faltered, but Tom made her continue.

"I saw him again. He followed me into my dreams. I'm sure he's trying to kill me."

David sucked in his breath but said nothing. He grasped the guardrail of the bed until his knuckles were white. In a flash he was seeing everything he had built and planned for start to crumble.

"Why do you say that?" Tom asked in a soft, sympathetic voice. He was a therapist; he was a friend.

Sandy answered.

For the next twenty minutes without pause she told them what she remembered of Christmas Day: the pull toward the cellar, and her entry into the house.

And the dreams that followed. All the dreams. Of the tunnel, the blackness, the creatures. The devils that were so very real and tactile. She told them her suspicions of having died before.

After she had finished, she sat silent for a long moment. Perspiration beaded her forehead and her breath had quickened.

Tom looked at her through pitying eyes. She was like a confused, frightened animal.

But inside him, something suddenly clicked and began to make sense. The exfoliative dermatitis *may* have fitted into its proper place in the pattern. The key word, though, was "may." Nothing, he knew, was certain.

She held her arms out, momentarily forgetting the texture and color of the skin. She spoke each word separately, moving her hands with her words.

"The dreams did not feel like dreams. They were so very real," she repeated with a bitter fervor.

She looked at her hands and turned them palm to back. It was as if she had never seen them before. Then her glance fell on her arm and remained there as she talked.

"They were the most horrible creatures. Hideously ugly. Deformed. Touching me. Raping me." She choked.

"Take your time," Tom said soothingly.

Sandy became more agitated as she recalled the demon sights, as if talking about them would bring them on again, and her voice rose with her fear.

"They came from nowhere. From thin air. With just one purpose. To get me. There was no one else. Just them and me. I felt them. Touching them was like touching fire. There were electrical shocks. Bites."

Tom absorbed what she was saying.

"I'll be honest with you," Sandy continued. "For the first time in my life I feel absolutely out of control. I don't know what to do. Lying here all day, afraid to sleep, afraid to dream, to think. I even thought of suicide. To run from it all. To try to escape it."

She laughed derisively. "Three days ago I was renting skis and now I'm contemplating killing myself. What's stopping me is the fear of what I saw. I don't know if I've been through it or if I'm destined for it. I just don't know."

Her voice was raised, excited. There was a note of desperation in it that Tom had recognized in many of his deeply troubled patients.

And Sandy was.

Tom chose his next words carefully. He needed to keep her controlled until he could be with her for a time to try to sort through all that she had seen, dreamed, and remembered.

"It *was* a dream, Sandy." His voice was soft, full of compassion. She had to strain to hear it, which was what he wanted. "And a dream is the mind's attempt to solve a problem."

He got up and crossed to the window. He peeked out and then perched himself on the vents. "Because you are dreaming and remembering, shows you are opening. As unpleasant as the nightmares are, it is a good sign. It shows your barriers are coming down. Very few dreams are faithful translations of dream thoughts. What you see in your dream has gone through a considerable change in your mind before it emerges as what you finally see."

"It's symbolic?"

Tom nodded. "In a dream, a person, or an event, or an object never has a single meaning but rather a convergence of thoughts, memories, and feelings, all representative of something else. Yes. Symbolic. Because you dreamed this tunnel and these"—he hesitated before using the word, but decided not to avoid it— *"demons,* it doesn't mean you have lived through the death experience. It is probably something totally different. The whole Wallford story, which is unraveling itself to you, quite possibly has meaning somewhere else. It's probably less a 'realistic' dream than a symbolic one."

He took a breath and thought to himself, *father-daughter relationship.* It couldn't be clearer to a first-year psychology student. But maybe he was being too simplistic; nothing was absolute.

"You didn't die, Sandy," he continued. "And you're not living through a vision of death to come. That's nonsense, and I think you know it."

There was fear in her voice.

"I want it to be nonsense." She trembled. "But I know what I saw."

"If you want it to be nonsense, then you can make it nonsense. You created these dreams and visions for yourself and you can be rid of them too. It may take time, but you will do it." His voice was firm, steady, convincing. "When you come to grips with your past. You yourself know there are things you can't remember because there is a blockage. We'll try to break through this barricade your unconscious has put around itself, and once we do, the dreams and the visions will stop."

His words were reassuring, but suddenly she tensed, as if fully realizing what he had been suggesting. She tried to make it compute, but it did not.

"Tom!" she said strongly. "I saw Eben Wallford in that house!"

"Sandy," Tom said softly. "You did see him. And the others. I'm not saying you didn't." He lowered his voice even more. "What I am saying is that I don't think they were real."

Tom saw Sandy trying to back away, deeper into the bed, as if trying to disappear.

"No. Oh, no—" she said.

"Listen to me, Sandy—"

"No! I'm not crazy. I know what I saw. I didn't dream him. I didn't hallucinate him. He was in that house. I was drawn to the house. *I was in the house.*" Her voice was becoming louder, more desperate, as she fought a portion of herself that was responding logically to Tom's words, becoming more defensive, supporting a position she was beginning to waver from. Her eyes darted back and forth between Tom and David as if searching for the punch line to this horrible joke they were telling her.

"You were in the house, Sandy," Tom said. "I'm not disputing that. And you were hit by the car when you came running out of the house."

"Because *he* was after me." Were these people stupid? Why weren't they listening to her? Her eyes were wild. She suddenly closed them tightly.

And then it came.

The one sickening, terrifying moment of realization. That he *couldn't* be in the house. He was dead. Dead a hundred years. David and Tom saw it all on her face, and in that same moment Tom knew she had taken the first step toward recovery. Then came the flood of relief that none of it was real. She didn't die. She had dreamed the demons, not experienced them. And that was okay, because she knew the dream demons were symbolic of something else. They weren't real. And that was good.

She was suddenly drained. She needed words from Tom. Something solid, something real, something to hold on to, because in that one moment the only reality Sandy could swear to was David, Tom, and the itching, scaling skin that was falling from her arms.

Her face was pallid, her upper lip trembled, and she bit it until it hurt. None of this could be happening to her. Was it possible? To hallucinate what she had? Eben Wallford chasing her? *No—it wasn't possible. He did chase her!* Her head buzzed. It was all so inconceivable.

"Tom, just tell me it's going to be all right. I'm not very strong now."

"Of course you're going to be all right." Tom's words were simplistic, but his tone conveyed the strength he wanted it to. So often the patient needed that bit of hope the doctor could offer. When all else failed, hope was still something to hang on to.

"Sure," Sandy said. "You just have to commit me, that's all."

Somehow, the most incredibly strange feeling passed over her. Without knowing, she knew that she was going to be there a long time. But that was all right, because she'd be able to stay home from school. The hidden thought made her smile.

She turned to David, and with dry humor in her voice added: "Wonderful, David. You're marrying a crazy."

"You're making yourself crazy," David said softly. He fought to keep his voice from cracking. "And knowing you, you can do it."

Good, Tom thought.

She was quiet for a moment.

"Why don't you listen to Tom?" David suggested.

She digested the conversation of the last several minutes.

"I'm sorry. You're right. I'm sorry. It's just awfully tough, you know . . ." She trailed off, lost. What cascaded through her mind was unmatchable in experience or imagination. She groped to see what the ending of it all might be.

Tom moved close to the bed and held Sandy with his eyes. His gaze was intense yet compassionate, a practiced look that promised nothing but good.

"Sandy," he said gently, in a voice that sang with confidence. "You don't believe me now, and there is no reason why you should, because I'm certain those hallucinations—those *visions*," he emphasized, "—were very real."

He saw her nod in confirmation.

"But just think about what I'm saying and you'll have to see it makes sense. Everything is interconnected. The dreams. The visions. All the thoughts of your father—"

She looked up sharply. He had hit a nerve.

"A portion of your memory that was forgotten until now, lost to you, is surfacing. Painful memories, I promise you, and I think you already know that. I think you also know that until those memories pull free, it's going to be hell for you. You've had a taste of it already."

"Understatement," she muttered.

"I pray the worst is over. We have to find out what's coming. And *why*. Then we can deal with it."

"As a mental case," she said derisively.

"That's not going to help," Tom prodded gently. "Now, is it?"

"No," she conceded. "And it's infantile to boot." She smiled. "Couldn't I just believe in one little ghost?"

David suddenly noticed life in her eyes that Tom missed. A flash and it was gone. But it was Sandy.

Tom did not allow himself to return her smile. "We will try to find out what is causing everything." His eyes were wide, encouraging. "Right?"

She nodded and forced a smile, but her voice was small, distant. "I guess I'm your patient, huh?"

"If you want to be."

"I want. I want."

She closed her eyes and put her head all the way down on the bed, so that the sides of the pillow framed her tired face. "Oh, how I want."

Tom looked at David, who nodded.

"I'll see you tomorrow, Sandy. Right now I'll wait outside. You two can be alone for a few minutes."

"Thanks, Tom," she said. "And I'm sorry if I screwed up your vacation. You need this like you need goiter, right?"

Tom shot her a reassuring thumbs up and left the room, closing the door gently behind him.

David smiled at her. Both were more relaxed and at ease with each other.

"You know, you're a mess," he said.

"You should be with the U.N.," she shot back. "Always the diplomat."

"What about *my* vacation?" he challenged. "I don't hear you running around apologizing for lousing up mine."

"Yours deserves to be loused up. If we had gone to the Caribbean, none of this would have happened."

David frowned inwardly. She was right, but who was to know?

"Yeah," was all he could say.

"So next year when I—" Her nostrils flared, her lips quivered, and suddenly she broke down. "David, I can't continue with this banter." She covered her eyes with her hand to hold back the tears. "I'm sorry. Banter is easier."

"It's all right," he said, forcing a half-smile. But he knew the words sounded phony and hollow. They hung in the air.

"I've never been so scared, David."

She looked like a frightened pup.

"I know."

"Is it possible to just crack like this—? Of course it's possible. I'm doing it, aren't I?"

David didn't know how to answer. All he could do was look at her.

"I just want to say 'be gone!' Go away! Take the piece of my mind you want, but just go!"

"Sandy—"

"I'm sorry, David. My getting hysterical is not going to help either one of us. I'll stop. I'll be good, I promise. You're trying to help me, you and Tom. I'll let you help. I'll do whatever you want, but I just have to know there is something at the end of all this. The return of my sanity."

Her voice was intense, and he knew she was fighting to believe.

"They were all so goddamned real!"

There were tears on her face. He felt so helpless.

"I can't go through this much longer."

He watched her close her eyes and steel herself. When she opened them, she had regained control. He so wanted the right words to come, but try as he would, they would not. Words of encouragement, Tom had said. Shit—he couldn't even find his tongue.

With an unconscious gesture he reached for her hand, but then pulled back. He wanted to take it, but pulled away, half from not wanting to disturb it, half from his own distaste. He immediately felt guilty and reached to take it nonetheless. As if reading his mind, she drew her hand away.

"You don't have to," she said. "I know *I* wouldn't."

"I'm not so sure of that."

"Whatever." She turned away from him. "I'll be all right."

"Of course you will," he said automatically, and regretted that his years as an editor hadn't given him a better command of English. There was so much he felt he wanted to say; *should* say, but the words just wouldn't come. Somehow doctors always knew how to respond, but they were never close to the patient.

"I'll be all right," she repeated, half to herself.

David walked around to the other side of the bed and knelt down so he was level with her. Their eyes met, and he saw the fear deep behind hers.

"You *will* be," he said firmly, more forcibly, as if the very words would make it so. "And then we'll get you home."

"Home," she sighed. "If I hadn't been so pigheaded, that's where I'd be right now, instead of in this hospital bed watching my skin rot and my mind snap."

David held her with his eyes. "The skin will clear up," he said with certainty. He was careful with his voice. The slightest wavering would create doubt. It was as if he were staring into the eyes of a cobra about to strike, holding them hypnotically with his.

They looked at each other for a long time, communicating without words. His love for her spilled over. He turned away first, before the tears started to form. He didn't want to show her any weakness. He didn't know if she could handle it. The room felt suddenly cold. He felt detached from his body; felt that he was looking at himself and Sandy as a distant spectator. That none of it was real.

But it was.

"We'll be back in the morning," he said, standing.

"Okay," she said simply, and followed him up with her eyes. "Do me one favor, okay?"

"Sure."

"Say 'pleasant dreams.' "

She smiled at him, but it was a vacant one.

"I love you." He turned toward the door.

"Yes," she answered, and then hesitantly added: "Don't let this come between us. Promise."

"If you think this could ever come between us, then there was never anything there to begin with. All right?"

She nodded.

"Tomorrow," he said simply, and slipped out the door.

She watched the door close slowly behind him. Outside it was completely dark and the lamp in the room washed over her with a weak yellow light. You could talk yourself into anything, she thought. Even into thinking you had died.

She allowed herself to follow a curative thought process. Tom was undoubtedly right. He was a psychiatrist, wasn't he? Her dreams of death were obviously of something else; her dreams of Eben and Suzanne, the same. The hallucinations? There were reasons for them. They would just have to find out what.

She had often wondered what kind of a person went to a psychiatrist. Now she knew. Anybody.

The sensation tickled her nostrils again. It smelled as though someone in the hospital cafeteria had burned the dinner. But she was used to the odor by now; it was part of her.

She closed her eyes, but would not let herself fall asleep.

She thought of her father and the good times they'd had when she was small. The good times . . .

The accident. The stupid car accident. Why did he leave her?

Suddenly she felt very alone.

CHAPTER XXV

Tom and David walked silently down the hospital corridor. There was noise around them as dinner was being served and visitors shuffled back and forth. Tom noticed that David's brows were furrowed deeply, as if he were trying to comprehend all that was happening. It was tough, Tom knew, and for the first time he did not seem to have words that could reassure. Somehow telling his friend "she's going to be all right" would have sounded empty and all wrong.

As they neared the entrance to the hospital, David stopped and turned to Tom.

"I can't go back to the ski house yet," he said. "Can we go somewhere and talk? Do you mind?"

"Get drunk?" Tom suggested.

David shook his head. "I couldn't. I've got to remain clear tonight."

"You think less when you're loaded."

"I know. And it's tempting, believe me. But I've just got to talk this out with you. Okay?"

"Sure. Let me call Gail and let her know we'll be late." He moved to a pay phone near the reception desk. "Hey, shall I ask Bob to reimburse us for missing dinner?"

"Yeah," David said ruefully. "And for Sandy too. She'll be having her meals here for a while."

Tom started the car with a roar that sent a shock through the quiet evening air. He let the motor warm; the engine idled and coughed brown exhaust.

"Any thoughts?" he asked David.

David smiled wanly. "That's what I thought you were here for."

Tom shook his head.

"About where to go," he said with a smile. "To eat."

"Oh. I guess I'm jumping."

"And jumpy, I'll add."

David looked over toward Tom in a "Can you blame me?" pose and Tom shook his head in silent response.

"Someplace light and cheery," David said. "Nothing dark. Nothing atmospheric. Someplace where I can look at you and perhaps see reason."

Tom thought for a moment. "That limits us to the Dunkin' Donuts or the Star Light Cafe."

David answered immediately. "The Star Light. I couldn't stand swivel seats and chrome counters right now."

"You got it," Tom said, and backed the car out of the space.

They made small talk on the way to the restaurant, David not wanting to broach anything substantive until he had Tom's complete attention in the cafe. Tom wanted to give David his own time to become calm, to think.

A light, snowy mist had started to fall, although no appreciable accumulation was expected. The flakes danced in the glow of the headlights. To David, they were almost hypnotic, and he forced himself back to alertness.

The diner's parking lot was only half full when they arrived. They were quickly seated, and menus were left for them by a bored waitress who grunted something incomprehensible as they sat.

Waiting for the busboy to bring water glasses, napkins, and silverware, they each pretended to study the decor. A carousel of cakes was rotating next to the entrance; David followed a half-cut cheesecake that was making the rounds, giving it more attention than it deserved. A long counter was piled with cookies and Danish, and two mackinaw-clad truck drivers were sipping coffee and flirting with a waitress. A tabletop jukebox from somewhere down the aisle of booths was playing a tinny "Night Fever," which traveled lightly throughout the diner. David found himself drumming his fingers on the table, thinking back to when he and Sandy had danced to the song.

As the music ended and the jukebox shut off he noticed Tom looking at him.

"I thought we'd lost you," Tom said.

"No. I'm still with you." He forced a smile.

The waitress returned to take their orders.

"Cheeseburger," David said, almost automatically, not even knowing if he was hungry.

"The same." Tom nodded to her and handed back his menu. She collected David's.

"Anything to drink?"

"Coke."

"Coffee."

The waitress scribbled on her pad and turned toward the swinging double doors that led to the kitchen.

Bob watched her go and then looked squarely at David.

"Talk to me."

"There's no ghost," David said simply. It was a statement of fact, almost a summation, not a question.

"No," Tom said directly. "I would say there is not."

He held David's glance and would not break away. "She had lost reality, and that's something we have to face. But because she was able to sit and talk with us as coherently as she did, I have hope for an eventual full recovery."

David picked up his glass as a diversion and started to sip water he didn't really want. He knew he needed Tom's help, but for some reason he felt uncomfortable in his presence. As if he were speaking to him not as a friend but in a professional capacity, as the fiancée of a patient. For perhaps the first time, he saw Tom Landberg, psychiatrist.

"Something is surfacing," Tom said. "The dreams. The visions. The voices."

"The skin?" David asked.

The psychiatrist exhaled and pursed his lips. "That's possibly an expression of the body to expose what the mind is afraid to. Because what it is facing is too threatening." He raised his eyebrows. "If you hate your job or your boss, it may be your ulcer that finally gets you to quit."

He took a sip of the soda and let an ice cube roll around in his mouth and dissolve.

"David, the mind is a very powerful, very complex, very unknown entity. With circuits that permit a multitude of simultaneous body functions and maneuvers, physical and mental. And while it's our greatest ally, frequently our only ally, it can also be our own worst enemy."

"You're talking about psychosomatic illnesses?" David offered.

Tom nodded. "So much of what is wrong with us cannot be linked to anything organic. Yes. A lot is psychosomatic—stomach ulcers, migraines, boils, twitches —skin eruptions. All in our heads. We use them sometimes as defense mechanisms."

"A kid gets a cold on the day of a test so he has to miss school? Something like that?"

"Or an executive gets sick on the day of a crucial

business meeting and has to postpone it. And as soon as he's postponed it he begins to feel better."

"I know about some of those," David said smiling.

"An expression of the body to expose what the mind is afraid to," Tom repeated. "But I'm not saying that the ulcer, headache, rash, wart, sneezing, whatever, and any pain or symptoms derived from the ailment is not real. It's real enough, and the pain frequently and unhappily is very real. Doctors treat and control the ailment and the pain, but maybe in too few cases try to get to the underlying causes."

Tom paused as the waitress deposited two cheeseburgers in front of them. The feeble-looking french fries that came on the platter were wet, from water or grease or both, and David decided he really had no appetite.

"In times of stress, David," Tom was saying, "we all react in different ways. An illness or injury might incapacitate one person and have only a minor effect on someone else.

He touched his temple with his index finger and said flatly, "So much is controlled from up here. And for many of us there are indeed physical manifestations of emotional problems. A typist, for instance, grows to greatly resent her job and either suddenly or over a period of time develops pain or cramps in her hands that intensify when she's typing but vanish when she's not. There may indeed have been a real strain and a proper diagnosis of tendonitis or tenosynovitis made, but quite often in cases such as this you can trace the ailment back to the psychological problem or anxiety-producing situation."

"Fine," David said, leaning in over the untouched food. "A typist can't type because of pain in her fingers, but is it possible for the mind to actually 'will' the skin to peel off?"

"Where is the difference?" Tom asked. "Resentment

in the typist's head manifests as tendonitis in the hands. Something within Sandy—guilt, fear, anger, resentment, whatever, could be resulting in the skin's malfunctioning.

"Mental tension can bring on a number of physical ailments. Leg cramps in a frightened athlete so he doesn't have to compete. A woman gets a headache so she can avoid sex and not feel guilty about it."

David forced a smile.

"There are even those few who have caused themselves to suffer the stigmata every Easter. Their hands and feet start to bleed, welts appear on their backs. Hives, asthma, and allergies are frequently psychosomatic. There is a theory, for example, that asthmatics may have a deep, unconscious fear of being separated from their mothers, and the attack could be the manifestation of a repressed cry for the separated mother. But nothing is absolute. Sandy's skin problems could very well be psychosomatic. Believe me, I have seen similar instances."

He leaned against the high back of the booth and let David absorb all that he had just said.

David looked absently down at his plate and swirled a french fry around the now damp hamburger roll.

"I can't dispute anything you've said, Tom," he said slowly. "This is your field and you explained it all in words I could understand, which was a feat in itself."

Tom smiled and shook his head. "But—?"

"I don't buy it."

"You don't buy it, or you don't want to buy it? There's a difference."

"I don't want to," David said reluctantly.

"I understand. That's *your* defense mechanism. You don't want to accept that Sandy may be doing this to herself. It's easier to accept a spirit entity, a phantom Eben Wallford, a ghost, coming from beyond to terrorize a girl who disturbed the peace of his house."

"Please don't laugh at me, Tom," David said.

"I'm not. Goddammit, of course I'm not!" Tom raised his voice and then, as if sensing his was the only voice in the room, quickly lowered it to a hoarse whisper. "How can you ever suggest that?"

"I'm not, Tom. I'm sorry. I don't know what anymore."

Tom held back and let him continue. David looked as if he were groping.

"What she said before. About her death experience. I've read the Dr. Moody books on 'life after life.' Have you?"

"Yes."

"She hit all the points of the life-after-life journey. The tunnel. The light. The feeling of peace. The voice saying 'it isn't time,' and the return. That she would have known from her own reading." He looked up toward Tom searchingly, frightened. "The rest of it, though: the demons, the horrors. What do you make of it?"

"Right now, David, I don't know enough to make anything of it."

Tom leaned in toward him to punctuate the point. "She *dreamed* she had a death experience, David. She didn't die and come back. It's real to her, but you have to know it didn't happen."

"Then *what?*" David said fiercely, teeth and fists clenched in frustration. "Give me something."

Tom sat back and watched a waitress spray whipped cream onto a hot fudge sundae. The cream ended up everywhere but where it was intended. He finally spoke.

"I'd like to hypnotize her, David."

"What?"

"I use it with many of my patients. She seems to remember fragments from her life with no unity. Perhaps through hypnosis we can tie the pieces together. And once we've learned the *why,* we can start on the cure. Sometimes it's very effective."

David looked at him, suspiciously. "That sounds too easy."

"I promise nothing, David," Tom said quickly. "It's not a cure-all and nothing is guaranteed. I don't even know if she'll let me hypnotize her."

"She will," David answered with assurance.

"There's a defense mechanism within her unconscious that may not want to release what I'm going to be asking for. Patients sometimes keep me out and they sometimes purposely deceive."

"When?" David asked. He didn't want to talk about failure.

"I'll talk to her doctors tomorrow."

"Let's do it," David said, and reached for his hamburger, suddenly feeling better. The feeling, though, quickly passed as he bit into the now cold meat.

It was the sound of snoring above him that awoke Tom.

His eyes opened and suddenly he thought of Sandy's first dream.

She had seen Eben Wallford.

Was he symbolic of her father? Tom wondered.

At first she had reached out to him. And then pushed him away. Fought against him as he tried to push her into the mausoleum.

The simultaneous attraction to and retreat from the man. There was something threatening that made her push him away. But at the same time he obviously fulfilled some need, because she kept on bringing him back in later dreams. A need to be with him? And then a fear of it as well?

But why the fear?

Why the self-destruction?

Why the demons?

Tom dragged himself from the warmth of the bed, groped in the dark for his slippers and robe, and walked down to the living room. The fire was dead and the room was cold. He shivered as he switched on a lamp, which filled the room with a late-night eerie yellow. Sitting in one of the large old chairs, he reached for a piece of paper and started to jot down notes.

GUILT he scrawled in big bold letters. Then he wrote WHY and a big question mark: WHY GUILT?

He next scribbled, "approach/avoidance." She had been drawn to the house, to the basement of the ski house. Her need to go to both places was obviously greater than her fear. But whenever the presence of Eben Wallford became too threatening to her, she quickly came back to reality.

Why the familiarity of the drowning? The death of the mother? The precognitive dream that followed? Was there some sort of linkage there? He circled the sentence three times and put a large question mark over it. Was it important?

It was over an hour later when he had finished his jottings.

CHAPTER XXVI

The venetian blinds were lowered and the insistent light that trickled in was muted. Tom had not wanted David to sit in on the hypnosis session, but Sandy had demanded it and Tom had relented. Also, Dr. Spinner was in attendance, inconspicuous in a straight-back chair in a far corner of the room. He had wanted to be present in case he could be of any medical help, but Tom suspected he was just plain curious. Which was all right. Because that was what Tom was as well.

He had spent a half hour relaxing Sandy and explaining to her what he was going to do. The disease had weakened her somewhat, but she understood, relaxed, and agreed to cooperate.

Tom produced a small flashlight from his jacket pocket. "A prop," he had told David. First-time patients almost expected it. A light. A watch. Something. After they'd gone through several sessions he would hypnotize them with voice alone, and when they became comfortable, he could put them under by mere suggestion.

He passed the light slowly before her eyes and bade her focus on it. He spoke to her softly, in an even voice, well modulated. It was calming, soothing, steady.

Hypnotic.

"Keep your eyes on the light, Sandy. Concentrate on the light. I am going to count backward from one hundred, and as I do you are going to feel yourself getting tired . . ."

Except for Tom's steady cadence, there was silence in the room. Neither David nor Dr. Spinner had ever sat through a hypnosis session that wasn't performed in a nightclub where some volunteer would end up prancing around the stage like a chicken.

". . . each part of your body is getting heavier and more tired in turn. Your feet, Sandy . . . your legs . . . your arms . . . your hands . . . your fingers . . ."

David felt himself nodding off, and smiling sheepishly to himself, straightened up in the chair.

". . . your neck . . . your eyes. . . . Your eyelids will get heavy. They will want to close. You will close them as you hear only my voice counting."

Tom paused. Sandy's already heavier and steady breathing filled the room.

"I am counting now, Sandy: one hundred . . . ninety nine . . . ninety eight . . ."

Sandy's eyelids began to flutter and droop. Tom watched her eyes roll upward and then close. He did not break his cadence. He wanted to make certain she was fully under.

". . . ninety seven . . . ninety six . . . You hear only my voice . . . ninety five . . . ninety four . . ."

David was the first to see it and spoke out harshly, sharply.

"Tom!"

Glaring, Tom turned to silence him, but David could only point. Tom and the doctor turned simultaneously. He was pointing at Sandy's leg. Her nightgown had fallen to the side and her right leg was exposed. The skin from the knee down was scaling freely as they watched.

"Ninety three . . . ninety two . . ." Tom continued,

more loudly. His concern for Sandy grew, but he did
not want to pull her out. There was a tension in his
voice that had been absent the moment before and he
fought to control it. He could not alarm his sleeping
patient. Modulating his voice downward to an even
softness, he continued counting, but made his way
slowly across the room to the dermatologist.

"Let me finish," he whispered. "Can we?"

Spinner nodded. It was not an emergency. He could
apply medication when Tom was through. He motioned
for him to continue.

David was perched at the edge of his seat, looking
questioningly from Tom to Spinner. Tom held up both
hands in a calming gesture to indicate the situation was
still under control.

". . . eighty nine . . . eighty eight . . ." He paused.
"Sandy, I am going to stop counting now, but should
I wish to awaken you I will count to three and clap
my hands. Upon the sound of the clap you will awaken.
Do you understand me?"

First her head shook back and forth, from front to
back, and then she found her voice.

"Yes." The voice was small. It was Sandy's, but it
was not.

"On the count of three, Sandy, you will open your
eyes, but you will still be asleep. You will hear only
my voice. Is that understood?"

Like a recording of the previous response, her stiff,
dull answer came back. "Yes."

"Good," Tom said gently. "Now, Sandy, no matter
what happens, you will hear and respond only to my
voice. Do you understand?"

"Yes."

"All right. I want you to open your eyes."

Her eyes opened as wide as a carnival clown's. David
and Spinner watched intently as the skin on her right
leg started to scale. The color was a weak yellow.

She was a good subject, Tom thought. Easily hypnotizable. Didn't awaken to David's interruption. Didn't know the disease had suddenly appeared on her leg.

"I am going to ask you some questions, Sandy."

She nodded easily and almost looked as if she were eager to respond.

But suddenly there was a change. She moaned, as if something had grabbed her from within, her neck jutting forward violently, her veins bulging, her muscles taut, almost as if they would rip apart.

The voice came. Strong. Fierce. Not the weak voice of the hypnotized girl. A desperate cry that welled from deep within her and flowed out through tightened vocal cords and lips.

"Fight him! Fight him!"

David jumped out of his seat and surged forward.

It was as if Sandy were at war with herself. Her head rolled backward almost as if in whiplash.

"Sandy!" Tom commanded.

"What is it?" David shrieked.

"Quiet!" Tom ordered. "Sandy!"

Spinner sat frozen in place.

"Sandy! You will listen to me!"

Sandy tightened again as once more the voice fought its way through.

"Fight him! Fight him!"

She moaned again, an exhaling cry through her opened mouth. Tom didn't know if Sandy was back or if the moan came from—

"Sandy!" he snapped loudly, and suddenly she stopped. Her head dropped to her chest as if her muscles had relaxed. Tom cupped her chin and gently raised her head to a neutral position.

"Jesus!" David gasped. "What is it?"

"It's okay," Tom whispered in hoarse response. "Stay quiet."

Spinner tugged gently at David's sleeve and coaxed him back to the chair, where they both sat stiffly. Frightened.

Tom spoke reassurance to Sandy.

"You are relaxing, Sandy. You are feeling no pain. Nothing can harm you." He repeated the words over and over again in a calming voice. The voice, he realized, was perhaps more for him than for the girl. He felt his own heart rate slowing, his pulse normalizing.

He knew that under deep hypnosis or age regression spontaneous traumas and violent emotional reactions could arise as memories and emotions were released. All of that is within normal bounds, as frightening as it may be when it occurs. Tom sometimes got his finest insight into a patient's problems when it did occur. He never had anyone else in the room with him during a session. Especially not a loved one of the patient. He could have kicked himself for not being adamant with David, but Sandy was not disturbed and he would carry on anyway.

He had an opening.

He stood close to her and asked softly. "Fight who, Sandy? Who should you fight?"

The skin on the lower half of her right leg continued to scale and fall. It was worse than the peel of a bad sunburn because underneath the remaining skin was rough and yellow-white. Other areas were red.

"Who should you fight?" His voice grew stronger, meant to be shocking. "Who should you fight?" he repeated loudly.

Sandy rolled her head off to the side as if in conflict with herself. Her head tilted in the other direction.

The skin above her right knee started to scale. Tom watched it with growing alarm.

"Sandy, listen to me. We are going to recreate the night this whole horrid nightmare began. You will relive it, understand it, and then we will leave it. Do you understand?"

As she struggled to answer, the voice once again was weak.

"Yes."

"Good. The children were missing. Do you remember looking for the lost children?"

"Yes."

"You crossed the field behind the Stoneham house. It was snowing. Do you remember?"

"Yes."

"Good." He paused and wet his lips. He felt the tightness in his throat relax. She was back in his control again.

"You found the children but then went into the house. You felt compelled to enter the house."

Sandy nodded as she recalled the draw to the Wallford mansion. She began to sway gently back and forth in place.

"Sandy, you are now in the Wallford basement. Do you see yourself in the basement?"

She nodded.

"What do you see?"

"It's dirty and dusty," she said in a small voice. "There is a mannequin and a griffin and furniture."

"Good," Tom said. "Now you are walking up the stairs. You are standing in the dining room. There is food on the table—"

"Cake," she interrupted.

"But no one is there. . . ."

"David."

"Yes. David is there. But then you leave him. You run up the stairs and David doesn't follow. You go into Eben Wallford's bedroom. Sandy—you are in Eben Wallford's bedroom."

Her face tightened again as she was thrust back into that terrible room. Her fists clenched and unclenched in rhythmic motion, and despite Tom's commands she was far from relaxed.

"What do you see, Sandy?" Tom prodded.

"I see Eben Wallford," she cried. There was fear on

her face and her voice rose two octaves. "He's looking at me . . . staring at me."

Suddenly she threw her head back sharply. Her face froze with a start in a contorted sneer and the foreign voice emerged again.

"Fight him! Fight him! Fight him!"

Tom responded in turn by raising his voice. He didn't realize it, but he was practically screaming at her.

"Sandy, stop! Sandy, stop! You are no longer in the bedroom."

"Fight him! Fight him! Fight him! Dear God——!"

"Sandy, stop! When I count to three you will move away from this memory!"

"He's coming toward me," she suddenly shrieked as she reacted to something she alone was able to see.

"One. Two. Three."

"Eben Wallford! He's coming to get me! He wants to kill me!"

Tom clapped his hands sharply.

"One. Two. Three."

"Don't let him kill me!"

Her screams filled the room. Hospital personnel appeared at the door. Spinner ran to the door, barricading it, indicating that no one should enter. He assigned an orderly to stand guard outside.

"Don't let him!"

"One. Two. Three. Do you hear me, Sandy?"

Once more the moan came, and the other voice. Her breath came in spurts as the voice struggled to free itself. It was almost as if another entity had taken temporary control of her being.

And indeed, when the words came next, that was what the others in the room believed.

"Daddy . . . don't . . . don't . . . no! . . ."

"Sandy, do you hear me?" Tom repeated the words systematically, continuously. It was practically inconceivable that she had not by now responded to his controlling voice.

*"Daddy . . . don't. . . . I don't wish to come back.
. . . I'm happy here . . . it's pretty here. . . ."*

Once again the voice took on a quality of desperate
fear. The blood coursed fiercely through her neck, the
skin was exfoliating freely from her right leg.

"There's no pain. . . . I want to be dead. . . ."

"My God!" David screamed. It was as if the moment
couldn't possibly exist. He wanted to close his eyes,
disappear, anything to make time move backward. He
couldn't believe he was watching his fiancée writhing
and moaning on a hospital bed as a voice other than
her own emerged from her lips. How could this be
happening? If Spinner hadn't been holding him in
place, he might have bolted from the room.

"Why do you want to be dead, Sandy?" Tom tried to
be gentle, but his voice took on a tightness. He was
disarmed; he'd better lead her somewhere else. "I am
going to count to three—"

*"Daddy, come with us. . . . Come inside. . . . come
through the barrier. . . ."*

No— He'd better let her finish.

Her breathing rose to almost orgasmic intensity.
Her head bobbed back and forth on her fragile neck,
chin wavering, shoulders heaving uncontrollably. She
sounded asthmatic.

*"You did nothing wrong . . . you didn't know . . .
you didn't. . . . You can be with us now, with mother
and me. . . ."*

"Suzanne!" David yelled in sudden realization.
"That's Suzanne speaking!"

"Grab the light, daddy. . . ."

"We were wrong, Tom!" David was becoming more
frantic.

"Shut up!" Tom ordered, and begged the girl to
answer him. "Why do you want to be dead, Sandy?"

*"Grab the light. . . . Don't punish yourself this
way . . . don't torture yourself . . . don't torture the
girl. . . ."*

Then an unearthly screech pierced the air. Tom grabbed Sandy and held her.

The door burst open and the chief resident and hospital administrator entered, followed by three burly orderlies.

"Get out!" Tom shrieked. "Don't give her anything. I'll pull her back!"

But frozen in horror and fascination, no one moved. The door remained open as staff and patients alike struggled to look inside.

"Goddammit! Shut that door. David!"

David would not remember getting up and pushing the others out of the room.

Sandy started to cry. Tears flowed freely down her face. Her mouth opened. The sound was the wail of a mourner.

"Don't damn yourself. . . . We'll never be together-rrrrrr. . . "

The skin on her left knee started to fall from her body, the underlayers roughened and fishlike.

"Don't daddy! Don't kill her . . . don't damn yourself. . . . We'll never be together."

Sandy's body shook, as if the physical motion alone would banish the invaders from her spirit and corporeal self. Her head hung at a dangerous angle to the side and Tom held her, afraid she would do damage to her neck.

And then as the disease spread unstoppably on her leg, she opened her mouth as might a python about to swallow a victim alive and whole, jaw muscles relaxing beyond the range of tolerance, it seemed; and with a scream Tom could almost see rise wavelike from her throat, she threw the word directly into his face.

"NO!!!"

She collapsed into his arms and he patted her neck gently.

No more questions. It was time for reassurance.

"You are all right, Sandy. There is no danger. You are all right."

Her body heaved against his, her crying continued.

"You are all right. I will now count to three . . ."

"I'm sorry," she sobbed.

Tom heard the words, but in wanting nothing more than to bring her around, he misunderstood.

"One . . ."

Her voice was soft, in lost repentance, as if trying to make it all right and knowing she never could.

"I'm sorry, Daddy."

Tom stopped counting. He knew something was about to happen, but not what. The sudden silence in the room was unnerving. He knew now was the time to probe.

"Why are you sorry, Sandy?" he asked gently, and lifted her chin up to face him.

"The dream," she said, as if trying to explain the obvious. "There was the truck. I saw the truck."

"What truck, Sandy? What truck did you see?"

"The truck," she said again, as if he were stupid.

Suddenly she sat bolt upright in his arms, eyes bulging, throat tight. Perspiration cascaded from her face and her hair was matted wet against her forehead.

Skin continued to scale from her extremities.

"Fight him. . . . Fight him. . . . Don't let any part of you become part of me . . . don't let him. . . . I don't want to come back!!" And then in a voice of absolute blue-black terror as Sandy's body seemed to rise above the bed: *"Don't let him damn himself. . . . Stop him! . . . Stop him! . . . Make him hear me. . . . You can—"*

Tom turned hurriedly to Spinner. "Get me something. A hundred milligrams of thorazine."

"Right." Spinner tore himself from the chair and left the room. David heard the sounds of the people outside.

"Make him hear me . . ." the voice repeated again.

"Sandy!"

"Make him . . ."

"Sandy!"

". . . hear me!"

And then without knowing why, perhaps instinctively, but in an action that went against everything he believed, Tom screamed at the top of his lungs:

"Suzanne!"

The word silenced her.

Once again she started to sway and moan. The voice was doleful, mournful, a voice on the Day of Judgment pleading for eternity.

"Daddy don't. . . . Daddy don't. . . . Daddy don't. . . ."

Her head rolled in anguish from side to side.

"I don't want to come back. . . ."

"Suzanne," Tom said in a compassionate voice. "Why does your father want you to come back?"

"You didn't know . . ."

"Why does your father want you to come back?"

"Don't," she implored.

"Why, Suzanne?"

Tom shook the girl.

"Why?"

No answer.

He shook her harder.

"Tell me why!" Damn it! He felt he was close.

"You're hurting her, Tom." David was off the chair.

"WHY??"

Her body offered no resistance as it wobbled at his touch.

But Sandy was silent, as if she, or Suzanne, or both, had reached the point of exhaustion.

"Sandy," Tom tried again in a muted voice. "Do you hear me?"

Sandy slowly nodded yes, as she had in the very beginning of the session.

"I'm going to bring you out now."

Tom fought the rush in his voice. He wanted to end the session so he could try to correlate what he had heard.

"I'm going to count to three, Sandy, and then I'm going to clap my hands. You will awaken refreshed, as if from a nap, and *you will remember nothing from this session.*"

David wondered if that was possible.

"You will feel good and be at ease. Your skin will stop flaking from your body and all will be well. Do you understand?"

The slow nod, the soft voice. "Yes."

"Good. I'm going to count now. One. Two. Three."

Tom clapped his hands sharply together, and in a flash Sandy was with them. Tom pulled her quickly to him so she would not notice her legs. The skin continued to scale and the dry thickness spread. Spinner returned with the medication.

"You've had a rough go of it, Sandy," Tom said. "And I'm going to make you sleep."

"What happened?" she asked weakly.

"We'll talk tomorrow," he said. "You're going to be all right."

As the hypodermic needle sank into her arm, Tom relaxed his grasp on her. As she lay back she caught a brief glimpse of the condition of her legs but was not able to respond before the drug took hold and she was asleep.

"Jesus!" was all David could say. "Jesus! Jesus!"

He too was drenched in perspiration that clung coldly to his body.

"Let's bring ourselves down," Tom said, and the others quickly agreed.

CHAPTER XXVII

David sat with Sandy as she slept. Even in sleep the disease continued. There was a fascination in the thickened skin as small, thin yellow scales continued to flake from her body, from arms and legs, until most of both arms from the elbow and legs from the knees down were red or scaling.

He had often thought the unthinkable. The testing of a true love. Could he indeed remain with someone who might become injured, paralyzed, disfigured? As he stared down at Sandy's inert body, his own fingers passing millimeters above hers as if drawn to the color and texture of the skin, he knew that nothing could separate him from her. If he had to bathe her with corticosteroids, he would do so. Of course, at this point, he realized as he looked down at her beautifully serene face, it was still easy.

Tom came for him and they returned to the ski house.

Dinner was in progress and as they passed through the kitchen into the dining room, the conversation around the many tables suddenly stopped. As if he had the plague, David thought. As if the house were a morgue.

From the far corner of the head table, Bob stood up.

"We just started. We've saved two places for you. Over here."

As David and Tom crossed the dining room, David felt all eyes in the room on him. Only the sound of an occasional fork lightly brushing against a plate broke the silence.

"Roast beef today," Bob said, delaying the talking an instant more. He speared a piece and put it on David's plate.

David looked at the slice of meat with detached wonder. A wave of revulsion passed over him. The color of the meat was the same as the color of Sandy's arms.

Bob noted the change of expression. "What's the matter? Meat not well done enough for you?"

David nodded. He couldn't possibly know. "How can you people eat meat that's oozing blood?" Once again the mixed conflicting images filled his mind.

Around them people had started to converse once more in hushed, tentative tones, as if sensing there wasn't going to be any announcement.

From behind a full mouthful, Bob broke through with a grin. "Only way to eat roast beef," he said. "Rare, rare, rare."

He turned to Ricky, who was sitting on his left. "You know how we cook roast beef here?" he asked the girl.

Ricky shook her head.

"We take a cow," Bob explained, "and walk it by the oven just once."

"Aren't you going to eat, David?" Tom asked with some concern.

David pushed the meat around on the plate, a thin layer of juices easing out toward the edges. The corner of his mouth twitched involuntarily and he shrugged.

"Not hungry, I guess."

Tom liberated the slice of meat from David's plate. "Well, I certainly am." He leaned over and whispered into David's ear: "Hey—wallowing won't do anything, okay?"

David looked up, turned to him and slowly nodded. "No. It won't." He rubbed his hands together and turned to Bob. "How was the skiing today?"

Bob smiled sadly. "The best, David. The absolute best."

David absorbed the answer and then said softly: "Well, I don't get out much anymore." Immediately he regretted the words and tone and moved to apologize. "This is still your vacation and I'm not going to mess it up for you. I'm sorry. I'll be reasonably pleasant or split. I promise."

"It's all right, David," Bob said, not knowing what else to say.

"Thanks. But it isn't."

"How is she?"

Tom picked it up. "Her skin disease—the exfoliative dermatitis—is still spreading. The doctors think it'll be another couple of days." He would talk with Bob later, if David would allow it. Nothing else had to be discussed in public. No one in the house had to know about the session.

David felt hands massaging the back of his neck. It wasn't until he felt the fingers working the knotted muscles that he realized how tense he really was. He let his head roll back as the soothing fingers dug deeper and deeper into his skin, pinching the muscles and breaking up the spasms.

When the motion stopped, David turned around.

"Hey—!" he said to the girl with the short blond hair who was smiling at him. Her eyes were light blue and warm and familiar and they met his. She stretched her hands out against each other to rest her fingers. The knuckles cracked audibly.

"Thanks, Audra. How are you?"

"You needed that," she said.

"That's the understatement of the millennium."

She winked at him. "More after dinner. I promise."

He smiled. "Thanks."

Bob, from the head of the table, noted the interplay but said nothing.

"When did you get here?" David asked her.

"This afternoon." There was an awkward pause. "I heard. I'm sorry."

"Thanks."

She smiled at him. "See you after, okay?"

He watched her go into the living room. "Yeah."

Dessert was baked Alaska. A huge mound of iced cake was brought in on a tray. The serving platter was placed on the head table and all the members gathered around Bob as he cut through.

The cake was gone in thirty minutes, with even dieters coming back for seconds and thirds. The best dessert of the winter was not the time to start counting calories. And after all, you could always take an extra run tomorrow and burn them off.

As the members finished their dinner they filed into the living rooms for Ping-Pong, chess, lounging, and sleeping. Very few traded words with David as they passed his chair. Not even Stan. But that was understandable. They were embarrassed and didn't know what to say.

When the dishes were cleared away, Tom leaned in to David. "Care for a walk?" he asked.

David stood waiting for Tom on the kitchen stairs.

The night was cold, although not excessively so, and he was able to go bareheaded. There was a slight haze in the air that indicated the possibility of snow—or dreaded rain—the next day, and a silvery mist surrounded the moon. Only a few stars were visible as the swirling clouds slowly drifted across the sky.

David stared at the outline of the Wallford house, mesmerized, almost possessed by it. Although he admitted to himself he almost felt neutral about it by now. Resigned. The hate had passed. At least for the moment.

If only he knew what was going on.

Almost as if on cue, the screen door banged open and Tom walked out.

"Hey—warm!" he said.

"Yeah."

"Didn't need the sweater after all. Ah, well. After a half hour out here I'll be glad I have it with me." He danced down the steps. "Where shall we go?"

David shrugged.

"I mean, toward the house, or away," Tom said pointedly.

"It's only a house," David said flatly.

"And remember that, will you?"

"That I'll remember," he answered. "What's inside, though . . ." He trailed off, in no mood to rehash.

"David, the house may have been the catalyst, but it's still Sandy herself."

David looked at Tom and thought the psychiatrist suddenly looked much older and wiser.

"Yeah," he said, not fully convinced.

"Come on," Tom said, and started down the driveway, already three steps ahead of David, who was forced to jog to catch up with him.

They turned left at Route 93 and walked away from the house, briskly toward town. Owlsfane was closed tightly. The gas station was dark, with a silent pickup truck nosed toward the garage doors. The post office was decorated with a lonely Christmas wreath and tired hanging tinsel. Josiah Stoneham's general store was dark, with a "Be Back at 7:30" clock affixed to the door. That was the center of town.

It wasn't until they crossed the truss bridge that Tom let himself get into it.

"I'm sorry that I haven't talked to you before this," he said.

"I understand," David said.

"I think the session was almost as traumatic for us as it was for Sandy. Perhaps more so, because she doesn't remember anything from it."

"I'm probably going to sound like a naive nerd for saying this, but here goes anyway." David paused. "The mind is incredible, isn't it?" *Naive nerd,* he thought glumly. Well, Sandy said he was good at alliteration.

"It is," Tom answered soberly. "And when we finally find what makes the whole thing tick, it will make all other contributions in all other areas of science, medicine, and the humanities miniscule by comparison."

They walked in silence for a moment, single file, as a line of cars shot past them on the two-lane highway. The taillights disappeared over a hill, the road was once again becoming dark. Tom flipped on a flashlight he was carrying. They were out of range of the Owlsfane streetlamps.

"What was the voice, Tom?" David asked. His own voice sounded young, innocent.

Tom shook his head. The movement was barely discernible to David, who was walking beside him. "I can't say for certain. Not yet. But I would still think not Suzanne," Tom answered. "If that's where you were headed."

"Then what?"

"She may have regressed herself back to the period in her life where there was the greatest trauma and she was reacting to it. I once had a patient in hypnotherapy who took himself back in time to a heart attack that almost killed him. And relived the experience right in my office."

"What happened?"

"I pulled him back before he managed to kill himself. Which he obviously wanted to do. But believe me when I say I was in trouble for a few minutes there."

David whistled. "I can imagine."

"I mention this," Tom said, "because there is a pattern of self-destruction in Sandy."

David looked questioning. "You think she wants to kill herself?"

"I don't, no. But there is a consistency to her dreams, her visions, her recalls. She's drawn to scenes of self-destruction. Really, she creates them for herself. She has an intense curiosity about death.

"And look at the disease she's manufactured," he went on. "Remember the dreams she had about the burning of her skin. Now there's the exfoliative dermatitis where the skin is peeling off."

David exhaled sharply as Tom continued.

"I spoke with Spinner this afternoon. We believe there's a good possibility there's a psychological basis to the disease, although it's not a certainty. It's good, because we can probably rule out one of the more ominous diseases like leukemia or hypoproteinemia and everything else."

"Why would she be self-destructive, Tom?"

"Perhaps she's harboring unconscious guilt. Of major proportions. Which seems to revolve around her parents. Perhaps she was powerless to save her mother from drowning and now she's punishing herself. The death of her father ties in, although I don't know where as yet."

"What was she saying?" David asked, " 'Fight him, don't damn yourself, the truck'—" He stopped and looked at Tom blankly. "What does all that mean?"

Tom shook his head. "Right now, I just don't know."

"What do you have to do?"

"Continue."

"No—."

"She's not going to cure herself; you'll agree with that."

"Yes."

They walked in silence for a few moments. David kicked up a spray of snow with his boots and watched the flakes bunch up on the tops of his shoes. He tried to walk stiff-legged to keep as much snow on as possible, but he very quickly tired of the game.

"I would like to regress her in time."

David nodded. "Where are you going to take her back to?"

Tom thought for a moment. "I think the first real trauma in Sandy's life was her mother's drowning. She dreamed it, remember? And the dream itself felt familiar. Anything else could have followed from there."

"Yes," David agreed.

"David, I think there are patterns emerging and things will all fall into place, believe me." He had an idea of where to begin, but that was not something he would share with David.

"Can I sit through tomorrow's session?" David asked.

Tom hesitated. He didn't want him to. He had no idea what he would discover the next day, but he needed to keep Sandy as calm as possible, and if having David there helped in any way . . ."

"You won't say anything during the therapy?"

"Nothing," David promised.

"No matter what?"

There was a beat of hesitation. "Promise."

Tom squared his jaw and nodded. "Okay."

"Shall we go back?" David offered. "I didn't bring an extra sweater, and it's getting a bit chilly out here."

"Let's," Tom said, and did an about-face.

They started to walk into the wind and the going was less pleasant. The temperature was dropping. For the others, there would be snow.

They had progressed about a mile down the road, almost as far as the second truss bridge. Nearby they heard the rush of the icy waters, a hollow, lonely roar, the only sound in the cold, silent Vermont night.

CHAPTER XXVIII

David felt frightened and alone. He needed to hold someone. And she was there.

They had come back from the walk to a buzz of excitement in the house. The revised weather forecast had come through, and indeed it was going to be snow all the way. Another snowfall on top of the one before Christmas! That was something almost unheard of during the usually snow-sparse holiday week. The members were heading upstairs early so they could get an early start for the mountain in the morning.

Tom started up the stairs to join them. Sandy was exhausting him. David came in from the hallway and lightly touched his arm as he rounded the first landing.

"Tom, I didn't say it back there, but I just want you to know I'm sorry."

The psychiatrist looked into David's eyes. "For what? What are you talking about?"

"Getting you into this on your vacation."

"Will you knock that off, David," he said with a tinge of annoyance. But he wasn't annoyed. He wanted to help the girl.

"I owe you," David said pointedly. "I don't know what I'll ever be able to do to repay."

A warm smile broke on Tom's face. "David, we'll think of something, okay? But for now, forget it. I should be thanking you. This may be one for the journals, wouldn't you think?"

David nodded grimly. "Yeah. I would think."

Tom gently released David's hold on his arm. "Get some sleep, will you. She's going to need both of us alert and awake. There's no predicting what's going to happen tomorrow."

"I'll be up in a few minutes."

"See you in the morning," Tom said, and turned up the stairs.

"Yeah. Good night."

David wandered into the empty living room. He was not ready to go to sleep. He tried to stir up the cold fire but was not successful and gave up. He put a Paul Simon album on the stereo, turned the volume down so he wouldn't disturb the others, put his feet up on the coffee table, and slouched down into the warm softness of the old couch. A throw pillow propped up his arm.

He concentrated on his breathing. His stomach, rising and falling rhythmically, held him in mindless fascination. Then he looked at his arms, skin clear and pale, and thought of Sandy's. He shuddered and tried to erase the sight.

Fingers were playing on his hair. The touch was familiar. He twisted his head around and looked behind him. Audra smiled down at him then knelt next to his reclining figure.

"How are you?" she whispered into his ear.

"Frightened," he answered softly.

"Want company?"

Without hesitation David answered her. "Yes."

She sat down on the couch next to him, her legs tucked underneath her. Her head rested on the couch close to his.

"How is she?"

David continued to stare into the fire and didn't look at her. "That's a hard question."

Audra nodded silently. "But she'll be all right?"

"Yes. She'll be all right." David felt his answer lacked conviction.

"Good," she said anyway.

They were silent for several moments until David asked, "Aren't you going up to sleep?"

"Aren't you?"

"Soon. But I don't have to get up and ski tomorrow."

"I'm not that tired," she said. "I met some friends on the mountain and spent half the day in the lodge." She paused and smoothed his hair across his head. David didn't move. Her touch felt good. As if sensing his pleasure, she continued.

"Does Sandy know I still have the hots for you?"

"She knows about us," David said.

"I hope you didn't supply her with any graphic details." Audra smiled.

"No."

"I won't either. Once I get to meet the competition."

"That's good to hear. I had hoped you wouldn't. I didn't want to give up coming here after we broke up, and I know you didn't want to either. Peaceful coexistence is good. I'm glad we can do it."

She let her hands twirl around his ear. There was excitement in his body and he didn't turn her off.

He knew that she still more than liked him, and one of them was probably wrong for coming back to the house where they had had such a marvelous season past. But both liked the place and the people in it and felt they could do it. He had called her after Thanksgiving and told her he would be sending Bob the membership dues. And he had told her about Sandy.

It had just not worked for him. It had gone so far and would go no farther.

She had been a new member the previous year. It

started when he offered her a ride to the mountain after
her car refused to start one sub-zero morning. They
skied together and went dancing that night. They spent
the week together, the rest of the season, and saw each
other in the city as well.

It was all okay, but that was all. For David there
was a spark missing. He couldn't define what, just that
there was something lacking between them that time
would never bring. He knew it; she did not. He felt it
instinctively, kept it to himself, hoping, and then finally
had to voice it.

He had tried to make it work, knew how much she
liked him, and very honestly tried to come up to her
level. But it couldn't be forced. So in the late spring
he had called it off.

They remained friends and saw each other casually
throughout the summer. Audra had not really believed
it was over until Sandy happened. She had tried to get
him back, but knew it would be an uphill, if not impossible, struggle once she saw the glow that Sandy's
presence brought to him.

"So she knows about us," Audra said now.

"No reason to keep it a secret."

"No," she agreed.

"Enough people knew. Someone was bound to say
something."

"You really thought I was going to be catty, right?"

David tried to detect sarcasm or venom in her voice,
but there was none. He knew she would do nothing to
hurt him.

"I never thought that at all," he said honestly.

"Liar," she smiled.

He shrugged. "I had hoped you thought more of me
than that."

Her face clouded. "You know I do," she said softly,
and trailed her fingers down the back of his neck. The
fine hairs tingled. Her touch traveled the length of his
body and centered in his groin. She knew how to get to

him. A fleeting sensation of guilt emerged from the grottoes of his mind, but innocent of wrongdoing, he suppressed it. For some strange reason he realized he should check in with the office and see how next week's issue was progressing.

"I've missed you, David," she said, and there was sincerity to her voice.

"Audra, please don't," he said. "Not now."

"When, then?"

David immediately regretted what he had said. He knew the words came out in innocence but was ashamed at how they could have been interpreted. He took her hand from his neck and put her fingers to his lips. He kissed them.

"Please," he said. "We talked last year."

"*You* talked last year. I listened."

He turned from her. "I shouldn't have come up here. I suspected it wouldn't work, but I wanted it to."

"Stop that," she said, and paused before slowly continuing. "I want it to work too. I also wanted you to see me again as we were when it started. That was stupid. I should have known better. I'll leave. I'm the newcomer. You've been the member for five years."

"You don't have to."

"I know I don't have to. I just will. Okay?"

"No. It's not okay. Okay?"

"We'll see," she said offhandedly, and then added, "You've got to admit one thing."

"What?"

"I haven't made any scene up here. Like throwing my arms around you and dragging you bodily to the bedrooms."

"That was good of you."

"I'll probably even like Sandy, which from the woman scorned is a big admission. I'd probably even give her painkiller before I scratched her eyes out."

"Please don't do this to either of us."

Audra leaned her head on the back of the couch and

stared wistfully at the ceiling, letting her eyes follow the plaster cracks and jagged paint chips.

"I remember one thing you said to me. It was during one of our heavier moments."

David wanted to go upstairs and not listen to what she would say. He was afraid it might give rebirth to memories he wanted to remain dormant. But something stopped him from moving, and he knew it was the need to be next to her.

"We were talking about love. No, that wasn't exactly right. I was talking about love. You were pretending to pay attention. I had said something idiotic about thinking that I loved you."

David didn't answer. No matter what he said, it would have been wrong.

"You then said you didn't even know if you knew what love really was. Or if you had the capacity to love."

"I remember," David said softly.

"You were absolutely convinced you'd never get married. Hell, I would have asked you right then and there if I wasn't so certain you'd say no."

"I would have."

"I knew you would have. And I knew before you told me too." Her eyes were moist. "A lot of things said between two people are never said at all. They're felt. Through movement. Gestures. Expressions."

She once again placed her hand on his neck. He made no movement to take it away.

"I wonder," Audra said wistfully, "if it was I who opened you up and gave you that capacity to love. And then Sandy wandered along and benefited from my hard work."

"Sandy didn't wander along. I went after her."

He remembered what a struggle *that* had been.

"The mechanics don't matter. Am I far from the truth?"

"I don't think I'd tell you either way."

"No. I don't suppose you would."

Yet he wondered. The more he had gotten to know Sandy and understand her past (Jesus! only a fraction of her past), the more he realized they were two people alike. Neither had loved before the other. At least not a strong "this is it, the rest of my life" kind of love.

He had drifted in and out of relationships; afraid to commit himself, perhaps subconsciously fearful of love and what came with it. Perhaps there was a grain of truth to what Audra was saying. But perhaps it wasn't she who had kindled the feeling. Perhaps it was Sandy. And perhaps now something beyond their control was going to pull her away.

"We're all so very fragile," he said to Audra.

"What?" His comment lacked definition. She knew she was fragile. The proper words from him would send her reeling.

"I need you right now, Audra. Perhaps as much as you need me. But in a different way." He felt his voice crack, and he ran the risk of breaking in front of her. But he didn't care. Right now he was almost as vulnerable as his fiancée lying in the hospital, and he didn't care who knew it.

"Please hold me, Audra," he said gently. "I'm not going to give you what you want, but if your feelings for me are as you say, you'll hold me. Right now I need to know someone cares about me."

Audra put her arms around David and pulled him to her.

He shifted on the couch and buried his head in her chest. She softly patted his head and looked off into the empty room. In that one moment she knew that no matter what, she would never win David back again.

Yet her memories were so firm and full. She didn't pull away when she felt him start to cry. Rather, she snuggled him and rocked him softly in place.

"Who loves ya, baby?" she whispered.

* * *

It probably will be one for the journals, Tom thought grimly as he prepared himself for bed. He hated to go into a case thinking it would be special enough for an article; he preferred to concentrate on the patient and leave his own literary and professional ego completely aside. He was always fearful of manipulating a case toward the sensational; but in the case of Sandy he didn't even know if he could manipulate it away from the extraordinary.

He pulled up at the end of the bathroom line, his towel slung over his shoulder, toothpaste, brush, and soap clutched in his hand. He knew that he mustn't trust his memory. He had to start keeping accurate diary notes and tapes of the sessions.

Gail emerged from the corner bathroom drying her hair from shower.

"You're back," she said to Tom.

"We walked up the road about a mile. Talked. Analyzed. Thought."

Gail knew her husband like an open book. "This case has got you, hasn't it?" she asked.

"It has," Tom admitted. "Hook, line and thinker."

Gail shuddered. "It's difficult to think of Sandy as a case, you know?"

"I know," Tom agreed. "But believe me, it's a beaut."

"I don't want you to tell me about it," Gail said pointedly. While he was always open and shared most of his cases with her, she didn't know any of his patients. Knowing Sandy made it all different, and he was grateful she had respected his work and the oath of patient confidentiality enough to voice it first.

"Thanks," he said simply.

"Just tell me how she is."

"Not good," Tom said softly, voicing the thought for the first time. "The skin disease is debilitating. She's running a fever. She has no appetite. It's also running her down mentally."

"I'm sure," Gail said soberly.

"It's a constant, visual reminder of her problem. I can only be with her several hours a day. She's got herself for twenty-four." Tom pursed his lips. "Her unconscious defenses are working to keep me out."

"You've had resistance before."

He nodded shortly. "I don't think she's going to respond easily to my posthypnotic suggestions. It's going to be rough."

"Don't say that."

"I shouldn't. I'm a better doctor than that." He quickly held up his hand. "No need to comment or reaffirm. Just that today I felt more than once that I might be in trouble."

Gail kissed him on the lips. "I'm here."

"I know."

One thing Gail had never done in their marriage was mutter empty words to her husband. She cringed when she heard other doctors' wives casually say "I'm sure your patient will be all right" or "I'm sure you'll make them better." To her those words were a dismissal, revealing a lack of interest in his work, when what she wanted to lend was needed support. If she could trivialize her thoughts down to a "Don't worry, you're a good doctor," she feared that she might be able to trivialize their marriage as well.

"Don't forget," she added. "You have a daughter who has forgotten what her father looks like."

"I've been bad," Tom agreed.

"Her ski school classes end tomorrow. She's been looking forward to skiing the rest of the week with you."

"Why? By now she probably skis better than I do."

Gail placed her fingers across Tom's lips to silence him. "Don't duck it," she said knowingly.

"I'll talk to her," Tom said. "I think she can understand that I've had to be busy with Sandy. She had a bit of a nightmare the other night too."

"More than a bit," Gail said, the image of her daughter thrashing and screaming on the couch crisp in her mind.

"She'll be okay," Tom said. "She's not been bothered since. By now she's probably forgotten about it." There had been no recurrence of the bad dream—a good sign.

Gail nodded. "Probably."

"I might even combine our talk with a little lecture on professional responsibility. Good idea, wouldn't you agree?"

"Anything. Just as long as it's not about the facts of life." Gail pretended to shake. "I don't think I could handle my baby's knowing just yet."

Tom's smile was broad. "You can stop shaking. She already knows."

"You're kidding. Thank God. I can grow old in peace." She clutched her hands to her chest. Then she furrowed her brow. "How come she never mentioned it? Or rather, how come *you* never mentioned it?"

Tom saw his "out" as a door behind him opened. "Hey, an available john."

Ricky, in a long dressing gown swept past them and waved good night.

Gail looked after her escaping husband. "Get all the sleep you can up here," she said jokingly. "Back home, it's the couch."

"See you in the morning," Tom chirped cheerfully, and then called back to her from behind a half-open door. "Hey, I was lying."

The towel she threw at him bounced off the closing bathroom door. As she bent to retrieve it she heard the metallic snapping of the lock in place and she sensed the satisfied grin from the other side of the door.

"Bastard," she muttered.

Tom opened the bathroom door. "Who are you calling a bastard?"

"You, you bastard," Gail answered with a nod. "Who else is here?"

"Get in here and tell me to my face."

He grabbed her arm and pulled her into the bathroom, locking the door behind him.

"I'll say one thing about the Kanon bathrooms," Tom said when he and his wife were alone.

"What's that?"

"They've seen more action than Iwo Jima."

He took her to him, pulled her once more into the shower, and made love to her under the rushing water.

The voice, whispering in Judy's ear, woke her from sleep. It was an anxious voice, desperate, plaintive.

Get away from this place before he gets you too.

The words were muttered hurriedly, urgently.

Judy's eyes came open. She looked up, expecting to see someone standing by her bed. Perhaps her mother, gently prodding her from sleep, stroking her hair.

No one.

The room was sleeping soundly around her. But she had heard the woman's voice and she had woken up. She frowned. It was dark, the middle of the night. Why would she be woken up?

And there wasn't anyone there. It had been a dream.

She strained to try to remember what had preceded the voice but came up empty. She shrugged. Back to sleep again. Maybe she would shake free the dream and find out what the warning words meant.

CHAPTER XXIX

Snow was falling silently on a windless, sunless day. Sky and land were indistinguishable. Overcast clouds hung low to the ground, obliterating the horizon; a gray mass of quiet desolation. Tiny flakes fell rapidly, quickly accumulating in tightly packed layers. Cars sported headlights and streetlamps were turned on to give false daylight to the twilighted noon. Beyond the parking lot, children were rolling in the fresh-fallen snow, oblivious of all else, the flakes too dry and fine to make an effective weapon when balled, disintegrating to powder at the touch.

Sandy stood by the window of the hospital room peering out. The snow was comforting. There was safety in the forced isolation of the storm. The involuntary solitude was welcome. She wanted the wind to pick up so the snow could pound against the window with driven fury, imprisoning her for all time in the womblike tomb she had created for herself.

The lights in the room were turned off and it was dark. Her eyes were adjusted. She wanted it that way. An opened paperback, spine up, pages down, sat expectantly on an orange-colored visitor's chair, where Sandy had been sitting, reading. Trying to read, rather.

Her attention was scattered, her mind elsewhere. *And she wondered where the hell it indeed was.*

She couldn't concentrate on the Agatha Christie. Whole pages slipped by and she would not remember what she had read. She threw the book down in frustration and went aimlessly fidgeting to the window. She was just killing time. No thought was required to stare out at the falling snow.

It was snowing the first night she had gone into the Wallford House . . .

. . . so long ago.

Her legs and arms were swathed in plastic wrap so the medicated gel could work more effectively. For half a day they wrapped her skin, and still there was no improvement.

If anything, it was getting worse, spreading. When she had awakened that morning she noticed that overnight, skin had scaled from her upper arms and stomach. The medication was not working.

She had looked at her skin with bemused detachment. As if it weren't hers; as if it weren't there. It was incomprehensible. Like trying to comprehend infinity, or the tragic death of a baby. But it no longer frightened her, no longer shocked. She was resigned to it, she felt, in the same detached sort of way. It was spreading—ho hum.

The first rush of fear was over. The unknown was more terrifying. Once the first wave of skin had scaled from her body and then the second, it was now more or less accepted. She was giving up and would let what would be, be.

She could not understand her feelings. There was an indefinable, unbelievable sensation of relief. But did the relief come from the hope it would all soon be over, or from the resignation that it would not?

But damn it! She didn't want to give up.

She shivered and stared desolately out of the window, at one with the grayness of the day. She followed the paths of random snowflakes, losing them in the morass of the others as they piled anonymously on the white ground.

The door to her room creaked slowly open and a zebra plant was thrust through. A voice followed. Tom's.

"Are you decent?"

Sandy turned to see the white-veined plant bursting with life and fullness and touched her own Saran Wrapped legs. "I'm gift-wrapped," she said.

Tom entered, shutting the door behind him. His coat was wet from the melting snow and he was shaking his hair dry.

"Hi."

"Hi."

"For you." The way he held the plant reminded her of a peace offering.

"It's lovely," she said. "Please put it over there."

Tom moved the water pitcher and a cardboard box of hospital tissues and set the plant on the night table next to the bed.

"You have to water these little sons of bitches every twenty minutes, I think. Otherwise their leaves droop and—" He broke off.

"Fall off?" Sandy finished.

"Yeah," Tom said with a sheepish grin. "Crummy gift, huh?"

"Actually, no," Sandy said with a sad, introspective smile. "Next you can get me a parakeet and we can both molt together. Or better yet, a mackerel," she added ruefully, running a hand lightly over her fishlike skin.

"That's our Sandy," Tom said with a broad grin.

Sandy studied her scaling arms for a moment and then sadly said, "No, Tom. This is not our Sandy."

"Hey," Tom said with cheer. "I give up a day of skiing and you're going to be self-pitying?"

"I'm sorry. I'm doing that too much. But I just

don't feel overly jovial." Then, as if dismissing the thought, she asked, "Where's David?"

"I sent him to the mountain. I think he's worse than you are."

"Oh?" she asked. "Is his skin falling off too?" She pursed her lips apologetically. "I'm sorry," she added quickly.

"It's all right."

"No. It isn't." Then she asked. "Tom, do all your patients hate themselves as much as I do?"

Tom furrowed his brows. "What do you mean?"

"I mean I must hate myself really bad to be doing this, don't you think?"

"What?" He tried for confusion.

"I know it's not an allergic reaction to a drug. It's me."

"No," he said with assurance, ignoring her second comment. "I most definitely do not think you hate yourself."

"Even deep down in my unconscious. Under brain matter that I don't even know is there. There must be the most concentrated pocket of little hate cells swimming murkily and devilishly sending commands to my skin to drop off."

"You don't believe that, Sandy."

"Then tell me what to believe." There was no more sarcasm or humor in her voice and her eyes were frightened. "The dreams have stopped, Tom, but when does this whole nightmare end? I don't think I can take much more of it."

"Soon," he said in a low, comforting voice.

"But the hypnotism failed, and wrapping me in Baggies doesn't seem to be doing the trick either."

"The hypnotism didn't fail, Sandy."

Sandy silently held out her arms.

"It was just one session," Tom continued patiently. "There will be more sessions. Exploratory sessions, where we try to bring to the surface what's troubling you so. And once we know, then we can go back in there and try to rectify the problem."

Her question came coldly; was cold: "What if I'm dead by then, Tom?"

"What?" His face rose in surprise and confusion.

"Exfoliative dermatitis has a thirty-percent mortality rate. I checked a book. Plus possibility of infection. Pneumonia." She paused. "Suzanne had pneumonia, you know."

Tom took her hands and looked deeply into her eyes. "We're going to lick this, believe me. You think you're the only person around who has repressed emotions?"

"No. I think I'm the only person around who has psychosomatically produced scaling skin and has seen dead people who weren't there." Her lips curled into a wry grin. "That was a laugh-line, Tom. Why aren't you laughing?"

"Sandy, fighting me is not going to help."

She broke free from him and walked to the window. She held her arms up and fought the nausea that threatened.

"You know what I've been thinking all day?" she asked.

"What?"

"Now this is really sick. Even you will have to admit it."

"Tell me," Tom said softly. He took a step toward her. Both were framed in the reflective window as though in a mirror. He brushed the hair back from over her eyes where it had fallen and slipped a hand around her waist. She leaned against him.

"I was thinking about dying."

"We've been through that, Sandy."

"No. Not in relation to the dreams of my having died. Correction: of my symbolically having died. Nothing like that. It was more general. About people. Anyone. That I'm now what? Twenty-two?"

"Go on," Tom said uncertainly.

"If I didn't die, I'd have, say, another forty or fifty years ahead of me. Maybe a little more." She shrugged. "So I asked myself, What's forty or fifty years when stacked against eternity? If I died tomorrow, so what? It really doesn't seem to matter much, does it?"

Tom nodded. "I understand."

"Is that sick?" she asked.

"No. I've heard it before. Mostly from patients in acute, chronic pain. Back pain. Pain from sciatic nerves." He hesitated, but continued anyway. "And from others who couldn't cope. Every one of them looking toward death as a release."

"There's no pain in death."

"Nor responsibility."

"No."

"Yet every one of them," Tom continued, "held on to life nonetheless. Every one fought to try to ease the pain and try to go on with a normal life any way they could." He held her at arm's length and looked at her. "I didn't lose one to suicide," he said pointedly.

"Oh, not to worry about me." She held up her hands. "Promise."

"Good."

"I'm still too frightened about the possibility in my dream to do anything like that."

"Good," he repeated, and then, holding her with his eyes, added sincerely. "Just to finish, Sandy. Each one of those people who wished for death held on to truly wonderful moments in their lives and the lives of their families that made those fifty or sixty or even five years terrific years and worth cherishing. And you can't balance that against an eternity of the unknown."

"Family," she muttered derisively. "How long is David going to hang around with *this?*" She turned her arms in front of her. In the distorted reflection of the window, the scales appeared as a myriad of tiny bumps on her body.

"If you don't withdraw and drive him away, he'll be there," Tom said. "Believe me."

"You've been asking me to believe a lot, and all I've got to show for it is . . ." She kicked up a leg and trailed off.

"Well, that's what we're here to talk about. The next hypnosis session."

"Going for strike two?" She turned to face him. "I'm sorry. You don't need this from me."

"I really don't." His smile was genuine and his eyes warm and comforting. "The more positive attitude you show on any level, conscious or unconscious, will help me and help yourself."

"I know. You got me. All that crap about dying?"

"Yes?"

"It's bullshit. I don't want to. I want to get the hell out of here with all of my skin cells, get to a warm climate, and marry that son of a bitch who got me into this mess in the first place. Now, what about the next session?"

"I want to take you back in time."

"Age regression?" She looked skeptical. "You mean like Audrey Rose?"

"Take you back in time and try to reconstruct what you saw and experienced. From your mother's death, to your father's death and whatever else we discover. It's all in there."

"Audrey Rose didn't have a very happy ending."

"I have no intention of regressing you to a former life. I even question it being done."

"What happens? Do I start talking like a child?"

"No. I'm not going to put you into that deep a trance." The session of the day before flashed in his mind. The voice she had assumed so intensely unnerved him. Also the fact that she had gotten away from him for a while and was regressing herself. "You'll remember clearly. Sharply. You'll talk in the past tense. 'I saw . . . I did' . . ."

"I died?" She held up her hands in apology and he smiled.

"If I don't get what I want the first time around with you recalling your past experiences, then we can really send you under so you can relive everything. I don't like to do that, because it is sometimes traumatic for the patient, especially when he relives moments of fear or terror."

"And I must have plenty of those," she said with a toneless smile and a circular motion of her left arm.

Tom did not return the smile but said simply, "Yes, Sandy, you must."

"Yeah," she said, and there was a silence.

"Then," Tom continued, "once we have dug up and analyzed the offending matter, I sort of go to work with a little mumbo-jumbo reassurance on the unconscious and try to implant positive suggestions."

"Commandment number eleven? Thou shalt not cause thy skin to scale?"

He smiled. "Something like that."

"Sure," she said. "Anything you want. Let's do it. When?"

"This afternoon."

"You got it," she said, and prayed that the big mouth she always thought she had would open to a past she no longer recalled having lived through.

Two orderlies were quietly posted outside the hospital room. They were instructed to keep the door closed and under no circumstances let curiosity seekers —patients *or* doctors—inside the room.

Tom was nervous, yet did all he could to mask it. He performed hypnotherapy on his patients as a matter of routine. A patient not coming out from under hypnosis was inconceivable—*impossible* by all known standards. A person who has allowed himself to enter a hypnotic state will allow himself to return from it as well, or simply fall asleep and awaken naturally.

Sandy's getting away from him bothered Tom, and at the first sign of any uncontrollable problem he would immediately bring her around. Or if he had to, sedate her.

The venetians were drawn and the low-wattage lamps were lit.

Dr. Spinner sat on the orange chair, a silent observer. David sat next to him on a straight-backed chair. He was perched on the edge, his elbows on his knees, chin cupped in open palms, peering out expectantly through small, intense eyes.

He had spent a few minutes alone with Sandy before the session was to begin.

He had walked in with flowers and a plastered smile frozen on his face.

"You have food between your teeth," she said quietly, trying for a joke.

He crossed the room to her, and fighting the sight of her dry, scalelike skin, encircled her with his arms, the flowers unnoticed in his hands. She melted and cried on his shoulder. A good cry. Tears of built-up frustration, fear, and isolation wet his shoulder.

He patted her back lightly and repeated over and over: "It's going to be all right." The words began to take on a strange sound and lost their meaning, but he kept his voice steady and repeated the now nonsensical syllables.

He broke the embrace and pulled a handkerchief from his pocket and wiped his eyes. His own tears threatened to fall. He realized he was all she had. He shuddered. At a time such as this it must be terrible not to have parents.

Her tears stopped.

"I can be a commercial for color television," she said, and a light, hysterical giggle started to break forth. "My skin is yellow-white and my face is red."

He looked at her.

"I think I've lost my mind," she continued.

"Hey, don't lose it until we've found it, okay?"

"Okay," she said, and the crying stopped.

If the eyes were indeed the mirror to the soul, Sandy looked as if she had lost hers.

They held each other for a long moment, David peripherally receiving and rejecting the scene with Audra. Sandy was the person he wanted, this girl with the multicolored scaling skin he held in his arms.

He suddenly started to laugh and his face grew red. Sandy looked at him queerly, wanting to hear what was so funny, but every time David opened his mouth to share the thought, he choked with laughter and swallowed the words. The laughter, with its base in tragedy, fed on itself and became contagious in the tension of the hospital room. Sandy smiled as well and then started to laugh.

David's shoulders bounced up and down, and he had to hold his stomach with his left hand it hurt so. He doubled over, his hands dropped to his knees and then he straightened up.

"What's new?" he was finally able to sputter, laughing at the sad absurdity of the question. He thought of the cartoon of two men with long, flowing beards stranded on a desert island with the same caption.

Sandy found the sad humor in his question and joined him in full-blown laughter. They were roaring as Tom entered the room.

Now he was repeating his instructions to her and David was pulled back.

". . . And when I count to three, you will awaken. Do you understand?"

"Yes."

"Good." He paused before continuing. "Now, Sandy, we are going to look back into your past. To a portion of your life long ago. We are going back in your life to when you were twelve. Think back, Sandy. Think back to when you were twelve. Do you remember being twelve, Sandy?"

Mixed memories cascaded through her mind as she sought out that section of her brain marked Childhood.

"When you were twelve, Sandy . . ." Tom's soft, mellifluent voice purred.

David watched him with fascination. Tom could be a stage actor, he thought, the way he turned his voice on and off.

A smile gingerly played across Sandy's face as within her mind the circuits locked into place and she saw herself first hazily and then clearly as a girl of twelve. She folded her hands in front of her and tilted her head sideways as pleasant recall flowed over her.

"Do you remember being twelve?" Tom asked.

"Yes."

"Tell me what you see."

Her smile widened. "A house at the beach. We spent our summers at the beach since I was very young. It was a small house. Wood. There were two rooms. A kitchen and a bedroom. We all slept in one bedroom. My mother. My father. Me."

Her eyelids fluttered as she went deeper into herself. David relaxed. The session was starting off well.

"Tell me about the beach, Sandy. What did you like about it?"

Tom had a pad at the ready, prepared to take shorthand notes of her recall. The tape machine was recording.

"I liked playing in the sand and going in the water with my father and eating ice cream and hot dogs from the stand and . . ."

As she continued, David noted the sound of pure joy in her voice. The voice was grown-up Sandy, the recalls a child's memories. She seemed more at peace in this one moment than over the last several horrendous days.

". . . we saw boats in the water and people swimming. . . ."

"Now, Sandy," Tom coaxed gently. He spoke slowly, cautiously. He was about to ask her to enter areas he knew would cause trauma. "I want you to remember something else for me."

"What?"

"I want you to remember the day your mother drowned."

There was a visible change in the girl as the color drained from her face. A small tic developed at the corner of her mouth and her closed eyelids began to twitch.

"No."

"The day your mother drowned, Sandy. Tell me about it. What was it like? What did you do that morning? Do you remember?"

A tension filled the small room, and David felt his stomach do flip-flops. He swallowed and fought a tightness in his throat. Spinner stole a glance at him and then turned his attention back to Sandy.

When she spoke, her voice was different. It was heavier, throatier, and came uncertainly, in spurts, as the day unfolded before her closed eyes.

"We got up as always," she began. Her head was thrown back, her slender neck elongated, and she seemed to be searching the air. "It was early morning . . . we had breakfast outside. We talked about going to the movies that night. I remember that." Her voice began to quiver and she swallowed continuously. "We never went to the movies, though."

"Tell me about the drowning, Sandy."

"I was playing on the beach. Building sand castles as I always did. The waves would come and knock them down and I would always see how close to the edge of the water I could build them and not have them destroyed."

David relived the moment with her. He saw the image of a girl playing in the sand. It was not Sandy. Just a girl. Any girl. A faceless girl sitting with a play pail and shovel and a lopsided sand castle, patting sand in place, shoring walls, constructing fragile buttresses. Water cascaded toward her as the waves lapped at the sand to their deaths, soaking into the beach, creating depressions and gullies and rivulets. The girl's foot might have been in the soft, wet sand. And her hands, as she scooped the sand to provide building material for the castle.

With pain on her face Sandy swayed from side to side. They trained their eyes on her and knew she was seeing the death of her mother.

"Arms waving . . . like two sticks far out in the water. . . At first I didn't see . . ."

Her voice tightened; she clenched her fists in helplessness.

"I didn't understand . . . the faint call for help. . . . I heard her. . . . I continued playing like I didn't hear. . . . Then my father running out to her, stepping on my sand castle, breaking it. . . . I watched him run out to her . . . watched the arms wave and—"

She started to cry as the impact of the drowning hit her. It was difficult to watch her and not be moved. David choked and held back his own tears. A lonely chill coursed the length of his spine. He could not imagine witnessing anything more horrible than what his fiancée was describing.

The skin on the soles of Sandy's feet began to peel free in thin layers. No one noticed.

"I stood up and walked forward. . . . I didn't see the wave coming. . . . From nowhere it seemed . . . it knocked me down, and my head fell into a pool of water. . . . I couldn't see. . . . I couldn't breathe. . . .

The anguish was on her face. Her nostrils flared. Her jaw stiffened. The nervous tic was more pronounced. Her eyes squeezed tightly shut, as if trying to blot out the vision she was forced to see.

"I coughed and tried to breathe. . . . Then I saw them pulling my mother out of the water. They carried her by her arms and legs and placed her on the sand.

They leaned over her. I was so frightened . . . I couldn't move. . . . I sat down and watched them. . . . I started to play with the sand. . . . Someone came to me and held me. . . . She covered my eyes with her arms so I couldn't see. Then I saw my father walking past me . . . walking slowly past me. . . . I could only see his legs, but I knew it was him . . . walking slowly past me. . . ."

She broke off as the tears came.

Tom's voice was soft, comforting. "That's good, Sandy. Real good."

"That's all I remember." She brought her hands to her closed eyes as the tears fought to escape.

"Tell me, Sandy. How did you feel at the time?"

Her mouth started to quiver, but no words came.

"What were you thinking, Sandy?"

"Thinking?" she asked, confused. "I—I watched it happen."

"Did you feel you wanted to help her?" Tom asked gently.

"I—I couldn't," she said. "I heard, but I—I couldn't." A frantic tone started to creep into her voice, almost as if she wanted to say something. She didn't. But Tom was listening. "I couldn't," she repeated. "I didn't know how. I was too late." Then her face went blank, her voice flat. She was stating fact. "My mother drowned. I couldn't help her."

"Good," Tom said. "Now I want you to leave that memory, Sandy. I want you to sleep. But you will still hear my voice. Do you understand?"

"Yes."

"Sleep, Sandy."

There was quiet in the room as Tom gave her a moment to rest. He walked softly across the floor and whispered to David and Dr. Spinner. "She's doing well. Next I want to take her forward in time to the first time she had the dream of her mother's drowning.

David shot him a thumbs up, and Tom crossed back to Sandy, who sat quietly, almost motionless on the edge of the bed. Her face was at peace, muscles quiet, breath regular and even. Her eyes were lightly closed, lids fluttering slightly, and there was no tension in her expression. Her hands were folded at ease in her lap and there was no stiffness to the fingers.

"Sandy," Tom whispered. "Were there times when you dreamed about your mother's drowning?"

He sensed her eyes searching inwardly, looking for the answer to his question.

"Yes," she said. "I dreamed of my mother's drowning."

"Do you have that dream often?"

"Often?"

"Once a year? Once a month? Ten times? Twenty times?"

"No. Not often."

"One time?"

"No. More than one time. A few."

"Good. Let's move to a particular time. A time when you first dreamed of your mother's drowning. A dream you had, Sandy. That's what I want you to remember. Do you understand?"

"My mother's drowning?" came the weak response. There was hesitation in her voice, uncertainty.

"One memory I want you to find for me. One frail moment in your life. You remember it, Sandy. I know you do. Because it was significant. Very significant. One memory. The first time you dreamed about your mother's drowning. Go to it, Sandy. Search for it. Find it for me."

For the first moments she didn't move. It was as if Tom had not spoken to her or she had not heard, or chose to ignore. Then there was a slight tilting of her head, as if the motion would jar free the memory. Her eyes appeared to be at work under the closed lids as she searched inwardly, trying to please the doctor who was asking her the questions.

"The first time you dreamed your mother drowned

. . ." Tom repeated the words in hypnotic monotone, and Sandy struggled within herself to recall.

The scaling continued from the soles of her feet. David noticed, and with an intake of breath pointed it out to Spinner. The doctor acknowledged it with a silent nod of his head. But he would not interrupt Tom.

Suddenly Sandy stiffened. Her back went rigid, her head straight. Her nostrils opened wide and her breathing became sharp.

Tom was right there.

"What do you see, Sandy?"

Her voice was almost triumphant. "My mother drowning . . . in a dream . . . I see it." She started to sway in place. "No . . ." Her breathing came faster, her voice excited, as she relived in her mind the scene of horror she had just articulated to them.

A shadow crossed David's face.

"How old were you, Sandy?"

"Thirteen. I remember."

"Good. Very good. Now tell me what you see."

"My father walking slowly past me. . . . I could only see his legs. . . ."

The words were the same as before, the tone as intense. Tom knew she was there again. He moved in closer to her, his warm breath almost on her face as he pushed to bring her through it and beyond.

"What else did you dream, Sandy? What else did you see? First there was your mother drowning. Then what else? What else happened? What did you see?"

Tom knew where he was going. He hoped for verification of a dream she had had earlier that week. That verification might be the first important step to his understanding.

He pressed. "What else, Sandy? What else do you see in that dream? Remember. It's important."

"I'm trying to remember," she moaned, and then the one word came. "Bicycle . . ."

"What?"

"I was riding a bicycle." The words came faster as she remembered. "My father had bought it for me. It was red . . . bell on handlebars. . . . I dreamed I was riding the bicycle. . . ."

"What about the bicycle? Think. What about the bicycle?"

"I was riding. I was pedaling uphill and I knew I was tired. Exhausted. I couldn't pedal any—"

Her face suddenly changed expression; her eyes struggled against the closed lids and popped open. Her breathing became sharp, intensified. She looked as if she wanted to escape from herself.

"Daddy . . . don't . . . no!"

"Sandy!" Tom ordered.

"No! No!" The sound broke from her in a scream that pierced the room.

"No!"

"Sandy!"

"Daddddeeeee." The voice was mournful. Tears rolled from her eyes and her hands were out in front of her as if begging. "Daddddeeeeee."

"Sandy. You are on the bicycle. Return to the bicycle. Close your eyes and return to the dream of the bicycle."

Her words came out softly. There was fear in her voice. Fear for someone else. Fear for her father. As if she alone were able to see and were desperately trying to convey what she saw.

"Don't damn yourself, Dad-dee."

The voice dropped to a lost, frightened whimper. It was almost like a child speaking—a frightened child faced with something beyond her control. Faced with a vision of unspeakable horror.

The skin on her neck turned yellow and rough. Thickened scales fell onto her nightgown, where they lay. A flush of red stretched toward her breasts, which were hidden by the nightgown.

David turned from the sight. "Dear God," he sighed, and fought the urge to vomit.

"Return to the bicycle, Sandy. Close your eyes and return to the bicycle." Tom's voice droned.

Her expression was one of confusion. Then suddenly her eyelids fluttered and slowly lowered, the shocking interruption of the previous moment suppressed. From her rigid position she slowly slumped in place. Tom caught her to prevent her falling forward. Her breathing eased.

"The bicycle," Tom continued, in metronomic voice. "Return to the dream of the bicycle."

"The bicycle?" The voice was small and lost. Confused. But it was a question that she answered for herself. "I was tired."

She spoke slowly, the voice of a moment before buried within her. But there was a cracking to her speech, an uncertainty, as if the hypnotized girl knew intuitively that the fear and the voice were not within her control and might return at any time. "But then I reached the top of the hill and started down. I was coasting, not pedaling."

Tom breathed in relief. He had her back again. Jesus! What was it she could not escape from, that kept invading her mind and possessing it?

"There was construction," she continued. "A hole in the road. It wasn't deep, but I saw it coming. I tried to turn the handlebars but the bicycle didn't turn."

There was strain and disbelief. Her breathing was shallow. "The wheels didn't respond."

She began to race as her mind recalled the dream events. Tom watched her arms stiffen and try to turn the bicycle. But as in her dream, her arms were frozen in place, unresponsive. Tension lines appeared on her face, and her throat tightened. Her voice quaked. "I knew I was going to fall if I went into the hole, but I couldn't stop myself . . . I couldn't turn. . . ."

Self-destruction, Tom thought.

"Go on," he prodded gently. It was painful, but she had to go through it.

"I was going fast now . . . down the hill . . . I couldn't turn . . . I couldn't stop. . . ."

Like the skiing.

"I knew I was going to hit the hole. . . . It was all so real . . . so vivid. . . . The front wheel entered the hole . . . it skidded out . . . I started to fall—"

She screamed and swooned and threw her arms up protectively to guard her head.

"What happened next, Sandy?" he asked, although he felt he knew. It would be the same as the ski fall. He held her tightly so she would not fall from the bed. "Did you ride your bicycle the next day?"

She nodded her head weakly. It was coming back. "Yes."

"Tell me what you see."

"Construction. A hole in the street."

She had probably known of the construction before; it already had its place in her mind. As with the skiing, there may have been less psychic precognition than wish fulfillment, the unconscious desire to be self-destructive.

"It was like it was in the dream, wasn't it?"

He saw her arms tighten again. She swallowed and bobbed her head up and down.

"Yes."

"You saw the hole. You tried to turn the wheel, but you couldn't?"

"No. I wanted to turn the wheel, but my arms wouldn't listen. I wanted to turn the wheel but I couldn't. The wheel didn't turn."

"And then you fell?"

"I fell on my arm. I broke it."

"It was all like it was in the dream?"

"Yes."

Good, Tom thought. Time to go further.

"I want you to rest, Sandy. To sleep. Nothing can hurt you. Nothing can happen to you. You are safe." He constantly reassured his patients during times of emotional recall and pulled them away when the memories became too painful. Or at least tried.

Tom silently paced the room. His head was tilted upward in thought and analysis. He went to the window, separated the venetian slats, and looked out. The snow was falling heavily, the flakes larger, hitting the windowpanes, warmed from the inside and quietly melting, lost in time and memory; the water droplets that crept slowly downward a short-lived memorial to what was.

He stretched and allowed the built-up tension to flow from his body. He shrugged his shoulders tightly, painfully, bringing his head to his back, to break up the spasm in his neck. He turned to David and the doctor, momentarily masking a look of fascination on his face, and he shook his head. A memory engulfed him. Of the man who had gone back in time to his own heart attack. He silently prayed that nothing similar had happened—*or would happen*—to Sandy.

He questioned whether hypnotherapy was the right approach for this particular patient. He looked at her. Her head was resting in a slightly upraised neutral position on fragile vertebrae, her breath heavy in her hypnotic sleep, and her skin—scalelike yellows and patches of white, with erythema from her neck to her upper body, and over her legs. He was aware of the scaling on the soles of her feet, but it didn't register. He gently pulled apart the nightgown and saw that the redness covered much of her torso, the scaling occurring on her arms, legs, and now her neck.

Only her face remained her own. But for how long? Yet he knew the dangers in the hypnotherapy were balanced by the benefits. He might be able to uncover so much more so much faster than through conventional therapy, and looking at her, he knew he had to move quickly.

The self-destruction. Perhaps she felt she was unable to help her mother and now she was punishing herself. He knew there was more, and it was time to unlock it.

He turned back to her. "Sandy," he said gently. "I want you to remember. There was another time. The *next* time. Another time that you dreamed of your mother's drowning. I want you to go to that time and remember."

She started to recall almost immediately.

"Mother drowning . . . another dream . . ."

"When was this, Sandy? How old were you?" He needed a time reference.

She seemed puzzled at first and then remembered. "Fifteen."

"What happened after you dreamed of the drowning?"

"Dream of glass . . . a window . . . a window in a door . . ."

"A glass door?" Tom offered.

She nodded vigorously. "Something on the floor . . . something slippery. I was walking, carrying something . . . I tripped. . . ."

Her face froze at the memory of the crash through the sliding glass door. The pain was written across her face. She started to pull at her face, as if trying to remove imaginary shards of glass from it.

"I saw myself fall through the door. I screamed and woke up."

"Then what, Sandy?"

She remembered. "It happened."

"Just like in the dream?"

"Just like in the dream." she repeated. She looked confused as if sifting through brain matter to separate dream from reality.

"It all happened, didn't it?" Tom asked again.

"Yes," she said, and shook her head up and down.

"I fell through the glass, just like in the dream. It was three days after the dream. I fell through the glass." She repeated over and over, parrotlike, "I fell through the glass . . . I fell through the glass. . . ." Her voice cracked.

"You will leave this memory, Sandy," Tom ordered. "And you will rest. You will go to a happy time in your life."

A smile broke across her face and she was suddenly oblivious to the painful memories that had held her moments before.

Tom too smiled. The session was going well. It was time to press forward. With an acknowledging nod toward David and Dr. Spinner, he indicated he was on track.

"The next time, Sandy," he said. "Tell me about the next time you dreamed of your mother's death. The next time . . . the next time . . ."

Her breath quickened almost immediately, as if she had expected the question, and her mind at once directed her to time and place.

"I dreamed my mother drowned," she said loudly. "That was the signal. I got the warning signal from her. She came to me to warn me something was going to happen."

Tom reacted. Her last comment was significant. What *warning* signal? He was temporarily thrown. He had been seeing the dreams as self-destructive.

"What do you mean by warning signal?"

"Whenever I have the dream something happens. . . . My mother comes to me to tell me something is going to happen. . . ."

"Why do you think that?"

"I don't know. I—don't know," she floundered. She wanted to answer, but nothing would come.

Something told Tom that this recall would be important.

"You will relax, Sandy," he said in a soft, controlled voice. "There is nothing to fear and nothing will harm you. You will recall a time in your past, that's all. A memory long gone. . . ."

She seemed eager to talk. "It was raining . . . a big storm . . . My father and I were driving up a hill . . . a steep hill. . . ."

"How old were you, Sandy?"

She ignored the question. "The wipers were on high speed . . . going furiously back and forth. . . ."

Tension spread across her body. Lines were in evidence on her face, and she looked as if she had aged years in the seconds since the memory unfolded. As she talked she swallowed and licked her lips. Her nostrils flared and her breath was loud. Her hands were out in front of her as if steering a bicycle—*no*—clutching a steering wheel.

"How old were you, Sandy?"

"We were coming to the top . . . there was a truck in front, around the bend—"

David and Tom glanced at each other. The truck! *There was the truck. There was the truck,* she had said.

They were there!

"What about the truck, Sandy? Tell me about the truck."

"In my dream I saw the truck . . . big as a house. . . ."

Terror crossed her face and her eyes fought to remain closed. Her hands shook as she fiercely held to the imaginary wheel.

"It was in our lane. . . ."

She suddenly screamed, a shrill sound of helplessness and hopelessness. Her face turned beet-red.

"My father swerved—"

She threw herself from the bed to the floor before Tom was able to prevent her fall. David and Spinner were up in a flash rushing to her. "We missed the truck!"

Yes, this was it, Tom thought. If only he could calm her enough to allow her to tell it.

They helped her back to the bed, her hands still clenched in front of her.

"It's all right, Sandy. It's all right."

He held her to him and struggled to unclench her hands. She resisted, her mind locked on the recall.

"What happened next, Sandy?"

Her voice was small, weak. As if she were begging forgiveness from those in the room. "I tried to tell him . . . I tried to warn him. . . ."

"Your father?" Tom asked.

But Sandy had gone into a world of her own. "It was raining and he wanted to go visiting. . . . But I didn't want to go. . . . I told him about the dream . . . about my mother . . . about the warning . . . but he wouldn't listen . . . he wouldn't . . . ."

Sandy's head bobbed from side to side. Her face was long, her expression mournful.

"I tried to stop him. . . . But he told me I had to go. If I didn't, I would always be afraid of riding in a car with him. He didn't not believe me, but what he said made sense. . . ."

She gulped fiercely. Her eyes popped open in unseeing surprise. Tom tensed.

"It was raining hard . . . just like in the dream."

Her voice became more excited, more desperate. The memory was flooding her mind and she was talking quickly, spitting it all back as it opened mercilessly to her.

"We were going up the hill . . . it was the same hill as in the dream. . . . I recognized it. . . . Even then I tried to tell him. To stop. To turn back. It was all there. The sound of the wipers . . . the road signs . . . the mountain. I told him—!"

Her hands started to stretch out in front of her as she grabbed once again for the steering wheel.

Suddenly there was a change. Her breath came in short, shallow gasps, her eyes widened in terror. It was as if she were looking at something unimaginable in the room with them, but Tom knew she was looking deep within herself.

"The truck!" she shrieked, and the word came out like a gunshot. "The truck! I see the truck!"

It was only a fraction of a second before Tom knew what was wrong. She was no longer remembering what happened. She was reliving it. He had to stop her. He did not know what would come.

"Sandy, I'm going to count to three—"

"Daddy, the truck! Oh, my God, the truck!"

The tears flowed; the hands shook in desperation. "Stop! Please stop! We're almost at the top. There! There's the sign I saw. Daddy, the truuuuck!"

Her breath rose from her stomach. Her eyes looked as if they could burst wide open.

Tom's voice was firm, controlled, with fist-pounding clarity. He had to get her out of there. She had regressed herself to the moment of her greatest trauma. "ONE . . . TWO . . . THREE . . ."

The clap was sharp but had no effect.

"SANDY!" David yelled, desperately hoping the word would have its effect on her.

Spinner had already reached into his bag and was readying a tranquilizer. Tom waved him off; not yet.

They watched as Sandy turned fiercely to the left, her hands still outstretched. "The wheel, Daddy. Give me the wheel!"

Sandy struggled with an unseen figure for control of the car. Simultaneously she tried to grab the steering wheel and fight off a father obviously trying to steady her.

"The truck! The truck!" she kept on crying in a last voice of terror before the end.

Then obviously she had gained control of the wheel, because she whipped it fiercely to the right and once again tumbled to the floor.

"We're going over the edge. Daddy! Daddy!"

She threw her hands up instinctively to protect her face.

"The car is skidding over the edge."

She screamed and hit her head against the floor as if to simulate her jostling in the car. "We're turning over and over and over and—"

Suddenly she was still, the car having come to rest at the bottom of the incline.

David and Spinner moved to her, but Tom motioned them away. She was quiet. He had to see what would happen next.

Her hands moved about her body, tentatively at first, in exploration, and then more rapidly, touching her shoulders first, her chest, her legs.

"She's checking for broken bones," Tom whispered.

She looked up and around her, staring directly at David yet not seeing him. Her hands moved out in front of her and stopped, boxed-in, as she hit the window of the car.

She made a motion to release her seatbelt and tried to shoulder her way out of the car. The door was jammed. The three watched in fascination as Sandy got up from the floor and eased herself out of the car window. She saw something and waved fiercely.

"The horseback riders!" she cried. "Help! Help!" she called in a voice that filled the hospital room. Her arms were held out and above her as though people were helping her away from the car.

"My father!" she shrieked in desperation. "Save him—! Please!" It was a moan the likes of which David had never heard. He watched his fiancée sink to her knees and throw her head back and her mouth open.

"Please—!" she wailed in high-pitched mourner's agony.

Then she screamed. "It's exploding! The car's exploding!"

"Dear God!" David cried. "I had no idea."

"It's on fire. Save him! Please save him!"

Sandy started to run for the door.

David and Tom moved to restrain her, but she screamed again and struggled to free herself from their grasps, as though thrusting herself through the open car window. "I've got to save him! Daddeeeee—!"

She broke free from them and flailed her arms desperately. Suddenly she cried out in pain. "My arms! They're on fire!" She waved her arms back and forth furiously as David and Tom moved to capture her again and ease her back onto the bed. "The pain! The pain!" she moaned.

She threw her head back all the way and opened her mouth wide in agony. "Dear God! Look at my arms. The skin is black and burnnneddddd. . . ."

David and Tom looked at each other—the burning girl that she had seen in the Wallford house! Was this the origin?

Sandy moaned for a last frightful time and collapsed in a dead faint onto the bed.

It was over.

Tom quickly injected her with the tranquilizer and they put her to bed.

Drenched in sweat, they made their way from the hospital room, past the incredulous orderlies and the others who had heard the desperate screams. In the doctors' lounge they practically bathed in the cold water as they threw it against their faces and hair.

David had never known his heart to race so. He was breathing as if he had just finished running a mile. He leaned against the wall and then allowed himself to find a chair and fall into it.

"I can't believe it," he muttered over and again. Tom and Dr. Spinner sat next to him.

"Is that it, Tom?" he asked. "Is that why she's like she is today?"

Tom too was catching his breath. He rubbed his

eyes with his fists and tried to calm himself. He felt as though he too could use a tranquilizer. Or better, a drink.

Spinner had the same idea and quickly produced a bottle of Scotch. They each had a glass, the warm, fiery liquid trickling down their throats, relaxing them.

For long moments no one spoke, and then David asked again. "Was that what you wanted, Tom?"

Tom nodded thoughtfully. "In part."

David looked surprised. "You think there's more?"

"Yes."

"What?" He was incredulous. "You've got it all. The fire. The crash. Her father's death. The truck."

"Elements, David. That's all we have. We still have to put them together."

"What more do you have to do?" he asked fearfully, almost antagonistically, already knowing the answer and afraid of hearing it.

"Another session."

David swallowed. "You can't. Can't you work with her conventionally with what you have?"

"David, I really can't," Tom said softly. "I need more for myself before I can work with her."

"Jesus," David sighed, and covered his head with his arms. He started to cry.

CHAPTER XXX

Cal's bar was a local place.

Vacationing skiers would hit the tourist spots and discos closer to the access road and leave bars like Cal's to neighbors and friends. There was rarely an unknown face in Cal's. And that was okay by Cal and the regulars.

The mahogany bartop was rubbed to a brilliant sheen from years of lazy linseed oiling. It reflected all above it, even defining wrinkles and denoting pie-shaped bleary eyes when someone had had enough.

A few tables with rounded pedestal bases dotted the plankboard floor, and straight-back chairs were tilted against them, awaiting use. A broken pinball machine stood darkly next to the door near the jukebox, which was stacked exclusively with country western, although seldom played on weekday nights.

The weekday barstools were unofficially reserved, almost sacrosanct; someone else could sit in yours, but was expected to vacate when you came in. And you would do the same for him.

Barstools were also inherited.

Among the regulars, clockwise from the john in the

rear sat Hank Sweeter, a real estate broker whose list-
ings nonexclusively included Glendon, Owlsfane, and
a number of the other local bordering towns. He was
on his fifth and downing strong. With no family, no
one to go home to, Cal's had become his home, and
the regulars were his family. His feet dangled freely in
a never-used waitress station, for there was no waitress.
Next were Gilbert Sims and Hawley Elbers, two truck-
driving partners who worked for a local soft-drink dis-
tributor. Then there was Josiah Stoneham, and Nathan
Abraham, who had come to growl habitually into his
beer and look forward to the hours at Cal's to break
up his never-ending day. He still did not have work.
He cursed G.E. for moving the plant, cursed big busi-
neess in general, cursed Owlsfane for being a shithole
he would never leave, and cursed his teenage son for
being out of his control.

The empty seat was for Chet Riley, whose wife had
been giving him a hard time of late for being away
from home too much. Enough kidding had passed back
and forth to the effect that if your wife looked like
Chet Riley's wife you wouldn't be home that much
either.

Chet Riley often led the kidding himself and then
shrank home.

Usually about this time of night either Gilbert or
Hawley or someone else in on the gag would look at
his watch and chirp out something lewd about Chet
Riley being at home to do what his wife needed being
done to and which shopping bag was he going to throw
over her head tonight. Then they'd all laugh and jab
each other and order another round, and they would
sip their drinks to get themselves through the long, cold
Owlsfane nights.

And as he did each night, Cal rubbed his rag of
linseed oil over the aged, sheened surface of the bar
in a motion he could reproduce while asleep, a lazy

movement that kept him occupied and filled him with a sense of accomplishment as the bartop darkened and shone to a deep-brown mahogany gloss.

His business was secure. The tired feel of the room aside, he knew the men of Owlsfane really had nowhere else to go. So he rubbed and polished and he listened and he talked. And this was life in Owlsfane, Vermont, and everybody complained and nobody meant it, because there was none better.

Tonight it was Hank who had news.

"Had a client today inquire about the Wallford place," he said casually.

There was surprise around the bar. People rarely, if ever, asked about the house. No reason they would. There was no "for sale" sign in front of it and the brokers in the area knew it wasn't on the market. It was just there, because Josiah left it there. He and the others of the town respected the privacy of the man and the house. And there were those, Josiah Stoneham among them, who actually feared him.

Josiah was suddenly alert. "What did you tell him?"

"The place wasn't for sale," Hank said flatly, and looked thoughtful. "Wish you'd change your mind about that place, Josiah, you being the heir to the executor. Could bring an awful lot of money."

"I'll never sell that house," Josiah said. "You know that, Hank. I'll never sell that place so long as Eben is in there."

"With owners like you, a broker could starve," Hank said with a cold, cutting smile. He knew the commission on a house that size would be many thousands of dollars and that Josiah would give it to no other broker but him.

"I'm not the owner," Josiah said.

"Yeah?" Hank shot back, goading. "Then tell me who is."

"Eben," Josiah said calmly.

"Eben's dead. His whole family's dead." Hank

rapped on the bar and turned to Gil and Hawley for support. But they weren't taking sides, because they didn't know.

"He's in there," Josiah felt compelled to say. "How can I sell his house?"

Suddenly, in his articulation of it, hidden feelings of foolishness came in a chalkboard chill running up and down his spine.

Deep down he knew he should really sell the place and turn the money over to charity or—what the hell—keep it himself. He knew he was no longer bound by the will, which had specified that the house could never be sold. Only his feelings and beliefs in what was right kept him from selling. Because what was legal might be one thing; what was moral, something else. And as long as Eben was in the house, or might return to it, then the house would remain his to live in or come home to. Whatever, there were no two ways about it.

Hank looked down the bar. "You really believe all that?" he asked, as if having read Josiah's thoughts. "About Wallford being in there. And all the other stories?"

"Lots of people believe it," Josiah said firmly, yet calmly. "You know that, Hank."

It was true, Cal thought. People believed, but indeed few ever talked about it. Just did what they had to do, like keep the grass cut or walk up the center of the road. You did it; everybody did it. But you didn't make mention of it. It was hard to sit in a room and discuss an alleged ghost that no one had ever really seen.

"Even the stories?" Hank asked, raising an eyebrow in a gesture they all knew marked skepticism. His question came to goad, to clarify, as well as to try to keep the conversation moving so that perhaps Josiah might reconsider. The prospective buyer had already made an excellent offer on the house after Hank had shown him around inside. And there hadn't been any ghost! Hank knew that by negotiating the offer Josiah could realize a hundred thousand easily for the house and land. It was obvious that was what the guy expected to pay when he came in with an offer of ninety-two five. Even on that Josiah could close up the grocery shop and retire for the rest of his life.

But Josiah would not waver. "My grandfather believed, as did your grandfather, Hank," he said. "My father believed. And I believe." He shook his head up and down with certainty, convinced of the absolute truth of the stories about the disappearing food and the blinking lights. "And remember, I found that girl up in his daughter's bedroom, burning and mad!" He didn't tell them about the girl from the ski house.

"She was probably half mad to begin with," Hank Sweeter mumbled.

"Nope. No record of that. I suppose she set herself on fire too?"

"Sure," Hank answered uneasily with a shrug, not really knowing. "But that all happened sixty years ago. Who cares anymore?"

"I care," Josiah said with conviction. "And as long as I care, the house remains Eben's. So please tell that to anyone else you take to the house before they inquire about it."

"That's what I'll have to do," Hank answered. "But do me a favor, Josiah, and think about it. Please. It could make us both a lot of money."

"I'll do you a favor," Josiah answered. "I'll think about it. And you have my word on that."

As conversation continued around him, Josiah stared into his half-empty glass. The beer had become warm, and he signaled Cal for another one. As he sipped the brew, he let his mind wander. For as many years as he could remember, he had tried to decide between Darwinian evolution and the creation of the world as dictated by his own religious upbringing. He had finally come to peace with his soul and accepted both on different levels. Also, for as many years he had watched his father before him and then his wife and himself clean the Wallford house and prepare food for the family. On one level he wondered if he was a foolish old man believing and doing foolish things.

But on the other level, to go to Church was to fervently believe in God, which was to believe in life after death; and that was to *believe*. And to believe was to fear; and in this case, to fear was to care. After sixty years of caring for the house as if it were his own, because that's what the Stoneham family did, he would not let the prospect of money dangled in front of him alter his deep-set beliefs.

If the stories were fictitious, then he had been wrong. Nothing really had been lost. But if they were all indeed true, as he knew they must be, then he was doing right. And he would meet Eben Wallford on a higher plane and would be able to face him with honor.

No. He would not sell the house or let anything disturb the peace and sanctity of the house or the unfortunate family.

Sleep would not come to David that night and he didn't even try to fight for it. He lay awake in his lower bunk. His eyes were open and he stared at the springs of the bed above him. His hands were clasped tightly under his head; his elbows framed his face.

It was late, and the house was quiet around him. He had stayed up later than the others, spending the evening quietly, unmoving, sunken into one of the Morris chairs. At first he had thumbed idly through a ski magazine, as if the diversion might occupy his mind. Next he had tried the transient conversation that drifted past him in whispered waves, catching words against an amorphous background din. Finally he had tried a game of chess with Bob. But in the middle, when he suddenly realized that after a lifetime of playing he had forgotten the move of the knight, he decided he had had enough for one evening.

Audra had left for home that day, directly from the mountain.

Returning hermitlike to the chair in the corner, he watched the others slowly tire and climb up to bed. Still, they held him at arm's length, uncertain in his presence, helpless, murmuring things like "I know you'd rather be by yourself." Everything had been said and said again, comforting words sounding meaningless and forced, and they were nervous. Even Stan, with whom he had been close for years, looked to escape and found avoidance in early bed, backgammon, and discoing at the mountain. David understood and forgave, wondering how he would react if the circumstances were reversed.

He knew he was bringing down the tone of the house and apologized for it.

"Bob, I could find a motel," he had said. "I'm not doing much for your repeat business."

"Forget repeat business," Bob had said in a genuinely angry tone that showed David the words were not emptily uttered.

He had not questioned Bob again, but did try to become more invisible, more open, and more outwardly cheerful.

Yet he knew he was failing miserably.

When the living room was empty, peaceful in its after-hours disarray, he shut off all but the light offered by the conquistador and tossed an extra log on the fire. It caught almost immediately. He watched the flames consume the wood.

Consumed by that which it was nourished by . . .

The words of the Shakespearean sonnet danced through his head. He thought sadly of Sandy consuming herself from within.

His defenses marched on overtime. He kept on telling himself that at any moment there would be a call from the hospital. They would tell him a terrible mistake had been made. That Sandy was all right and he could come and take her home.

His mind moved backward in time. To the week before. When they were driving north and he was telling her of the Wallford house. "Sounds like fun," she said. Right— The vacation in Vermont was going to be so perfect, so idyllic.

He trained his eyes on the fire; and lost himself in the flames that were leaping upward in graceful ballet twirls. The new log shifted in the hearth, blackened, and settled to the floor, sending upward a whirlwind of gray ashes and soot. The fire was softly comforting, yet . . .

He suddenly sensed the flames were laughing at him, mocking him, the tongues of fire taunting him. Their gentle dances of a moment before had become ominous, hellish, triumphant. As if the flames had won.

The flames had burned her arm and killed her father. They had come to her in her dreams. And the very flames were now burning the skin from her body.

It was all so inconceivable. The flood of nightmares, the ghostly visions, the unconscious mind at work stripping her bare. A lifetime of buried pain and guilt bursting forth in one unstoppable rush. A wave of torment unleashed by powerful internal feelings. All stirred loose by—what? The Wallford house? Eben Wallford? And of course the key question: What was the connection? How did the house and the man come into it? They did not have all the answers yet and David knew that Tom was right. They had to go back for another session.

He shuddered, chilled in spite of the warmth of the fire. Could she take another session as painful and agonizing as the one she had been through today? Something told him, *there are more secrets, more pain.* In the suddenly smaller, suddenly darker, quarter-lit room, he was afraid.

So much now made terrible sense: The discomfort and uneasiness whenever she talked about her father. It was nothing she could ever articulate, and now he knew it was nothing she ever felt on a conscious level. It was her unconscious that had closed the gate, and now, of course, the gate was opened.

As much as he dreaded the hypnosis session of the next morning, he knew he could not stay away. Approach/avoidance. Tom had used the phrase in regard to Sandy. It had a place here as well. He didn't want to attend the session, yet he was still drawn captive to it. He knew she needed him there, but, even stronger, it was a case of fascination. Had it not been Sandy, it would have made for a remarkable spectator show. Given the opportunity to attend he would not have missed it. Although he knew he had no business being there except that Sandy wanted him there. Suddenly he felt very ashamed.

But no, he told himself. There was nothing abnormal with his fantasy. He remembered that one of the most common of nonsexual fantasies was envisioning the death of one's loved ones. He prayed it would never come to that.

The last of the sparks became silent. The hearth was now a quiet, smoldering gray-black. David went upstairs, hoping to fall into oblivious sleep, to wake rested and ready for the next morning.

But he could not sleep.

Thoughts of Sandy paraded unchecked through his mind. In his inner ear he heard her voice, her laughter, her sighs, and her sobs and screams of the last several days. He saw her in the dark above him, remembered her as she was just a week before, and he thought of the good times they had had together.

It had taken him all of fifteen minutes after being introduced to her by the managing editor to make an absolute jackass out of himself, all of thirty minutes to ask her out to lunch, all of an hour and a half to fall

crazy for her. He had wondered all this time if the
bubble was ever going to burst, if he was ever going to
wake up and not find her next to him.

And now he heard her voice, coming to him from
out of the dark. "Listen, jerk. Staying awake and
worrying is not going to help either one of us, okay?"

"Okay," he said out loud, and was suddenly embarrassed lest someone had heard.

But the room remained undisturbed, the sounds of
sleep ever present around him. He stretched his entire
body, from fingertips to toes, grasped on to the bedposts, and tried isometrically to pull the bunk down
around him. His muscles tensed, then rested, and he
closed his eyes, praying for escape into sleep. But his
eyes burned. In front of him danced visions of eternal
flames and the solemn face of a gray-haired man.

His eyes sprang open to banish what his mind was
seeing, yet each time he closed them again the visions
returned. It was not until hours later, as the sun first
threatened to peek beyond the distant mountaintops,
that exhaustion finally took hold and he fell asleep,
restlessly dreaming of holocaust and Armageddon.

BOOK IV

The Link

CHAPTER XXXI

The third hypnosis session began as had the others. David and Dr. Spinner assumed their places. Sandy was in a straight-back chair with arms to offer some protection against her falling.

She was frightened. She knew the skin was not improving. The disease was spreading. Except for her face, upper arms, and thighs, her entire body was either reddened or scaling. Her self-confidence of the day before had diminished, even though Tom had met with her before the therapy session to relax her, to tell her how well he thought the hypnosis was going; that he felt they were close. Even though she knew he was telling the truth, the visible evidence stood overwhelmingly against what the psychiatrist was saying.

Within seconds she was under.

Tom was sweating, and already bands of perspiration had formed under his arms. He knew the session today was going to be fierce—indeed probably had to be if he was ever to get to the true cause of her remarkable feelings of guilt. Although he had a strong inkling . . . She hadn't been able to save her mother and then she hadn't been able to save her father either.

". . . Sandy, we are going to return to what you remembered yesterday."

Tom felt a tightness to his voice and hoped it wasn't noticeable. His mouth was dry, and there was a burning feeling in the pit of his throat. He poured a cup of water for himself from the pitcher on the night table. His eyes fell on the small zebra plant, unwatered from the day before. There was a weakness to the plant, a limpness to the stalk, a hesitancy to the leaves, as if all their strength had ebbed from their dryness and they were about to give way to gravity.

He quickly sipped the water and poured the excess over the plant. The soil immediately absorbed the water droplets and appeared to beg for more. He drained the pitcher into the pot and watched the water soak through. He knew that by the session's end the stalks would be strainingly erect, the leaves would be strong, upright, defiant against gravity, and the plant would live for another two days.

He turned his attention back to Sandy, who sat sharply in place, a look of expectancy on her otherwise placid face. Tom suspected that the calm exterior was masking a subconscious ready to explode at his question or command.

". . . there was the accident," he droned softly. "The car had gone over the cliff. You crawled out, saw the horseback riders—"

The moan escaped unrestrained from her slightly parted lips. She remembered.

"Your father was caught in the car. You tried to save him. You put your hands through the flames to get to him—"

"Save him," she moaned. *"Save him. Why won't they save him?* Oh my God! My arms are on fire. My arms!"

In less than a second she was thrust back into the living nightmare, then was once again silent, a look of peace on her face.

She might have fainted, Tom thought. From the pain. From the shock.

"You then awoke," he tried. "Where were you when you awoke? Tell me where you were and what you saw and did."

"I awoke in the hospital." Her voice was calm, clear. It betrayed no emotion. She was stating fact, retelling what she had been told. "They put me there because my arms were burned." She winced at the memory. "They told me my father was dead . . . he had been burned in the car."

"What happened next, Sandy?" Tom coaxed.

She swallowed. A pained look appeared on her face.

"What happened, Sandy? You remember."

"I dreamed again. That night."

David watched her, fascinated. In front of him, a mind closed tight for five years was opening to Tom's voice.

"Was it your mother warning you?"

She licked her lips.

"No. Not my mother." Her face tightened, tension lines forming where seconds before there had been no expression. The corners of her lips twitched. She grasped the arms of the chair in unconscious support.

"What, Sandy? If not your mother, what did you dream?"

"I dreamed . . ." She swallowed again; hesitated. She remembered, but she was fighting herself.

"What, Sandy? What did you dream?" He repeated the question over in a lower voice and knew that it was stirring that portion of her mind within his control. She wanted to tell him, yet she was afraid to articulate it.

"The accident," she gasped. "I dreamed about the accident again." Her voice came out in spurts as her breath quickened. "It was all the same. The hill . . . We were going up the hill . . . the rain . . . the road signs . . . the mountains . . . the—"

She broke off, and her eyes suddenly opened wide in

desperate fear and recall, a lost, sickening feeling invading her stomach. Her mouth was wide, her voice full.

"I thought I saw the truck coming into our lane. I grabbed for the wheel. I turned the car, forcing it off the road. But then I realized. I didn't see the truck. There was no truck! There was no truck!"

Tom was startled. "What, Sandy?"

"There was no truck . . . in my dream. . . . The car went over the edge . . . down and down and down it rolled, over and over and over." Her arms came straight up and she shook her fists. "I wasn't hurt. . . . I crawled out the window. . . . I saw the horseback riders. . . . All the same as it happened. All the same . . . the explosion . . . my arms! My arms!" Her eyes stared out zombielike, the size of half-dollars. "But there was no truck!"

Going from dream to reality to dream, Tom thought, she had somehow lost the truck.

"I woke up . . . my arm hurt terribly . . . I remembered the dream. . . . I remembered everything. . . . But I couldn't remember the truck. . . ."

"You will rest now, Sandy," Tom said gently. "You will go to a pleasant memory and you will rest. You're doing very well. You're working very hard, and now we're going to have a chance to rest. Close your eyes and go to a happy time in your life."

Her eyelids closed, but she started to sway in place.

"No truck . . . no truck . . ." she moaned again. "I tried to remember . . . all that day I thought back to my dream and to the accident and I tried to remember . . . but I couldn't. . . . I couldn't remember the truck. . . ."

Tom abandoned his directive for her to rest. He decided to forge forward, to let her continue. He worked as if David and Dr. Spinner were not in the room. Indeed, in that moment of his therapy with the girl, they were not. His total concentration was on his patient.

Sometimes in the more difficult sessions, when he was physically as well as mentally drained, he found he had lost two or three pounds.

"Go on, Sandy," he said, urging her on, but she needed no urging.

"I had the dream again and again. . . . Each time it was the same . . . the rain . . . the hill . . . the explosion!" The tears came and then a moan, as if from the damned. Her face fell, and at the same time her skin began to scale.

David closed his eyes to avoid looking. The disease was spreading to her entire body. He lowered his head into his palms and repeated to himself how much he loved her.

Her next words were loud, delivered in a sudden onrush of escaping emotion.

"Oh, dear God! There was no truck! I killed my father! I turned the wheel and killed my father!"

Tom spoke to her gently. "But, Sandy, you thought you had seen the truck. You didn't intentionally turn the wheel. You received the warning signal from your mother. Like the times before with the bicycle and the glass door. It was the same. The dream came to warn you of danger. Your mother never lied to you and you had no reason to think that anything was other than in the dream. You saw the truck in your dream and you thought you saw it on the hill. You weren't trying to kill your father. You were trying to save him. Your feelings of guilt were never justified. You thought you were saving him." His perspiration turned cold and his body became chilled. "Anybody would have wanted to help, and in your own way you did too, but perhaps you just don't remember."

"I woke up. My arms hurt. The nurse came into the room. 'Aren't you going to the funeral?' she asked me. 'Yes,' I said. I went to my father's funeral and I saw it all again, over and over and over again. The car rolling over the cliff. Standing there while I watched them bury him, throw dirt on him, and all I could see over and over was that there was no truck. I was responsible. I killed him."

She choked, and the tears flowed freely. "The warning dream was wrong . . . there was no truck!"

Tom's face was inches from hers. "Maybe your other dreams were wrong, Sandy. Maybe there *was* a truck that you saw. But in your dreams after the accident you didn't see it. Perhaps you were confused. That's possible, isn't it? There was a lot going on. You were in the hospital. On medication. Perhaps it was difficult for you to remember."

"No."

She looked as if she were trying to escape the painful memories, but at the same time refusing to give them up. She squirmed in the chair, and Tom stood in front of her lest she bolt and do damage to herself.

"How can you be so certain?"

"There was no truck on the hill. I couldn't remember it."

Tom would momentarily let it be. "What happened next?"

She opened her mouth a fraction of a second before the sound emerged. It was a scream, louder and more fierce than any of the others in the previous days. The black voice rose from deep within her. Her neck muscles bulged. Her eyes again popped open wide in fearful recall. Her arms started to shake.

"Guilt—" she cried out, as if being strangled from within.

Tom knew she was expressing the raw emotion that was consuming her.

"I killed him—"

A useless emotion, guilt. Yet such a damaging and all-powerful one. The key to so many of his patients' mental—and physical—disorders.

"Couldn't live—" she choked. "Couldn't live with the guilt."

Perhaps quite the contrary, Tom thought. Perhaps she had learned how to be comfortable with her guilt and was able to reinforce it by excluding the truck from her dreams.

"But you had nothing to feel guilty about," Tom tried again. He tried to be conversational with her, not to preach. "You did what you thought would help."

"Dream . . . same dream . . . over and over . . . daytime too . . . I saw it over and over . . ."

She had kept on hallucinating the accident even while awake.

"The funeral . . . the bus . . . in the street . . . anywhere. I saw it all again . . . always the same . . . the rain . . . the hill . . . I grabbed the wheel—"

Her hands reached out in front of her and held on tightly to Tom's arms as if trying to right the steering wheel that had sent her father to his doom.

He watched in horror as the skin around her eyes started to exfoliate and drop to her nightgown. Her once pretty face was now marked with the fishlike scales, and for a half second he wondered what the hell he had gotten himself into. Only for a half second, for then he was back with his patient and trying to free himself from her strong grasp.

David was on his feet, as was Spinner, and they hurriedly crossed to Tom, each taking one of her hands and pulling the fingers free.

"My God!" David exclaimed. "What did she do to herself?"

Tom motioned for quiet as Sandy again started to shake.

"Couldn't sleep . . . couldn't escape . . . couldn't live . . . couldn't . . ."

"What did you do, Sandy?" Tom asked.

"Couldn't escape . . . couldn't live . . . couldn't continue to live . . . I killed him. . . ."

Her voice changed. The edge was off. It was now a voice of quiet, fearful desperation. A voice of explanation, asking for forgiveness. A long sigh looking for confirmation that she had not sinned, that she had done the only thing that made sense. . . .

"Pills—" she said through her tears.

"You took sleeping pills?" Tom asked.

She nodded fiercely up and down.

"Whole bottle . . . with Scotch . . . wanted to kill myself . . . tried to kill . . . had to escape . . . The music! It was soft, inviting. It called to me. I followed the music. . . ."

She suddenly froze in absolute terror at the realization of what she had done and its outcome.

"I see them!" she shrieked. "I see them coming to get me. I was wrong. I shouldn't have killed myself. The guilt. I still feel it. The dream. I can't escape the dream." She sobbed uncontrollably and sucked in her breath in a powerful snort.

"Dear God!" David cried out, and wished he were somewhere else.

"The faces. The devils. Can't escape. No escape. They won't let me be free."

At once David knew she had regressed herself to a death experience and was reliving the horrors of her suicide attempt.

Tom had to try to bring her out. "When I count to three, Sandy, you will wake up."

"Crawling with blood. Pus. Bugs. The fire—"

"ONE—"

Her body contorted, as if trying to escape the fearful images that only she could see.

"TWO . . ."

"—burning me . . . licking at me . . . The noise! I can't escape the noise!"

"THREE . . ."

"I've done wrong! I've done wrong!" she screamed at the top of her voice, ignoring him, as the visions of her guilt-ridden hell engulfed her.

David broke from his chair and ran to her. He

slapped her hard across the face. It whipped to the side; she offered no resistance. He raised his hand to strike her again. As if the sudden force would free her from her memory. Spinner stopped him in midair. David fought against the doctor. He had to do something to rescue Sandy. Something. No one else was. Spinner wrestled him back to the chair and forcibly held him in place. David's breathing matched Sandy's. Strangled sounds emerged from his mouth. Spinner tried to calm him, afraid he might hyperventilate.

"Sandy—" David moaned from across the room, and tears streamed down his face.

"Can't move," she suddenly yelled. *"They're coming to me. They're surrounding me. They're moving closer."*

The others in the room could only try to imagine what the girl was seeing.

"No! I'm not one of you! I'm not one of you!"

David had never known a sound like the one that emerged from her throat. It was a sound that had its origin deep in the ground, from the underworld, the dead.

"Sandy—!" he screamed to her in a voice of pain. "Don't! No!" But he didn't know what he was referring to. Everything she was seeing, everything she was saying, had happened years before.

Sandy's eyes were open wide, staring inwardly, oblivious of all around her. She was reliving a private hell.

"We'd better sedate her," Tom said to Spinner, who nodded. He readied the injection as David stared on helplessly.

"I see myself," she shrieked. *"Like one of them. I'm becoming one of them. My skin is old, wrinkled. The pain. They're touching me. Electrical shocks. Fire. Don't! Stop! I'm not one of you. I'm not one of you. I didn't mean to kill myself. I'm sorry. I'm sorry. I didn't mean to—"*

Tom held her as Spinner bathed her arm with alco-

hol. He was about to inject the needle when suddenly
Sandy was silent. Spinner looked at Tom, puzzled, and
Tom waved him off.

The terrors cleared from her face, as if bathed with
holy water. The demon fears of a moment before were
replaced with blessed relief. The lines disappeared and
her lips stopped quivering. Her arms stopped shaking.
It was, as if she had been exorcised.

"I was spared," she said softly. "I heard a voice. 'It
isn't time,' the voice said, and I came back." Her exal-
tation was apparent. "I came back," she repeated, in a
voice of joyous triumph. "God spared me and I came
back. I didn't die. I didn't die. I didn't die—"

Her smile was radiant. "I didn't die—"

"You will close your eyes now, Sandy, and you will
listen to me. When I count to three, Sandy, you will
awaken. Do you understand?"

"Yes." Tom had her back.

"Good. One . . . two . . . three."

Tom's sharp clap brought her around

Skin fell freely from her forehead.

CHAPTER XXXII

David was in the doctors' lounge.

He had spent the day with the sleeping Sandy trying to look at her and tell himself he still loved her. The scaling had spread to her forehead and eyelids, and to her palms and scalp. More hair had fallen out, as if she had been getting chemotherapy. A blood test had been done, as there was fear of an anemic complication.

A nurse had come into the room to hook her up to an IV. She was refusing solid food. The nurse indicated to David it was time for him to leave, which he did, with a reluctant wave Sandy could not have seen. He stepped out of the room into the harsh glare of the corridor light and squinted after the soft lamp-glow of the hospital room. He leaned against the door and breathed in deeply, carefully inhaling to fill his lungs and exhaling so he wouldn't cry. But he finally felt all cried out. Tears would solve nothing.

Standing alone in the hospital corridor he suddenly realized with an aching knot in his stomach how much he did love her, and how guilty he felt for even doubting his affection. He turned to go back into the room, to tell her, to scream into her sleeping ear that he was there, he was hers, he would always be there. But he was met by the nurse coming out, who blocked his entrance. He hit his forehead with his fist. He needed to tell her, perhaps more for himself, but now he was too late.

"Do you need help?" the nurse asked, concerned.

David shook his head. He couldn't even speak to her.

"Why don't you come and sit in the lounge?" she offered, and David silently followed her.

The coffee helped. He was finishing his second cup, staring blankly at the opposite wall, when Tom came into the room.

"They told me you were here."

"Yes," David said with no enthusiasm.

"I've gone through my notes and listened to the tapes again," Tom said. "I think I may understand what's been happening, but do keep in mind that I don't know for certain yet."

"Thank God," David said, choosing to ignore Tom's qualification.

"Let me get some coffee and we can go through the notes." Tom moved over to the urn and poured himself a cup. Stirring in milk and sugar, he returned to the couch where David was sitting and spread the notes out on a small table in front of them. He gulped the hot coffee as David sat in hopeful expectation.

"Okay," Tom said. "Let's back up to the beginning and bring it all forward."

"Shoot."

"Sandy comes up here to the ski house. There's no indication of anything out of the ordinary. The first night, Bob tells us the story of the Wallford family." His voice lowered. "It's a tragic story, full of pity, self-torture, excessive guilt. Eben Wallford carried with him to his death the painful knowledge and tremendous guilt that he had buried his daughter alive. This is all conveyed to Sandy, and the way Bob tells the story he lays it on really thick—the guilt, the anguish. Enough to penetrate very deeply. As Sandy listens to the story, all of a sudden she begins to get funny feelings." Tom flip-flopped his hand. "They're strange feelings. Alien. Inexplicable. Nothing she can define and therefore nothing she can relate in words. Except that she is drawn to this house. This man.

"She doesn't understand the peculiar pull to the house, but it's strong and she can't fight it. She has to go with it. There might be an identification with Wallford, David. They share a feeling between them— guilt. And she goes to him because she thinks he will be her friend. She may have been exploring her own guilt through his."

Tom made a motion with his hand as if sticking a pin into a balloon. "And now her unconscious has been pricked, her defenses stripped. There is a hole, an opening for a very repressed past to start slowly seeping through. All triggered by the story of this man and his guilt."

Tom sipped the coffee and sorted through his notes. Little pieces of paper were scattered across the table.

"Then come the visions and the dreams. Of Eben and Suzanne. After the discovery of the premature burial, Eben goes to the mausoleum and listens. Possible translation: Sandy, full of remorse, is hoping to hear her own father's voice." Tom clenched his fist in emphasis. "Guilt!" he said. "As well as a strong unwillingness to bury the dead. The same as Eben.

"Next there is the drowning dream and the precognition of the ski fall. We know now that she had perceived that as a warning dream of sorts. And as before, with the bicycle and the glass door, the dream was borne out. She fell. But when she took the car accident dream to be precognitive—well, in real life we know it just didn't work out that way. She grabbed the wheel in anticipation of the finish. But instead of just swerving, the car went over the edge and her father was killed. Something had gone very wrong. Irreparably wrong.

"And when she relived the horrors of that day in her subsequent dreams and visions, she realized she didn't remember there being a truck. The warning dream had been wrong. She had anticipated something that never materialized. In her mother's death she unconsciously knows she heard the cries early enough to run for help. Heard them and ignored them. Here, she didn't save her father, just as she hadn't saved her mother. She had failed again."

Tom crossed the room to the coffee urn and poured himself another cup. David sat on the couch, frozen, trying to absorb what Tom was saying.

"And then she undoubtedly started to go through the what-ifs: What if there really had been a truck? Would her father still have been killed? What if the truck had stopped? What if her father had swerved the car? What if the truck had swerved? It grew, and she came to realize that by taking control of the car she removed all other possible alternatives. She had caused the death of her father. And the guilt took hold."

David nodded.

"Then perhaps she compounded her mistake," Tom continued. "Instead of acknowledging that the warning dream may have been faulty, or accepting that perhaps she was confused and didn't remember the truckless dream accurately, or even because she was feeling comfortable with her guilt in that she had learned to live with it after her mother's death—she chose to blame herself again and shoulder the new guilt.

"But she couldn't. Believing that you have killed a parent is guilt of a major proportion. It began to haunt her as nothing before and soon became something she couldn't cope with."

"So she decided to kill herself?" David asked.

Tom nodded. "It was tearing at her. She had to end

it all as a means of escape. She combined the pills with the alcohol and . . ." He trailed off. They knew what it had led to.

"Do you really believe she actually died, Tom? If only for a few minutes before resuscitation?"

Tom exhaled. "I don't know. We'd have to find out what hospital she was taken to."

"I guess what I'm asking you is," David said tentatively, "do you think the horrors she saw were part of her death experience?"

Tom tightened his lips and then spoke. "I can't answer that. No one can. I don't know. All the life-after-life research reports the pleasant experiences people have: the long dark tunnel that leads to the Godlike light at the end, the warmth, the overall feeling of security and well-being. What Sandy envisioned Suzanne going through. The research doesn't really involve itself that much wtih the question of suicides, except to report that people who have been brought back after suicide attempts, for the most part, hazily remember having unpleasant, negative experiences and the strong knowledge that they have done wrong. Like Sandy. Some envisioned they were falling into fire pits or something of an equally unfortunate nature. But those are the rare exceptions, and while they can't be dismissed, they're definitely not the norm. But then again, neither is suicide. I don't know of any reports of anyone's experiencing what Sandy did. Which is not conclusive either way. I don't think we can make a judgment about whether it was a true death experience or a symbolic dream. The demons could be part of her self-destructiveness. Whatever, the sights were too frightening for her, too terrifying, to even imagine, and she repressed the incident. As might other resuscitated suicides. I don't know."

"How absolutely horrible," David sighed.

"She may have repressed the entire episode leading up to the suicide, going back to the warning dreams and her taking control of the car. Her father died in a car accident; that's all she knew."

"What about the skin, Tom?" David asked.

Tom thought for a moment before answering. "Let me suggest the following as a possibility: the real Eben Wallford, in the way he chose to live the rest of his life, punished himself, right? There's no argument. And Sandy knows all of this."

"Right."

"Perhaps the Eben Wallford of her dreams and visions is a punishing element, representative of the guilty side of her psyche, coming to punish her. Her father was burned in the fire. In her dreams of hell her skin is burned off as well. Eben Wallford reached out from the cellar to burn her arms. She envisions a girl on fire. David, her defenses are coming down; she can no longer call on them. Her body undergoes chemical changes and the skin peels freely.

"But we have something else: the voice. What we have called Suzanne. The voice of reason. Ordering her to stop. 'Daddy . . . don't. Daddy, don't,' it called out. Don't *what*? Don't harm the girl. 'Sandy,' it is perhaps saying symbolically, 'don't harm yourself.' Sandy would like to be free of the guilt she is carrying. Suzanne is telling Eben to leave her alone, meaning *leave me alone*. Suzanne is speaking for her. She's saying, 'Sandy, I've been carrying this guilt for too long. It's heavy and I want to free myself. Sandy,' Suzanne is saying, 'don't punish me, because I really haven't done anything wrong.' " Tom's voice had grown soft and kindly. David nodded. He understood.

"What do we do?"

"Unfortunately we have to work with 'Suzanne,' who is not real. But I'm going to have to work through her to get to Sandy. And then perhaps we can finally bury Suzanne for good." Tom realized what he had said and smiled sheepishly.

"But as I mentioned, hypnotherapy is not a miracu-

lous cure-all. I'm not going to march into her unconscious, tell her to relax, she's going to be all right, and
expect immediate results. It's going to take time, work,
and suggestion."

"How long?"

Tom pursed his lips. "No way of telling."

"When do you start?"

"Immediately. Tomorrow."

Finishing the coffee, he crushed the styrofoam cup
in his fist and tossed it expertly into the wastebasket
across the room.

CHAPTER XXXIII

They were riding horses: a man and a girl of eleven high-stepped through the tall grass. The sleeping girl responded, smiling lightly to herself as the horses entered the shady lane, the overhanging trees a canopy above, sun sneaking in through treetops like dazzling pinpricks.

The point of view shifted continually, as it often does in a dream. First she was on the horse, trees and fields rushing by as the animal picked up speed and followed hidden paths. Then she was an observer, from a dozen different angles, as if cameras had been set up to film the action sequence in one take.

All around her was color and light and sound: the turning of the trees in the crisp October air, the crush of the dead fallen leaves under the pounding of the horses' hooves, the whistle of the sharp breeze through partially bare boughs.

The girl called out to the man. "Look, Papa. I can jump," she said, pointing in front of her to a cross-barred gate waiting in the distance.

"Be careful, Suzanne," the man called back to her, as he pulled his horse up to watch his daughter jump.

The young girl took the jump, the hooves of the

horse flying six inches above the top of the gate. Her father applauded loudly.

From the other side of the gate the girl in the dream turned in the saddle and spoke again. But it was different this time. It was as if a camera had gone in for a tight close-up and she was framed in the screen. She was not speaking to her father as she had before; she was speaking directly to the sleeping girl.

To Judy.

The voice was familiar; Judy had heard it before.

Please, the girl on the horse implored. *Please.* Her face was turned downward, as if a mask of sadness and despair had slipped over it. *You've got to listen to me and leave this place. He sees you too! Don't let him hurt you too!*

The image of the man suddenly filled the screen in close-up, replacing the picture of the girl. His eyes were deep and so very appealing. Almost spellbinding. They hooked onto Judy's.

Judy drifted up from sleep, the face of the gray-haired man fading from view, the voice of the girl lost in her wakeful state.

Her eyes opened and Judy remembered something odd: the young girl in the dream looked a little like herself, with straight black hair parted down the center and almond-shaped eyes. She tried to remember her other dreams, wondering if she often dreamed about herself. But nothing would come.

Sandy slipped into a hypnotic trance with only a word from Tom and the gesture of his flat palm over her eyes. David and Dr. Spinner assumed their places in the corner of the room and Tom was ready to proceed.

"Sandy," he crooned softly, and her head cocked in his direction. "I want you to feel very relaxed today. I want you to go into a deeper and deeper trance. I want your whole body to be relaxed." His voice took on a gentle, melodious quality. "I want your arms to remain heavily by your sides and your feet to be cemented to the floor. Do you feel tired and relaxed, Sandy?"

She swayed gently in place. "Yes."

"Good. Now I want you to open your eyes, and when you do you will be prepared to listen to what I am going to say. Listen and absorb. Your mind will be restful and open and we will talk. Open your eyes, Sandy."

Unlike the times in the previous sessions when her eyes would spring open wide in fear, the lids lifted upward easily and slowly, and a strange, remote softness radiated from her. She looked calmer and more rested than on any of the previous days. Tom hoped she would be communicative and receptive.

"You've had many dreams over the past several nights and they've been frightening."

Her nostrils flared slightly. He sensed her breath quickening. He hurried to reassure her and spoke in gentle tones.

"You should not be afraid, Sandy. The memories cannot harm us. Nor can the dreams. They were only symbolic."

For only a fraction of a second Sandy perceived a grayish flickering shadow. It was amorphous, airy, transient; and as quickly as she thought she had seen it, it was gone.

"What is the symbolism of Eben Wallford, Sandy?" Tom asked softly. "What does he mean to you?"

"I saw him. . . ." Sandy said. "He is dead . . . he wanted me dead . . . he came to kill me . . . to punish—"

"To punish, Sandy!" Tom seized on the word. "He came to punish you. Why do you think he came to punish you?"

She swallowed before the words would come.

"Bad . . . I was bad . . . had to be punished . . ."

Tom's voice brimmed with confusion. "Why were you bad?"

"Bad," she repeated. She passed her tongue over her dry lips.

"Why were you bad?" Tom asked again.

"My father," she said, and the word came out as a whimper. "I killed him. . . ."

"Why do you say that, Sandy? You were trying to help your father."

"No truck . . . no truck . . . He wouldn't be dead if I hadn't turned the wheel."

She tightened as her guilt closed in on her and won. Tom saw that she was straining to remain calm, as she had been directed.

"But you *believed* there was, didn't you?"

"My mother——"

"Yes. Your mother. Your mother had come to warn you, as she had twice before. And because she was right both those times you believed again. Your mother never lied to you." Tom was gentle, supportive.

"There was no truck. . . ." She was floundering, a lost child.

"But you couldn't have known that. Everything was as it had been in the dream. You told me that yourself. The rain . . . the hills . . . the sound of the wipers. Next you would see the truck. You *believed* you saw the truck."

"I believed I saw the truck," she mimicked.

She was thrown back into the car once again. Tom's words faded under the sound of the groaning engine.

As soon as the car started up the incline she knew they had made a mistake in coming. It was all as it had been before. The rain beat down like a waterfall over the windshield; the wipers made the very same familiar sound she had heard in the dream. The signposts were the same. The curve and top of the hill were ahead of them.

The truck——

"Stop!" she yelled to her father.

But the car didn't stop.

They once again neared the top of the road, where it curved inward along the ridge of the rising mountain, to the spot where the truck would inevitably come hurtling down at them.

To the others in the room, her face took on the strain of the memory. But it was more than a memory. She was once more in the car.

"Stop!" she continued to yell. "The truck! The truck!" She moaned as she relived the seeds of her guilt.

She wrestled with her father for control. She grabbed the wheel and turned. The car skidded over the edge. She threw her hands up instinctively to protect her face as the car flipped over once and then again and again until it came to rest at the bottom of the incline.

Nothing was broken; there was no pain. The seatbelt held her securely in place.

"You thought you were trying to save him." Tom's words came through in a hazy cloud and countered the scene that buzzed through her head. "I don't know why you should feel guilty."

She released the belt and tried the door: jammed.

"You didn't mean to kill your father."

She eased herself out of the opened side window.

"You believed your mother when she came to you in your dream. So why wouldn't you try to save your father the best way you knew how?"

Her father groaned, still alive.

"You loved your father. You wouldn't hurt him."

The horseback riders came running toward her, helping her away from the car.

"My father! My father!" she cried, and tried to break free to run to him.

The explosion knocked them all down; the car became an inferno. She ran back to the car, around to the driver's side, and tried to get to him, to put her hand through the fire to release the seatbelt.

"Your father forgives you, Sandy. You should forgive yourself now."

When they pulled her out, her arm was on fire, her skin already charred and red and raw.

"No—" she moaned in place as the memory was complete and she knew her father still remained in the burning car, dead.

"Do not feel guilty," Tom's voice droned gently on. "You thought you saw the truck. You believed your mother, who had come to you to warn you. You were trying to save your father. It was an accident. God's will. We can't blame ourselves for accidents."

"An accident . . ." Sandy repeated.

"An accident," Tom said again in a louder voice, as if the shock of the word alone could break through resistant brain cells and home in on that section of her memory embedded in guilt and pain. "An accident, Sandy, and you can't blame yourself for the accident."

She stood beneath the portrait in the bedroom.

The fire was burning. The flames crackled and arched upward. She turned from the fire as Eben Wallford entered the room.

"I see him," she said, her eyes wide in surprise.

There was a strange, sad smile on the man's face as he entered the bedroom and saw the girl standing next to the fire.

Tom, misunderstanding, asked: "Your father?"

"Suzanne," she heard him say. "You've come home."

"Please, no—" Sandy said, and in her mind took two steps backward toward the fireplace as the man walked slowly toward her. His arms were open and outstretched as if in preparation for an embrace. But so many things are perceived from different points of view, and the arms that came toward her seemed threatening to her, arms that would seize her, arms that would kill.

"I see him," she repeated in a voice that was loud and fearful. "Coming to get me."

"Who do you see, Sandy?" Tom pressed.

"Eben Wallford."

"Who do you think Eben Wallford is? Is he your father? Could he be your father?"

Sandy did not hear the question as she backed against the fireplace grill. The heat from the flames reached up and touched her and she tried to move away from the fire. But the man she saw was next to her, reaching out to her, his hands moving to caress her cheek.

And suddenly she knew.

David saw the skin scale and fall from her face. Chills double-timed the length of his spine. His hands unconsciously lifted to cover his eyes and remove for all time the sight of his fiancée willing the life from her body to assuage mistaken guilt.

"No——" she said, and her face pulled away. Her chin was in a military brace as she fought to move from the man who was torturing her so.

"I'm sorry, Suzanne," she heard him say.

"Do you see your father?" Tom pressed.

"Suzanne," the man said. He trailed his hand down her cheek toward her chin.

The skin exfoliated freely from her face. All Tom could do was to continue. His voice was kindly. He was a friend. "Sandy, you're punishing yourself under a false impression of guilt."

The warning dream came to her in a flash.

The rush of waves cascaded before her eyes. The swirl of white foam was more violent and pronounced than she had ever remembered it being.

The girl was playing in the sand; *she* was playing in the sand. There was frenzy to her castle building as she struck repeatedly at the buttressed walls with an open palm, a flat *thwack, thwack* sound until her arms hurt and she could swing no more. Above her were marching clouds, rolling downward in angry upheaval. The sky was dark, low, more than threatening.

Her mother's arms flailed in the distance, pink flesh sharply contrasted against the purple of the horizon. Her father stepped over her to go to the drowning woman—

The scene shifted. The foreshadowing began.

She saw herself in the cemetery; she was *in* the cemetery.

Lost, frozen headstones, half buried in the fallen snow, decayed and decrepit, signaled to her. There was electricity in the air as the dark blue-black sky shifted above her. Clouds folded under themselves, as if giant hands were trying to hold them back. A cold wind blew and chilled her. Her dress billowed up and around her. There was movement in the cemetery as the surrounding tombstones freed their sculpted stone figures of death and time. They flew at her from all sides, rushing past her in swirls of air, disappearing before impact, leading her forward up the path toward—

The mausoleum.

Eben Wallford stood in front, a conflicting mixture of joy and sadness on his face. He had come to bury his daughter. He had come to free his daughter.

The voice came from inside the mausoleum, a low moan of desperation and doom.

"Daddy, don't . . . Daddy, don't . . ."

It was heard in the room as it fell from Sandy's mouth.

"Daddy, don't . . . Daddy, don't . . ."

Tom seized on the moment as Sandy twisted away in front of him. Her body became contorted, doubled over, as she tried to escape the beings that were flying at her. But she was held in place by them as they prodded her closer to the mausoleum on the top of the hill.

"Talk to her, Suzanne," Tom implored. He tried to reach through to that portion of her psyche that was striving to save her. "Tell her she is not guilty," he said.

"Don't damn yourself," Suzanne wailed, and the lost voice welled from deep within her.

"Don't," Sandy said, as she walked trancelike toward the man who was waiting patiently for her in front of his mausoleum. She was under his control. The voice of Tom was powerless next to him.

"Your daughter is dead. I am not your daughter." The words dropped from her lips, and she didn't know if he even heard her. The man touched her head.

"Suzanne," he said, and in a moment of frozen time, Sandy didn't know if he was talking to her or to the girl inside.

Skin reddened and fell from her face. Her entire body was scaling. Hair fell from her head in clumps, as if cut by unseen hands.

She swallowed fiercely and started to tremble. She knew she was taking her final steps. In less than a moment she would be inside the mausoleum, the door forever closed to her.

"Noooo—!" The scream pierced the air and caused David to jump. Spinner reached for his bag to prepare an injection. Tom waved him off.

"We can't. We've got to continue."

David saw her hair fall around her in tufts. He shook his head, lost, withdrawn. He wanted to run, but he couldn't move. He fell to his knees and covered his eyes with his hands.

In the cemetery, Sandy stood next to her tormentor, who reached in front of him and slowly eased open the door to the mausoleum. She was rooted in place, incapable of moving. Her mind willed it, but her feet refused to obey. She was being overridden.

"Help me," she said to those in the room. The words were little more than a whimper, for that was all the voice she could find. "He's going to kill me. . . . He's going to kill me . . . he's going to . . ."

Inside the mausoleum there was only darkness, a

black hole of night, of death. She felt the touch on her shoulder.

"He's pushing me in," she suddenly shrieked, as if her last efforts were being used to summon a voice she doubted she had. She started to push against Eben, who was standing in front of her.

Tom fought to hold her arms steady, but as he struggled with her she tried to free herself from the man who was condemning her to a premature burial.

She felt herself moving backward under his push, backward into the mausoleum.

The voice continued from inside. *"Daddy, don't . . . Daddy, don't . . . don't kill her. . . . You did nothing wrong. . . ."*

"We can't blame ourselves for accidents," Tom tried, not letting go of his firm hold on her.

"Don't damn yourself. . . ."

All alone on the top of the hill she could struggle no more. She knew she would have to submit to him, to give in, give up. To be pushed into the mausoleum the way he wanted.

"Grab the light, Daddy. Grab the light. Don't punish yourself. . . ."

The hands were insistent upon her.

"Eben Wallford!" Sandy cried in a shaky voice as the skin fell from her nose where it had brushed against him. Now all of her face, all of her body, was riddled with the disease. David sobbed into his arm; Spinner stared in horrified disbelief at what he was witnessing.

"He's pushing me into the mausoleum," she cried. "No—!"

She was inside and the door was closing.

Tom was startled. The mausoleum? What was she doing in the mausoleum? He had to steer her clear.

"You are not in the mausoleum, Sandy. Do you hear me?"

"Stop him! Please! The door—" Her alarm was evident and genuine.

The column of light became slimmer as the door was pushed closed on old rusty hinges.

"Don't leave me in here!"

She started to claw at Tom, whose face had become the door to eternity.

"Daddy, don't . . . Daddy, don't. . . ." There was a helplessness to the voice, a last desperation and acceptance of what was meant to be. *"Don't damn yourself. . . . We'll never be together. . . ."* A final appeal before the heavenly decree.

"Help her, Tom. *Please,*" David cried from across the room. Spinner took David's head to his chest to hide him from the sight.

Sandy's arms stretched upward as her fingers dug into the closing door to keep it from entombing her alive. The slender stick of light became gray and then black as she fell forward in the dark hole.

"Sandy!" Tom said in a sharp voice that whip-cracked through the room. Her nails dug into his face, but he overrode the pain.

"Sandy! Has Eben Wallford done this to you?"

"Help," she moaned in a last, lost cry. "Please help me. Please help me."

Blood dripped from Tom's face. He wiped it away quickly with the back of his hand.

"Has Eben Wallford pulled the skin from your body?"

". . . don't punish yourself this way . . . don't torture the girl. . . ."

"IS EBEN WALLFORD DOING THIS TO YOU???"

Sandy's screams filled the hospital room, and outside in the corridor others started to gather.

"YES!!!"

She collapsed into Tom's arms, exhausted, sobbing.

"Eben Wallford!" Tom commanded in a shrill voice. "You will leave this girl alone. You will torture her no longer. You will stop pulling the skin from her body."

The strangest feeling flooded Tom's mind. He was not certain if he was commanding the symbolic Eben Wallford of Sandy's subconscious guilt to leave the girl in peace, or the real Eben Wallford. But he knew it didn't matter at that moment whom he was talking to. They were one and the same. It was just what Sandy chose to make of it.

He would try once more. He was in danger of losing her.

"Sandy, you will listen to me. You will hear me and remember what I say."

It was cold in the mausoleum. . . .

"Eben Wallford is dead. He cannot communicate with you."

She felt her skin become clammy; start to crawl.

"He cannot touch you!"

Fear knotted her stomach and robbed her mouth of saliva.

"He cannot hurt you!"

Her fingers froze in false rigor mortis as they tried to bore into the heavy bronze door.

"You can banish Eben Wallford from your mind! You can fight him!"

She felt scratches on the wall, a century old, and knew they belonged to Suzanne.

"I see her nailmarks!" she gasped. She ran her hand quickly up and down the cold markings on the wall, palming the wall frantically as if blind.

"What else do you see, Sandy?" Tom pressed, and in that one moment he believed that part of her might just be inside the Wallford mausoleum.

"They buried you alive! You were alive!" she cried. Her voice trembled. Her throat locked. Her head dropped to the side.

"You can fight Eben Wallford!" Tom boomed. He pounded his right fist against his left palm. "You can stop your skin from peeling off and your hair from falling out! Listen to Suzanne!"

She looked around but could see nothing in the darkness. She was rooted to the spot, frozen, as if to move would be to lose her last solid connection with the bronze doors, and her only hope.

"You did nothing wrong!"

Then came the realization.

"Oh, my God! That's what he's doing to me! He wants to bury *me* alive!"

Tom reached out to her.

"Sandy!" he commanded loudly. "You will come out of the mausoleum and be well! You can fight Eben Wallford! You can banish him! You can stop your skin from peeling off! You did nothing wrong!"

But his voice did not penetrate.

Suddenly she felt a hand from the dark. It touched her shoulder. Tom's hand, but to Sandy it came from another. She stiffened and froze.

"Don't touch me, Suzanne!" she shrieked.

She whirled around and saw it—

"I will count to three and you will come out of the mausoleum. You will start to get better again!"

"*No!* Dear God, no!"

"ONE . . ."

"He can't! He can't!"

"TWO . . ."

But she never heard Tom finish the count, because she was lost in a blood-chilling scream. She fainted into exhaustion. Her final sight before blacking out was the vision of what she knew would now be her destiny.

CHAPTER XXXIV

The conquistador lay at the foot of the stairs. With strength and fury he didn't know he possessed, David had rushed into the house and seized on the statue to devastate it. He didn't remember bolting from the hospital room, or driving home in a blind, helpless rage. His breathing was intense, his whole body heaving, as he took in great gulps of air and ferociously expelled them. He stared downward at the statue, which had been chipped from the fall, the Burger King hat squashed under the stone figure. It was Bob's property, but at that moment he felt no remorse, because nothing mattered anymore.

"Damn you, Wallford! Damn you!" he spat out.

He looked around the room, lost, as if seeing it for the first time. There was destruction in his eyes and an uncontrollable tenseness to his arms. His glance went from object to object in the antique-laden room. He seized an axe that stood next to the fireplace. He shouldered the axe and ran from the house.

In blind, thoughtless action he raced up the road toward the mausoleum. He stumbled up the snowy steps until he was level with the statue. He raised the axe again and again and began to hack away at the petrified stone.

Ice chips flew in all directions as the axe found its way home. Again and again. First at Eben Wallford's arm. Then at his trunk and head.

The head of the axe was blasted to bits by the hard stone, but still David kept up his futile efforts; and when the axe head finally flew off, David went at the statue with the wooden handle.

Tears streamed down his face and froze in his mustache. He was swinging blindly, not seeing, not thinking.

"Damn you, Wallford! Rot in hell!" he screamed over and over again in a voice that wasn't human.

The handle flew from David's hands and he went at the statue with his fists, pounding at the cold, hard, unforgiving stone. His hands hurt, but he suppressed the pain. All he could see was the vision of Sandy in her hospital bed, skin reddened and scaling, and her reported vision of the man coming to pull the skin from her body.

A hand grasped his shoulder.

David whirled around.

"David!" Tom screamed.

David looked at Tom and saw only Eben Wallford. He started to swing at Tom, who grabbed at his arms in midair and tried to wrestle him to the stone steps.

"David, stop! It's Tom. Listen to me. Listen to me!"

They both struggled to the ground. David was more wild than accurate, and Tom managed to pin his arms off to the side. The breathing of both was intense, the struggle even more difficult in the cold air.

"Let me up," David cried frantically, and kicked outward as if in a tantrum. His gaze kept falling on the statue, which remained standing, reminding him of unfinished business.

"No," Tom answered. "You calm down."

David tried to free himself, but Tom, suddenly

stronger and having the advantage, held his grip tightly and forced David to struggle against himself. He slapped David hard across the face. Surprised, David lay still, exhausted. Tom slowly eased off.

He stood over David and watched him in the snow. His breath was slowing, his fists unclenching.

"There's improvement," Tom said, inhaling sharply to catch his breath.

"What?"

"I just spoke to Dr. Spinner. . . ."

David's face lit up with hope.

"There's a stabilizing of the condition."

"She's better?"

"No. Not yet. Just no worse. But she's on her way."

A grin spread across David's face. "You did it, Tom! You did it!" His eyes shone. He pounded the snow. "Son of a bitch!"

Tom smiled. This was what it was all about.

"Her will to get better is stronger than the destructive, punishing influence of the Eben Wallford part of her. She can control him. With luck, as I directed, she can banish him. You might say that Suzanne is winning. Sandy is freeing up her guilt, acknowledging to herself she did nothing wrong. That the crash was an accident. That she was not to blame."

"What next?"

"More of the same. More therapy. Reinforcement."

"But it's downhill from here?"

Tom ducked the question; that was not one he wanted to answer. He looked at David lying in the snow. "Hey, aren't you cold down there?"

David nodded. "Yeah. Help me up, will you."

Tom stretched out a hand, which David grasped firmly. Tom pulled him to his feet.

David looked once more at the statue of Eben Wallford. He no longer had any power.

Back in the house Bob broke open a bottle of champagne in celebration.

David raised his glass high. "Let's toast the best psychiatrist in the world."

A smile opened on Tom's face and he touched glasses with David. But inwardly he was troubled. A feeling was coursing through him. A sense that something was not right.

It was very late, the pit of the night; closer to dawn than to dusk, closer to daylight than to midnight. When outdoor movement is rare, when darkness seems denser, cold more intense, sleep deeper.

Something strong woke Judy Landberg from sleep. It bade her get out of the bed. With great reluctance she threw off her covers. It was the time of night when her body temperature was lowest, and she was cold. Yet something was making her leave the warmth of her bed.

She remembered the face of the man. The gray-haired man. She had seen him before she awoke. She had looked deeply into his eyes, *had locked on them,* and had seen what was behind them: terror, and a deep, lost hopelessness buried far within. The eyes burned sharply at her and called her from sleep. The eyes spoke to her, the *man* spoke to her. Not through words—*she heard no words*— yet somehow she knew they were linked nonetheless. His thoughts were hers.

She was the girl he wanted.

She sensed desperation within those eyes, and somehow she knew the man had but one last chance; his hope was slender. She was unable to share his emotion, having no identification with anything remotely similar. But she knew this desperation was a powerful one that burned to his core. An eternal one.

The hall light burned brightly, and she shielded her eyes as she left the women's dorm room. She still saw the man, still saw his forceful eyes blazing inexorably at her. She was following those eyes, going where they were leading. Unquestioningly.

They were leading her down the stairs to the living room.

Her slippered feet made no sound on the hall rug. There were no other sounds in the sleeping house. But she wasn't really aware of anything other than the man.

The living room was cold, as if a mat of frigid air had settled over it.

The fire crackled high in the hearth. That was odd; with no one downstairs, the fire should not have been burning. She watched it as she walked down the stairs. The flames were slender fingers reaching out to her, beckoning to her, pulling her to them. And she went.

Even the blazing fire could not warm the room.

(She wondered what it would be like to walk into the fire, to be on fire, to let the heat scorch her skin and blacken it; what it would be like to burn to the bone, to be incinerated.

She stood at the bottom of the stairs, her back straight, her chin high. She peered deeply into the fire, hypnotized by the alluring flames. She was not afraid; it was where she had to go. Where he wanted her to go.

The familiar burning smell was strong.

Slowly she approached the fireplace.

There was a buzzing in Tom's ear, and suddenly in his sleeping mind it all came together and made sense. Something woke him with a start: a precognition of terror? A warning? He didn't have time to analyze, only act. He had to get to his daughter.

He remembered.

Judy looked like Sandy: same eyes, same hair. Like Suzanne. What if he had been wrong? What if Eben Wallford *had* been telepathically removing Sandy's skin? If the skin had stopped peeling from Sandy, it might continue to come from someone else: Judy.

Her will was not now as strong as Sandy's. Tom had not programmed her with resistance. There had not

been a need to. She was vulnerable. Eben could turn
to her.

He jumped to the cold tile floor. He raced to the
dorm and looked in Judy's bunk.

Not there.

"Judy!" he called loudly, and tore out of the room.
No one answered him. "Judy!" he continued to yell,
and the house reacted to his voice and came awake.

Something intuitive told him he had to find her immediately, otherwise he'd be too late. The same inner
voice seemed to whisper: *downstairs*.

He saw her from the landing. She was inches from
the fireplace, staring into the fire, holding her hand
out, testing it. The flames were licking hungrily at her
fingertips.

"Judy!" he screamed again, as if the word would
wake her from her trance.

He took the last steps in one leap and was across the
room to pull his daughter's hand back out of the fire.

The fire seemed to heave and shudder and tried to
follow her, to grasp her. But Tom had pulled her far
enough away. He slapped her fiercely, calling her name
loudly over and over.

The others came running down the stairs. Gail
stopped at the landing, her hand to her mouth in horror.

Finally the girl's eyes opened and she looked at her
father.

"Daddy?" she asked weakly, and then fell sobbing
into his arms.

Tom spoke rapidly. "I want both kids out of here
now. Gail, dress them and take them home. Don't let
them fall asleep until you're all home. And you all stay
together tonight. Don't leave them alone until you hear
from me."

It was then that they noticed how cold the living
room was.

* * *

Nobody went back to sleep. Gail had Scott and Judy dressed and ready to go within twenty minutes. Bob would follow them in Tom's car as far as the highway. *Until they were out of Owlsfane.*

Tom dropped to the couch. It was the first time he had had to stop and reflect since jumping out of bed a half hour before. He had questions for himself: Why had he awakened from a deep sleep at precisely the right moment and with the right conclusions?

Then suddenly he remembered what it was that had awakened him: an anguished female voice shouting warning in his inner ear.

It was a half hour later when the telephone rang. Bob was not yet back, and Tom ran for it, grabbing it, thinking something had happened on the road. The other house members gathered around.

He listened grim-faced.

"Thank you," he said finally, and hung up the phone.

"What is it?" David asked. "What's wrong?"

"That was the hospital," Tom said slowly. "Sandy's condition has worsened. The skin is peeling again."

He looked at David and spoke softly. "We may have been wrong. We have to find out for certain."

Tom poured the boiling water into two cups of instant coffee and quickly added sugar and milk. His fingers grasped the cup and he downed half of the hot liquid.

David just stared at his cup, a distant expression on his face. He waited for Tom to finish his coffee.

"Sandy resisted the hypnosis, David. Purposely. At times violently. The skin disease spread at an unexplainable rate and didn't respond at all to the medication. Let's suppose the disease is not organic or purely psychological in origin. Then what? Then we look at what else we have: the voice of Suzanne."

"Meaning?" David asked.

"Meaning we cannot exclude the possibility of an otherworld psychic connection. Eben Wallford and Suzanne. What Sandy was reporting as happening might have actually been happening. Perhaps there was no symbolism to her seeing Eben Wallford. Perhaps she did see him. And perhaps we really have been listening to Sandy speak in the voice of Suzanne."

"That's a big admission for you," David said.

"I'm not going to say that her background is separate and apart from the possible Wallford connection. Without one, there may not have been the other. Her repressed past came through to us under hypnosis; there's no question and nothing supernatural there. Sandy probably never would have gone into the Wallford house in the first place if it hadn't been for her own past's having been recalled to her by the story Bob told. Nor can we at all ignore everything we've learned about her. But that's all to be dealt with in therapy later."

He paused to sip the rest of his coffee.

"However, now we have the following possibility: Sandy is drawn to the Wallford house. Eben is in there. He *sees* her. He reaches out to her. He comes through to her. In her dreams. As a ghost. He has been in psychic contact with her since the first night she got there. As has Suzanne."

He paused ruefully. "Now, we've all been in that house before, right?"

David nodded.

"So why Sandy?"

"The portrait," David said immediately, suddenly seeing everything more clearly. The distorted TV picture had just locked into place with a flip of the horizontal hold.

"Yes, the portrait," Tom said sadly. "The one bloody clue we all chose to ignore because we didn't know what to do with it. The similarity was more than coincidence, we allowed that. But what was it? No one ever defined it. Perhaps now we know. Sandy Horne looks just like the dead Suzanne. Bingo! A reason for Eben Wallford to come through to her.

"Which brings us to Judy. Eben was losing the struggle for control over Sandy's subconscious. She was resisting him, successfully fighting his pull on her skin. That's why he turned to Judy, a little girl with the misfortune of having the same hair and shape of eyes as Sandy. As Suzanne. Whom Eben also saw. She didn't know enough to resist; she suspected no danger. Nor did we," he added sadly. "Eben was leading Judy to the fire to burn off her skin when I broke his telepathic possession of her and snapped her free. So in desperation he had to turn back to Sandy, who is still susceptible to him, and struggle with her. And now, in his fierce panic to do what he has to do, his telepathic influence is proving stronger than Sandy's strength of will to keep him away."

Tom poured another cup of coffee. The rational part of his being fought this psychic connection, but now he knew he could not dismiss the possibility. The evidence was strong and the circumstances demanded investigation. There were so many positive indications.

"Up until now we had thought of Sandy's condition as being psychosomatic—self-induced. There is now the chance that telekinetic forces are involved. Eben Wallford could be telepathically causing her skin to peel off, to *burn* off. Sandy's symptoms could be *tele*somatic in origin. And coming from beyond the grave."

Tom paused. "Why is Eben doing this?" He looked straight at David, almost through him, before adding, "As Sandy/Suzanne has said, to reconstruct his daughter and bring her back."

CHAPTER XXXV

It was evening when the doorbell rang. They had just finished dinner, and while his wife carried the dishes into the kitchen, Josiah Stoneham went to open the door. Startled, he looked into the face of Bob Kanon.

"Hello, Mr. Stoneham," Bob said graciously.

Josiah lowered his head in polite, but distant greeting. "Mr. Kanon."

"May we come in?" Bob asked.

It was then that Josiah noticed the two others who stood behind Bob.

"Just for a few minutes. It's very important."

Josiah stepped aside and held the door open to them. They stamped the excess snow from their boots and entered the house.

"We'd like to talk to you about Eben Wallford," Bob said.

"What about Eben?" Josiah asked. There was surprise in his voice, alarm, and he was suddenly defensive. His eyebrows flared upward and he looked at them with suspicion. "Just what is it that you gentlemen want to talk about?"

Before Josiah could change his mind, Bob had his coat off and hung on a peg by the door. Following his lead, David and Tom slipped out of theirs, handing them to Bob, who hung the parkas over his.

"Mr. Stoneham, this is David Thomas, a member of the ski house. And Dr. Tom Landberg, a psychiatrist."

Josiah resisted the efforts of both men to shake his hand.

"May we sit down?" Bob asked, indicating the couch in front of the fire.

"Only for a minute," Josiah said. "We're rather busy."

Mrs. Stoneham appeared from the kitchen door.

"Oh," she said in surprise, and then said politely, with warmth, "Hello, Mr. Kanon."

Bob quickly made the introductions before Josiah added, "They can't stay long."

Taking their chairs into the living room, Bob started it off.

"Josiah," he said, hoping to put the old man at ease by using his first name, "you know we all believe in the story of the Wallford family."

Josiah snorted. "Didn't know that. Certainly don't show any respect."

Bob chose to ignore his last comment. "Although we've never really talked to you about it to hear some of it firsthand."

"Why? So you can laugh at it back in that ski house of yours?"

"It's important," Bob said. "Please."

Recognizing the urgency in Bob's tone, Josiah softened and nodded. He was feeling a little awkward about his outburst the other night. He really wasn't like that. Not even with strangers. He could talk to these people—it didn't matter. "My grandfather was executor of Eben's will and, of course, his friend. Probably one of only a few. Eben was the land baron of this area and was regarded by most more as a curiosity than a friend. And of course I only knew of him. He died years before I was born. Although," he added, suddenly thoughtful and introspective, the conversation with Hank Sweeter ringing fresh in his mind, "I feel I do know him—at least his presence—living so near his house all my life."

Tom weighed his next words carefully. "Have you ever seen him or talked to him?"

"No," Josiah said with certainty. "Never seen him. Never talked to him." He was suspicious. "Why?"

"Yet you think he's in the house?" Bob offered.

"Know he's in the house. Or at least coming back to it." Mrs. Stoneham nodded vigorously in agreement.

"Have you ever made any attempt to contact him?"

Mrs. Stoneham looked genuinely surprised. "Heavens, no. Why would we do that? We don't want to go looking for ghosts."

Ghosts, Tom thought. Poor unfortunate souls, trapped in limbo between this world and the next, unable to escape the problems that hold them here, looking for someone to guide them to the next plane of existence.

Stoneham agreed. "No sense turning things up that best be left alone. We've come to a pretty good understanding, Eben and I. He don't bother me and I don't bother him." He winked confidentially at David, who exploded.

"Well Eben happens to be bothering—"

Tom silenced him by asking loudly: "Do you ever go into the house, Mrs. Stoneham?" He already knew the answer, but it was the only question that came to mind.

"Well, of course," she said. "To clean. Dust . . ." She trailed off, uncertainly.

"You dust the whole house?" Tom pursued. "Downstairs as well as up?"

"Whole house gets dirty."

"About how often are you in there?"

Mrs. Stoneham looked hesitantly toward her husband, who nodded that she could continue.

"I'd say once a month or so. Maybe more in the spring, less in the winter."

"And yet you never made any attempt to contact him, or vice versa?" Tom asked softly.

"No."

"When you go upstairs, do you ever notice anything unusual?"

"You mean, Dr. Landberg, where is he when I go up there?"

"Yes."

"I don't know. And I make no attempt to find out. We do what we've been doing for more years than I can remember, or care to, and what Josiah's family did before that—"

"The cake you put out," Bob asked casually. "Is it ever eaten?"

"Don't answer that!" Josiah snapped suddenly, and his tone was hostile. Any pretenses of friendliness were dissolved. He owed these people nothing.

"Gentlemen," he said with restraint. "There is more than idle curiosity to your questions. We've told you what you wished to know. More than we cared to tell. Now what is it you specifically want from me?"

There was an edge to his voice and Tom knew they would get nothing more from him. It was time to tell.

But David was talking already. Blurting, perhaps, might be more accurate.

"Your Eben Wallford, whom you've never seen or talked to, has taken over my fiancée's body and is stripping the skin and hair right off her."

Josiah Stoneham was on his feet. "What?" His gaze was hard and he looked as if he could drip acid.

"You heard me," David said, standing. "If you don't believe me, you can just come and look at her for yourself." He turned to Tom and noticed the look of warning on his face. He collapsed back onto the couch, crying into his hands. "I'm sorry," he muttered. "So sorry . . ."

"Mr. Kanon," Josiah said sternly. "I think you'd all better leave my house."

"Wait," Bob protested. "Listen to Tom. You've got to hear all of this and we've got to talk."

Tom quickly told them all he knew. From Sandy's first entrance into the house, to her dreams, the hypnosis session, and the exfoliating skin. Josiah and his wife exchanged glances from time to time. Mrs. Stoneham's face showed pity for the girl; Josiah was stoic, betraying no emotion.

"What do you want from us?" he asked when Tom was through.

"We have to find out if Eben is the cause."

"I can tell you right now, Eben is doing no such thing," Josiah said with finality. But inwardly he wondered. About the girl who had come running out of the house.

"You can't tell us that," Tom said wearily, the strain of it all finally beginning to come through in his voice. "Because you don't know. No one does."

"You're right. I don't." Josiah said. "How do you plan to go about finding out?"

Tom was careful. "Sandy is very weak, Mr. Stoneham. At the rate the disease has spread, she is wide open to complications. She could die."

"I ask again," Josiah said. "How?"

"What we have to ascertain is whether or not Eben Wallford is tearing the skin from the body of Sandy Horne to reconstruct his dead daughter."

"How?" Josiah repeated, louder, once again on his feet.

"By exhumation of the dead girl's body," Tom said.

Josiah's eyes opened wide in disbelief. His mouth moved in confusion before his voice came out.

"You're mad," Josiah hissed.

CHAPTER XXXVI

Nighttime.

The small-town hospital swung into its quiet routine. The overhead corridor lights were dimmed to a filtered orange. From the nurses' station in the center of the floor, one could look in either direction toward the inky blackness of the night beyond the institutional cross-barred windows. Porters were silently sweeping huge mops across tiled floors. The light splash of dirty pail-water, the sound of wringing and dripping, the whooshing backdrop of mop against floor, echoed up and down the lonely corridor. The phones were silent, the patients asleep. The floor nurse was settling in for a nighttime of routine. From time to time her eyes glanced upward from her paperback novel toward the patients' callboard, which was silent and unlit.

She sensed a fragmented motion and was suddenly chilled by invisible currents of frigid air, which swept over her in ominous waves. She shuddered and looked around at dim corridors she had seen and memorized and stared unseeing at hundreds, if not thousands, of similar nights. There was no one near her save the porter, almost frozen in time and motion over his long-handled mop, abstractedly moving dirty water about, thinking of other times, other places, other lives.

No one, and nothing but the strange feeling of . . . *something*. Something queer. Something lurking. Something invisible; sensed, not seen. A hidden presence announcing itself through shadowed recesses of frightened minds.

The nurse on duty coughed nervously, and the porter down the hall was pulled from his reverie. As if he suddenly remembered where he was and his function, his idle mop sprang back into motion and all of a sudden filled the hall with life and purpose. Inwardly embarrassed, without cause, the nurse shifted her eyes back to the callboard then to the novel. She fought the urge to glance behind her, fearful of what she might discover had invaded the normalcy of the hospital corridor.

There was something there. That they all knew. But whether it would be just in *her* room, or throughout, they didn't know. In an hour the nurse on duty would make her rounds. Look in on the patients. Usually an obligatory drudge. Tonight, for that one room in particular, in the half-lit empty corridor, it was a function she did not wish to perform.

Whose skin did he want next?

In Sandy's room, there was the sound of even, drugged breathing. Air encountered resistance in her nostrils and pushed out through a half-opened mouth. There was a heaviness to the hospital room, as if the particles of darkness were moving slowly against each other. An invisible sluggish turbidity punctuated by the steady, rhythmic in-and-out of passing air.

To someone who had heard the stories making the rounds of the hospital, the room might have appeared colder than the others, as if the desire to create and see (*yet not see*) would summon the presence as a wish fulfillment. To anyone else, it was a room of sleep, like any other room in a small country hospital settled in for a night of unbroken routine.

Sandy was dreaming.

Of a girl bathed in a white light of warmth and brilliance, a light that beckoned, a light from which no one would ever turn or return. A light of forgiveness, of understanding. Of life in death.

The girl was whole and happy. She was surrounded by others. By a woman who had drowned. By a man killed in the flash of a burning car. And others. As far as the eye could see. Yet the eye was not really seeing. That was only within its frame of understandable reference. *The mind was receiving.*

Yet there was someone missing.

The girl in the dream spoke, and the words were carried forth through invisible circuits, crumbling barriers hairbreadth-thick, yet solid and unbreakable. And one way.

The words were perceived more than heard. As were the visions that preceded them. A sense of reality (it was more than a dream), yet an equal sense of timelessness, of diffusion. The slightest quiver would disintegrate the picture already beginning to waver and wane.

But before the vision was lost, the words were heard in a light call. The voice was familiar to the sleeping girl, but the tone was softer, like spun silk. The voice no longer sounded a warning; instead, it reached out to her, beckoning to her.

Come to me, Sandy, the lilting voice said in a color of light, refreshing sea-blue. *Bring him to me. . . .*

An arm unfolded and stretched outward, palm open and up, in invitation and greeting, fingers slightly curled inward to a tightening fist.

And then the dream ended.

CHAPTER XXXVII

The county coroner would hear the case for exhumation. It would be an informal hearing. Tom, who made the request, would state his case; any others who wanted to speak would do so. The coroner's decision would stand unless appealed in court.

Josiah Stoneham was confident. The coroner was from Bartsbury: *one of them.* He had grown up with the Wallford ghosts as neighbors; he knew their tragedy. He would not rule against them. Certainly not for such a ridiculous, *terrifying* request as exhuming the body of Suzanne Wallford. Good God! Did they have any idea what they could be opening up? What might be in there waiting to be let out? He could only try to imagine what his grandfather and the others had seen when they opened the mausoleum to inter the body of Eben's wife: the daughter, arms outstretched above her, as if reaching out from quicksand; her fingers bent and twisted in a paralyzed claw trying to dig into the cold bronze door; her nails broken, streaks of blood running to the floor; her mouth hanging open and contorted, tongue stiff and dry, a last voice lost within the hollow of the mausoleum; her eyes frozen open, final realization written on cracked pupils. No—the coroner would not rule against them. That was inconceivable.

The hearing room was overly warm. The hiss of the radiator penetrated like a poisonous snake coiled and about to strike. The windows were fogged over from inner condensation, and already the air had grown stale and sticky. Clothing was strewn about, as layer upon layer had been shed as the room became more crowded and uncomfortable. The double doors in the rear were swung open to try to catch a passing breeze from the corridor windows.

Even more people packed into the small room, and many had to stand or perch on the wide windowsills. It had the feeling of a meeting late in getting started—one that no one wants to attend, yet one from which no one can stay away. The courthouse in the county seat of North Johnston had not seen so much excitement since Keith Acton had gone on trial for the rape and murder of one of Townsend's housewives three years before, when people lined up for hours before the ten A.M. *oyez,* braving wind chills in the double minus figures for choice seats to "the trial of the last two decades," where tickets were ultimately scalped as the proceedings continued toward their climax and the verdict of guilty. *This,* however, would be a one-day-only sale, they all felt; and as word of the request and hearing spread like wildfire through the neighboring towns (the clerk had called Josiah, whose wife had called Mrs. Amsterdam, and that was as good as if it had gone out over the radio, the small-town grapevine being very ordered and efficient), plans for the upcoming holiday weekend were shunted aside as the more exciting event unfolded and took precedence and spectators crowded into the small hearing room.

The members of the ski house filled one of the hardback benches, the townspeople the others. Josiah Stoneham, seated in the second row, was determined to battle the request fiercely and had the support of others. Some voiced shock, but secretly hoped it would

come to exhumation: *this was news!* They were curious
to peek into a mausoleum they had passed in wonder
and awe all of their Vermont lives. Perhaps now there
could be verification of a story long told and half believed. Most likely, though, they conceded, there would
be nothing.

But the hearing itself was still something to break
the tedious Owlsfane (Bartsbury, Townsend, North
Johnston) routine, and still something to discuss at
New Year's Eve gatherings with the same people you
see daily: when you're really all talked out on everything else, and talk of prices and city people and the
long-gone G.E. plant no longer holds your attention,
and the fact that the mountain is floating a new bond
issue is not really so interesting or pertinent to your
life, because you don't have the money to buy a bond
and you don't ski anyway. The exhumation request
also legitimatized the whole Wallford legend: it was
now okay for you to talk about something you never
really talked about for fear of being labeled silly or
superstitious (although it was okay for Josiah, because
he was *in the house,* and a little old and possibly senile
anyway, but for anyone else it smacked of belief in
ghosts, and that really wasn't something you went
public with, you know?).

Hank Sweeter even expected to see "Eben Wallford
Lives" buttons, bumper stickers, and iron-on T-shirts
sold in front of the courthouse. He was a little disappointed an enterprising local didn't take advantage
of an obvious situation.

Hank really didn't know what he wanted to see
happen when they opened the mausoleum, vis-à-vis
Josiah's changing his mind about selling the Wallford
place. If they found nothing unusual, then there would
be nothing conclusive either way, hence a *status quo.*
But if they opened up the doors and found what everybody was saying they were looking for—well, that
would be proof that something was going on in that

house after all, and Josiah would never consent to sell.
When Hank Sweeter pieced this all together he realized
that "heads he lost, tails he lost." Either way it had to
work against him, and that meant ten thousand big
ones shot to shit.

Tom was already in the courtroom as the spectators
filed in. They looked at him as if they had come to
see a show, and he knew he was it. He also knew he
had to be concise and convincingly good. It was the
Friday before New Year's weekend. It would be five
days before another hearing could be held. Any number
of complications could set in for Sandy in that time,
including pneumonia or heart failure. Her body temperature was already unstabilized, and some transfusions had been required as anemia developed. Her
condition was being listed as "guarded." A complication could drive it to "serious," a severe setback to
"critical." There was an urgency to this request, jeop-
ardy to Sandy's life.

Tom also knew the odds against bucking the local
superstitions were high.

He was dressed in the best clothes he had brought
with him for the holiday week in Vermont, where high
fashion was not *de riqueur*. He hoped a dark turtleneck
worn under his old tweed jacket with the black elbow
patches would create the proper image mix of medical
knowledge and legal razzle-dazzle. Although he acknowledged he knew precious little about the law, less
about courtroom procedures, and what he was about
to present to the county coroner relied little on his
medical knowledge at that.

He had to know if there was indeed a psychic override in the case. The possibility seemed so foreign, so
alien to all he had been taught and practiced. But the
possibility existed nonetheless, and if borne out would
lend definition to something that appeared undefinable.
Although he wondered if he was being foolish. *Psychic*

override, he thought derisively. Sandy's past was extraordinary! More so than that of any of his other patients, perhaps extraordinary enough for a dozen lifetimes. Was he admitting defeat as a psychiatrist that he had not gotten through to her in one therapy session? Patients had willfully opposed him before, their defenses attuned to keeping him out. Most times he had eventually succeeded. Given time, he might succeed here as well. But he knew there was more than that here; there was mounting evidence of *something else:* the other sessions, the reality-based dreams, the portrait, *his daughter.* It was all too coincidental, too ordered, not to be explored. He and Spinner concurred. They had never before seen a case as extreme or swift in development as Sandy's. And therefore, as baffling. Perhaps it was too easy to look for a supernatural explanation, but it had to be investigated, if only to be eliminated. Tom realized that it all came down to one question: Did Sandy hallucinate Eben and Suzanne? Or were they actually coming through to her? Tom didn't know which answer he hoped to find. If there was no evidence of a psychic override, the hypnotherapy would continue, as would the corticosteroids, the skin dressing, and transfusions if required. If there indeed was the other-world connection—well, in that case, he honestly didn't know what he might do, short of a psychic rescue circle to free the earthbound Eben Wallford.

The coroner gaveled the room to order. The voices quietly stopped with a final "They're crazy if they think they can do that" cracking the air. The coroner ran a hand through his short gray hair. Nothing of so explosive a nature had ever been before him in his forty years as a county official. He wondered if someone should have called the local press, but knew they were better off without the publicity. They didn't have to be known nationwide as the town who hunted for ghosts. First thing, they'd find themselves on *Real People,* and then Mike Wallace would be nosing around.

The room was silent except for the hissing steam. The coroner began to speak in his perpetually hoarse, scratchy voice. He should give up cigarettes, he knew, and he would—the same day he gave up breathing.

"Dr. Landberg," he said, addressing Tom, who stood up respectfully. "Why are you petitioning for exhumation of the body of Suzanne Wallford?"

Tom angled himself so that he half faced the coroner and half the expectant room. He felt as if he were addressing a jury.

He quickly repeated the entire story, skipping psychiatric details, covering only what he had to, from Sandy's first entrance into the Wallford house—

(*"Where she had no business being,"* Josiah interjected.

"Josiah, please, *let him continue,"* the coroner admonished)

—to the results of the last hypnosis session.

He cited the portrait, the resemblance, and the peeling skin. Many in the room did nothing to mask their revulsion at Sandy's condition. An older woman excused herself from her aisle seat and left.

Tom was sweating as he started on his conclusions. He almost felt as if he had stepped aside from himself, an observer to what he was saying. The thoughts and words were his, that he knew; but they were delivered by someone else, it seemed, as if he were back in medical school listening to his professor recite a clinical history.

"From the very first moment Sandy Horne stepped into that house, it was as if she were in a different world. From that first moment, the spirits of Eben and Suzanne Wallford swirled around her, homed in, and began to come through, each trying to use her to reach the other. They obviously cannot contact each other psychically and are trying to do so through the living medium, Sandy Horne.

"From what I've gathered from the stories surrounding the Wallford family's deaths and from what Suzanne"—he caught himself—"*Sandy* said under hypnosis, I can suggest the following possibility for what might be happening to her. I may be right; I may not be." His voice rose, and there were pauses between each of his words. "But we will have to exhume the body of the dead girl for confirmation!"

He paused and breathed tightly, eyeing the hostile room. He knew he had only one shot and had to sound convincing. Suddenly he realized he was not detached from himself, not watching a professor deliver a case history. He was Tom Landberg, M.D., and he alone had the responsibility for the life or death of Sandy Horne. He felt a surge through his body and a warmth in his groin. *Ego,* he thought ruefully: he had it too.

David stared into the faces of those around him. Most were tight-lipped, but willing to listen to Tom. Others appeared to be openly belligerent. David hated those who hated them. Opening that mausoleum could not touch their lives, could not harm them. But it could help Sandy, and he would not let them block that. If the ruling went against them and they did not have the time to appeal, he would find a way into the mausoleum himself. Even if it involved grave robbing at midnight. Somehow he would get in there so they could look at Suzanne.

"The Wallfords were a close family," Tom continued. "That we all know. The unit was shattered, though, when Suzanne took ill and died. Doubly so after the death of his wife. Eben's wife was dead, his daughter was dead, and he was alone to think about how the girl was mistakenly buried alive. All of this eventually led a guilty Eben Wallford to take his own life and—"

Josiah Stoneham was out of his seat, defensive over the death of his grandfather's friend.

"He did not!" Stoneham shouted, and for a moment wondered why. But he knew why. He knew if the exhumation took place he would be betraying a trust.

"Lost the will to live, then," Tom countered with a scowl. "There's little difference."

"Eben didn't kill himself!" Josiah repeated. "There are religious teachings—"

The coroner banged down the gavel. "Josiah, it's irrelevant. Please sit down."

"He was a religious man," he said, before taking a seat. He turned to Hawley Elbers, who was beside him. "He would never have killed himself."

Hawley only nodded in neutral response. This was all very interesting.

Tom waited for Josiah's mutterings to fade before he continued.

"In life they were all together," he said. "And in death, Eben always expected them to be together still. But they are not together. The family has not come back—or, rather, did not stay behind. The food was eaten from only one plate: Eben's; the lights, according to eye-witness accounts, have only appeared in one room: *his*. If Eben Wallford is in that house, I contend he is in there alone."

Tom's voice became lower, almost tearful, full of pity for the troubled man.

"He is desperately trying to reach his family, to be with them where they are. But he cannot. And Suzanne is trying to get through to her father, but his guilt is a wall around him, keeping her out."

He allowed his eyes to glaze over as he searched inwardly and remembered the words of Suzanne/Sandy. Suddenly something intuitive told Tom that it had to be so.

"Death is pleasant for Suzanne, who died tragically,

in pain." He moved to a tape recorder on the front
table, cued and set. He flipped it on. Sandy's voice
filled the room—deep, distant, resonant in fear—
Suzanne's!

*"Daddy, come with me. Come inside. Come through
the barrier."*

David remembered how she had appeared in the hospital, only hours before, it seemed. The last week had
become one day for him, one unending, painful day.

*"I don't want to come back . . . I like being dead . . .
It's pretty here . . . I'm happy here . . . there's no
pain . . ."*

The words had their effect. The people in the room
sat stunned, expressionless, except for a creeping horror deep behind their eyes. There was no register of
disbelief. It was now more than an amusing circus.
With the realization that they were listening to the voice
of a girl a hundred years dead, one of the women in
the back row swooned and fell to the floor. Two others
helped carry her out; her family, presumably, for no
one else moved from his chair. The echoing voice of
the dead girl faded as Tom flipped off the machine. He
was glad now that he had decided to tape the sessions.
The evidence was strong. There was no doubt in the
minds of the religious people of the central Vermont
county that they were listening to a voice from the
afterlife.

Tom faced the spectators and spoke gently. "Suzanne
is calling to her father to join them. To leave his pain
and self-imposed guilt *here* and go to them. And Eben
wants to join them, we know that. More than anything
in this world or any other—"

He let his voice hang in the silent room, then emphasized his next words. "But Eben won't let himself fully
leave this world. He is a poor, tragic soul half in this
world, half in the next—"

A woman in the hearing room gasped. It was spontaneous; the reaction of all.

"There are many unfortunate spirits such as Eben's, held earthbound for whatever reasons—unfinished business, guilt—or those who might have died suddenly in violent accidents, who do not understand they are dead or cannot accept the transition to another world. There are those people who have condemned themselves to relive over and over the problems they had at the time of their deaths, not allowing themselves the release that death so sweetly offers to us all. Eben Wallford is keeping himself rooted in this world by what he took with him to his death—and beyond—the guilt that he buried his daughter alive. That is what is preventing him from being free and going to his eternal reward."

Tom leaned in toward the townspeople. His fists were clenched, his voice strong. He truly believed what he was saying. There was no more ego; it was real.

"We have to help Eben Wallford as much as we have to help Sandy Horne. The manifestation of a ghost is a cry for help. He is calling our attention to him to help him leave this world and enter the next." He stared straight out at Josiah in the second row and tried to melt him with his words. "We can't deny him this help. It would be morally wrong. If *I* were held in limbo between the two dimensions of existence, I would want the help others could give."

The spectators were silent, held suspended by his words. Then they began to stir uncertainly. They were terrified by the incomprehensible possibility of eternal limbo. Their thoughts went to their own lives: What might there be within each of them that might hold them earthbound against their will after their deaths?

"After the tragic discovery of Suzanne at the door of the mausoleum, Eben Wallford lived in hell on earth. He withdrew from people. Into himself. Josiah will bear me out on that. . . ."

Josiah's face was impassive. He was listening, absorbing, but not yet publicly agreeing. Although he knew he was softening, that his position was changing.

If Eben was in trouble, he had to help. If he chose not to, then that would be *his* eternal guilt, and the cycle might continue. The thought of his own suspended existence chilled him.

Tom continued. "And he carried that hell with him after his death. What he may have envisioned as punishment for his sin, he is now experiencing in the afterlife." He paused heavily. "And for Eben that punishment is eternal solitude, while he is desperately trying to escape. But unfortunately he doesn't know how, and his solution is tragically wrong.

"Suzanne forgives her father. *We heard her say that.* We heard Suzanne plead with her father not to damn himself. That *now* there is still hope they will all be reunited. It's all on the tape; I can play it. But not if he continues doing what he is doing to Sandy Horne."

Tom's voice rose and he spoke excitedly. "And what is he doing to Sandy Horne that merits damnation? He is ripping the skin, the flesh, the *life,* from her body! All in order to overcome the tremendous sense of guilt he feels over the premature burial of his daughter."

Voices immediately filled the room, a discordant buzz as from a nest of hornets, with people all speaking at once, analyzing, questioning, *understanding.*

Tom's voice was heard above the others. "What Eben Wallford is doing in an attempt to assuage this guilt is to bring his daughter back—to try to undo what he so tragically did—through the reconstruction of her body from the skin of the look-alike, Sandy Horne. To somehow, through whatever mistaken notions he had, try to do the seemingly impossible—to breathe life into his daughter and bring her back!"

Exhausted, Tom sank into his chair as the buzz in the room began again, louder this time.

"He's crazy," a man shouted from the back of the hearing room. "You can't believe that drivel. Bring her back—?" he spit out. "Isn't that right, Josiah?"

But Josiah didn't answer. He was thinking of the girl

who had been burned. The girl in the house. Half mad, they thought she was, to set fire to herself and burn off her skin. But she hadn't set fire to herself, had she? Nor had she been half mad. It was Eben Wallford *then,* as it was *now.* And it was so. No. Josiah did not answer the man from the back of the hearing room.

The coroner leaned over the table toward Tom, his hands folded in front of him, and the room was suddenly quiet.

"A few questions if I may, Dr. Landberg."

"Of course."

"There's no denying the tape. We all heard it. I also understand there are enough witnesses in the hospital to bear out what we all just listened to. It's not a joke, I think we can accurately say. The girl is sick, quite sick, I'm sorry to hear, and you wouldn't be wasting our time or your own unless you really believed there was something to what you've been saying. And your words are moving, troubling."

Tom nodded. A rational man, he thought. Unlike some of the others they could have come up before.

"This disease she has—the exfoliative dermatitis— there could be a purely physical reason for the disease?"

Tom nodded. "Unfound as yet, but indeed possible."

"There could also be, as you have suggested, a psychological basis for the disease, outside of the paranormal. The girl is very troubled. It could be of her own device; psychosomatic?"

"Yes."

"Or it could be—as you think it might—of a tele-pathic, psychic nature? You're asking me to believe, therefore, that all of this is really happening to the girl—not just that she thinks it is."

A woman's voice rose out of the crowd, high-pitched, fearful. "If the girl's crazy, let her be crazy someplace else. Don't let them go digging up our graves, disturbing our dead."

The coroner signaled that the woman be escorted from the room.

"That's what they're doing——" she wailed as she was led through the doors.

The coroner turned his attention back to Tom.

"Dr. Landberg," he said simply. "I could not live with myself if I did not grant your request." He banged down his gavel.

Josiah Stoneham did not protest; nor did anyone else.

CHAPTER XXXVIII

Afternoon.

In their barns, the horses snorted nervously, restively pawing the ground in fearful anticipation of the thunderstorm. Threatening, heavy gray-black clouds hung low in the southeastern sky, swirling elliptically and moving steadily northward. A warming air mass had been coming in from the south since early the previous evening, meshing ominously with the cold New England air, and the haze-fringed moon had only been visible through infrequent breaks in the oncoming storm clouds.

It was dark at two P.M. The rain had held back for the morning, giving the clouds more time to compact, coalesce, and build. Electricity crackled in the air even before the first bolts of winter lightning descended.

A perfect day for an exhumation, David thought ruefully as he eyed the darkened sky.

The tips of the Green Mountains surrounding the Vermont valley were no longer visible, snow-capped whites having been replaced by storm-cloud purple, evergreened forested peaks and snaking mist now joined as one; a strangling, turbid cloud quilt suspended from above.

Timorous silence. The town of Owlsfane in the eerie throes of the calm before the storm could listen only to the sounds of the anxious animals in their barns and the occasional whine of a passing car on Route 93.

In the cemetery there was silence.

The driver of a car slowed and stopped to watch. From the crowds of people stretched out below the mausoleum and the lineup of cars along the shoulder of Route 93, he could only conclude that this was a funeral of a respected Owlsfane local. He watched the people milling around aimlessly, silently, as if waiting for something to happen. For the casket to appear? For the interment to begin? But then the crowd parted as some men walked through it, and it struck him: *How odd! There was no casket!* He left his car by the side of the road, moving closer to see what was going on.

No casket . . .

The townspeople were all there; half afraid to have shown up, half afraid not to. Some were curiosity seekers, awed nonetheless by what was to happen; others, like Josiah, were uncertain of their feelings. *Did they want to see something in there or did they not?*

From the mausoleum mount Josiah Stoneham looked behind at the Wallford house. It looked larger, almost sinister, against the dark backdrop of the hillside and the low-hanging sky. He trained his eyes on the front bedroom window—*the room with the bars*—as if hoping to see something—a light, face, *something* to reassure him he was doing right. But he knew he was. He had always suspected that Eben haunted the house; just didn't realize he was crying for help. Had he known this, he would have done whatever was needed years before. But at least he was finding out now, when there was still time for something to be done. Too bad the girl had to be sick, but God works in mysterious ways, doesn't He? It was all only speculation, he knew, until the coroner swung open the mausoleum doors and they looked inside. The huddled statue of Eben Wallford stood in silent judgment, and Josiah could not bring himself to look at it for fear there might be condemnation written on its stony face.

The coroner stepped up to the mausoleum doors as the first drops of rain started to fall. Umbrellas went up; nobody left. In the distance, the low rumble of thunder broke the silence in the cemetery. Barren tree branches waved accusatory fingers at the frightened people. The wind whooshed coldly through the trees, making whining cries—devil sounds. The coroner's hands trembled as he reached out tentatively to touch the ring handles in front of him. His face was the color of the snow on the ground.

"Let's get on with it," he said softly, to no one in particular. It had been easy to decide this was to be done; to do it was something else.

A crack of lightning split the sky with a slithering flash of light. The coroner instinctively pulled back from the door as if the heavenly sign had been meant for him.

A child wailed from the bottom of the hill, a loud shriek followed by staccato sobs. The mother hurried her crying baby to a parked car, the people as one wondering how any mother could bring a child to a happening such as this.

With purpose, the coroner seized the handles of the bronze doors anew, as if to show those below him, as well as himself, that he was not afraid. After a half second he started to pull them open. The people reflexively stepped backward. David swallowed and bit his hand. His teeth dug into his skin, but he felt no pain. Josiah stood motionless. The rain fell on his bare head, but he made no move to cover himself. More cars stopped below and more people walked up the mausoleum mount.

The coroner opened the doors wider. People strained to look into the blackness, yet no one wanted to be the first to see.

A woman in the crowd suddenly screamed.

"You can't!" she said in a voice that pierced the air. "You can't let them out. They're dead. Why don't you let them rest in peace!"

Her cry was the wail of a mourner. She dissolved into tears. Another gently led her away, a protective arm around her shoulder to quiet her as they walked down the path to the Owlsfane church.

The mausoleum doors stood open: the first shock was over. There was no body on the floor or affixed to the door. But then there wasn't supposed to be one.

Light streamed hungrily into the mausoleum, where it had not been for almost a century. Three caskets squatted inside.

Tom, David, and Josiah followed the coroner into the tomb. Bob remained outside. The other people flocked forward, but no one else would enter.

The casket on the left bore the inscription "Suzanne." The coroner gently put his hand on the oakwood, as if afraid of being burned. He lifted his eyes heavenward—

"God help me," he said.

—and started to raise the lid.

In her hospital room Sandy dreamed. The scenes marched distinctly, one to the next. They were sharp; there was no distortion.

There was a girl. She was riding a white-spotted horse through a snow-covered field. She dismounted to walk by a stream. Ice broke apart beneath her, catapulting her into the frigid waters. She contracted pneumonia and died. She came back to life and crawled painfully forth in blackness to die again. She was closed in a casket, in a mausoleum. She was framed by a burning white light.

The casket was opened and the light filled the blackness. The girl rose out of the light to take another girl by the hand. The second girl looked like the first; they

might have been twins, they might have been soul
mates. She led her to the light that was burning bril-
liantly inside. Both girls went into the casket. Only one
came out.

Sandy stirred and woke.

The coroner lifted the casket lid in a smooth, unhur-
ried motion. He assumed a nonchalant air to mask his
fear. David steeled himself and fought his rising stomach. He tried to prepare himself for what might be
inside.

They saw the girl's burial gown first: a long dress of
off-white silk, a red sash for a belt, which David would
later remember having seen in the portrait over the
fireplace. But he would not know that now, because
now there was more to look at: folded arms and a face.

The shock was fractionally delayed. Somehow it was
less frightening the way it was—to look into a coffin
and see not a skeleton but a person, not a skull but a
face.

There was skin where there should have been none.
A thin, almost transparent layer of yellow-white
stretched tautly over cheekbones and forehead plate.
It was not healthy skin; it was jaundiced and appeared
as scales. The mouth was sealed, but instead of lips
there was a thin brushline of cracked, caked white.
Patches of familiarly colored hair clung limply to the
head. It was parted in the middle, straight. It framed
an oval face. There were no eyes; just holes, sunken
holes of black that led to a spirit long departed.

Yet somehow it was still enough to know.

The body was Suzanne's but it could have been
someone else inside the casket. And somehow it was
more frightening, not less, when the person seen dead
in a coffin is a person alive and breathing still, in a
hospital room twenty miles away.

Their eyes traveled the length of the corpse. As they
watched, nails began to appear on finger tips where

moments before there were none. Eyebrows darkened. Hair filled in bald spots.

The coroner was surprised there was no odor. He was also surprised that *that* was what he noticed when confronted with everything else.

Josiah Stoneham turned from the casket and vomited.

The first audible reaction was the scream of realization from David.

Within moments everyone outside knew it was so.

CHAPTER XXXIX

"We have to make contact with Eben," Tom said. His flat statement drew no surprise from David or Bob.

They were in Spinner's office on the first floor of the hospital. Upstairs, Sandy was asleep in her room. Her heartbeat was regular, her breathing even. Encouraging signs, but they didn't know how long she would remain stabilized. Unless they went for an immediate solution, they didn't know what might happen next to destroy the tentative equilibrium. A layer of skin stretched across the dead Suzanne. They didn't know if there would be any danger to Sandy's internal organs from the otherworld, or further complications from the dermatitis.

"How?" David asked in an even voice. He was open to anything. He held a styrofoam cup of coffee in his hands, idly twirling it, getting the liquid fractionally to the top and not letting it spill. Anything but drinking it. A Danish was untouched in front of him; he had no appetite.

"Through Sandy," Tom answered. "I'll hypnotize her. Put her into a trance and through her be in touch with Eben. Suzanne can't get to him, but I think we can.

Explain his earthbound predicament to him and free him of the guilt that holds him here."

Spinner looked at the psychiatrist in partial disbelief. His eyes were small, almost closed, his lips curled upward in a thin smile. "If you had said this three days ago, Tom, I would have seriously doubted your medical competency. Hearing this today, I can almost believe it's possible."

"It is," Tom answered. "And I'm not speaking as a doctor here. There are ghost hunters and psychic researchers as well as laymen who, with trance mediums, contact troubled, trapped spirits, help them see the reality of their situation, help them understand that the problems that are keeping them earthbound have no more meaning, and help them into the next world. Most times the haunting stops and the ghost is never heard from again. The ghost has passed upward. Prayer has freed earthbound spirits. As well as calm reason. It's my intention to talk to Eben. Sandy will be the medium.

"We have to end Eben's troubled, tragic hold over her. Save him and save her. Remember, Eben Wallford is not evil. Just frightened and misdirected. We have to help him to help Sandy."

"Not evil," David growled. "As I said before, we should just burn his house down and drive him the hell away from here."

"To where, David?" Tom asked. "No. That would change nothing. We have to persuade Eben to leave. We can't destroy his house and force him out. It wouldn't work. It would probably have a deleterious effect, the opposite to what we want. With no familiar place to be, it would frighten the already frightened spirit all the more. He would probably intensify his efforts to rectify his earthly mistake and that might cost Sandy her life." He paused, then added, "And Eben his soul."

"What do we do?" Bob asked.

"Take Sandy into the house. That's where he is. We have to set up the psychic link where the forces are strongest. Tonight." He paused. "I will not promise anything, gentlemen, but we may all even get to see Mr. Eben Wallford."

There was a quiet tenseness in the hospital room as evening approached and passed with a darkening whisper into night. Sandy was sedated, asleep. In her dreams there was a light, and in the light a girl. The girl reached out from the light, and there was a voice the sleeping girl recognized.

"Come to me, Sandy. Bring him to me," the voice said. But the sleeping girl did not understand. And because she did not understand, she did not tell the others. And they did not recognize or suspect the dangers when they came to wake her and dress her.

And that was where they made their mistake.

CHAPTER XL

This time they went into the house through the front. Josiah used his key and opened the double glass doors for them.

The steady pelting rain had continued throughout the afternoon. It softened the ice, melted the snow, and muddied the roads and paths where it mixed with the dirt and salt laid down by the state dump trucks. It was now night and it was colder. The rain had turned to sleet. It fell in stinging needles, icing the ground in a thin, slippery layer. David and Bob carefully made their way one slow step at a time up the path to the Wallford house. They carried Sandy on a stretcher. Tom held an umbrella to protect her face. Spinner followed behind.

The house, unlocked, seemed to suck them in. Too eagerly? David wondered. Mockingly? As if it had its own plans for them? Perhaps he would have felt differently if the doors had stuck, the lock refused to spring open, or the key jammed. It would be better, he thought, if the house were frightened of them, more so than the other way around. He needed to feel they were in control, but he couldn't feel this way because he didn't know. It was with this uneasiness that he entered the Wallford house for what he hoped would be the last time.

Josiah's flashlight broke the path to the drawing room. He had never been in the house at night before. He felt the trembling in his hand and saw the long cylindrical beam of light shake noticeably. Somehow, the furniture he knew so well in the daylight took on sinister shapes in the dark of night. He pulled long candles from his pocket and put them in the holders on top of the hearth. Tom quickly produced a match and set the candles ablaze. The yellow light cast long, lonely shadows throughout the room, the flickering flames bringing them faintly, eerily alive with deceptive movement that was all the more frightening. The room had the feeling of a fortune-telling parlor draped in funereal black. All that was missing was the crystal ball; but somehow, David thought, in that house, they didn't really need one.

Josiah Stoneham felt hollow with fear. He knew what they were going to do and he knew he had given his approval. He was as guilty as the others; even more so, as he could have chosen to oppose and exercised his right as executor of the estate, but he did not, in the belief that he was doing right.

He did not want to stay in the house. Until he turned the key in the lock he had not made up his mind: to stay and observe or to leave. How complex life becomes, he thought. Before the girl had gone into the house and opened up the Pandora's Box, he could have gone to his grave secure in the knowledge that he had done all he could in his lifetime to watch over the spirit of Eben Wallford.

But he knew he had to be there to bear witness. If what they said might happen, indeed did, he had to be present to see the friend of his grandfather's, the spirit for whom he had cared his entire life, go to his eternal rest.

And that made him feel very good inside.

Yet despite the apparent sense in everything the psychiatrist had said, and despite the warming glow he tried to nurture full to life, there was still the gnawing feeling that burrowed from deep within his God-fearing soul: Were they tampering where they did not belong? And would there be a payment for their transgression? This is what frightened him; this is what chilled him. *The not knowing.* His skin prickled and was cold with gooseflesh. A lump formed in his throat and he swallowed continually. It was as if an electrical current were surging through the air, stinging him. He felt as he had the night he had awakened dreaming of Eben. Eben's presence felt very strong to him. Very near. Anticipation hung thickly in the air, but he conceded that it might be his more than the spirit's, and perhaps only a self-fulfilling prophecy at that.

The not knowing. It was more frightening than the happening itself.

Sandy had been bundled warm and well. Before leaving the hospital she had been given another transfusion of whole blood. A long surgical bandage was wrapped around most of her face to protect it from the weather. Only her eyes were exposed. There was a puffiness to them and a yellow tinge to her lids. Her face was sallow. Only a few isolated patches of hair were left hanging limply from her head. Her scalp produced dandrufflike scales that fell around her. Her eyebrows seemed plucked clean. Her lips were dry and cracked. Her temperature was almost a hundred and three, but her condition was deemed stable. She was weak, but strong enough to undergo the hypnosis, Tom felt. They hoped there would be no abnormal strain to her heart; they knew she was vulnerable.

She was awake in the ambulance for the ride to the Wallford house. Tom told her all he suspected. David held her hand as Tom spoke, as if his strength could pass through to her. Her eyes were fixed on Tom as he talked calmly to her, explaining what they would do.

What he said made sense. She understood. Tom would speak to Eben Wallford through her and free him to enter the next world. She knew about the next world: she had had two glimpses of it already. Under hypnosis, in a trance state, she would not remember what transpired during the rescue circle unless directed by Tom. She would be the conduit; she was the medium. She continually passed her tongue over her chapped, split lips, in a vain attempt to moisten them. Her sharp lips hurt her tongue. She suspected the danger she was in.

She forgot to tell them about her dream.

David's nostrils flared as the thick, pungent smell of the house assaulted him immediately: the odor of wasting away, the stagnant presence of decay and death, the musty, sickly odor of age and time. He remembered the house as it was on the first night they had gone into it, and his impressions of a virulent cancer that seemed to ooze like slime from every chip in the wall, from every burr in the foundation. Tonight as well. It felt as if a giant hand were holding the dying house firmly in its ever tightening grasp, strangling it, choking the fast-ebbing life from it.

He glanced into the dining room and saw the chair he had tripped over when Sandy had first broken from him for her run up the stairs (*the run that started it all*), the goblet and decanters in the glass-door cupboard that she had been attracted to and touched with recognition. The house seemed as if it were almost ready to give up, but for some unexplainable reason still needed to hold on—perhaps for a final victory or, he prayed, a last defeat.

Something was watching him. He sensed it lurking invisible in the air, breathing on his neck. He whirled around to trap it. Nothing. Except perhaps in the dark corner of the room where the candlelight did not illuminate. An imagined *thump, thumping* seemed to pulsate from it. Like a heartbeat; but he didn't know if it was a palpitation that was dying or growing stronger with their presence. With Sandy's presence. *Would they be successful in stopping Eben?* He thought he saw a movement in the darkness, but shook free the vision. His imagination was running double time, and there would be no relief until they had finished. Then he would consider burning down the house. But then there would be no reason to. Eben would be gone. The house would stand empty and cleansed. The dust would settle for all time.

The sleet pinged steadily against the window.

Tom lifted one of the candles toward the blackness of the second-floor stairwell.

"Upstairs," he whispered. "To Eben's room. That's where Sandy saw and heard him."

The others silently nodded.

"Can you walk?" he asked Sandy.

"I can make it," she said. "I'm not dead yet." Her joke rang feeble and hollow, and she wished she could take back the words. "Let's go," she said.

She leaned on David for support as they climbed the stairs to the second floor. Her head buzzed and the steps exhausted her. She had to rest partway up. She touched her face; she was burning up.

They turned toward the front of the house and walked down the hallway to Eben's bedroom, where it had all begun.

Tom pushed open the creaking door and thrust the candle inside. A golden haze surrounded the flame and slowly brought faint light to the room. The door closed on him, and he jerked his hand backward, susceptible in the dark. The movement caused the flame to wither to a tiny glowing pinpoint of light, an isolated speck in the darkness, threatening to extinguish fully. Tom held his hand steady to nurture the fire back to life. Josiah followed him in with his candle, and then Spinner and Bob with theirs. The four candles illuminated the room. David helped Sandy inside.

The door closed behind them.

They were in his room.

The bedposts were reflected like Egyptian obelisks on the far wall. A looking glass propped on the fireplace mantel murkily distorted Bob's features as he approached it from the side with the flame held in front of him. He jumped back, thinking he was looking into the face of a ghost or a shrouded presence. He reminded himself that even he, who told the story year in and year out, was not immune to the power of suggestion.

There was an unnatural coldness to the room, indicative of a spirit presence. Tom noticed it. The others as well. Something would happen, they knew.

Bob wished they could light a fire in the hearth, but there was no kindling available. Although he wasn't certain if even a fire could warm the room.

Their eyes rose to the portrait that haunted the bedroom. They all felt the cold, boring glance of Eben Wallford; but whether the eyes spoke in appreciation or condemnation, they couldn't know or even guess. Josiah wished he could throw a sheet over the portrait.

David looked at the girl in the portrait: Suzanne as she was, Suzanne as she was again becoming. He looked into her eyes, as if trying to see life. As he walked toward the bedroom window he sensed the eyes following him: the Mona Lisa eyes of a girl long dead, being brought back. He shook himself free from the haunting feelings.

From the bedroom window the flickering streetlamp faintly illuminated the mausoleum across the road. Sleet fell slantwise across the stone statue, so stalwart against the elements. Suddenly the light from outside died: the storm had caused a power failure in the town of Owlsfane. The windows of the ski house down the road were also dark. The heavy country night bore down on them and the candles seemed to strain to break through the blackness that settled shroudlike over them.

Tom sat Sandy in the Morris chair and passed a hand over her eyes. The mere suggestion put her under. She was ready. He was ready. From different vantage points around the room the others watched.

The rescue circle was to begin.

"Eben Wallford," Tom said evenly. "You will come through to us and let us speak to you. Through the girl."

Sandy swayed in place. "Eben," she moaned softly.

"Eben," Tom repeated. His voice was suddenly stronger. It was a command for the spirit to appear.

The room grew colder still. Bob pulled the zipper on his parka up to his neck. The air within moved, although no doors or windows had been opened. The candle flames flickered darkly. Shadows roamed across the ceiling and walls. In the quivering light, halos seemed to form over the objects in the room, giving them almost living auras of flaring yellows and oranges.

There was a gurgling sound. It came from Sandy.

"Find him," she finally said. The voice was hoarse, distant. Familiar. It was not Eben. It was Suzanne. *"Find him. Let him come through."* There was a faint quality of hope to the voice that had been missing from the previous hypnosis sessions. As if Suzanne suspected she would soon be reunited with her father through Sandy. *"Find my father. Bring him to me."*

"Eben Wallford!" Tom commanded again. "Do you hear my voice? Acknowledge!"

A thin white mist seemed to float above them; a faint, almost invisible spider-webbing that hovered just beneath the ceiling. Airy. Ethereal. It may only have been smoke from the candles that drifted upward. But it wasn't, they knew. Josiah's eyes were wide as he backed himself into a corner to search the room, cautious that nothing could appear behind him. His throat was constricted, the way it was in nightmares when he knew he needed to scream but couldn't. Were he to open his mouth, dry and tight, he suspected no sound would emerge.

"He's here," Tom whispered. He looked back toward Sandy. Her eyes were closed; her head rested at an acute angle to the left. Her hands were folded in her lap. Her breathing was even; her mouth twitched only slightly. All appeared normal.

"We've got him. Suzanne too."

Spinner sat spellbound.

"Eben Wallford, you will hear me," Tom said. His voice softened; it was almost kindly. The tone stroked rather than stabbed. David knew he was going to try to reason with the spirit.

Suddenly Sandy's eyes burst wide open. *"Bring him to me!"* she shrieked in the voice of the dead girl. Her hands clenched tightly, balled into fists. Her whole body tensed and shook in frustration: so close, yet so far. *"Don't let him damn himself! Dadddeeeeeee—!"*

Bob watched with curious horror. He was only able to imagine what had transpired in the previous sessions.

"Suzanne," Tom begged. "Leave the girl alone." He stroked Sandy's arms, a steady up-and-down calming motion. Her shaking ebbed.

(A girl sat up in a coffin. . . .)

"Eben Wallford," Tom said. "We are here to help you. We want to help you go to your family. Your daughter is calling to you. She is waiting for you."

"We must pray for him," Josiah said, and bowed his head. *"The Lord is my shepherd,"* he began. He dropped his voice to an undertone.

"You must leave this world," Tom said. "You cannot accomplish any more here. You have to see that. You can only bring harm to yourself and to the girl. Your time in *this* world is over. You must free yourself and enter the next—"

He restoreth my soul

(There was a brilliant light. . . .)

"Your daughter forgives you. You have been separated for a hundred years. It is now time for you to be together with your family again for all eternity—"

(Suzanne reached out toward her to take her hand. . . .)

Yea though I walk through the valley of the Shadow of Death

"Free yourself from your hold on this world and go to them!"

(Sandy touched her. . . .)

There was a tragic change.

Sandy's breathing was suddenly strained. Rasping. Labored. Her eyes bulged wide, as if she were being choked by ghostly fingers. Her hands tightened and rose to her chest.

Tom knew that something that had made sense moments before had somehow gone awry.

"Bring him to me!" Suzanne shrieked as Sandy toppled forward into Tom's arms.

Spinner raced to her side.

Josiah silently continued the prayer.

Sandy's face was chalk-white. Spinner grabbed her wrist. "She has no pulse!" he shouted.

"She's gone into cardiac arrest," Tom said.

"He's killed her!" David cried.

"Quiet!" Tom ordered. They quickly carried Sandy to the bed. Spinner tilted her head back and opened her mouth. He jutted her chin forward and put his mouth over hers to send air into her lungs. Tom leaned on her chest. With flat palms he tried to squeeze her heart between her ribs and spinal column to start it beating.

Sandy heard the voice calling to her. It was now soft, sweet.

And very close.

Sandy, come to me, it said. Sandy remembered. It was the voice from her dream.

Tom pressed down on her chest. Firmly. Steadily. Despite the chill of the room, perspiration beaded his forehead. He quickly wiped it away with his sleeve. Spinner continued the artificial respiration. His face was puffy and red.

Sandy saw them and heard them: Josiah Stoneham, a small, huddled white-haired figure standing over the Bible, lips moving silently; David and Bob at the foot of the bed, hanging on to the reeded bedposts, concern and fear etched into their faces; Tom pushing down on her chest, his shoulders heaving in even motion; Spinner breathing into her mouth. But she felt nothing. Except confusion.

"I'm here," she tried to call to them, but she realized she had no voice.

She floated above them, out of her body. Weightless. She looked down at herself lying on Eben Wallford's bed, feeling that somehow she had to get back into her body. With a sick feeling she realized that she did not know how.

Yet it was pleasant. She felt no pain. No fever. No weakness.

"Bring her back," she heard David say.

Until those words, it had not occurred to her that she had died.

"Talk to Eben, Tom!" David cried. "Make him bring her back."

Tom never stopped the heart massage. "It isn't Eben," he said. "It's Suzanne. Trying to reach her father the only way she knows how. To have Sandy bring him to her."

Sandy was in the tunnel. The voices in the room grew fainter and fainter behind her. The blackness opened up before her, concentric circles in clockwise movement that were ever widening, pulling her through. She was horizontal, her feet touched nothing solid. Her movements were not her own. Soft recorder music piped around her, within her. She had once before heard and followed the music. She had been in the tunnel.

The tunnel! The music!

She was suddenly terrified. *The tunnel!* She knew what awaited her at the end: the faces, the devils, the pain, eternal hell.

The voice in front of her coaxed softly. *Come to me, Sandy. Bring him to me.*

"There's a defibrillator in the ambulance," Spinner suddenly remembered. "Bob, go and get it."

"Right." Bob raced from the room.

Sandy raced through the tunnel, deeper and deeper, her speed and direction controlled from without.

In the far distance she saw a pinpoint of light.

The heavenly barrier!

Suddenly her fears dissolved. She recalled the peace of Suzanne's death experience. It would be good this time for her as well. It would be good. There was full relief. There would be no demons, no faces, no pain. She was not destined to hell. She was moving toward the heavenly light.

But first she had to get there.

She was suddenly swimming in a murky grayness that surrounded her like a sticky webbing. It was where she remembered seeing Eben Wallford the first time in her dream—confused, trapped, hopelessly puzzled, and disoriented. She was there now too—in this region of eternal limbo, suspended between the two states of existence.

In the bedroom the doctors worked.

David held on to the bedposts until his knuckles were stiff and white. His fingers were almost one with the wood. Then suddenly something made sense. How had Tom missed it?

"Suzanne can't let her die!" he said in triumph. "She would be damning herself." His voice brimmed with realization and relief. "Sandy will bring them together and Suzanne will send her back."

Tom didn't answer. He was not as confident as David. He kept massaging Sandy's chest. Still no response. Her heart was silent. They had only a few remaining moments to get it started and pump oxygen to her brain. Beyond that they could still try, but the result might be irreparable brain damage.

Eben Wallford loomed out of the gray mist in front of her. He smiled and held out his hand to his daughter.

Suzanne's voice continued to ring telepathically in Sandy's ears. Eben didn't hear it; that she knew. It was for her alone. Intuitively she knew why. Suzanne was there to guide her through the gray suspension. And she had to follow. Otherwise there would be no escape.

Bring him to me.

And she knew she had to take Eben with her. It was his only way to his daughter on the other side of the light.

Come to me. . . .

Suzanne's voice was growing weaker. Should it fade completely, Sandy knew she would be lost for all time in this region of turmoil. Downtrodden souls milled aimlessly, purposelessly, about her. Their heads were earthward, their eyes lowered in continuous search for solutions to problems that followed them beyond their deaths. They were destined, she knew, for an eternity of hopelessness.

They were ghosts.

She reached out and took the hand of the old man. He quickly pulled her toward him in embrace. His daughter had finally come.

I am not your daughter.

He held her tightly. His eyes were wide in joy. She struggled to hear the guiding voice of Suzanne. She knew she had to pull free from Eben. Before it was too late for both of them. She had to go to the voice.

To the light, which was growing dimmer in the far distance. The gray nothingness swirled heavily around her. It was like trying to see through fog at twilight. They had drifted farther away from the light, the voice.

Confusion rifled Eben's face. This was his daughter. Why was she distant? Age lines and fear replaced the happiness in his eyes as Sandy tried to pull free from him.

Bring him to me. Come to me. . . .

She strained her ears and found the direction of the spirit voice. She pushed herself from Eben to go toward it. It was like struggling under muddy water. She tried to swim through the mist that surrounded her like a sticky thread.

Bob raced up the stairs with the battery-operated defibrillating unit. Tom hurriedly readied the shoes.

They were at arm's length, Eben and Sandy. Only their hands still touched. She could not let go of him for fear of losing him in the fast-thickening murky gray. She would never be able to find him again. She had to bring him with her. To his daughter. To the next world.

He tried to pull her closer to him. *This* was his eternity. This was all that he knew. All any of them knew. But Sandy knew of another place, a better place, a place of light and heavenly peace. She had been there before. She had seen it. She had to get there again.

Others came to her. They surrounded her in welcome as one of them. They swirled about her. Their inner thoughts buzzed in telepathic chaos through her. Did she know so and so? Did she have any word? Where were they all? When were they coming? Where were their loved ones? Did she know? Their hands caressed her in hope; their thoughts hers.

Her heart went out to them: these lost, hopeless creatures. People once, who had gone to their deaths tragically, in guilt, in confusion, lacking forgiveness

from others for earthly sins, their business left unfinished.

But she had to save herself. Eben could come or not.
She strained to hear Suzanne's directions through the
Babel clatter that filled her thoughts.

But no—

She could not leave Eben there. If she was to be
saved, it was Suzanne who would save her. She had to
bring her father to her. The light twinkled dimly ahead
of her. She saw it. She moved toward it.

On the defibrillator Tom turned the dial to 5000
volts.

"Stand back!" he ordered. The others gave him
room.

Sandy felt shock and confusion. What was happening to her? The light before her weakened. She suddenly
wanted to turn back. To go back through the tunnel to
David and life on the other side of the blackness. But
she was lost in the gray. She didn't know how to get
out. She didn't know the way back. In trying to save
her they were confusing her. They were damning her to
eternal limbo.

Another shock surged through her as electricity
flowed through her corporeal body. The body on the
bed arched upward.

"Stand back!" Tom ordered, and shocked her again.
They watched Sandy's body twitch involuntarily.

Bring him to me.

Suzanne's voice was only a whisper. Of desperation.
Of realization that all might be as it was. Sandy had to
go toward it. She had to follow the voice. She was surrounded by the gray figures. She could no longer see
the light. The urge to go back to life was stronger. Her
confusion was heightened. She didn't know which way
to turn. She could go nowhere.

She was suddenly terrified she'd never be able to
leave this awful place.

. . . to me . . .

Suzanne's call was merely a thought, scattered by roaring winds.

She threw total concentration to the distant voice.

Eben clung to her. Questions were written on his face. Why was his daughter trying to leave him? He had been waiting so long.

I am not your daughter, she tried to project. *I am trying to take you to her.*

Intuitively she knew what had to be done. She had one last chance, then all would be forever lost. The light was gone. The voice was gone. The others huddled about her. No way out.

She pushed through the spirits to where she remembered hearing the voice.

Suddenly a pinpoint of light was visible. She reached out toward it.

Come.

Suzanne's thought.

She was shocked again as 5000 more volts ripped through her.

She fought the pull to return to life and the drag of the elderly man. She propelled herself through the masses toward the direction of the light. No one else saw it. No one else followed her. They had lost interest in her. Another had come.

Slowly. Then faster still. To stop or turn or hesitate was to be lost. She held tightly to Eben.

The heavenly light grew larger and closer. Its pull was stronger.

She was at the barrier.

She was through the barrier.

She was in the light. As was Eben.

She was at peace. At one with the light. The universe. No devils attacked her. No noise assaulted her.

Electricity surged through her once again. The ever stronger desire to return. But she couldn't return. She had to stay where she was. She could not go back and risk the next time—the demons, the limbo. She would not have the aid of Suzanne.

Why were they trying to bring her back? She liked being dead! She didn't want to go back!

Suddenly Suzanne materialized before them. Hazily. Distantly. Her features became defined. Sandy didn't know if they were drifting further into the light or if Suzanne was coming to greet them. But it didn't matter. They were all there.

Beneath her she saw lush gardens, trees, flowers, lakes of calm blue.

Don't! she cried out. *I don't want to go back. I'm happy here. It's pretty here.*

The word-thoughts were familiar: Suzanne's!

Suzanne reached out to her father and Eben knew. He went to his daughter and they embraced. Suzanne, framed against the heavenly light, was radiant. She had succeeded. Her father had come.

Another shock.

Sandy tried to hold firm. She could not go back!

From out of the light she saw her father come toward her in welcome. Behind him, her mother. All asmile, her father reached out to her. He forgave her, she knew. Not that he had ever blamed her. She grabbed on to him, to her mother. The three held tightly to each other in reunion. They moved deeper into the light, trying to will her to stay. But then a voice rang out:

It isn't time.

She knew the voice. She had heard it before. She could not stay. Her time on earth was not over. She could not remain falsely in heaven.

The pull to return was suddenly stronger. Her fingertips brushed with her father's for the last time until the next time. But she knew intuitively there would be a next time in this heavenly light.

She had saved the soul of another. She had been pardoned.

And Sandy knew she now had seen what awaited her after death. She had the precognition of an eternal life of peace and heaven.

But for now it was time to go back.

There was another shock.

On the bed Sandy coughed and spat. Her head arched off the bed. Her chest rose. Saliva dribbled down her chin. Tom pulled the defibrillating shoes from her.

"She's back," he said simply, and suddenly the room felt warm.

The candles stopped their quivering.

Sandy breathed steadily. Normally.

It was over.

When the Wind Blows

A chilling novel of occult terror!

John Saul

author of *Suffer the Children* and *Punish the Sinners*

To the Indians, the ancient mine was a sacred place. To the local residents, it was their source of livelihood.

But the mine contains a deadly secret—and the souls of the town's lost children. Their cries can be heard at night, when the wind blows—and the terror begins.

A DELL BOOK $3.50   (19857-7)

At your local bookstore or use this handy coupon for ordering:

THE NATIONAL BESTSELLER

THE CRADLE WILL FALL

by Mary Higgins Clark

"Buying a Mary Higgins Clark book is like buying a ticket to ride the roller coaster."—*The Washington Post*

"She has given us a truly villainous villain, a young and attractive heroine…a diabolical scientific experiment and a terrifying, spine-tingling climax. As current as today's headlines"—*The Denver Post*

"An instant classic…superbly plotted."—*Los Angeles Times*

☐ **THE CRADLE WILL FALL** $3.50   #11476-4

Other bestsellers by Mary Higgins Clark:

☐ **WHERE ARE THE CHILDREN?** $2.95   #19593-4
☐ **A STRANGER IS WATCHING** $2.95   #18127-5

At your local bookstore or use this handy coupon for ordering:

 DELL BOOKS
P.O. BOX 1000, PINE BROOK, N.J. 07058

Please send me the books I have checked above. I am enclosing $_____
including 75¢ for the first book, 25¢ for each additional book up to $1.50 maximum
postage and handling charge.
Please send check or money order—no cash or C.O.D.s. *Please allow up to 8 weeks for delivery.*

Mr./Mrs._____

Address_____

City_____ State/Zip_____

A true odyssey of love and evil
by the author of <u>Blood and Money</u>

SERPENTINE

by Thomas Thompson

A chilling factual account of exotically handsome,
demonically charming mass-murder. Charles
Sobhraj. "Shocking impact...marks Thompson
as one of the finest nonfiction writers of the
decade."—<u>Philadelphia Inquirer</u>

"The most bizarre true-crime narrative since the
Manson story <u>Helter Skelter</u>...Grotesque,
baffling, and hypnotic."—<u>San Francisco Chronicle</u>

A Dell Book $3.50   (17611-5)

Bestsellers

- [ ] **THE RING** by Danielle Steel $3.50 (17386-8)
- [ ] **INGRID BERGMAN: MY STORY**
      by Ingrid Bergman and Alan Burgess $3.95 (14085-4)
- [ ] **SOLO** by Jack Higgins $2.95 (18165-8)
- [ ] **THY NEIGHBOR'S WIFE** by Gay Talese....$3.95 (18689-7)
- [ ] **THE CRADLE WILL FALL** by Mary H. Clark $3.50 (11476-4)
- [ ] **RANDOM WINDS** by Belva Plain $3.50 (17158-X)
- [ ] **WHEN THE WIND BLOWS** by John Saul $3.50 (19857-7)
- [ ] **LITTLE GLORIA . . . HAPPY AT LAST**
      by Barbara Goldsmith $3.50 (15109-0)
- [ ] **CHANGE OF HEART** by Sally Mandel $2.95 (11355-5)
- [ ] **THE PROMISE** by Danielle Steel $3.50 (17079-6)
- [ ] **FLOWERS OF THE FIELD**
      by Sarah Harrison $3.95 (12584-7)
- [ ] **LOVING** by Danielle Steel $3.50 (14657-7)
- [ ] **CORNISH HEIRESS** by Roberta Gellis $3.50 (11515-9)
- [ ] **BLOOD RED WINE** by Laurence Delaney....$2.95 (10714-8)
- [ ] **COURT OF THE FLOWERING PEACH**
      by Janette Radcliffe $3.50 (11497-7)
- [ ] **FAIR WARNING**
      by George Simpson and Neal Burger $3.50 (12478-6)

At your local bookstore or use this handy coupon for ordering:

DELL BOOKS
P.O. BOX 1000, PINEBROOK, N.J. 07058

Please send me the books I have checked above. I am enclosing $_____
(please add 75¢ per copy to cover postage and handling). Send check or money
order—no cash or C.O.D.'s. Please allow up to 8 weeks for shipment.

Mr/Mrs/Miss _____

Address _____

City _____ State/Zip _____